Thailand
Cold Rain

A Novel of Love and Passion

J. F. Gump

© 2008 by J. F. Gump & Sabai Books
North American Edition
ISBN: 978-0-9714855-4-9

First English Version Published by:
Bangkok Book House, Bangkok, Thailand
Previous Title: The Farang Affair
Distribution Rights in Southeast Asia
ISBN: 974-85123-6-3

Cover Photography by Rene Ehrhardt
www.flickr.com/photos/rene_ehrhardt/2391312758/
ehrhardtrene @ yahoo.de

Published by Sabai Books, P.O. Box 138, Kings Mills, Ohio 45034

www.JFGumpNovels.com

Printed in the United States of America.

About This Book

Cold Rain. Those two words strike a sharp contrast to the tropical heat that is the essence of Thailand. Yet these words also describe the emotional turmoil that drives the characters in this novel. People haunted by their pasts; victims of decisions made long ago. When fate brings them together, a maelstrom of raw human passions are unleashed and their powerful needs to be loved are laid bare.

This story transports you to exotic Southeast Asia where you will meet characters so real you can hear them breath and see them sweat. Characters with hopes and dreams that have been shattered by mistakes they can't change and events they will never forget. Walk with Chalamsee, Somjit, and Mike as they discover the true meanings of love and forgiveness.

Cold Rain is the second of three books in set in exotic SE Asia. If you haven't read Siam Nights, the lead book of this trilogy, you should order it now. Cold Rain stands alone as a story and a novel, but Siam Nights offers insights to the Thai culture that will enhance your understanding of the people who live there and the foreigners who travel to Asia for work or play. Visit my website for a list of available Tropical Heat novels.

(www. JFGumpNovels. com)

Acknowledgements

Thanks to everyone who has supported my work. A special thank you to readers who bought my trilogy from Bangkok Book House, and to my family who allowed me uninterrupted time to write. Your support gave me the courage to continue.

~~ J. F. Gump

Chapter 1

Mike Johnson stared down at his shoes. Mud rimmed the manmade soles and part of the leather uppers. A swash of wet brown stained his trouser cuff where a shoe had brushed unnoticed. It rarely rained in Pittsburgh in mid August, but it was raining today. There was no thunder or lightning, only a steady drizzle that dampened everything unlucky enough to be outside.

Across from him a Methodist preacher was doing his best to be inspirational. Mike hardly noticed. He was beyond inspiration. Mostly he was just tired – tired of all the bullshit that came with life.

A casket perched on a short metal frame separated Mike from the preacher. Carefully placed cloth and floral wreaths hid Susan's final resting place. She had been dead for four days now; four days of living hell. He had never in his life had to identify the body of a dead person. Certainly he had never had to identify the mangled body of his wife.

His sister Carol, ever the steady one, had been his constant companion through it all. Without her the funeral would never have happened. His old friend alcohol had joined the madness less than an hour after he'd identified Susan's body. Carol took care of funeral details while his old friend kept him numb.

The preacher ended his prepared speech and said amen.

Mike wasn't sure what he was supposed to do, so he simply stood and walked away. Carol chased after him but he brushed her off. "I want to be alone right now, but I want to see you tomorrow. Can you meet me at my house at two o'clock?"

"I have to work, but I can be there if it's important."

"I'm meeting a real estate agent and an attorney. I'm selling everything. There'll be papers for you to sign."

"What about Josh?"

"What about him?" Mike's tone turned harsh.

Carol didn't answer. Instead she said, "Some people from your work brought food to my house. You should come; they're expecting you."

He opened the car door and slipped inside. "I'm not in the mood for those people, especially Jess Ankrom."

Carol's eyes flicked to the Jack Daniel's bottle lying on the front seat. "I thought you only drank beer."

"I'll see you tomorrow at two."

"Are you going home?"

"I can't sleep there anymore. It was never my home anyway."

"Where are you going? I might need to get in touch."

"I'll see you tomorrow."

He started the engine and drove away.

Chapter 2

Somjit Chutima glanced at her watch; it was almost eight. Daylight had faded and the geckos, frogs, and other night creatures had started another evening of chirping, croaking, and mating.

She stirred at the overcooked food she had been nursing on the hotplate since seven. She knew she should throw it away but was afraid to do that. Her husband would be hungry when he got home. He would be angry if his supper wasn't waiting. She grabbed a piece of the pork with her chopsticks, brought it to her nose and sniffed. It wasn't anything her husband would eat, she was sure of that. She put the bite in her mouth, chewed once, and then spit it back into the pan. Nothing she wanted to eat either.

She glanced at her watch again. If Nong came home soon, there would still be time to buy food from a street vendor. It wouldn't cost much and it would be a lot better than what was on the hotplate. She reached into her pocket. She knew from the shape and size of the coin that it was a ten baht piece, about 30 U.S. cents. Not enough, even for the cheapest of meals.

Somjit considered her options. If she threw the food away and Nong didn't have thirty or forty baht in his pocket, there would be no dinner and he would be angry. On the other hand he would be just as angry if she kept the food and he couldn't eat it. If he was angry enough, he might even make her eat it. The thought of having to eat the overcooked pork made up her mind. She switched off the hotplate, picked up the pan, and walked to the door. The baby kicked hard as she stepped outside. With a kick like that she was sure it would be a boy.

She looked down the street. In the dim glow of the streetlight she saw the neighbor's dogs lying at the edge of the dusty lane. She walked over and dumped the steaming food on the ground. The dogs sniffed cautiously and then proceeded to eat. The way they curled their lips away from the heat made them look like they were grinning. She smiled and turned back toward her house. At least the rats wouldn't get it.

Rats. Somjit hated rats. Rats had killed her parents. Not directly, but the rats had killed them just the same. They had died from leptospirosis, a disease known to Thai farmers as rat fever, caused by rat urine and open wounds in rice paddies. She had been sixteen at the time and their deaths changed her life. The few relatives who made room for her demanded her meager rice-paddy wages in return for their hospitality. Eventually she took a job as a construction laborer and left her relatives behind. It was in the labor camp where she had met and married Nong. They both worked hard and lived a simple but happy life.

Everything changed when Somjit got pregnant. First Nong refused to be seen with her in pubic. Then, when she could no longer do a laborer's work, their income was cut in half and there was never enough money. She had reviewed their budget a thousand times and was sure Nong was spending money on drugs again. She had accused him of that once and had been rewarded with a beating that left ugly bruises for everyone to see.

A movement to her left shook her from mental meandering. It was her friend Nok, a young girl from down the street. "Hello, Nok. How are you?"

"I'm okay," the girl answered. "I came to see if my husband it here. He didn't come home from work."

Somjit sighed. "Your husband isn't here. Nong didn't come home either. Maybe they had to work late or something."

Nok's face twisted to pout. "Maybe, but I don't think so. I hope Prem's not with another woman. He's done that before and I hate him for it."

Somjit was worried, too, but not about another woman. She was worried about her own husband's other vices. "I'm sure our husbands will be home soon." Her words came out more confident than she felt.

"I hope so," the girl said. "If he's with some whore, I will kill him. "

Somjit didn't know what to say, so she said nothing.

After an uncomfortable moment, the girl finished her thought. "First, I will cut off his penis."

Somjit smiled. "That's like cutting off your nose to spite your face. Don't you think?" She had heard that saying somewhere and now seemed an appropriate time to use it.

The girl squirmed. "Well, maybe I wouldn't do that. But if he brings home a disease, I will kill him."

Somjit nodded her understanding. "Me too."

After a long silence, Nok left without further comment. Somjit stepped through the doorway into her labor camp room.

When Nong arrived thirty minutes later, his eyes were bloodshot and his pupils dilated, but Somjit smelled neither whiskey nor beer on his breath.

"Sawasdee ka, good evening," she said, her voice soft and controlled. "You're late. I was worried about you."

"I'm hungry," His words came out slurred. His eyelids drooped half over his glassy stare. "I haven't eaten since this morning."

"Teeluk, darling, if you have thirty baht, I can buy some food from the cart down the way."

"I gave you money this morning." He stepped closer, his posture neither threatening nor affectionate. "What about that?"

Somjit eased away. "I bought food and I cooked your supper, but you are home very late." His face took on a look she had seen before and her chest tightened in response.

"Are you saying this is my fault, you fat water buffalo?" His right hand lashed out and slapped hard against her cheek. It balled into a fist as he brought it back to his side.

It had happened so fast that Somjit didn't have time to react. She had seen him tense, but didn't realize he was swinging until she felt the sharp crack of his hand. The blow sent her reeling. She staggered and fell. "Please, Nong," she pleaded, "I'm not a good wife. I promise to do better. Please don't hit me. You might hurt our baby."

"It's not *our* baby," he hissed. "It's *your* baby and I hate it." His left foot snapped toward her in kick-boxer fashion. He aimed it toward her swollen stomach.

Somjit tried to move away but was too slow. His kick hammered full force into her body. Oddly, she felt little physical pain, but the thought that he could have hurt the baby sent her into a rage. She saw the pan lying near from her hand. With surprising speed for a pregnant woman she grabbed the pan by its handle, rose to her feet, and turned to face Nong. At that moment Somjit was not Somjit—she was a mother protecting her child. Her every instinct was focused on killing the man who would harm her unborn baby. She had no thoughts of love or hate or anything other than protecting her baby. A loud, inhuman cry erupted from her throat. The pan rang as her swing collided with Nong's fist. She recovered and swung again.

Nong was surprised when Somjit returned his attack. He parried with the heel of his fist and the pan rang in response. The blow should have hurt, but he felt nothing except rage. She had ruined their lives by allowing herself to get pregnant. He should have made her get an abortion as soon as he found out. He would end it now before the baby was born. He caught her arm on her next swing and snapped the pan from her hand.

"I will kill you," he roared. His fist shot toward Somjit's face; his whole body participated in the powerful blow.

She turned her head at the last moment and his fist caught her just behind her left ear. She went down like a sack of wet rice.

"Get up, damn you," he shouted. "I will kill you and your baby both."

He stepped over and kicked her again and again. "I will kill you both," he screamed each time his foot dug into her stomach.

THAILAND – COLD RAIN

~~~

A solitary monk ambled up the dusty street lined with labor camp shacks. A small, purse-like bag hung loosely from his shoulder. His face was solemn, his eyes pointed straight ahead. His shaved head and saffron robe made him an unmistakable sight.

It had been a good day. He had spent the afternoon with his mother and father, and the early evening with a childhood friend. This was the first day he had taken from his religious duties in over four months. Now he was heading back to the temple, his home as long as he devoted his life to God and Buddha.

The evening was warm but not overly so. An occasional gnat buzzed near his ears. He felt mildly lightheaded from the two beers he had shared with his friend. He knew it wasn't proper to drink while he was in service to the monkhood, but today was special. Having a couple of beers with a friend wasn't the same as getting drunk. No one would mind.

He stole an occasional glance at the people sitting in front of the shabby shacks that lined the narrow street. They were construction workers, nomads who wandered from place to place following their companies to wherever there was work to do. Most of them had little education and their career choices were few. They did what they had to do to survive. He felt sorry for them but there was nothing he could do. There were too many of them for one man to make a difference.

A painful wail from a nearby house sent a hard chill down his back. It was followed by an male voice threatening to kill the wailer and her baby. He picked up his pace.

A young boy of maybe fourteen stood listening to the dull thuds and loud threats. The monk grabbed him by the arm. "Come with me." He pulled the boy toward the house.

Without hesitating he pushed the door open and stepped inside. He flinched at the assault taking place. "Stop," he shouted.

The man turned. Thick veins pulsed deep purple on his neck

and forehead. "Fuck you, bastard of Buddha. Get out of my house or I will kill you, too."

The monk drew back at the wild look in the man's eyes. Here was a monster capable of anything. The pregnant woman on the floor was proof of that. By reflex he assumed a Muay Thai stance he remembered from his teen years. "Leave now and I won't hurt you."

"Fuck you," the man snarled. Without further warning he attacked, swinging and kicking like Satan himself.

By luck more than skill, the young monk averted the worst of the assault. At an opportune moment he delivered a sharp blow and the man reeled. "Leave now, before I really hurt you."

Nong tried to remount his offensive but fell in the attempt. After a moment of confusion he abandoned his rage and staggered out of the shabby hut.

The monk took the boy by both arms and shoved his face close. "Get an ambulance and hurry. Then get the police—I want that man arrested."

The boy stood unmoving, stunned by what he had just witnessed.

The monk shook him hard. "Do it now!"

The boy nodded and ran from the room. His cries for help started as soon as he was outside.

The monk knelt beside the woman, pulled her blouse up and the waistband of her slacks down. Already huge blotches were forming on her stomach. She twitched and spasmed in the manner of the unconscious.

He pressed his ear tight against her lower abdomen. He heard one heartbeat and it was strong. He didn't detect the fainter beat he strained to hear.

He pulled a half-empty water bottle from his shoulder bag, dampened the hem of his robe and wiped gently at the woman's forehead. After a minute her twitching stopped and her eyelids flickered. A siren screamed in the background. Her eyes opened briefly then closed again. A pitiful moan came from her mouth.

THAILAND – COLD RAIN

He took her by the hand and whispered softly, "Everything will be okay." He prayed he was right.

At the hospital he forced his way into the emergency room against the wishes of the doctors on duty. They gave way to his saffron robes and his insistence. He watched as the doctors examined the woman. She woman had carried the baby for a long time, over eight months if his guess was correct. Their expressions said what he hoped wasn't true.

"You will take the baby from her?" he asked.

"She has no money and no insurance," the doctor answered. "The hospital has rules."

The monk noticed a trace of resignation in the doctor's voice. "I want her to have proper care. The cost isn't important. "

The doctor regarded him neutrally, "You have money?"

The monk nodded. "My father is Isara Horungruang."

The doctor proceeded to take the dead baby from Somjit.

The next day the young monk went back to the hospital, paid what was owed, and took Somjit to the safe house at the temple. She did whatever he told her, but she didn't talk. She was in a state of physical and mental shock. The brutal beating by her husband and the loss of her baby had destroyed her.

The monk could see the dark depression on her face. She was his patient in his care and he was losing her. For the first time since entering the monkhood, he replaced his saffron robes with civilian clothes and hired a taxi to the nearest pharmacy to buy antibiotics and antidepressants. He treated Somjit with a passion he had never known.

Chapter 3

Pittsburgh, PA

Mike Johnson awoke to the phone ringing in his ears. He pulled a pillow over his head to muffle the irritating noise. It didn't help. He reached out, lifted the receiver, and then dropped it back into its cradle. The ringing stopped but the throbbing in his head didn't. His bladder ached, stretched to the point of exploding.

He forced himself out of the bed and toward the toilet. A wave of nausea swept through him as he walked. It subsided a little as he sat lady-style on the toilet. He felt horrible. He was sick and his head pounded. He finished draining his bladder, rinsed his mouth, and went back to his bed.

Mike felt his heart doing somersaults. Holiday heart syndrome someone had called it: Too much booze and too little food. Inside, his liver and kidneys ached with the pain of alcohol destruction. He was surprised there was anything left to hurt. So far his body had survived every assault he had thrown at it.

He pulled a Marlboro from the pack on the nightstand. His first drag sent him into a spasm of coughing. How long, he wondered, could his body take the abuse he subjected it to before something really important stopped working? Weeks? Months? Years? He hoped something quit before he ran out of money.

The last year of Mike Johnson's life had been shit. A year of shattered dreams, personal loss, and blinding depression. It had started with the death of a young Thai lady named Math—his lover, his soul mate, the woman he wanted to spend the rest of his life with. She had never been his legal wife, but she had been the woman he loved more than any other.

Math had died nearly a year ago in a motorcycle accident. Her death had devastated him. At the time he had prayed for his own death, but every known god and prophet had ignored his prayers.

Less than three months after Math's death, Mike lost his job. It hadn't been anyone's fault, only a slowdown in business, but he'd blamed his boss anyway. Jess Ankrom hadn't terminated him in person, but he knew the fat prick had a hand in it.

Four weeks after being laid off, Mike lost his only son Josh. It had started as a stupid argument and ended with Mike kicking Josh out of the house. It was the last time he had seen his son. Actually, Mike had lost Josh to drugs long before kicking him out; it had just never seemed so permanent before.

Susan, his wife and long time tormentor, had screamed, cussed, and cried at Mike for making Josh leave. What little self-esteem he had left had quickly evaporated at Susan's unrelenting placing of blame. In a state of depression heavier than he'd ever known, Mike had attempted suicide with an overdose of valium and alcohol. It hadn't worked. He had managed to get a broken nose when he fell down the stairs, but he didn't die. His failure had left him even more depressed.

But there had been one bright spot in his suicide attempt, Susan had stopped her never-ending attacks. More than that, she had started being nice. He had been wary at first, but soon realized she was trying to change. As he watched, she became the woman he had married so many years before. Soon, they began making love again for the first time since he had returned from Thailand. Sometimes it was passionate. To his own amazement, Mike began falling in love with Susan all over again. He was surprised there could be anything left after so many years of numbness.

Three months after being laid off, and two months after Josh had left home, Mike's old company called to say they had picked up a new project and would be calling him back in a few weeks. Jess Ankrom, his ex-boss, had said little about the job except it was out of town. Mike didn't care; he was happy to be working again even if was only temporary.

That afternoon Mike called Susan at work and told her everything Jess had said. He wasn't sure how she would react to him being out of town again, but she seemed truly happy for him. He suggested they go out for dinner that evening and she said yes.

After dinner, Susan said she had a surprise. She opened her purse and pulled out an envelope. Her smile faded as she handed it to him. "Before you open this I have something to say. It's about when you were in Thailand."

Mike glanced down at the envelope. He had no idea what it contained, but divorce papers came instantly to mind. He looked up, uneasiness etched his face.

Susan kept her voice even. "When you went to Thailand, you were gone for a very long time. You never said anything, but I think you fell in love with another woman." She paused, blushing in self-embarrassment. "I should hate you for that but I don't. If you did find someone else, maybe it was my fault. I understand that now and I'm trying to change." She paused again, closed her eyes for a moment, and then looked back up, "I love you Mike and I never want to lose you, but I need to be sure it's me you want. We have reached the age where we owe each other total honesty." She took a deep breath. "Now you should look in the envelope."

Mike lifted the flap and pulled out an airline ticket. In the dim light of the restaurant, he couldn't see the details. He stared up at his wife.

She took his hand and squeezed tight. "It's to Bangkok. It leaves next week." She paused for a moment then added. "If you come back, it will be to me."

"And if I don't?"

"It's better we know that now instead of two years from now. I can't spend my life competing with a dream. I bought this ticket so you can decide what you want."

Mike was overwhelmed. He had never told Susan the truth, but he knew how her suspicions tormented her. Except for intuition, there was no way for her to know that Math had ever existed. The last thing he expected was for her to insist he go back to Thailand alone. His words came out a hoarse whisper, "Will you go with me?"

"I don't understand," she responded, disconcerted.

"I love you and I don't want either of us to hurt again. I will be hurt if you tell me no, and you would be hurt if I go alone. If I don't come back, at least you will know the reason why. What do you say, will you come with me?"

Susan smiled. Tears formed in her eyes. "How can I say no?"

Later that night they made love with a passion they hadn't felt since they were much younger. She responded to his every touch and he responded to her every movement. He basked in the glow of her pleasure as he rushed to the end of his own physical desires. Afterwards they fell asleep holding on to one another.

Early the next morning Susan bought airline tickets for herself and then went shopping to get *a few things* for their upcoming trip. She never came home. A deer smashing through the windshield at sixty-five miles per hour can do unbelievable damage.

Mike remembered very little about that day, or any of the days which followed. He remembered identifying her body. He remembered trying and failing to find Josh. He remembered the funeral, but only vaguely. He got drunk immediately after the funeral and never sobered up. His sister, ever the efficient one, took care of the legal crap that haunted people after they died. He signed whenever and wherever he was told. His sister tried to talk to him about his drinking but she stopped when he told her to fuck off.

As soon as it was cleared, he put their house on the market, furniture included. He didn't want anything except his clothes and a few personal effects. The house sold in two days. Total net assets after nearly thirty years of marriage—$92,159.28!

He put half of the money in a trust fund for Josh and the rest in his own account. Then he rented a cheap hotel room where he could get drunk and feel sorry for himself in peace.

J. F. Gump

During the last few weeks he had graduated from beer and wine to bourbon and vodka. He left the room only long enough to buy more booze and cigarettes. He took a bath whenever he couldn't stand his own odor. Sometimes he ate.

He looked at the cigarette dangling between his fingers, took another drag, and then stubbed it out in the ashtray. He picked up the half empty bottle of vodka and took a short swig. His stomach twisted with a sharp spasm that gave him a newfound respect for vodka. He knew it would pass after the alcohol dulled the same pain it had caused. He leaned back and waited.

Before the vodka had time to take effect the phone rang again. This time he answered. "Hello."

"Damn you, Mike! Don't hang up on me again."

It was Jess Ankrom. "How did you find me?"

"Your sister Carol. She's quite worried about you. Damned if I know why. By the way, I'm not very good at this sort of thing, but I want to say I'm truly sorry about Susan. I met her a couple of times and she seemed like a nice lady. Are you okay? No, of course you aren't or you wouldn't be staying in that shit-hole of a motel. Look, I still have that job coming up next month. I need you to come to the office for a week or two and catch yourself up on the project. Can you be here tomorrow morning?"

One thing about Jess Ankrom, he didn't let etiquette stand in the way of direct communications. "I'm not interested, Jess. Goodbye."

"Wait! I forgot to mention something. The job is at the refinery in Thailand. You know, the project we did a year or so ago. I didn't mention that before; thought it might cause problems. Know what I mean? They asked for you specifically. Damned if I know why. It's only for a couple of months, but maybe we can stretch it a little. It's up to you."

"I already have two tickets to Thailand," Mike said, remembering the tickets Susan had bought. He wasn't sure they were still good.

THAILAND – COLD RAIN

"Well, now you have three. Sorry, but this one's coach class. The refinery has a new controller and he's a real tight-ass. It was all I could do to get a car and a driver out of him. Your sister thinks it will do you some good to get away from here for a while. I think so, too. Are you interested or not?"

Thailand! Not so long ago he would have given anything to go back. Now he had no reason to go. *Thailand!* Somehow the word had a magical effect on him. It lit a spark he thought was dead. Suddenly he wanted to go back. Maybe it was his chance to start living again. He felt a rush of anticipation that he hadn't felt since Susan had died. He screwed the cap back on the vodka bottle and set it aside. "I'll be there this afternoon."

Mike showered, put on his cleanest dirty clothes, and drove to the office. The assignment was a cakewalk. He would have it done in three or four weeks, but told everyone it would take ten or twelve. Jess Ankrom rolled his eyes, but for once he said nothing.

Mike collected everything he needed from the office and went back to his motel room. He called the airlines and asked about his and Susan's old tickets. With the death and all, the tickets were still good and there wasn't a penalty. He rearranged everything, threw in a few frequent-flier miles, and upgraded himself to business class. His flight would leave in ten days. He would be two weeks early but he didn't care. He was ready to get away.

He drove to the nearest mall and blew three hundred dollars on new clothes. On the way home, he bought a pizza and a six pack from Antonio's. By nine o'clock he was asleep.

Chapter 4

Chiang Mai, Thailand

Surat Duansawang awoke as dawn overtook the dark Thailand night. He rubbed his eyes for a moment and then stared into the heavy grayness.

His room was one of two in the painfully small house. The concrete floor and corrugated tin walls made it more like a shack than a house, but it was his home.

His cot took up nearly half the space in the room. A small dresser and an assortment of boxes crammed with personal belongings filled the rest. The second of his two rooms was almost identical except they had somehow managed to fit a sewing machine into the already cramped space.

Near the door sat the small bag his wife had packed for him the night before. Hanging from a wire stretched along the ceiling were the clothes she had selected for him to wear. He smiled at the thought of his wife asleep in the room next door.

In a moment he slipped into a pair of well-worn shorts, grabbed his towel, toothbrush and razor, and then stumbled outside toward the bath. Today would begin a three day assignment driving a German couple to tourists sites in the Golden Triangle area of northern Thailand. It was easy money.

When he was sure his teeth were as clean as they would get, he abandoned the brushing for a bath. The cold water he ladled over himself shook away the last shreds of the drowsiness. As he toweled himself dry, he caught sight of himself in a mirror hanging on the wall. Surat wasn't a vain man but he had always taken pride in the light color of his skin and the green flecks in his eyes. It made him look aristocratic, high class. Even better, he looked younger than most of most men in their late thirties. Lucky genes he figured. He shaved and then hurried back to his room.

Quickly but quietly he dressed in his neatly pressed slacks and white shirt. Both would be wrinkled within an hour but that was okay. He was happy his wife had taken the time to iron his clothes to help him look professional.

Chalamsee was his wife's given name, but everyone knew her as Nuang. They had been married for nearly seventeen years. In all that time they'd never had children. He had often wondered if it was him or her who was infertile. Now he knew it was neither.

Nuang had become pregnant months ago. He remembered the day clearly. She had just returned from visiting her brother in Pattaya and wasted no time letting him know she wanted to have sex. He had never seen her so aggressive. It was like she was possessed. Surat had been surprised at the way his body responded. That night they made love for the first time in months.

The following week they made love every day, but Surat knew it was that first night when she became pregnant. It had been magic and Nuang carried his child as proof. He could hardly wait for the baby to be born so he could brag to his friends. He didn't care whether it was a boy or a girl, or what it looked like, as long as the baby was healthy.

Surat knelt beside his wife and laid his hand on her stomach. His touch was light. She stirred but didn't awaken. He stared at her for a minute, and then leaned over and kissed her cheek.

Her eyes flicked open and she smiled.

"Sawasdee krup, teeluk," he whispered. "Good morning, love."

"Sawasdee ka, Surat," Nuang answered. "What time is it? Are you going to work now?"

"Yes, it's very early but I must go. I don't want to be late. Will you be okay until I return?"

Nuang smiled at her husband, "I'll be fine. The baby won't be born before you return. I will make it wait for you."

Surat laughed. "I think the baby will come when the baby wants to come and you can't make it wait."

"Not yet born and already I have a disobedient child," Nuang responded. "Sort of like his father, don't you think?"

"I would say more like her mother." Surat teased.

Nuang slapped him playfully on the shoulder. "Get out of here and let your fat wife finish her sleep."

Surat laughed. "You're not a fat wife; you're the most beautiful woman in Thailand. I'll be back in three days. If you need anything, call me on my cell phone."

Nuang's smile faded into seriousness. "Please drive safely."

"I always do," he said. "I'll be home as soon as I can. Goodbye, teeluk. I love you."

"Goodbye," she whispered as Surat picked up his small bag and left their house. "I love you, too."

Nuang shut her eyes and tried to sleep but couldn't. Instead she lay there thinking. The last few years of her life had been full of surprises. Her brother had opened his own business in Pattaya, her next younger sister had married a man from Scotland and moved away, and her second youngest sister had fallen in love with an American. Her own pregnancy was the biggest surprise of all. No one had expected it, especially herself.

But there had been tragedies, too. Her mother and father had separated, her brother-in-law and her nephew had drowned in a freak accident, and her sister who loved the American had died in a motorcycle accident. Nuang wondered what would come next, a good surprise or another tragedy.

A sharp pain interrupted her thoughts. She'd had stomach cramps like that before—just last week in fact. She had been sure she was going into labor and Surat had rushed her to the hospital. After a series of tests and measurements the doctors had diagnosed her pain as gas and sent her home. The baby wouldn't arrive for another two or three weeks. Nuang's embarrassment had been complete. She wouldn't go to the hospital with gas pains again.

THAILAND - COLD RAIN

As the cramp eased, she turned her thoughts to the day she had told Surat she was pregnant. She had never seen anyone so happy. From that moment on he had become a different man than the one she had been married to for most of her adult life. Surat had started working harder than ever before, and when he was home he doted on her entirely. He had even started offering to send money to her family in Phitsanulok.

Nuang couldn't believe the change in her husband. If only he had been like this forever, she thought, their lives would have been much different. During the months she had been pregnant, she and Surat had rediscovered their love for each other. She prayed their happiness would last.

Nuang dozed on and off, but never fully slept. By ten o'clock the tropical Thailand sun had heated their corrugated tin house to uncomfortable levels and she'd begun to sweat.

She left the bed and turned on the oscillating fan. She wanted to go outside and wash, but the thought of anyone seeing her pregnant body embarrassed her. She would bring a bucket of water inside later and wash herself in private. Surat wouldn't be home tonight so she wasn't concerned that she might smell bad.

She slipped into the clothes she would wear for the day and then propped open the oversized shutters set into the front wall. In a few minutes the fan cooled the house a few degrees and she stopped sweating.

She stood in the doorway and watched the cars, trucks, and motorcycles passing by. Down the street, a sidewalk vendor was setting up for lunch. The vendor's name was Noy and she was an excellent cook. Nuang's stomach rumbled at the thought of food.

As she reached for her purse, a familiar terror gripped at her senses. Her eyes darted through the house but she saw nothing. She strained her ears but didn't hear the voices. If they were here, they were quieter than usual.

She glanced at the strips of aluminum foil hanging from the ceiling. She had put them there to ward off the demons, and they were fluttering out of position. At once she turned off the fan and the aluminum strips stopped moving. She went to the door and cautiously stuck her hand outside. Nothing. The voices were silent.

She picked up her purse, pulled the door shut, and waddle-walked to Noy's sidewalk restaurant.

"Sawasdee ka, good morning," Noy greeted her politely. "You look wonderful today."

"Khop khun ka, thank you," Nuang smiled. "But I don't feel so wonderful. I think maybe I'm hungry."

"I can cure that," Noy smiled. "My special today is cashew chicken on rice. It's very good."

Nuang had eaten Noy's cashew chicken before and it was good. "Okay, I'll have that and a bottle of water."

As Nuang waited for her meal, another contraction twisted her insides. She nearly cried out at its intensity. Maybe not a gas pain, she thought. She turned away so Noy couldn't see the grimace on her face. Suddenly she felt hot and flushed. Beads of sweat formed and ran down her face. Her head spun. For a moment she thought she might faint. The contraction subsided about the same time that Noy delivered her food.

"Are you okay?" Noy asked, seeing the look on Nuang's face.

"I don't know. My stomach is cramping and I feel dizzy. I'm not sure I can eat."

Noy touched Nuang's forehead. "You're warm but you aren't fevered. I'll put your food in a bag so you can take it home to eat later when you feel better. Are you having labor pains?"

"I don't know," Nuang answered. "I've never had a baby before."

"Never mind," Noy said, "You'll know soon enough. Let me take care of a couple of things and then I'll walk you to your house." She was back in seconds.

Nuang's cramps intensified when she stood and grew worse as she walked. Less than halfway home she stopped, a look of utter embarrassment covered her face.

"What's wrong?" Noy asked.

"I think I peed myself," Nuang winced in embarrassment.

Noy glanced down at the small puddle forming at Nuang's feet. "I think your water just broke. Is your husband at home?"

"No."

"Then you can forget going there. I'll get you to the hospital. Unless I miss my guess, you'll have a baby before the day is over."

"I must go home," Nuang forced her words between clinched teeth. "I need to bathe, and put on clean clothes. My shutters are open. Someone might steal my sewing machine."

"I'll close your shutters and you won't need clean clothes in the hospital. You'll go now and no arguing. Understand?"

Nuang nodded.

Two minutes later she was bouncing through the streets of Chiang Mai in a three-wheeled tuk-tuk taxi. The ride did nothing for her pain. As the tuk-tuk stopped at the front of the hospital, she heard the voices and they were laughing.

While Noy closed up and bolted down the house, she found a piece of paper and wrote a note for Nuang's husband. "Your wife has gone to the hospital to have your baby."

After everything was secure, Noy locked the front door and hurried back to her restaurant.

~~~

Nuang spent the next six hours at the hospital in periodic misery. The contractions came and went, but mostly they came. She never imagined labor would be so painful.

Throughout her lifetime Nuang had seen many women get pregnant and have babies, but it had never happened to her. She had stopped thinking about having a family years ago. Now she was in the final stages of labor and she was scared. Thirty-six was too old to be having a baby. It's definitely too old when you're not sure who the father is. The thought mortified her.

It's your husband's baby, she had been telling herself since she learned she was pregnant. *It's your husband's baby.* She knew the words could be a lie but she kept telling herself that anyway. Nuang knew who the father was if it wasn't Surat, yet she denied the thought every time it entered her head. She had once made love to a man other than her husband, only a few weeks before she learned she was pregnant. It was the only time in her life that she had been unfaithful. It had been a fluke, a twist of fate, a mistake. Women don't get pregnant from having sex just once, she had struggled to convince herself. She and Surat had made love many times. It had to be Surat's baby.

The doctor came into her hospital room and did some tests and measurements. "You'll be giving birth soon, Mrs. Duansawang," he announced. "You're a small woman and your delivery may be uncomfortable. I'm going to give you something for the pain, and then we can start to work bringing your baby into the world."

Nuang only nodded. Her latest contraction had eased but still wouldn't allow her to speak.

"Is your husband here?" the doctor asked, making conversation as he worked.

She managed a weak *no*.

"If you would like, we can contact him."

"No," she said again, her words stronger this time. "I don't want my husband near me."

"Okay," the doctor replied evenly, "It isn't uncommon for women to feel like that at about this time of delivery. You will feel better about him later. I see on your chart your nickname is Nuang. May I call you Nuang?"

Her contraction eased to acceptable levels. "Yes, that would be better. It's my name."

Five minutes later they had finished giving her an epidural and the pain had all but vanished. The relief was bliss.

At seven twenty-four that evening, Mrs. Chalamsee "Nuang" Duansawang gave birth to a daughter. What she saw when they brought the baby confirmed her deepest fears. There was no mistaking whose baby it was and it wasn't her husband's.

She made them take the baby away so she could think. The voices that had been tormenting her came back and they were louder than ever. They insisted she must run away. That night Nuang made her plans.

The next morning, against the doctor's orders and threats, Nuang left the hospital and took her newborn with her. She wasn't feeling well and knew she should stay, but the voices were unrelenting. Her mind was a blur, in shock from her labor. She was in even more shock from what had emerged from her womb. She couldn't let Surat see this baby.

Her first stop was an ATM where she withdrew most of the money from their bank account. Next she took a taxi to the Chiang Mai bus station and bought a one way ticket to her hometown. She found a seat away from the main terminal and began the three hour wait for her bus. She kept the baby's face covered with the blanket she had taken from the hospital. No one needed to know her baby had blonde hair and blue eyes. She breathed a sigh of relief when she boarded her bus and headed south toward Phitsanulok.

~~~

An hour outside of Chiang Mai the baby awoke and began to cry. Nuang wasn't sure what to do. She knew the baby must be hungry, but she had never breastfed a baby before. She rocked back and forth in her seat hoping the cries would stop but they didn't. Finally she knew she had no choice. She unbuttoned her blouse and put the baby's mouth to her breast.

It was an unusual sensation. Surat almost never touched her breasts, and had never taken one in his mouth, not even when they made love. The feeling wasn't unpleasant, just different. She kept the blanket pulled across her as the baby nursed.

The man seated across the aisle stared for a few minutes but lost interest when she kept the blanket in place.

Nuang and her baby arrived in Phitsanulok long after the sun had set. It was almost nine o'clock by the time she exited the bus terminal. She flagged down a taxi and gave directions to her mother's house. Two blocks later she changed her mind and gave directions to her sister's house. After a minute, she told the driver to stop at the nearest Seven-Eleven store and she asked him to wait while she went inside to buy diapers, wipes, and powder.

The driver didn't mind. He left the meter running and waited.

When Nuang returned, she gave him new directions. This time it was to the temple. As much as she wanted to see her mother and her sister, she wasn't ready to face the shame of having a baby from an illicit affair with a farang.

As the taxi made its way through Phitsanulok, Nuang changed the baby's diaper. It was only wet. She wondered how long it was before babies had their first bowel movement. It was something she had never thought about and something she didn't know.

The driver never looked back so he didn't see the baby uncovered; but Nuang did. As they passed beneath the street lights, she got a perfect look. Its skin was mostly red and clearly more foreign than Thai. Its hair wasn't as white as she had first thought, but it was far from being black. Its eyes were shut but she knew they were as blue as she remembered. Her baby wasn't Thai. It was farang, foreign, a half-breed, and it was hers. She stared for a long minute. Yes, it was definitely hers.

"Why are you going to the temple?" the driver asked, pretending nonchalance.

He was being nosy, but Nuang answered anyway, "I'm taking my baby to see her grandfather." It was a lie, but the truth was none of his business.

"Your grandfather is a monk?" the driver pried.

"My grandfather is the abbot," she lied again, hoping the driver would stop his questions.

"How long has he been a monk?"

Nuang didn't answer. Instead, she pulled the baby to her chest and sang a soft Thai lullaby. The driver took the hint and kept his mouth shut. Five minutes later they arrived at the temple. She paid her fare and the taxi drove away.

As she entered the courtyard, she heard faint chanting emanating from inside the temple. She was surprised. It was late, and the temple should be quiet by now. Probably some religious holiday she had forgotten. She saw a lone monk walking toward her. She wondered if he would speak to her or just ignore her.

"Sawasdee, krup," he said when he was within earshot.

"Sawasdee, ka," she replied. "Please excuse my bad manners, but I cannot wai while holding my baby." A wai is a polite greeting of respect, presented by pressing one's hands together in prayer-like fashion and then placing them in front of one's face. She knew she could put her baby on the ground and wai to the monk, but she didn't. "Please accept my apologies."

"Mai pen rai, never mind," the monk's eyes focused on the small bundle she held close to her chest. "Can I help you?"

Nuang guessed the monk to be in his late twenties. He was lean but not gaunt. His head was shaved. He seemed uncomfortable in his saffron robe. She suspected he was at the temple to do a period of service to Buddha and God, rather than making monkhood his life. It was common for Thai men to spend a few weeks, or even several years, wearing the saffron robes. Usually, they did it when they were younger, but some did it when they were older. It was a personal thing for each to decide.

"I have a baby and very little money," she said. "I need a place to stay for tonight. A man told me this temple sometimes helps desperate women. Please, can you help me?"

"How old is your baby? Is it well?" he asked, his tone gentle.

"The baby was born just yesterday," she answered. "Please, I need some place to lie down. Suddenly, I feel very tired."

It was true. This was the longest she had stood at one time since the baby was born and she hadn't eaten in two days. There was an itching and burning in her pelvic area. She felt nauseous.

J. F. Gump

"May I see your baby?" the monk asked.

Nuang pulled the baby closer. "No."

The young monk was taken aback. He had never met a woman who didn't want to show off her baby, no matter how beautiful or ugly. He studied her face. She wasn't young, but not old either. He guessed her to be in her mid thirties. The maternity dress bagged unflattering on her body. She looked exhausted. The baby hadn't moved or made a sound.

"Please come," he said. "I'll show you where you can sleep."

She followed him to a building away from the main temple area. The room was stark but clean. Most important, it had a bed. A deep chill gripped her body. She shook involuntarily.

"Are you okay?" he asked, stepping closer, extending his hand to touch her forehead.

Nuang pulled away. "I'm okay. Please, I want to sleep now."

"What about the baby? Will you need help? I can have someone take care while you sleep."

"No," the word shot from her mouth. She hesitated a moment and then said in a softer tone, "I mean no, thank you. I'll be fine."

She laid the baby on the bed, then turned and presented the monk with a very proper wai. "Khop khun mahk ka, thank you very much. Now I must sleep."

"Chai, yes. I will come for you in the morning to eat breakfast. It will be very early." He turned and left the room.

Another chill swept through Nuang. She never knew Thailand could be so cold. She slipped under the bedcovers beside her baby, pulled herself into a tight fetal ball, and shivered violently.

As she lay there trying to get warm, she realized the voices hadn't spoken since she left Chiang Mai. She prayed they didn't find her here. In a while the shivering calmed and she slept.

During the night an infection grew wild, uncontrolled. It ravaged her body to near death.

Chapter 5

Chiang Mai, Thailand

Surat's three day assignment to Thailand's Golden Triangle ended on the second day. The German couple he had been escorting had cut their trip short due to a family emergency. After making sure they had confirmed flights, Surat left them at the airport and headed home. It was nine o'clock in the evening.

The traffic was light and Surat reached his house in twenty minutes. A seed of apprehension sprouted when he found the shutters bolted and the door locked. He tapped lightly at the door and waited. Nuang didn't answer and he didn't hear her moving inside. *She is only asleep,* he tried to convince himself as he fumbled through his keys. In a moment the door was unlocked and he stepped inside.

He turned on the bare overhead light and walked quickly through the house. Nuang wasn't there. It wasn't like her to be out this late at night. In fact, for the last month she had hardly gone out at all. She had become extremely self-conscious and thought everyone was staring at her pregnancy. More than that, she had become paranoid. She was always talking about voices he couldn't hear, and evil spirits and other things that put cold bumps on his skin. No, she wouldn't be out this late without a good reason.

He searched the house again looking for any clue that would tell him where she had gone. This time he saw a note on the bed. He held it under the light and studied the writing. Surat wasn't an educated man, but he could read road signs and other simple words as long as they were written in very proper script. Beyond that, reading was a struggle. Whoever had left the note had scribbled so badly that he couldn't read a word of what it said.

After a few minutes he thought he recognized the words baby and hospital, but he wasn't sure. He folded the note and slipped it into his shirt pocket. His heart raced neck-and-neck with his thoughts as he hurried outside to the car. His employer didn't approve of him using the company vehicle for personal business, but sometimes he did it anyway. He started the car and sped to the hospital.

At the information counter, he spoke to the nurse on duty, "Kaw thort krup, excuse me," he said, very polite. "I need the room number for Mrs. Chalamsee Duansawang."

"It's past visiting hours," the woman responded.

"I know," he lied. He had no idea of their visiting hours. "She's my wife. I must see her right away. It's important."

The lady stared at him for a brief second then punched at the computer keyboard. In a moment she looked up. "Are you sure she's your wife?"

"Of course I'm sure," he said, irritated at her question. "What's her room number, please?"

"She's not here. She checked herself out this morning. It was against her doctor's orders. She didn't pay her bill before she left. You owe the hospital a lot of money."

"Did she have a baby?"

"Yes, she had a baby girl. Are you sure you're the father?"

"I told you once already. Thank you for your help. My insurance will pay for the hospital."

He returned to the car unsure what to do next. He wanted to revel in the joy of being a father, but the situation wouldn't let him. Why hadn't Nuang called his cell phone when she went into labor? Why did she check herself out of the hospital and where could she have gone? He couldn't tell if the feeling overtaking him was anger or worry or terror.

He remembered the voices Nuang had been hearing. Certainly that wasn't normal. Now he wondered if they could be dangerous.

Suddenly he wished he hadn't laughed at her when she had told him about them. He slid into the driver's seat and pulled away from the hospital.

He drove aimlessly through the streets of Chiang Mai trying to think like Nuang. There weren't many places she would go besides their home. In a while he had narrowed it to her mother's house in Phitsanulok or her best friend's apartment here in Chiang Mai. It took him less than five minutes to drive to Siriwan's.

Surat rang the bell at the bottom of the stairs leading up to Siriwan's room. A moment later a window opened above him. He looked up, "Sawasdee krup, Khun Siriwan. Have you seen Nuang?"

"I haven't seen Nuang in over a week," she shouted down. "Is everything okay? Have you lost her? "

Surat blushed at his situation. How many men lose their pregnant wives? "I was out of town for one night. While I was gone, Nuang had her baby and left the hospital. She's not at our house. I was hoping she had come to visit you."

"I'm sorry. I haven't seen or heard from her. Is the baby okay? Is there anything I can do?"

"I don't know about the baby except that it's a girl. If you see Nuang, make her wait here and call me. I think maybe she's afraid to be at our house alone. She thinks evil spirits are there."

"Maybe she went to her mother's house."

"I thought about that, but I don't think she would travel so far with a new baby." Memories of the evil spirits crept through his head. "But I will call and ask. If she's there, I'll drive down and bring her back. Thanks for your help."

"Mai pen rai, never mind," Siriwan answered. "I will watch for Nuang. If I see her, I'll let you know. Good luck, Surat. My prayers are with you."

He drove back to his house hoping Nuang would be there but she wasn't. He slid his cell phone from his belt and sighed. Nuang's mother didn't like him much and she didn't hide it from anyone. The old woman tolerated him only because he was her daughter's husband. His feelings toward her were mutual. Reluctantly, he dialed her number. He winced at the sound of her voice.

"Sawasdee krup, hello," he said with forced politeness. "I am Surat."

There was a noticeable silence before Nui spoke. "I know who you are. Did Nuang have her baby? Is she okay?" Nui didn't make any attempt at customary Thai politeness. She simply asked her typical pointed questions.

"Yes, she had a baby girl. Do you mean you haven't seen her?"

"How could I? You keep her locked away in Chiang Mai. You do know where she is, don't you?"

Surat's chest tightened. "No, I don't. She left the hospital, but she didn't come home."

"How could you lose your wife and your baby?" the old woman shrieked through the phone. "What kind of a husband are you? I always knew you were no good. I told you..."

Surat turned off his phone. He didn't want to listen to her ranting. He hadn't lost Nuang; she had lost herself and he was worried. If she hadn't gone to Siriwan's house and if she hadn't gone to her mother's, then he had no idea where she might have gone. On impulse he drove to the bus station. It was only a hunch, but maybe someone had seen her.

Buses arrived and departed Chiang Mai at all hours of the day and night, but the terminal was quiet when Surat entered. He approached the ticket counter and asked loud enough for everyone to hear, "Did anyone see a woman with a very young baby here today? I'm her husband. It's very important that I know where she has gone. She's not well and needs her medication."

It was a lie, but he didn't care.

"Does she have braided hair?" one woman behind the counter asked.

"Yes, yes she does. Have you seen her?"

"Earlier, when I first came to work, I sold a ticket to a woman with a baby. Her hair was in braids. She looked ill. She bought a ticket to Phitsanulok." The girl glanced at her watch. "She should have arrived there already."

A woman with braided hair and a baby. It had to be Nuang. Surat ran from the bus terminal. If he drove fast enough, he could be in Phitsanulok by morning.

At a stop light he counted the money in his wallet: less than 1,200 baht. Probably enough for gasoline and food, but just barely.

He stopped at an ATM to withdraw extra money from his account. It registered a balance of 200 baht. That wasn't possible. Over the last few months he had saved several thousand baht for when the baby was born. He tried again with the same results.

"Shit," he said aloud. Not only had Nuang ran away, but she had taken all of their money with her. He hoped she would spend it on the baby.

He ran their balance to zero and drove south toward Phitsanulok.

It was five o'clock in the morning and still dark when he coasted to a stop in front of Nui's house. He sat in the car and waited until he saw a light shine from inside. Then he walked to the door and knocked. In a moment, Nui pulled the door open. The old woman looked tired.

"Good morning," he said, his tone cordial. "May I speak to Nuang?"

"Why are you here?" she demanded, her eyes narrowed in contempt. "I told you last night that I haven't seen Nuang."

"I don't believe you," his courteous smile faded. "I want to see my wife, and I want to see her now."

Nui hesitated as if calculating her next remark. She tilted her head back and stared down her nose. "If you were a better husband, Nuang would be at your house and we wouldn't be talking."

Her words grated at his exhaustion. He checked the urge to retort. He knew he would never win an argument against Nui's sharp tongue. "Please just listen for a minute. Yesterday I went to work, and when I came home Nuang was gone. The hospital said she had a baby one day and checked herself out the next. A woman at the bus station said Nuang had bought a ticket to Phitsanulok. I thought she had come here. If she's not here, then I'm very worried."

"Nuang didn't come here and I am worried, too. Maybe she went to her sister's house. Neet has a baby of her own. I think that must be it. Wait for a minute and I'll go with you."

Neither spoke as they made the short drive. Neet was already awake and clearly surprised to see Nui and Surat together. "Is everything okay?"

"We don't know," Nui answered. "Surat has lost Nuang. We hoped she would be here."

Surat ignored Nui's intentional barb and explained about Nuang's recent odd behavior, and the voices that whispered in her ears. He told them how nervous she seemed every time they talked about their baby. He sensed something was wrong but he didn't know what.

For two hours they discussed Nuang's unusual behavior and where she might have gone. Later they called her brother Anan in Pattaya, and her sister Itta in Scotland. They didn't expect either to know more than themselves, but they wanted to let the others know what was happening in case Nuang contacted either of them.

With nothing left to do in Phitsanulok, Surat drove back to Chiang Mai. His boss was going to be pissed; he hoped he didn't lose his job.

Chapter 6

Phitsanulok, Thailand

In the days following her arrival at the temple, Nuang's body was ravaged by the mother of all infections. Her intensely high fever triggered horrifying hallucinations. Everything became so surrealistic she didn't know what was real and what was a dream. Vague images of her surroundings mixed with terrifying nightmares. She thought she heard a baby crying and people talking, and hands touching and cold things sharp as needles being pushed against her skin. It all seemed less real than the monkey-man who filled the voids of her delirious mind. Surely it was the same creature that had haunted her sister Math to death.

Finally the infection succumbed to penicillin and Nuang's feverish nightmare ended. She wasn't sure where she was or what time it was when she awoke. She didn't even know if it was day or night. The room wasn't familiar. It had no windows. A single lamp glowed in the otherwise dim room.

She touched her stomach. Flat. Yes, now she remembered. She'd had a baby. The thought caused her eyes to dart about the room. Where was her baby? For that matter, where was she?

Nuang stood from the bed and started toward the door. In less than four steps her legs buckled and she fell hard against the cold concrete floor. A small cry passed her lips. Immediately a man was at her side. She glanced up; it was a monk. He looked familiar but she couldn't place him. He lifted her from the floor and carried her back to the bed. It was only then that she realized she was undressed. As fast as she could, she pulled the blankets over her body.

"You saw me naked," she said, looking away from his stare.

"Don't worry," he answered, "it's not the first time."

Even in her confused state Nuang felt her cheeks burning. "What do you mean, *it's not the first time*? Where is my baby?"

The monk sat at the foot of the bed, well away from Nuang. "Your baby is fine. I'll bring her here later, after I am sure you are well. You have been a very sick young lady. You developed a severe infection from giving birth. You could have died. It has been my duty to care for you."

Nuang pointed toward her womanhood. "You mean I had an infection here?"

The monk nodded.

"And you looked at me there?"

He nodded again, blushing.

"I would rather die than have a monk look at me there."

"I'm a doctor."

"You're a monk."

"Yes, but first I'm a doctor."

Nuang's mind raced to recall everything. Piece by piece it came back. This was the same monk who had greeted her when she arrived at the temple. He had brought her to this room. She remembered him being very polite. Finally, she said, "Are you sure you're a doctor?"

The monk breathed a sigh of relief. "Yes, I am. I'm here only because my uncle was once a monk at this temple. He died while I was attending medical school in America. I promised I would devote six months of my life to Buddha in honor of his memory. In two months my promise will be fulfilled. After I leave the temple, I will open my own medical practice. I'm pleased for you and your daughter to be among my first patients." He smiled an impish grin, put his hands together in front of his face, bowed forward slightly, and presented her with a wai.

It was neither customary nor expected for monks to wai anyone except their superiors. Certainly they would never wai a woman. Nuang was surprised by his gesture. Even more she was flattered. "Thank you," she said, returning the wai. "May I see my daughter now?"

"Yes, I will have the woman bring her to you. Your baby is a beautiful little girl."

Minutes later a young woman came into the room carrying an infant.

"My name is Somjit," the woman said, eyes downcast, her voice barely a whisper. "I have been caring for your baby. Without me your baby might have died."

Somjit knew her pronouncement was unnecessary, but she said it anyway. She didn't care. Secretly, she had been hoping this woman, the baby's birth mother, would die. She wanted the baby to be hers. Her heart beat with jealousy as she handed the newborn to Nuang.

Nuang noticed Somjit's swollen breasts through her thin, silk-like, blouse. "You have been nursing my baby?" she ventured quietly, non-threatening.

Somjit looked away from Nuang's steady gaze. "Yes," she whispered. Her single word carried tones of both pride and pain. An embarrassed silence followed.

After a minute Nuang said, "Thank you for doing that. You must have a baby of your own. Is it a boy or a girl?"

Somjit didn't answer. She wanted to pick up the baby and run away, but she couldn't. "Mai pen rai," she tried to say; it came out as an unintelligible moan. She turned and rushed from the room.

Nuang heard gut-wrenching sobs filter in from the hallway. Then a male voice speaking low. In a minute the sobbing stopped.

Nuang pondered the woman's reaction. She wondered what she had said to upset the woman so much. She wasn't angry or bitter, though she did feel a small twinge of jealousy. But more than that, she felt a deep sense of gratitude. Certainly she hadn't meant to upset the woman.

She stared at her baby for a long time. There was no doubt the child was hers. Its nose, its ears, its mouth, and its chin could have come from no one else. Its skin was still red but less than she remembered from before.

She wondered what she would do after she and the baby left the temple. Going back to her husband wasn't an option. Surat would never accept a half-farang baby as his own, and he would never forgive her infidelity, no matter how or why it had happened. For an instant she hated herself and the baby. It was a fleeting feeling that was quickly replaced by depression.

At the age of thirty-six, Nuang was trapped by one long-past minute of unthinking passion in the bed of her sister's boyfriend. The idea that she could contact the baby's true father crossed her mind. Maybe he would send her money if he knew. A second later, she decided it was a stupid thought. What had happened was her own fault, and there was no sense ruining another life because of it. Still, the idea lingered.

She put her daughter's mouth against her breast. By reflex the baby engulfed a nipple and began sucking. At once Nuang pulled the baby away. She had been sick and she had been taking medication. What if her milk was no good? She might make her own daughter sick.

The baby cried at the interruption of its meal. Nuang cooed and sang a soft Thai lullaby, but the crying continued. In the hallway, Somjit's sobbing resumed. It was a woeful sound of emotional torment. Nuang's mind retreated from the screaming baby and the wailing woman. The room spun crazily. She wavered from sharp awareness to eerie confusion.

"Kill the baby," a voice inside her head demanded. The demons had found her. "Kill the baby before it kills you."

"No," she screamed at the top of her lungs.

The young monk ran into the room. Nuang's eyes shined wild. He snatched the baby from her arms and carried it from the room. He returned a second later. Nuang was standing naked by the bed screaming *no* over and over.

He grabbed a blanket and wrapped it around her body. "Shut

up and lie down."

Immediately, her cries ceased. "What happened?"

"I don't know." He eased her toward the bed. "Maybe you can tell me."

"Where is my baby?" she asked, her disorientation obvious. "Is my baby safe? The voices said to kill my baby."

The monk stared at her. He had read about people hearing voices and doing odd things, but he had never had contact with any of those patients during his medical training.

"Your baby is fine. What voices are you talking about?"

"Didn't you hear them?" Nuang pleaded. "They were right here in this room. They told me to kill my baby. Please say you heard them."

The monk took her hand in his, "Don't worry. Everything is okay now. I will protect you and your baby from the voices. When did you first hear them?"

Nuang was surprised. She had expected the monk to react like her husband had when she told him about the voices and the demons. Surat had laughed at her and teased her about being crazy, but this monk wasn't laughing. To the contrary, he seemed sincerely concerned. "The demons came in my sixth month of pregnancy. Sometimes they talk to me."

The monk nodded his head as he studied her face. Dark shadows highlighted the hollows beneath her eyes. She was just now recovering from an infection that had savaged her entire being. In the five days she had been here, she had drank little and eaten even less. Mostly it had been clear broth they forced down her during the periodic, semi-lucid, moments. He knew she was weak and confused from the lack of food and water.

"Don't worry. The demons won't hurt you or your baby while you're in the temple. Tonight you must get some rest. Tomorrow, after you eat, you will feel better."

He sat on the edge of the bed until Nuang fell into a fitful, exhausted sleep.

Chapter 7

When Nuang awoke the following morning, the young monk was standing beside her bed. She regarded him briefly then said, "I smell awful, and I'm tired of lying here. Please bring my clothes so I can go to the bath."

The young monk smiled, pleased that she was feeling better. He nodded and stepped from the room. A moment later a woman entered carrying clothes. She laid them on the bed and then left.

Nuang slipped into the clothes. They were the same ones she had worn the night she arrived at the temple, except now they were clean. She walked quietly to the door and peeked out. The woman who had brought her clothes stood waiting in the hallway.

"I will show you to the bath," the woman said, smiling.

By reflex Nuang smiled in return. As she followed the woman, she began remembering things about this part of the temple. She had been here nearly two years ago and it hadn't been a social visit. Her sister Math's ex-fiancé had beat her severely she had been brought here for safety and healing.

By the time they reached the toilets Nuang had regained her bearings and knew where she was. She took a very long bath. It felt wonderful to be clean.

The young monk was waiting when she arrived back to her room.

"Sawasdee ka. Good morning," she said, presenting him with a polite wai.

"Sawasdee krup," he smiled, without returning her wai. "You slept through breakfast, so I asked one of the women to save you some food. If you're strong enough, we can go to the kitchen. If not, I'll have someone bring the food here. Either way I insist that you eat."

His insistence was for nothing. Nuang was starving. "Thank you. Can we go to the kitchen now? I'm so hungry I could eat an elephant."

"Sorry," the monk laughed. "We have no elephants on the menu today. Only rice and fish, but we have plenty of both. Come, I'll show you to the kitchen."

Nuang remembered where the kitchen was and didn't need anyone to show her the way, but she didn't say anything. She didn't want him to know she had been here before.

As they walked, she hoped she wouldn't see anyone else who might recognize her face and expose her past. The thought that the monk already knew who she was crossed her mind. Her heart skipped a beat at the notion.

In the kitchen Nuang was given a glass of juice and bowl with rice and fish. The bowl was small and didn't hold much; certainly not enough to satisfy her appetite. She hoped the monk intended to feed her more than this. She ate as slowly and politely as her hunger allowed. Within minutes the food was gone. She looked up. "I'm embarrassed to ask you this, but do you have more?"

"It's best if you don't eat too much at once," he said. "Let's talk for a while, and then if you're still hungry you can eat more."

Nuang nodded. "What do you want to talk about?" She hoped he wouldn't ask her too many questions so she wouldn't have to tell too many lies.

"I want to apologize for what is happening."

His statement caught her off guard. She had expected him to ask about her baby and its non-Thai appearance, or maybe even announce that he knew who she was and where she was from. She hadn't expected an apology of any sort. "I don't understand."

"When you arrived, you were very sick and couldn't take care of your baby. Another woman came here just a few days before you. Her baby was...." He hesitated briefly, as if finding the right words. "Her baby was born dead."

Nuang pulled her hand to her mouth, "Oh dear Buddha, that is terrible. She must be very sad. I feel much pity for her."

It was true; she did feel sorry for the woman. At the same time she felt envy. How less complicated her life would be now if her own baby had been born dead. Immediately, she regretted having such a thought. She pushed it aside. "But she is still young, someday she can have another."

The monk looked away. With the brutal beating Somjit had suffered at the hands and feet of her husband, it was questionable if she could ever get pregnant again. His face flushed at the lie he was about to tell. "Yes," his eyes avoided hers. "Someday she can have another baby, but right now she is very upset. She wanted to take care of your baby until you were well. I let her do that and it was a mistake."

"What do you mean it was a mistake? I think she did a very unselfish thing. "

"It was a mistake," the monk whispered low, "because Somjit has adopted your baby as her own. When you leave the temple with your baby, she will be devastated all over again."

"I never thought about that." Nuang avoided his eyes. How twisted the world was, she thought. One woman, who so desperately needed a child, had none; while another, who wished she had never gotten pregnant, had a baby she didn't want. It was a cruel joke that fate sometimes played on people. "I think everything will be okay in the end," she said hopefully.

"I pray you're right."

They sat in silence, each contemplating what had been said. In a minute a soft chant floated to them on the mid-morning air.

The monk spoke first, "After you've finished eating, I'll take you to a doctor, a family friend. I want him to do some tests to be sure you are well from your infection." He was just as concerned about the voices she heard, but didn't mention them. He suspected it was some odd effect from her pregnancy but he wanted to be sure. "It won't cost any money," he added as an afterthought.

Nuang couldn't think of a good reason to say no. "Okay, I'll go, but only if you let me have more food."

The young monk smiled and nodded his agreement, "Go ahead, but not too much. I don't want you to get sick while we're in the taxi."

After an examination and a series of tests, the doctor confirmed her infection was in full remission. He found no immediate cause for the voices, but maybe her blood work would be more definitive.

The doctor suggested it might have been caused by her pregnancy and would likely go away as her body returned to normal. He gave her a mild anti-psychotic medication but suggested she not take it unless the voices returned. Overall he concluded that Nuang was in fine health except for being too thin. He made her promise to eat better and sent her on her way.

Later that day, at the midday meal, Nuang kept her promise to the doctor.

Chapter 8

Somjit had spent most of that same day in her room with the baby. She was embarrassed at the way she had broken down the night before. She had tried very hard to keep her composure and might have succeeded if the woman hadn't asked about her own baby. Her baby was dead and nothing could change that.

During the few days she had cared for the sick woman's baby, she had developed an incredibly strong attachment. She knew it wasn't her baby and that someday she would have to give it up, but that didn't make her pain any less real. Now that the woman had healed, she knew what was coming next. She cried from time to time, but in small shudders, quite unlike the massive wails of the night before. She missed the midday meal because she didn't want to see anyone. Just before sunset, Somjit came to terms with herself and her decision. She picked up the baby and walked purposefully to Nuang's room. The door was open and Nuang was lying on the bed. For a moment Somjit thought Nuang was asleep, but then saw that her eyes were open and staring at the ceiling. She stepped into the room. "Please excuse me for not knocking. My manners are very bad."

Nuang sat up. "Never mind." She noticed that Somjit was carrying the baby. "Please come in."

Nuang had spent the last few hours thinking. Her thoughts were clearer now than they had been for weeks. For a while she had thought about her husband, Surat. He would be worried about her, but she had no intentions of going back to him. It would never work. Later, she had thought about Somjit and her dead baby; it was depressing. She had spent a lot of time practicing what she would say to Somjit when she saw her again. Now that the girl was there, her prepared speech evaporated. "I'm happy to see you. Your name is Somjit, isn't it?"

"Yes," the girl answered, her voice barely more than a whisper. "Now that you are well again, I'm returning your baby. I think you must miss her very much."

Nuang's eyes watered. After her conversation with the young monk she knew how much this must be hurting the girl.

"My name is Nuang. Please come and talk for a while. I want to know the woman who will share my baby with me."

Somjit started at the words. What did this woman mean by *share my baby*? A glimmer of hope nudged her senses. Her heart fluttered. "I don't understand."

Nuang smiled despite her own emotions. "Neither do I. Maybe it's not important for us to understand. Please, tell me about yourself."

Somjit hesitated for a moment and then talked. She was surprised at how easily her past flowed out. She told about her young life and the death of her parents, and she talked about her great aunt and her marriage to Nong, but she didn't mention the beating that had killed her baby.

When Somjit fell quiet, Nuang told of her own life. She talked about her brother in Pattaya, and her sister, Math, who had died just one year ago. Briefly, she spoke about her husband, but she didn't elaborate. She mentioned neither her family in Phitsanulok nor the true father of her baby. In a while Nuang, too, fell silent. Neither spoke for a long time.

Finally Nuang broke the silence. "May I hold the baby for a minute before you go?"

"Yes." Somjit's face twisted with inner turmoil. She handed the baby to Nuang.

Nuang swayed back and forth, rocking the baby in her arms. She watched Somjit, wondering at the thoughts that must be tearing through the girl's head. "Somjit," she said. "Do you love this baby?"

Somjit looked up. "I don't know what to say. What do you want me to say?"

"Only the truth, Somjit."

"Yes, I love your baby very much. She is the most beautiful baby I have ever seen."

"Have you wondered at the color of her eyes and her skin and her hair. Have you ever noticed the baby isn't Thai?"

Somjit paused. She prayed it wasn't a trick question and that a wrong answer wouldn't dash the small flicker of hope building inside her. Yes, she had noticed the baby didn't look Thai, but the color of the baby's hair, eyes, and skin didn't bother her. In fact, she thought it made the baby even more beautiful. Most Thai women would die for skin as white as the baby's. How was she to answer? Nuang had said she only wanted the truth.

"I guessed the father was farang, but it isn't important. What matters is that the baby is healthy and her white skin makes her very beautiful. She will be the envy of all Thai women when she is grown. You must be very proud to have a baby like this."

Guilt cut through Nuang's heart like flashing swords. She had never considered her baby as anything other than an embarrassment. She looked down at her baby from a new perspective. "Her father was from America. He died the same month I became pregnant." It was a lie but Nuang said it to stop further questions. "I don't know what I'll do now. I have no money or job or anything. I don't know how I can take care of everything. It scares me to think about it."

For the first time Somjit saw Nuang as more than a woman with a baby. Now she saw a woman with feelings and fears, a mother caught in a situation with no easy solutions. "I'm sorry," she said.

Nuang sighed and looked away. "Never mind, it's not your fault. But now I have a baby and no husband. I need help." She hesitated, considering her next words carefully, "Will you help me raise our daughter, Somjit? I would like that very much."

THAILAND - COLD RAIN

Somjit couldn't believe what she was hearing. This woman was asking her to help raise the baby. "Yes," she wanted to shout it loud enough for all of Thailand to hear. She kept her composure. "It would be my honor."

Nuang smiled and handed the baby back to Somjit. "I'm very tired. I think I'm not completely recovered. You can help me today by taking the baby to sleep with you for tonight. Maybe I will feel stronger tomorrow."

Somjit was speechless. She tried to answer but couldn't. Instead she nodded, her face glowed with unbridled gratitude.

Nuang couldn't remember ever seeing such a happy person.

As Somjit reached the doorway, she stopped. "I don't know your baby's name." Her face flushed. "I'm so embarrassed."

Nuang was caught unawares. She didn't know either. She had never given her own child a name. With hardly a pause she said, "Her name is Tippawan, in honor of my deceased sister."

"It's a beautiful name," Somjit said.

Nuang blushed. "Thank you."

Somjit returned to her room with baby Tippawan in her arms. That night she cried at the emotions which overwhelmed her.

That night, Nuang cried too. She cried for her fears of the future.

As the days passed into weeks, Nuang and Somjit shared the duties of caring for the little Tippawan. Together, they learned to be mothers for the first time in their lives. More than that, Nuang and Somjit became friends. Before long, their trust of each other was explicit. The young monk seemed ever present. He watched as the baby healed Somjit's emotional scars and Nuang accepted her half Thai baby.

The voices returned to Nuang only twice, and the last time they had been less than a whisper. During the past three weeks, she had forgotten they ever existed. She stopped taking her medication after the first week.

Chapter 9

The young monk lay on his small cot thinking about his life at the temple. The last few months had been completely different from everything that had come before. Laht had grown up rich and was used to having everything he needed or wanted. Through his life he had never been deprived of anything reasonable. His father, Isara, had seen to that. But here in service to Buddha, he had learned to exist without the material trappings of the affluent.

Laht's grandfather had sired two sons. One was his father Isara, and the other was his Uncle Jum. More correctly, the other *had been* his uncle. Jum had been dead for more than a year now, but for as long as he could remember, his Uncle Jum had been a monk at this temple.

As Laht was growing up, he and his father went to the temple to visit Jum every week or two. Although it had seemed odd that his uncle was a monk, Jum had never acted like a monk around him and Laht rarely thought about it. He was in his final year of medical school in America when his Uncle Jum died. He couldn't come home for the ceremonies, so he had vowed to spend six months at the temple in honor of his uncle before pursuing his medical career in Thailand. It was his way of paying homage to a man he loved and respected.

But the night he brought Somjit to the temple had been a turning point in his life. He spent endless hours healing Somjit's physical wounds and emotional scars; more time than he had ever spent with any woman except his mother.

As the days had passed, the girl dominated most of his daytime thoughts and all of his nighttime dreams. He couldn't get her off his mind. He wasn't sure why. Maybe it was because he felt responsible after saving her from her husband's unimaginable assault; or maybe it was because she seemed so helpless; or maybe it was because he found her so overwhelmingly attractive. Whatever the reason, being near her made him feel good. Now that he was nearing the end of his time at the temple, he knew that leaving Somjit behind would be one of the hardest things he would ever do.

He lay in bed and considered his future. He wanted to ask Somjit to go with him when he went to Chiang Mai to begin his work, but what if she said no? What if his attraction to Somjit was nothing but a case of infatuation? Or what if his father became angry? He had always made decisions so easily, but now he had no idea what was right or wrong.

He got out of bed and walked toward the rooms where the women slept. He knew he had no business being in the women's quarters this late at night. Even with his special privileges, being here at this hour wasn't proper. He wasn't doing anything wrong, he told himself, but he needed to check on Somjit and the baby. It was his duty. He looked for any excuse to justify his actions.

He folded his fingers into a loose fist to knock at the closed door. His heart fluttered and his chest tightened as he pushed his knuckles forward. At the last instant he stopped. He turned and moved away from Somjit's room. Then, without hesitation, he went to Nuang's door and tapped lightly.

"Sawasdee ka, good evening," Nuang said when she saw the young monk. She noticed his flushed face. "Are you okay?"

"Yes, I'm fine," his words came out clipped. He softened his tone. "I have come to make sure you are well."

His voice and movements spoke of lies, but she let it pass. "Thank you for your concern. I am well. Would you like to come in?"

"Yes. I mean, no." His blush deepened. "I mean, can we talk?"

In the weeks that Nuang had known the young monk, she had never seen him like this. He had always been so calm and so sure of himself. Now he looked a man falling apart. "Yes, come in. I think we should talk."

He stopped just inside her doorway. To go farther into her room without good reason wouldn't be proper for a monk, even a temporary one. He searched for something to say but nothing came.

"What do you want to talk about?" Nuang asked after a short silence. "Is my baby okay?"

"Yes, your baby is fine." He shuffled his feet, looking more like a schoolboy than a monk. "I ah... I want to ask you about Somjit. You've spent time with her. What kind of a person is she?"

Nuang studied his face. It didn't take special intuition to see that the young monk was smitten with Somjit. She had noticed it before when she watched the two of them together. She wasn't sure if what she saw was love or lust, but she knew how embarrassed he must be to admit it might be either. She considered Somjit's situation before answering, "She is a good woman who has had a hard life."

Laht fumbled with the edge of his saffron robe, "Yes, I think she's a good woman, too." He turned to leave.

"Wait," Nuang said.

Laht paused, his eyebrows in question.

"Are you in love with Somjit?"

"I don't know." He left Nuang's room and pulled the door closed behind him.

Laht stood in the hallway for a moment before he realized Somjit was standing outside her door. He turned toward her. "I love you," he wanted to say, but his words came out, "Are you okay?"

"Why were you in her room?"

"I wanted to talk, but we said nothing."

Somjit stared at him for a long second before speaking. "Would you like to come to my room and say nothing?" She was surprised by her own words. She had wanted to say goodnight and that was all. To talk like that to a monk was contemptible. She thought she must sound like a whore.

Laht's face burned. Yes, he wanted to go to her room and talk and touch and hold and more. He wanted to walk to her now and take her in his arms. An image of him making love with her entered his mind. Hormones rushed through him in tidal waves and his manhood grew in response. He hoped it didn't show through the saffron robes.

"No, it's late," he answered. "I must go." For an instant he hated the clothes he wore. "We will talk tomorrow." He turned and hurried away.

Back in the safety of his own bed, he held and stroked at his maleness for a full minute before forcing himself to stop. In a while the hormones waned and his urges faded. He was amazed at the way he felt. He had never wanted any woman the way he wanted Somjit.

That night Laht didn't sleep. Instead he planned how he would tell his father that he had fallen in love with a peasant girl and failed his promise to his uncle at the same time. Laht was sure his uncle's spirit would be more understanding than his father.

Chapter 10

The next morning, ten days short of his six month promise, Laht slipped into his jeans, tee-shirt, and tennis shoes, and then walked away from the temple. He didn't say goodbye to anyone. He just left.

By ten o'clock he was at his father's law firm waiting for a minute of his time. Even as he waited, he hadn't decided exactly what he would say. It was almost noon before the receptionist escorted him inside. By then his nerves were worn raw.

Isara's office wasn't just plush, it was grandiose. Intricately carved teak furniture sat on colorful Persian carpets, which in turn sat on real marble floors. Isara sat in a black-leather executive chair, his lean body dwarfed by the oversized desk. On the wall behind him hung a larger than life portrait of the King of Thailand. To the left and right of the King stood bookshelves filled with legal tomes. The remaining walls were lined with an impressive collection of paintings depicting modern Thai life, Karen and Isaan handicrafts, and silk tapestry woven into surrealistic scenes of ancient Siam. On either side of the desk, large wooden elephants supported tabletops where someone had arranged ornamental vases of fresh orchids, roses, and other brightly colored flowers. A humidor filled with Cuban cigars sat on one corner of the desk and a small statue of Buddha sat on the other. A short pile of neatly stacked papers lay in between. Isara's upper body filled the space directly behind the center of the massive desk.

In a moment Isara stood, raised one hand, and casually motioned for Laht to come in. A polite smile brightened his face.

Laht wai'ed respectfully and tried to look calm. "Sawasdee krup, good afternoon father. I'm happy to see you. I hope you are well." He followed his father's silent invitation to enter.

"Sawasdee krup," Isara returned the greeting but not the wai. "Phom sabai dee, khop khun krup. I am well, thank you. I'm happy to see you again, too." He looked at his watch. "You are early."

Laht stared at his father, confused. "Early? I don't understand. What do you mean, *I'm early*. You didn't know I was coming, and it's past noon already. How can I be either early or late?"

"Laht, Laht, Laht," Isara replied. "I spent all of that money sending you to those expensive schools, and they didn't even teach you how to read a calendar. According to my memory, you were supposed to be at the temple for another ten days. I think that makes you a bit early."

"Oh, that." Laht felt his face flushing. His prepared speech disintegrated into jumble of disjointed thoughts. "I guess I need to explain."

Isara pointed to a chair at the front of his desk. "Have a seat. For you, I have all day."

Isara sat down, leaned back, and waited.

Laht sat but he didn't relax. His hips rested along the front edge of the chair, his back held straight, his hands folded into his lap. "It's no longer possible for me to live at the temple. If I stay, something terrible will happen."

Isara pondered his son's statement for a minute. "Let me be sure I understand what you just said. After nearly 180 days of devoting your life to Buddha, you can't stay another ten? If you do, something terrible will happen? Is that what you're telling me?"

Their conversation wasn't going near to what Laht had planned. He wanted to blurt out the truth but couldn't. Somjit wafted through his thoughts like fine silk threads. He wanted to talk about her, but in his whole life he had never talked about girls with his father. The very thought of doing it now made his face redden deeper. "Yes. It's very complicated."

Isara studied his son closely. He had never seen Laht so

nervous, so unsure of himself. He searched for clues that might reveal what was being said beneath words. Isara had always been good at sensing unspoken secrets about people. It was like a gift from Buddha and it had helped him tremendously in his business negotiations. In a moment he asked, "What is her name?" The expression on his son's face told him his hunch was correct.

Laht's chest tightened with unaccustomed anxiety. He wondered if he could speak. "Her name is Somjit," he managed on his second try.

Isara relaxed. To him, Laht's confession was a relief. As far as he knew, Laht had never had a girlfriend. For that matter, Laht had never even shown any real interest in women. Over the years Isara had started to worry about Laht's sexual preferences. Hearing that his son had fallen head over heels for a woman eased his doubts.

"Are you a virgin?"

The question flustered Laht further. "What do you mean?"

"Surely you know what a virgin is. I mean have you ever had sex with a woman."

Laht looked down at the tops of his American bought tennis shoes. "I don't mean to be impolite, but that is none of your business."

Isara smiled. He knew the answer was yes. He wasn't sure how the temple fit into this scenario, but he knew there was something. He was certain the truth would come later. For now he wanted to know more about the girl who had captured Laht's fancy.

"Yes, you're right," Isara responded. "I'm sorry for my question. It was bad manners. Please, tell me about this woman named Somjit."

Laht took a deep breath and talked. He described her beauty, grace, and charm with adjectives known only to those enmeshed in the throes of passion and love-sickness. If any details of her eyes or her mouth or her face were omitted, they were details not worth recalling. But Laht didn't tell his father everything. He didn't mention how he had met Somjit, nor did he say that she had a husband. In a while he stopped talking.

Isara could have been blind and still have seen the obsession on his son's face. Laht's words left little doubt about his attraction to the girl. Yet something didn't seem right; something wasn't being said.

"I can tell you have a very strong need for this girl. It's nothing to be embarrassed about. Every man feels like that at least once in his life. She sounds like a wonderful young lady. You should be running toward her instead of away from her. That makes me wonder, why are you running away?"

Laht squirmed in his seat. "There is one other thing I want to tell you. Somjit comes from a very poor family. She has no education except what a few people have taught her and what she has learned on her own, but she isn't stupid either. In fact, she is one of the smartest people I've ever met. But Somjit is from a lower class and I cannot embarrass our family by marrying a peasant girl. I'm not running away from her, father, I'm walking away before it's too late. I think you can understand that."

Isara pulled his face into a hard frown. Old memories of his brother Jum floated through his thoughts. Jum had once fallen in love with a woman of a lower class and their father had been unable to accept it. Back then, Isara had watched as his older brother rebelled against his father's stern demands and questionable Thai traditions. After a short tangle of wills, Jum had been disowned by his own father. The end of their father/son relationship hadn't come immediately, but the bitterness had driven a wedge between them that would never be removed. Eventually their father had simply stopped all contact with Jum—physically, financially, and emotionally.

By the time his father's and brother's battles had ended, Isara had decided he would never judge a person by their lot in life, he would judge them by their actions.

"No, I do not understand that and I don't understand you either," Isara said. "When you first came home from school in America, you told me you wanted to be the best doctor in Thailand. Not just for the rich, but for everyone. You don't know

53

J. F. Gump

how proud that made me. Now you're shunning the very people you said you wanted to help. No, I don't understand you at all."

Laht blinked at his father's response. His voice eluded him.

Isara leaned forward and softened his tone, "True love goes much deeper than a rich man's pockets. It transcends all boundaries of caste and education. Someday I might be embarrassed by whomever you marry, but not because God gave her to a working class family. I'm embarrassed right now because you think so low of me."

Laht wasn't prepared for what he'd just heard. He had expected fatherly praise for his mature decision to abandon personal emotions for family purity. Instead his father had scolded him. Strangely, he felt elated by his father's short outburst. "Are you angry?"

Isara sighed. "Only if you keep acting like a stupid water buffalo. I don't know what this girl has to do with you wanting to leave the temple, but I want you to stay until you have fulfilled your promise to my brother. However strong your reasons are for leaving, I believe there are stronger reasons for staying. Buddha is testing you, Laht. Be strong enough to meet his challenge. When you come home in ten days, we'll have a party to celebrate. Then we can talk more about this woman, Somjit." He picked up his pen and turned his attention to the stack of papers.

Laht sat for a few minutes while his father ignored his presence. He wondered just how strong he could be with his desire for Somjit burning from every pore. How embarrassed would his mother and father be if their son, the monk, was caught having sex with one of the women he had been charged to help and protect. An image of his humping bare ass sticking out of saffron robes etched his mind. How embarrassed would Somjit be if that were to happen. The thought of shaming Somjit quelled his raging hormones.

He watched Isara work for another minute and then stood, "Father, I must go now. I have promises to keep. I'll see you when my homage to Uncle Jum is fulfilled."

Isara didn't look up from his work. Laht turned and walked to the door.

Just before he left the room, Isara spoke, "Laht, I love you and I'm very proud of you no matter what you do. If I've been hard on you today, I apologize. Sometimes a man has nothing except his word, his beliefs, and his pride. I wanted to make sure you didn't lose any of those today because of some foolish idea that family is everything. Someday your mother and I will be dead. We don't want to die knowing we might have denied you some happiness through our own selfishness."

Suddenly, his father's desk seemed much smaller and the man behind it much larger. Laht wai'ed to his father. Then, without speaking, he stepped outside and pulled the door closed.

After his son was gone, Isara called his best staff investigator into his office. Her name was Pajeeka Wasiwat.

"My son has fallen in love with someone named Somjit," he explained. "I want to know everything about her."

Pajeeka nodded. No further information was given or expected. She left the building to do what she did best.

Chapter 11

Laht returned to the temple, put on his robe, and isolated himself for two days. He couldn't avoid seeing others at the temple, but he didn't interact with them beyond silent acknowledgements of their presence. He went through his religious duties as expected, but completely ignored his other assigned duties. It was an intentional act; he didn't want anyone or anything to interfere with his final decisions.

During the first day he recalled his entire life, examining every turning point, every decision, and every event which had led him to this temple. His grandfather being rich, his father being successful, his determination to study abroad, his uncle being a monk, his decision to put education ahead of love, Uncle Jum dying while he was in America, and his resolve to honor his uncle by giving six months of his life to God and Buddha, it was all too coincidental. It was as if some higher power was playing a role in this opera of his life. And Somjit, surely those same directors of fate had toyed with her life as well.

By the end of his first day of silence, Laht had convinced himself that their meeting was no mere accident, it was destiny. By morning he had decided his previous night's conclusions were pretty stupid. Despite his Buddhist upbringing, he didn't believe in fate. He believed that a man created and controlled his own destiny. Still he couldn't push aside the feeling that everything was as it was meant to be.

During the second day he shut out the past and considered what was to come. In a few days he would be away from everything he had known for the last six months: the temple, the safe house, the children, the monks, the ceremonies, and Somjit—especially Somjit.

His two days of avoiding her had only intensified his yearnings. He knew she had some feelings for him, else she wouldn't have been so bold just two nights ago. Still, his fear of her rejection made him weak. It took until mid afternoon to convince himself that all he had to do was ask and she would do anything for him, and go anywhere with him. By sunset Laht had built enough courage to do what he feared most—he would ask Somjit to love him.

At seven o'clock that evening, Laht bathed. At seven-fifteen he bathed again. At seven-thirty he walked to Somjit's door and tapped softly. This time there was no hesitation, no fluttering heart, no tight chest, no nothing; he was in control. There was no answer. He knocked again, harder this time. Still there was no answer.

A woman one room down peeked out at him but he didn't recognize her face. Suddenly he felt foolish standing there knocking on Somjit's door. "Sawasdee krup," he said, embarrassed. "Do you know if Somjit is here?"

The woman didn't answer. She pulled back from the hallway and closed her door.

Laht could feel his face burning. He turned and started back to his room. "What a fucked up night," he mumbled to himself, hoping neither God nor Buddha understood English slang.

"Kaw thort ka, excuse me," a voice came from behind him.

He looked back to see Nuang standing in the hallway.

"Please come here for one minute," she whispered urgently. "I need your help."

He stiffened involuntarily. The last time he had gone to Nuang's room, Somjit had seen him and seemed very jealous. "It's late and I shouldn't be here," he whispered. "I must go now."

"No, wait. It's very important, really."

He sighed heavily and walked to where Nuang stood waiting. He kept his voice low, "What is it?"

"I need to use the toilet."

"You don't need me for that," Laht managed after a flustered moment. "I think you're old enough to go by yourself."

Nuang almost laughed at the look on his face. "Let me explain. Somjit came to my room earlier and wanted to talk. She was very upset. She even cried some. Then she fell asleep. The baby is sleeping, too. I need to use the toilet very much, but I don't want to leave the baby alone and I don't want to wake either of them. Please, it will take only a minute. All you have to do is stand inside my room and watch Somjit and my baby until I return. Only a couple of minutes, I promise."

Laht's heart did mini flip-flops. Now he knew why Somjit hadn't answered her door. She had been asleep in Nuang's room. He forced a resigned expression, "Okay, but please hurry." He wondered if his excitement showed through his weak facade.

"Khop khun ka, thank you," she wai'ed gratefully.

She waited until he went into her room before heading toward the toilets. She was giddy at the idea of playing matchmaker. She knew it was the right thing to do for Somjit. She suppressed a girlish giggle. She would take her time in the toilet.

Laht stepped inside Nuang's room and pushed the door shut. He resisted the temptation to bolt it closed. He turned and looked at the bed where Somjit and the baby lay sleeping. Butterflies filled his chest. He walked to the edge of the bed and stared down. Everything he had told his father was true. Somjit was very beautiful. In another century, she would have been a goddess. He wanted very much to lie down beside her and hold her close, but he didn't. Here and now was neither the time nor place. Instead he knelt at her bedside and spoke so low it wasn't even a whisper. "Phom lak khun, I love you."

He stood and returned to the door. On impulse he pulled it ajar. Through the crack he saw the same woman he had seen in the hallway just minutes ago. She was staring at him. "May I help you?" he asked by reflex.

"I think I have the wrong room," she answered. She took one more penetrating look before moving out of sight.

THAILAND - COLD RAIN

For some reason the woman's unexpected appearance unnerved him. He didn't recognize her but that didn't mean anything; she could be a new guest he hadn't met. For the last two days he had been so self-absorbed that anyone, even Buddha himself, could have come and gone and he wouldn't have noticed.

He turned his attention back to Somjit but it was the woman in the hallway who dominated his thoughts. He would make it a point to meet her tomorrow. She was probably a very nice person who ended up here already pushed to the limit. That notion didn't stop his feelings of apprehension. He wondered if the woman would tell anyone she had seen him in Nuang's room, with Somjit lying on the bed. The thought pushed his discomfort to near panic.

He and Somjit hadn't done anything; they hadn't even talked. But that wouldn't keep people from believing what they wanted, and they would want to believe the worst. No doubt tongues would be wagging tomorrow; it was human nature. He hoped Nuang wouldn't be gone long. His nervous tension grew as the seconds ticked past. A line of sweat formed across his upper lip. Finally he heard footsteps nearing the door. He stepped into the hallway.

Nuang noticed the expression on his face. Just minutes ago she had been elated at getting the young monk and Somjit together. Now, she wasn't so sure. "You don't look well," she said. "Is everything okay?"

He forced a smile. Even without a mirror he knew it looked strained. He wiped at his lips with the back of his hand. "I think so. I'm not sure. A few minutes ago there was a woman standing outside of your door. She was staring at me. I didn't recognize her. I guess I let it bother me more than I should have."

Nuang studied him for a second. "It was probably the same woman who came to the bath while I was there. She's new here; she came just last night. She spent most of today by herself. I think she's very shy or very frightened."

"Yes, I'm sure you're right." He took a deep breath and exhaled slowly. He felt better at her explanation. "Earlier you said Somjit had been crying. I don't mean to pry, but why was she upset?"

Nuang could tell him everything she knew, but she wouldn't. Some things were better left unsaid. She would tell him only what he needed to know. "Everyone noticed you haven't come around for two days. Then today the rumors started. Someone said you were staying away because of Somjit. It upset her. She wanted to talk so she came to my room. That's all I know."

He sensed she wasn't telling the whole truth but he let it pass. "Thank you. I was afraid her depression had come back," he lied in return. "I'll check on her tomorrow anyway."

"Yes, that would be a good idea."

"I must go now."

The door to Nuang's room opened and Somjit stepped out. Her eyes darted from Laht to Nuang and then back to Laht. "Sawasdee ka, good evening," she said very quietly. "Why are you two standing in the hallway like this?"

At Somjit's appearance, Laht's whole expression changed. He glanced at Somjit then looked away, his face flushed.

When he didn't answer, Nuang interjected. "We were talking about the new woman who came last night. He wants to meet her tomorrow. He was just leaving."

Laht found his voice, "Yes, I have things to do." His eyes darted from one woman to the other. "I heard a rumor today and I want you to know it's not true. I haven't stayed away because of you. The truth is, I'm still here at the temple because of you." Without further words he turned and walked away, his face burned with embarrassment.

"What did he mean?" Somjit asked, after he had left.

"I think he meant exactly what he said," was Nuang's reply.

That night Laht made the biggest decision of his life. He was going to marry Somjit. For the next eight days, he did his every assigned duty. At the same time he ignored his saffron robes and wooed Somjit shamelessly. He knew he was a disgrace to the temple but he didn't care. None of the other monks said anything to him, but they avoided his presence. He barely noticed.

Chapter 12

Nuang left the temple only twice during the time she stayed there. The first time was her doctor visit with Laht. The second was the day she had an overpowering urge to see her family. It was a Saturday and the weather was cold and rainy—one of those days that pressed on peoples' spirits and lent itself best to inner reflections. At two in the afternoon she pulled her hair into a tight ball, covered herself with a saffron robe, and walked into Phitsanulok.

She stood near her mother's house for a long time but saw neither her mother nor her youngest brother. Later she walked past her sister's house. Neet and her two year old son were there, sitting in the doorway. Like herself they were bundled in extra clothes against the unusual coldness that had penetrated Thailand. Her desire to go to them was strong. Just as she was about to give in, another person appeared in the doorway of the house. It was Anan, her next to youngest brother. She hadn't expected to see him here.

Anan had his own advertising business in Pattaya and never came home for anything except family emergencies and funerals. Something was happening but she didn't know what. She wondered if someone had died.

She was edging nearer when yet another figure caught the corner of her eye. It was a man walking fast up the street. Nuang focused on him, it was her husband Surat. She stopped in mid stride. She didn't want to see him, or he to see her. She moved under the eave of a street vendor's cart and watched.

Neet and Anan didn't seem surprised to see Surat. That could only mean they were expecting him. Surat did most of the talking.

Sometimes her brother and sister spoke, but mostly they just listened. That was unusual for Anan, who had never liked Surat and usually went out of his way to avoid conversations with him. Anan wasn't smiling, but he was listening intently. Nuang strained her ears but couldn't make out their words.

At that moment Anan's eyes fixed on Nuang; his stare intense. She turned away from his scrutiny. Her paranoia of being discovered erased all urges to see anyone. She hurried away without looking back.

At the temple she stripped off the rain soaked robe and tried to make sense of what she had seen at her sister's house. She was sure it had to do with her. She wondered just how much Surat and the others might know. Probably only that she had disappeared with her newborn baby. It would be enough to make them worry. If they knew the truth, they would understand why she had run away, but they would never be able to forgive her for having a farang's baby, especially while she was still married to Surat. She had shamed more than her husband and herself, she had disgraced her whole family. Her tears fell as steady as the cold rain outside.

Later she went to the room next to her own and saw Somjit and the baby asleep on their bed. A small tug of jealousy pulled at her. Unlike herself, Somjit was a good mother, a true mother.

That night and the following nights, her dreams were a paradoxical mix of nightmares and soft visions of her daughter Tippawan.

Altogether Nuang spent six weeks at the temple. By the beginning of the fifth week she was going stir crazy. She knew she couldn't stay there forever, but she didn't know what she would do or where she would go if she left. She spent hours plotting and planning how she would survive once she left the temple. She discarded one scheme after another.

Thoughts of Surat entered her mind more often than she wanted. They had been married for over seventeen years and she missed him. While they had lived together, she had never considered what her life would be like without him. Now she knew and it hurt. She loved her husband more than she had ever realized. It dawned on her that she could leave the baby with Somjit and return to Surat and beg his forgiveness, but she couldn't bring herself to do that. It wasn't possible. She considered taking Somjit and the baby and going to her mother's house or her sister's house, but she quickly cancelled those ideas, too. She knew she wouldn't be welcome. They would probably make her give the baby away for adoption and then make her leave Phitsanulok so they wouldn't have to be reminded of the shame she had caused.

Nuang knew if she was going to survive and take care of her baby, she needed money. She needed a job that paid well but didn't require any special skills. That narrowed her choices to the tourist cities. The hotels and restaurants always needed people to work. She didn't know about the pay, but work would be easy to find. She considered Phuket and Pattaya, two popular beach resorts. They sat on opposite sides of the Gulf of Thailand, with Phuket on the far west side and Pattaya on the east. After a minute of self-debate, she decided on Pattaya. She had been there before, but she had never been to Phuket.

Her brother lived in Pattaya and that helped make up her mind. She didn't want to see him, but their chances of an accidental meeting were small. His advertising business took up most of his days and his nights were spent at home. Just knowing he would be close gave her a small sense of security. She would leave for Pattaya within the week.

Chapter 13

Mike Johnson spent the days before his flight to Thailand reviewing his work assignment and developing software routines for the refinery's process control computers. The software wouldn't be perfect but he could adjust it once he arrived on site. He spent his evenings looking for his son Josh. He hadn't seen Josh since kicking him out for selling drugs from the basement of their home. Josh had even missed his mother's funeral.

Mike went to every sleaze-hole bar in Pittsburgh asking anyone who would listen if they knew Josh. He ran into a few of Josh's druggie friends but none had seen or heard from him in months, except for one tattoed character with multiple rings piercings in his eyebrows and lips. He said his name was Rob and that Josh owed him money. Rob insinuated that Mike would never see Josh alive again if the debt wasn't paid. Mike retorted with a threat of his own: If Josh ended up dead, then the police would know who the prime suspect was. Rob backed away but hinted that Mike himself could be in danger. Mike told the guy to fuck-off but slept a little lighter after their encounter. He never saw Rob again.

Mike stopped looking for Josh three days before his flight to Bangkok. For all he knew his son was already dead. The thought hounded him, even in his dreams.

Chapter 14

On the same day that Laht had fulfilled his promise to his uncle, Somjit's life was turned upside down. It started with Nuang.

After five days of planning, Nuang had finally gathered the nerve to escape her life at the temple. That day she was feeling well and thinking clearly. There were no voices whispering in her ears, so her final decision was made with total lucidity. She set her plan in motion.

Early in the afternoon, Nuang found a cardboard box and packed the few clothes the monks had given her. Afterwards, she went to see Somjit and the baby. There were things she needed to confess, but she wasn't sure how to say them. Her heartbeat quickened as she neared Somjit's room. She reached up and tapped softly. In a moment the door swung open. "Sawasdee ka," she said.

"Please come in," Somjit motioned her inside. "Are you okay? You look upset."

Nuang struggled to make her smile natural. "I'm fine. How is little Tippawan?"

"She's asleep. Are you sure you're okay?"

"I have decided to be honest with you about my baby." Nuang's smile faded. "One hundred percent honest. I have never lied to you, but there are many things I never said. Things I have never told anyone. I trust you, Somjit, just like you are my sister. You are Tippawan's second mother so it's only right that you know the whole truth. I'm not sure where to begin."

Somjit tensed. A million bizarre thoughts streaked through her mind. Maybe Nuang had AIDS and had given it to the baby, or maybe she had been a drug user while she was pregnant, or maybe she had some disease and was dying. "What do you mean?"

"I lied about Tippawan's father. He's not dead. He's in America."

"I already know her father was a farang," Somjit replied, relaxing a little. "Whether he is dead or alive isn't important. If that's what you wanted to tell me, you're worried about nothing."

"No, there is more. Let me tell you a story—a true story."

Somjit nodded and listened.

"One year ago tomorrow, my sister was killed in a motorcycle accident. She was twenty-three years old. Her given name was Tippawan but everyone knew her as Math. I loved my sister very much. Not too many months before she died, she fell in love with a foreigner. I think he loved her, too. They came to visit me once in Chiang Mai and I was captivated by him. I don't know why. Maybe it was because he was so nice to me, or maybe it was because I was jealous of my sister. I was jealous because she was so young and she had found a man who could take good care of her. But I never said anything, I was embarrassed by own feelings.

"My sister was very religious, but she was also very superstitious. She used to have dreams of mythical demons whenever bad things were about to happen. I pretended her dreams were only a coincidence, but I knew they weren't. One night Math dreamed she would die. That same dream came back to her every night for a week. When she finally told me, she was frantic. She truly believed her death was imminent. We talked for hours.

"She asked me to do many things for her if she died. Most of her requests had to do with family, but one had to do with the American she loved. She asked to make love with him in her place if she died before they were together again. I said yes because I thought my sister's dream would never come true. I said yes because the idea excited me.

"Three months after I made my promise to Math, she was killed in a motorcycle accident. I was still in mourning when her American lover returned to Thailand. He came to have a ceremony for her spirit. He asked me to attend and I did.

"Before he went home I kept my promise to my sister. I made love with him one last time for her memory. But I did it for me, too. I had sex with him because I wanted to feel him inside me. I had never slept with any man except my husband and I wanted the American desperately. He didn't seduce me, I seduced him.

"That day we made love and baby Tippawan was conceived. He doesn't know because I never told him. I have thought about contacting him but decided it's better he doesn't know. What happened is my fault, not his. I'm not embarrassed for what I did, I'm only embarrassed at my stupidity for getting pregnant. I'm telling you this because I wanted you to know the truth."

Somjit was surprised and not surprised at the same time. "You didn't have to tell me all of that. It doesn't matter."

"I've never told anyone except you. You deserve to know everything."

Somjit nodded. Nothing that Nuang had done compared to her own life. There was much she should be confessing, too, but she kept her secrets inside. They sat in self-conscious silence, one embarrassed by what she had confessed and the other embarrassed by what she hadn't.

In a while Nuang kissed her daughter and returned to her room. She lay in bed and cried, agonizing over what she was about to do. Later she wrote a note and put it on the bed where Somjit would find it. Then, while everyone was busy preparing the midday meal, Nuang took her box of clothes and walked away from the temple. She still had most of the money she had taken from her and Surat's bank account. It wasn't much, but it was more than enough to get away from Phitsanulok.

She caught a taxi to the bus station and bought a one-way ticket to Pattaya. Without thinking, she gave her correct name to the ticket agent. It was a mistake but she couldn't take it back once the words were out. She chided herself harshly for her careless stupidity. She hoped it wasn't important. She paid the lady, then moved to a secluded area of the terminal and waited.

~~~

When Somjit returned from the kitchen that afternoon, she went directly to Nuang's room. Nuang hadn't eaten with the others and Somjit was worried. She remembered Nuang's expression when they had talked earlier. Clearly Nuang was depressed. She knew people sometimes did stupid things when they were upset. She hoped Nuang wasn't planning to do anything stupid.

She panicked when there was no answer to her persistent knocking at Nuang's door. With heart pounding, she let herself into the room. Nuang wasn't but she saw the letter on the bed and picked it up. Her hands trembled as she struggled with the unfamiliar handwriting.

"I have gone away," it read, "I will be back as soon as I can find a job. I love you both."

The short note gave no clues as to where Nuang had gone or when she would return. Only that she would be back after she found a job. With the Thai economy in shambles, Somjit knew that might be never. Nuang had deserted her. That harsh realization blocked out all other thoughts.

She stumbled back to her own room in a state of numbness. Her existence blurred into a tangled mass of confused depression. She lay down on her bed and let the black mood overwhelm her.

Somjit's depression was nearing climax when there was a soft knock at her door. She forced herself from the bed hoping it was Nuang. It was the young monk Laht. He was dressed in jeans and a tee-shirt. The meaning of what she saw escaped her.

"Sawasdee ka," she said, her words automatic. Her tone hid the turmoil ripping through her.

"Good evening," he responded, very proper and very polite. "I have come to ask you to go with me."

She heard his words but they barely registered. She had no idea what he was really saying. At that moment she wasn't capable of understanding. "No," she said aloud, but to herself she thought, *I cannot. I must take care of little Tippawan.*

He stared at her in disbelief; his face burned red through his light brown skin. He had just asked her to go with him and she had said no. With one simple word she had shattered his dreams. He reached out to touch her, stopped, and then let his hand fall. Without another word he turned and walked away.

It was only after she closed her door that she understood what had just happened. Laht had proposed to her and she had rejected him. She looked at the baby in her arms. For the briefest of seconds she hated the baby for the hold it had on her. At that moment she also hated Nuang for abandoning her with the baby. Her thoughts spun as a maelstrom of emotions ripped through her. In a minute she lay the baby down and left the room to find Laht.

She had gone just a few steps when she heard the baby cry; it froze her in mid-stride. Her heart pounded, torn in two directions. She wanted to run to Laht and tell him she loved him and wanted to go with him, but she couldn't leave the baby alone and crying.

She hurried back, picked the baby, and soothed it quiet. Her mind raced to decisions. She had to talk to Laht. She left the room and walked as fast as she could without jarring the baby. She went straight to Laht's quarters and knocked. There was no answer. She knocked again, louder. Still there was no answer.

She hurried back to the women's area and asked the first person she saw to hold her baby for a few minutes. Without having to worry about hurting the baby, she could run. She ran as fast as her legs would carry her. She searched throughout the temple and the grounds outside. Laht was nowhere to be found. She continued to run because she couldn't make herself stop.

One senior monk noticed her erratic movements and the frantic expression on her face. He caught up with her, grabbed her arm, and pulled her to a halt. "Are you okay?"

"I must find Laht. I have something to tell him."

"If you mean the young monk, he's gone. Someone in a fancy car drove him away. He's been gone for more than ten minutes. What's so important? Maybe I can contact him if it's urgent."

"I want to tell him I love him." She jerked her arm from his grasp. She knew that wasn't urgent enough for anything. She ran back to her room, closed the door, and cried. Everything she believed was gone; everyone she loved had deserted her.

She could understand Laht running away. He came from a wealthy family, he was well educated, and soon he would be a doctor in Chiang Mai. He had everything but she was less than nothing, a common laborer whose husband had killed their baby, an ignorant rebar buster whose formal education had been so hit and miss that it was practically nonexistent, a married woman who would probably be barren for the rest of her life. She was surprised Laht had ever noticed her in the first place. If she were him, she would have run away, too.

Nuang's abandonment hurt even more than Laht's. Her note had said she would be back, but Somjit knew it was a lie. Nuang had disappeared and would never return. She would find a new life without the burden of a baby and then forget her promise.

As much as Somjit loved and wanted this baby as her own, she knew she could never be a proper mother by herself. She thought about running away from the temple and leaving the baby behind. It would be the kindest thing to do. The baby would be put up for adoption. As hard as she tried to convince herself it was right, she knew it was wrong. She didn't want to stay, but she couldn't leave.

Deep melancholy overtook her. Her thoughts became hazy and disjointed. She sat on her bed and cried as darkness invaded her. For the first time since Laht had saved her life, she wanted to die.

In a while the woman brought Tippawan to her room. The baby was crying and nothing she did could make it stop. The noise rasped coarse across her raw emotions. At that instant she hated the bawling lump of flesh she held in her arms. Her loathing grew hotter with each new wail.

Why did the baby have to cry now? Her depression intensified beyond anything she had felt since the first day she arrived at the temple. If Buddha was punishing her for some past life sins, she wanted it to stop. She couldn't live like this.

With tears streaming, she picked up the screaming baby and ran to a small shrine in the courtyard. There she lay down and prayed for God to take them both.

Chapter 15

Pajeeka Wasiwat, Isara's investigator, had followed Nuang when she slipped away from the temple. It was partly out of curiosity and partly from her sense of duty. She wasn't sure what Isara would want to know, and she didn't want to risk disappointing him. She'd already learned much about Somjit but knew little about Nuang. She didn't understand the dynamics of this affair with Laht, but she knew Nuang was somehow involved.

Pajeeka lost Nuang in the cross-town traffic but her instincts told her the woman was going to the bus station. She arrived in time to see Nuang stepping away from the ticket window.

She waited until Nuang had taken a seat and then approached the agent. A two hundred baht bribe resulted in a name and a final destination: Chalamsee Duansawang—Pattaya, Thailand.

After leaving the bus station, she stopped at an internet café and typed her short report to Isara. She was finished by four o'clock. By four-thirty she was waiting in Isara's reception area and anxious to return to the temple. She didn't want to miss anything that happened in her absence. The minutes ticked past.

Isara was making her wait on purpose. She was certain of that. It was the same tactic he used on most of his clients. He always had to be busy, even when he wasn't. Considering that she was the only one waiting, she knew he wasn't busy today.

The waiting annoyed her, but only a little. Isara had always been good to her. He respected her for what she did and she respected him for treating her like a person. She had once told a friend he was the most honest man in Thailand, and she had meant every word. Besides, she was getting paid by the hour and he was approving her timesheets. She would wait the rest of the day if she had to. It was his choice.

A short time later the receptionist interrupted her thoughts, "Khun Isara will see you now."

Pajeeka crossed the waiting area and stepped inside his office. It looked bare compared to the last time she had been there. No pictures and no bookshelves, not even the wooden elephants she liked. The only thing that hadn't changed was his desk. Isara sat behind it, shuffling through a stack of papers. She waited for him to notice her entrance. After a moment he looked up.

"Pajeeka." His face broke into a smile. "Please have a seat." He motioned toward the solitary chair at the front of his desk.

She presented a polite wai and sat where he pointed.

Isara leaned forward. His practiced smile beamed. "I'm happy to see you are well."

Pajeeka couldn't stop herself from smiling in return. "Khop khun ka. Thank you." She let her eyes fall in deference. "I have been well. I hope the same for you."

Isara studied her for a moment. Pajeeka was the daughter of an old friend. He had hired her at his friend's request, and it had worked out well. He found Pajeeka interesting, even intriguing. By the age of thirty she had experienced enough for someone twice her age. Bar-girl, yaba head, small time drug dealer, heroin runner, and more. She had done it all. At the same time, she was one of the smartest people he'd ever met. He knew she was here to give her report on Laht and the girl named Somjit, so he got to the point.

"What have you learned?"

"I have learned that life is very complicated."

"I've known that for a long time." He fidgeted with a paper-clip. "What else?"

"Somjit, the woman your son loves, has a husband already." She paused for effect.

Isara felt his smile drop despite his best efforts to keep it in place. "Are you sure? Of course you are. Sorry I asked that. I know better than to question your observations. Tell me everything."

"The day Laht came to see you, he went back to the temple and avoided everyone for two days. Mostly he stayed in his room. I don't know what he was doing but it set tongues wagging. That girl Somjit was usually on the sharp end of the gossip. It made her easy to spot."

She paused, waiting to see if he had a response. He only stared. She continued.

"The girl is actually very beautiful. Quite shy, but a nice person. The way she talks says she is uneducated. I don't think she's stupid, but I haven't been able to spend enough time with her to know for sure. As I understand, she was very sick when she came to the temple. Laht spent days healing her. One woman said Laht was a bad doctor."

Isara tensed at the words. "Laht's had the best medical training money can buy. How dare anyone say he's a bad doctor!"

Pajeeka almost laughed. She had baited Isara and he had fallen for it. "She said a good doctor never falls in love with his patients."

Isara blushed, realizing what Pajeeka had just done. She wasn't so much different than himself. He stored their exchange away for future reference. "My son can fall in love with whomever he wants. Please continue with your report."

"Somjit is an orphan so to speak. Her parents have been dead since she was sixteen. If she has other living relatives, I'm not aware of it. For the last two years she's been working in Phitsanulok for a construction company. Her husband's name is Nong. Before the uh... before the incident, Nong was one of the biggest yaba heads in Phitsanulok. Rumor has it he has run away to Pattaya." She had learned those little tidbits from her street friends, but she claimed them as her own.

"What is this *incident* you mention?"

Pajeeka squirmed uneasily. Isara would learn the truth sooner or later; it might as well be now. She took a deep breath. "Somjit was pregnant before she came to the temple. Now she's not, but she has no baby. Her husband beat her savagely the night she came to the safe-house. His attack killed her baby." Unexpected anger

73

surged as she repeated what she knew. When she finished, she added, "Laht saved her life."

Isara was quiet. Pajeeka wasn't sure if it was because of the woman his son had chosen to fall in love with, or because of the way her baby had died.

In a moment he spoke, "Have you typed your report?"

She had more to tell, but nothing she hadn't already typed. "I have it on disc." She handed the CD to Isara.

"I think this information should remain private between us."

"Of course. What will you do?"

"I will do nothing. Laht is a grown man. If he asks my advice, I will give it. If he doesn't mention it, I won't either. I will just pray he makes decisions that are best for him."

Neither spoke for a minute. The silence grew oppressive. Finally Pajeeka said, "It's getting late. They will miss me at the temple. I must be going."

"You don't need to return to the temple," he replied. "There's nothing more I need to know. Today is Laht's last day of service to God and Buddha. I've already sent a driver to bring him home. Why don't you take a few days off? I'll call you if I need you."

"Khop khun ka," she said, wai'ing politely. "You're a most generous boss."

Isara nodded and Pajeeka walked toward the door. Before leaving his office, she turned and whispered, "I will pray for Laht."

As she rode the elevator to the ground floor, Pajeeka considered everything she had learned during the last week. Isara was right, it was a mess. She felt sorry for everyone. Especially she felt sorry for Somjit. She was truly a very nice woman whose entire life had beaten her into humble obedience and servitude.

She wondered if that was what Laht found so appealing. Some men liked that sort of woman. Usually they were the same men who were unsure of themselves and their own sexuality. Somjit would make someone a wonderful wife one day if she could learn to love again. Laht was probably the best chance she would ever have. She wondered what decisions he would make.

THAILAND - COLD RAIN

As the motorcycle taxi sped toward her apartment, she debated where she would go for her few days off. She considered Bangkok then discarded that idea. It was too big, too hot, and too expensive. Her second choice was Phuket, but it was too far away. Finally, she decided on Pattaya.

She had worked in Pattaya as a bar-girl when she was younger. She wasn't proud of that part of her life, but she wasn't embarrassed by it either. Besides, maybe she would see some people from her past. Even if she didn't, she could always have some fun teasing the farang tourists. It would be exciting after the boring nightlife of Phitsanulok.

After Pajeeka had left his office, Isara read her report. One name jumped out at him. That name was Chalamsee. He had once known a woman with that same name. Like the woman in Pajeeka's report, her nickname was Nuang. Memories as clear as yesterday flashed through his head.

Years ago, his brother Jum had fathered an illegitimate child with a married woman. That child's name was Tippawan "Math" Bongkot. There had been no scandal, but his brother had been so ashamed that he had left his life behind and entered monkhood. The reason for Jum's decision was a secret very few people knew. The Nuang he remembered had been the sister of his brother's illegitimate daughter. More important, that Nuang also knew the family secret because Jum himself had told her. Isara had never met Nuang, yet he knew her well.

Isara had last seen his niece Math Bongkot at his brother's funeral. That had been nearly a year ago. Afterwards she had just disappeared. He had never tried to find her because he never had a reason to. He had never forgotten her, either, but time had pushed her far into the background of his life and his thoughts.

Now, seeing the name Chalamsee and the nickname Nuang in print next to each other, he felt an irresistible urge to know what had happened to Math, his brother's only child. He had an equally powerful urge to know about this woman named Nuang who was now linked to his son. He wanted to find out if it was the same person he remembered. If it was her, he needed to make sure she and Laht never talked about their pasts. He didn't want Laht to ever know the true reason his brother had entered monkhood. He picked up the phone and called Pajeeka.

Pajeeka's cell phone rang as she stepped into her apartment. She knew without seeing the caller I.D. that it was Isara. "Hello," she sighed wearily.

"I read your report. You did a good job, very informative, but I have a question. It's about the woman who went to Pattaya, the one named Nuang. You said her given name was Chalamsee Duansawang. How do you know that?"

"I saw her leave the temple. She seemed very upset. Actually, she was totally stressed. She was carrying a box and she was in a hurry. I was curious, so I followed her. She went directly to the bus station. The ticket agent was happy to tell me her name in exchange for two hundred baht. You'll see it listed on my expense report. Is it important?"

"I'm not sure. I once knew a woman named Chalamsee with the nickname of Nuang, but her family name was not Duansawang. It was Bongkot. I need you to find out if it's the same person. If it is, I want you to learn everything you can about her."

Pajeeka could see her holiday disappearing before her eyes. "Can it wait a few days? I've already made plans for my time off."

"I'm sorry, but my instincts tell me this is urgent. You're good at this sort of work, so it shouldn't take more than a couple of days. When you're finished, I'll pay for your holiday. Transportation, food, and the best hotel. Everything."

She didn't need to give his offer a second thought, her vacation could wait. "This must be serious."

"It's personal," his voice tensed. "Whatever you discover must remain a secret between the two of us. This is no one's business but mine. Do you understand?"

"Yes sir," she answered, his tone had left no room for any

other response. "I understand. You shouldn't worry; I never talk about my work."

"I know that. I just wanted you to understand that this is very personal. I need you on this tomorrow."

"I'll start tonight, but finding her might not be easy. I know her name but that's about all. It might take more money that I have to chase this down. I have a friend with access to all sorts of records, but he won't do anything for free. Not even for me."

"Money's not a problem. I will pay whatever it takes. I'll have my secretary deposit 50,000 baht into your account. If that runs out, I'll deposit more."

Fifty thousand baht! Most people she knew made less than that in an entire year. Whatever was going on involved more than Laht screwing some peasant girl.

"One more thing," Isara continued. "If you learn anything about someone named Tippawan or Math, let me know at once." He hung up without waiting for a response.

Pajeeka looked at her watch. It was after six, too late to catch her friend at work. He was a system's analyst for the government in Bangkok and had easy access to all sorts of information; he wasn't above being bribed. She would call him at home later and pitch her offer. He would be more productive if he had all night to think about his reward.

Today she would start her search closer to home. Nuang had come to the temple in Phitsanulok, and Isara thought the name was familiar. It could be a coincidence, but there was also a chance that she or her family lived nearby.

Phitsanulok is neither the largest nor the smallest city in Thailand, but it's big enough that she could never search the whole city by herself. She pondered what to do, where to start. She guessed Nuang to be in her mid thirties. Isara had said he knew the surname Bongkot but not Duansawang. It was possible that Nuang Bongkot and Nuang Duansawang were the same person. She could have married and taken her husband's family name. If she had a husband, he would probably be about the same age. It wasn't much but it was something.

On impulse she decided to try the police. It was a shot in the dark, but it was better than running all over town asking people at random if they knew the Duansawang or Bongkot families. Police headquarters wasn't far away; she could be there in five minutes. She changed clothes, freshened her make-up, and left the apartment. She smiled when her motorcycle started on the first kick.

Chapter 16

The police station was surprisingly quiet. In fact, she was the only civilian in the place. Everyone went about their business and ignored her completely. Finally one man, a Lieutenant, looked in her direction, his eyebrows raised in question.

"Sawasdee ka," she said, presenting him a wai. He didn't return the gesture. She noticed his name badge; Viboon it read. "Lieutenant, I hope you can help me."

He motioned her to a chair at the front of his desk. "You have some problem?"

"No, no problem. My boss, Isara Horungruang, has instructed me to find someone, a missing person." The Horungruang family was well known in Phitsanulok. Pajeeka figured a bit of name dropping would help.

Recognition lit the Lieutenant's face, "I have met Khun Isara before. Truly a gentleman. You say you work for him?"

Pajeeka smiled, "I'm on his investigative staff. You and I are sort of in the same business." She pulled a business card from her purse and handed it to him. "May I call you Viboon?"

"If you want." He gave her card a cursory examination. "Who are you trying to find?"

"I'm looking for a woman named Chalamsee Duansawang."

He thought for a long minute then shook his head, "I don't know the name." He turned and announced loudly to the others in the room. "Does anyone know the Duansawang family?"

"I used to play soccer with a kid named Surat Duansawang," one officer responded. "I haven't seen him in years. I think he moved to Chiang Mai or something."

He turned back to Pajeeka, "Sorry. I guess we weren't much help."

"Mai pen rai, never mind. Khun Isara is looking for another family, too. Their name is Bongkot. Do you know them?"

"I've heard the name, but I can't remember where. What about first names?"

"Chalamsee, Nuang, Tippawan, or Math, do any of those sound familiar?"

The Lieutenant stiffened and leaned forward. "I know a Math Bongkot." He struggled to keep his expression nonchalant. "Nice girl, very polite, very smart. A year or two ago she had some problems. Domestic violence or something. Not too serious. She never went to jail. Her family is from Phitsanulok but I haven't seen her since the case was dropped. She must have moved away. That's not much help either, is it?"

"It's more than I knew before. Do you know if Math Bongkot had a sister named Chalamsee? Her nickname is Nuang. Khun Isara would want to know."

"From what I recall she had several sisters. It seems one was named Neet but I don't remember the others. One lived in Chiang Mai. I remember that because Math wanted to go there to look for work. If I think for a while, I might remember more."

"You have remembered much already. You've been most helpful. I will go now, so you can attend to your duties." On impulse she added, "My boss is offering a 30,000 baht reward to anyone who can provide a complete report on the Bongkot and Duansawang families."

It wasn't exactly true, but it wasn't a lie either. She had told Isara she might need money to open doors, and he had authorized fifty thousand baht. She was sure he hadn't expected her to spend so much of it on one bribe, but if it sped results she didn't care. It meant she could be on her holiday that much sooner.

"What sort of report?" the Lieutenant's eyes sparked to attention.

"One with as much detail as can be learned through police

access, local or otherwise. You know: family members, births, deaths, marriages, divorces, arrests, where they live and things like that. You seem like a smart young man. With your contacts, you could probably wrap that up in a day or two." She laid it on thick to bolster his ego. "Much faster than I could on my own."

"What do you get out of this?"

"I get to go on holiday as soon as my boss is satisfied." She smiled seductively, "With an extra 30,000 baht, you might want to go on holiday with me."

He smiled back. "With an extra 30,000 baht, I would buy my father a new motorcycle."

"Viboon, you *are* a very thoughtful son."

"Not really," he replied, "It's just that I have a very good father with a very old motorcycle."

She lowered her eyes coyly, and then looked up, "I still think you are a thoughtful son. You have my business card. Call my handy if you learn anything. I'm authorized to pay for incomplete reports, too."

"If there is anything I don't find, it's such a secret that no one can uncover it. I will call you as soon as I have something to report."

Pajeeka stood from her seat, "Khop khun mahk ka," she said presenting him with a polite wai. "I will wait for your call." She turned and left the station.

Viboon's mind whirled. Math Bongkot! Dear Buddha, yes he knew her. Just hearing her name caused feelings to gather in his chest. Not so long ago, he had been totally infatuated with her. At that time he had wanted to ask her for a date, but it hadn't seemed appropriate for him to socialize with someone in trouble with the law. He had often wondered what had happened to her. This was the perfect opportunity to find out and get paid for it. He went to the file room and pulled out Tippawan "Math" Bongkot's case folder.

That evening Pajeeka treated herself to a very expensive meal at Isara's expense. Later, she slept in her own bed for the first time in more than a week.

She spent the next few days duplicating some of the Lieutenant's efforts. As much as she was certain he wanted the 30,000 baht, she refused to bet her holiday on it.

Her friend in Bangkok had agreed to help for a fraction of what she expected, but the bits of information he emailed to her were minimal. Still, it was enough to help her know if any report Lieutenant Viboon might give her was fact or fiction. She had already decided to give Viboon a full week to do his investigation. If he hadn't called by then, she would contact him.

Chapter 17

Pattaya, Thailand

Nuang's bus departed the Phitsanulok station less than three hours after she left the temple. She breathed a sigh of relief as she started her journey south toward Bangkok. The entire time she had been in the bus station, she had worried that someone from the temple would come looking for her. Thank Buddha they didn't.

The bus reached the outskirts of Phitsanulok about the same time that Isara was instructing Pajeeka to investigate the Duansawang and Bongkot families. If Nuang had known that small detail, she would have been concerned. She was running away and didn't want anyone prying into her past.

She felt guilty for the way she had left the temple, but she hadn't been able to do it any other way. Despite her plans and her resolve, if Somjit or the young monk or anyone else had discovered her plan and asked her to stay, she would have. Instead of getting caught up in the emotions that come with hard decisions, she had simply disappeared. She had left a note for Somjit but it didn't say much. Only that she would return after she found a job. Nuang thought it might take a month or so but she knew it could be much longer.

She wasn't too worried though; Somjit and the baby would be okay at the temple. The young monk Laht would see to that. She knew by looking at him that he was hopelessly in love with Somjit. Even if she never returned, Somjit and the baby would be safe with Laht. She hoped Somjit would understand why she left.

By seven o'clock the sun had disappeared and the long

Thailand night had begun. Outside there was little to see except a sprinkling of houses and the glare of passing headlights. Every few kilometers small clusters of brightly lit restaurants and shop houses would emerge from the darkness. These roadside areas seemed ever alive with local families who came to eat, shop, and socialize with their neighbors. Most of them were farmers, rugged people with little concern for anything that happened beyond their own small piece of the universe.

Nuang thought about the lives these people must lead, isolated from the mainstream of the world. As remote as the temple had been, it was nothing compared to the seclusion these people faced each and every day of their lives. Yet the ones she saw were smiling, as if content with their fate. After spending her entire existence in the cities of Phitsanulok and Chiang Mai, Nuang couldn't imagine how life must be for these people living so far from the excitement of modern Thailand.

She tried to sleep but couldn't. The bus was comfortable enough but she wasn't sleepy. She passed the time wondering what she would do when she arrived in Pattaya. First she would find a hotel; that was an absolute must. Next she would look for a job. She figured she could find work as a waitress or a cook or a hotel maid. After seventeen years of marriage she had plenty of experience at all of those.

Pattaya would be gearing up for the so called tourist *high season* and finding a good job should be easy. Work was the least of her worries. She was more concerned about finding a place to live until her first paycheck. She had money in her pocket, but not much. It would be gone soon enough if she had to stay in a hotel for more than a few nights.

The bus entered the northern outskirts of Bangkok a little after midnight. The sky glowed from the lights of the city. With a population of over 10 million people, Bangkok was the largest city in Thailand. Chiang Mai and Phitsanulok seemed like midgets compared to this sprawling Asian megalopolis. As they neared the center of the city, skyscrapers sprouted by the dozens, towering high into the smog filled air. The bus exited the freeway and lumbered slowly through the busy streets. They reached Bangkok's eastern station at one o'clock in the morning.

Nuang purchased a ticket to Pattaya on the next bus with available seats. She wouldn't leave the Bangkok station for another four hours. She passed the time watching the other travelers milling around the terminal. They were an odd mix of Thais and farangs. Young and old, fat and thin, beautiful and ugly. They all looked as tired as she felt. She searched each face but saw no one she knew. She managed a few short naps but was afraid to fall into a deep sleep. She didn't want to miss her bus.

By five-fifteen in the morning, she was on her way south. Even at that early hour the streets were filled with traffic. She wondered what these people did for a living that would bring them out so early in the day. Maybe these were the people who slept by day and kept the city alive at night. Bangkok was a city of its own and not governed by the standards that ruled the Thailand she knew.

Nuang dozed on and off as the bus made its way down the eastern seaboard of the Gulf of Siam. Half waking thoughts and fleeting dreams replayed the other two trips she had made to Pattaya.

The first time was when her sister Math was critically injured in a motorcycle accident. Nuang had arrived just in time to see her sister die. Math's death had been devastating yet enlightening. Nuang had been happy because her sister would no longer have to bear the suffering that came with life. But she had been equally sad because she would miss talking and eating and laughing with someone she loved.

Forty days after her first journey to Pattaya, she had returned. That second trip had been to attend a sympathy ceremony given by Math's farang lover. He was an American named Mike Johnson. The man had sent a personal invitation and Nuang had accepted for reasons both selfish and not.

She had first met Mike Johnson when he lived with Math in Pattaya. Nuang had found him to be exciting, exotic, and alluring. That was part of the reason she had gone to Pattaya when he asked. But the main reason she had attended the ceremony was because of a promise she had made to her sister.

That second trip to Pattaya had been enchanted. Her emotions had still been supercharged from Math's recent death, and being so close to the man who had once loved her sister put her into an intoxicated state. At the ceremony, Mike Johnson had tried hard not to cry, but Nuang had seen the solitary tear that escaped his eye. It had affected her deeply. She had wanted to hold and comfort him but couldn't with her brother and his neighbors so near. Later, after the ceremony, she had kept her promise to her sister as she satisfied her own selfish desires. She had held him in her arms and made love to him one last time, just as her sister had asked. That afternoon of passion had changed her life. Indeed it had been magic, and she had left the proof with Somjit at the temple in Phitsanulok.

When Nuang finally fell into a true sleep, it was almost dawn. It would be daylight by the time she arrived in Pattaya.

Chapter 18

On the same day that Nuang's bus was leaving Phitsanulok, Mike Johnson arrived at the Pittsburgh airport. The only difference was that it was six o'clock in the morning in America and five o'clock in the evening in Thailand. He was two hours early for his flight but that was on purpose. He had a business class ticket and he intended to get his money's worth.

First class and business class passengers received special privileges including free drinks and snacks in the executive lounges and Mike intended to get his fair share of both. He figured he could drink two or three gin and tonics before his plane left, a couple of more during the flight, and at least one at the terminal in Detroit. He wanted to be well inebriated by the time his flight left for Tokyo. With luck he would be asleep before they served their first meal. This wasn't Mike's first flight across the U.S. and the Pacific, and the best solution he had ever found for surviving the trip was to sleep through as much of it as he could. Gin, he had discovered, worked much better than melatonin.

He collected his ticket at the front counter, passed security with his carry-on, and went to the executive lounge. Except for three other passengers and the bartender, he had the place to himself. The others, he noted, were drinking coffee. He ordered a gin and tonic.

His stomach rebelled at the first sip, so he ate a sweet roll and tried again. This time there was no reaction. Two drinks later he boarded his plane.

The commuter flight to Detroit had no business class section, so Mike was seated in first class. The flight was smooth and the service mostly personal. He managed to down three drinks in the short hop. He had two more at Cheers in the Detroit terminal before rushing to board his flight to Tokyo.

Mike had requested and been given an aisle seat. To him it was the only place to sit on an extended flight as long as you didn't have a seatmate with a weak bladder. His seatmate on this trip was a young man. Mike guessed him to be about twenty-five. He was relieved to see the young man wasn't drinking anything. It would be a good trip.

Mike took his assigned seat, adjusted his clothes to get comfortable, and fastened his seatbelt. He ordered Beefeaters on the rocks, then reached up and opened the air vent. A trickle of warm air oozed out. He closed the vent and turned to his seatmate. "Where are you headed?"

The young man looked up from his book. "Thailand."

"Me too," Mike said. "Ever been there before?"

"No, it's my first time. What about you?"

"Been there a few times. Lived there for a while."

The young man expression turned to rapt attention. "You've lived there? What's it like?"

"Hot," Mike answered. "Real fucking hot."

The young man smiled. "Yeah, that's what I've heard. Do you know the language? I bought a book and some tapes, but it all seems like gibberish. Have you learned to speak Thai?"

"Not really. Just little stuff like 'Hello', 'I don't want', 'You're beautiful', 'I love you', and enough other things to survive, but I don't speak the language. I think I'm too old to learn. Have you ever been in a foreign country?"

"I was in Kentucky once. They didn't speak English there either. Does that count?"

Mike laughed. "I have a few friends who would kick both our asses for this, but yes, I think it does count."

The young man smiled and nodded knowingly, "Me too. By the way, my name is Jim—Jim Dowling."

"Pleased to meet you Jim. My name is Mike."

THAILAND - COLD RAIN

Mike's Beefeaters arrived and Jim returned to his book. Mike flirted shamelessly with the stewardesses. This wasn't his first transpacific flight and he knew the value of a friendly flight attendant on a twelve-hour-plus plane ride.

In a minute the influx of passengers dribbled to a halt. The crew went through their routine of sealing doors and helping the few stragglers stow their carry-ons. One stewardess collected unfinished drinks but bypassed Mike as she did. Yes, a friendly flight attendant was worth her weight in gold.

Even before everyone was belted into their seats, the plane lurched in reverse. Jim Dowling abandoned his book at the movement. He stared outside until the plane stopped and jerked forward. "Have you been to any other countries in Asia besides Thailand?" he asked, making idle conversation.

Images of Vietnam flickered through Mike's head. He took a slow thoughtful sip on his gin. "I was in Nam once."

Jim sized Mike's tone thoroughly before speaking. "Were you there during the war? The way you said your words makes me think you're a Vietnam vet. Am I right?"

Mike didn't look at Jim as he answered, "Yeah, I was there during the war."

"What was it like?" Jim asked.

"Probably nothing like you were taught in school. Actually, I would rather not talk about it."

"I'm sorry if I asked a bad question," Jim said.

"Mai pen rai, Khun Jim," Mike replied. "Mai pen rai."

"Was that Thai? What does it mean?"

Mike laughed softly. "Yeah, Thai. It means *never mind*."

Jim pulled out a small notebook from his suit coat pocket, made an entry, and then returned his attention to Mike.

"What are the women like in Thailand? I've heard they are very beautiful and very sexy. I've heard they like foreigners, especially ones from America." He lowered his voice to a conspiratorial whisper, "I've also heard they're all very good in bed. Is that true or just a bullshit rumor?"

Mike clenched his jaw and fought back his initial response. The boy only wanted to talk man to man. It was an innocent question. Mike took another sip of his drink.

"The women in Thailand are just like women anywhere. If you're polite and treat them with a little respect, you will be treated the same. Treat them like shit or low class, then guess what? If you're a tourist, what I just said might not apply. Thais treat tourists nice because they want their money. If you're in Thailand for a long time, you'll get to know them as people and they will treat you differently. Not necessarily good, but differently. A lot of it depends on how you treat them.

"Are Thai women good in bed? Sure they are, but maybe I'm the wrong person to ask. You see, I happen to think American women, European women, Mexican women, Japanese women, African women, and most other nationalities are pretty damned good in bed, too. Who am I to judge? Pussy is pussy. Some just seems better than others."

Jim couldn't help but notice the tenseness in Mike's voice. Redness filled his face. "I guess I ask pretty stupid questions."

"Don't worry about it. Sometimes I give pretty stupid answers."

There was a long silence. Finally, Jim spoke. "Is it dangerous in Thailand?"

Mike took another sip of his drink. He wished mightily that he could smoke. "It's dangerous everyplace in the world. If you're wondering if Thailand is more dangerous than the States, I would have to say no. Just use a little common sense and you'll be fine. If you get hurt in Thailand, it will probably be your own fault for being stupid. My best advice is to stay away from the back alleys and the long-time expats. Don't trust either one. Most of all be afraid of the Thai women. They may not hurt you physically, but they're very good at stealing hearts. I've seen a lot of good men ruined by false love. Don't ever think you're immune to it."

The plane pitched forward and raced down the runway gaining take-off speed. Jim turned to watch out the window.

THAILAND - COLD RAIN

In a moment they were airborne. The plane banked to the right. Below, the city streets were lined with trees in the early stages of fall. Touches of yellow and red dotted the mostly green foliage. In a few short weeks the green would be gone. Not long after that the leaves would be gone, too; dead for the winter.

Neither man spoke as the plane climbed to cruising altitude. Mike worked his jaw to keep his ears clear while Jim thought about what Mike had told him.

When the plane leveled off, Jim turned and said, "I'm sorry if I offended you. I didn't mean to. I've never been to Thailand. I guess I'm a little worried. I don't know how to act, how to get around, or anything. You're the first person I've met who's actually lived there. You must know a million things I need to know."

Mike looked over at his seatmate. The boy was right, there were things he needed to know. "For what it's worth, I will tell you everything I've learned. It's not much, but maybe it will help. I'll tell you the easy things first. Baht is Thailand's local money. The exchange rate for U.S. greenbacks changes every day, but I'm sure you know that already. If you're offered a very high or low exchange rate, you're probably being ripped off one way or another.

"Until you've been there for a while you will be called a farang. If they never accept you as a person, you will always be a farang. Said in the right tone, the word can be an insult.

"Thinking about learning the language? Forget it! They don't want you to know, and you don't want to know what they say about you anyway. What you really need to learn is how to survive. You need to know that Thais drive on the opposite side of the road from the U.S. Left is right and right is wrong. For Americans, it can be confusing. What I'm telling you is to be careful crossing the street; look both ways before stepping off the curb. If you don't, you could end up dead.

"If you have a problem with a Thai local or a bar-girl, either forget about it or go to the tourist police. It's easier to just forget about it. It's even easier not to get involved in the first place. Thais have a strong sense of pride and it upsets them to lose face. I don't blame them; I don't like losing face either. Mostly they are a gentle people and have a lot of patience; but if they get pissed at you for whatever reason, then you have a real problem.

"I wouldn't recommend driving in Thailand unless you have nerves of steel or a death wish. Actually, there's no reason to drive. Bangkok has thousands of taxis, Chiang Mai and the north have three wheeled tuk-tuks and samlors, and Pattaya has baht-buses everywhere. They're cheap and you don't have to worry about finding a place to park."

Jim wrote furiously in his notebook and then asked, "Why do they call Thailand *The Land of Smiles*?"

"Because they seem to always be smiling. You'll see what I mean when you get there. But don't let their smiles fool you. They don't always smile for the same reasons that Westerners smile. One more thing, Thais are prolific liars. Next to eating, lying seems to be their favorite pastime. Usually it has to do with the saving of face thing, but sometimes it seems they do it for no reason at all. If it's a bar-girl, you can always assume she's lying. They do it to extract money from your wallet and they are very good at it. Just be aware that you'll be lied to and don't get insulted. Forget it and go on about your business."

Jim let everything Mike had said to sink in. After a long minute he said, "I've read all sorts of stuff on the internet about the bar-girls, but I can't tell where the truth stops and the lies begin. Since you've lived there, maybe you can tell me something. Do those women ever fall in love with foreigners? There's a great debate about this on some of the web boards."

Mike pondered Jim's question for a minute before answering, "Love in Thailand is a complex issue." Thoughts of Math flooded his mind. "But sometimes it can be very simple," he added, blushing. "Anything I tell you about love anywhere will be only an old man's opinions and could be wrong."

"I would like to hear anyway," Jim urged.

Mike took another sip of his drink. "Okay! My opinions only.

THAILAND - COLD RAIN

People fall in love everywhere in the world, even in Thailand. The bar-girls fall the fastest of all. Unfortunately, the first thing they fall in love with is your wallet. They can't help themselves and I don't blame them. If I were in their position, I would do the same thing. Think about it. Wouldn't you like to make a living having sex? I know I would. It doesn't matter anyway. Most men are too busy catching the disease to even care."

"Disease?" Jim's voice was deadly serious. "What disease?"

"The disease that comes when a man's ego gets inflated beyond reason. When they start believing a girl's love of their wallet equals true love. When they start believing they are sex gods instead of walking ATMs. When they start believing they are *oh so handsome and sexy*. If the disease is bad enough, a man will spend everything he has to keep the girl's love. The only cure is a healthy dose of reality. Like I said, no one is immune."

"Wow, that's pretty heavy. Have you ever had *the disease*?"

Math! Her image flashed crystal clear. She had been less than half his age and he had sent money to her after he went home. Weren't those symptoms of the disease? Was it possible he once had the illness but had been too blind to see it? He denied the thought; their relationship had been different. Math had loved him for more than his wallet. After a long silence he answered, "No, I'm one of the lucky ones. I've never had the disease."

"You mean you've never had your head turned by a Thai girl."

"I didn't say that. I only said I've never had the disease. I fell in love with a Thai girl once. I met her at a bar, but she wasn't a bar-girl. She was the most incredible woman I've ever met."

A sober mood overtook Mike as his life in Thailand replayed through his head. For reasons he didn't understand, he had a burning need to tell the tale that no one had ever heard. "Can I tell you a story?"

Jim saw the serious expression on Mike's face. "I would love to hear anything you have to say about Thailand."

Jim listened in as Mike told the story of a woman named Tippawan. She had been the love of his life, the woman he would judge all other women by until the day he died.

Mike talked about how they met, how they lived, and how they had loved. He told Jim about the problems caused by their cultural differences. He mentioned their fights only so he could talk about their make-ups. He talked about her unlucky life, their secret plans, and her tragic death. His words drew a larger than life picture of the woman he held above all others. More than once his eyes misted over as he talked.

Mike was careful not to mention Math's sister, Nuang, or what had happened between them after Math had died. It didn't seem appropriate and it was none of the boy's business anyway. Two Beefeaters later, he fell silent.

"She sounds like quite a woman," Jim said when Mike stopped talking.

"More than you'll ever know," Mike replied, his lips thick with gin, his words grating with emotion. "And it wasn't the disease." He shut his eyes and turned away.

Jim returned to his book but saw only the images of Thailand from the story that Mike had just told. In a while he said, "You should write a book. It's an incredible love story."

There was no response.

Mike awoke as the plane began its descent to Tokyo's Narita International Airport. The pain started just below his left ear and stabbed down behind his jaw bone and into his glands. He tried desperately to clear his ears. Yawning, swallowing, chewing, and more, but nothing worked. It had happened to him before and he knew what was coming wouldn't be pleasant.

As the plane descended, the pressure in his ears built from discomfort to pure agony. They cleared just before touchdown; the relief was immediate.

Jim stirred awake when the wheels bounced against the runway.

"Tokyo?" he asked, his voice hoarse from sleep and the dryness of the cabin.

"Yeah," Mike answered. "Welcome to Japan."

Mike led Jim through security and then to the Business Class lounge. "Where in Thailand are you headed?"

"Pattaya," Jim answered. "What about you?"

"I'm going to Pattaya, too," he corrected Jim's pronunciation. "If you're interested, we can share the cost of a taxi. I can get you a full fare receipt for your expense report."

"Someone is picking me up at the airport. I don't know who. I guess someone with a car to take me to my hotel."

Mike smiled and nodded, "If they don't show up, my offer of sharing the taxi still stands. Getting a room in Pattaya won't be a problem. Just let me know before I leave. Okay?"

"What do you mean, *if they don't show up*?"

"It happens sometimes," Mike answered. "To me more than once. I've stopped depending on anyone to meet me. It's easier that way. Just let me know if you change your mind and want a ride."

"Okay," Jim said. "Maybe you could ask me again before you leave the airport."

It was still daylight when Mike boarded his flight from Tokyo to Bangkok. He felt like he was chasing the sun.

Chapter 19

Pattaya, Thailand

Nuang's bus arrived at the Pattaya terminal at seven o'clock in the morning. She collected her box of clothes and followed the other passengers toward the street.

The sky had grown light with the new day. Already, cars, trucks, and motorcycles were zipping up and down the road toward scattered destinations.

This was the first time she had been to Pattaya without someone meeting her and she wasn't sure what to do. She stood and watched as the others hailed baht-buses and motorcycle taxis to wherever they were going. Before long she was one of the few people left standing at the curb.

Her box of clothes wasn't very heavy but she figured it was too awkward to carry on the back of a motorcycle. She flagged down the first empty baht-bus that passed by.

"I need a place to stay for a night or two," she told the driver. "Can you take me to the cheapest hotel in Pattaya?"

The driver smiled and nodded. "Ten baht," was his answer.

The sun had topped the horizon by the time the baht-bus stopped in front a seedy looking hotel. The driver waited while Nuang exited the bed of the truck.

"Ten baht," he repeated his fare, holding his hand through the open window.

She fished a coin from her pocket and handed it to the man. "Is this place clean?"

"I don't know," he shrugged. "I've never been inside. I only know it's cheap."

He drove away leaving Nuang to find out for herself.

The lobby was dimly lit and smelled of old wood and cigarette smoke. Two white painted wicker chairs sat against the wall opposite the reception desk. The boy on duty was asleep.

"Kaw thort, ka. Excuse me," she said, loud enough to awaken him.

He sat up with a start. "May I help you?"

"How much for a room?" she asked.

The boy looked around. "Will a farang be joining you?"

Nuang blushed at his question. Her smile didn't fade but her voice became terse, "I am alone."

"The cost is one hundred fifty baht. It's our special rate for Thais only. I'll give you our best room. It's on the fourth floor and has a very nice view."

She filled out the short registration form with false names, addresses, and phone numbers. She didn't want anyone to know who she was, and she didn't want to run the risk of someone, somehow, finding her. As remote as that possibility seemed, she couldn't take any chances. She had already made one mistake at the Phitsanulok bus terminal and she wouldn't make another.

She took the key, walked to the elevator, and pushed the button. After a minute or two of mechanical groans and clanking, the door opened. The car dropped a another few millimeters when she stepped inside. Her better judgment told her to take the stairs, but she pressed the fourth floor button anyway. The motor whirled for a moment before the elevator jerked upwards. A slight burning odor reached her nose. The clanking and groaning intensified as the car moved up the shaft. She was relieved when it stopped and the door slid open.

In the hallway stood a slender young lady dressed in a bright colored blouse and tight black jeans. Thick gold chains dangled from her wrist and neck. A heavy layer of make-up covered what Nuang could see was a beautiful face. She guessed the girl to be in her early twenties. Her body was what men called very sexy.

J. F. Gump

"Sawasdee ka," Nuang said politely as she exited the elevator.

"Sawasdee, ka," the girl replied, smiling.

"I think the elevator has a problem," Nuang said. "If I were you, I would take the stairs. That would be safer."

"I'm not worried," the girl responded and stepped into the waiting car. "I have taken it many times. It likes to growl like an old man's stomach." The door squeaked shut and the elevator clanged downward.

Nuang's "special" room was small and dingy, but at 150 baht it fit her limited budget. The wonderful view turned out to be of a window in another building less than three meters away. If she leaned her head out far enough, she could catch the slightest glimmer of Pattaya Bay. The TV didn't work, but that wasn't important. She would be here only a day or two and would be too busy to watch TV anyway.

The water was cold and more like an anemic trickle than a shower. Getting clean turned into a twenty minute ordeal. Afterwards, she put on fresh make-up and clean clothes, and then walked down the four flights of stairs to the lobby.

"Sawasdee ka," Nuang said to the girl who was now working the front desk.

"Good morning," the young girl smiled. "May I help you?"

"Yes, I need a map. I'm looking for the best hotels in town."

The girl's smile faded. A worried look crossed her face. "Is there a problem with your room? I can move you, if it's not okay."

Nuang was too polite to tell the truth, and the next room might be even worse than the first. She decided it best not to complain.

"I'm looking for a job. I hope some of the hotels are hiring for the tourist season. My English is good and I'm a hard worker. I want to work at the best hotel in Pattaya."

The girl relaxed a little but her smile seemed uncertain. She pointed at a stack of thin magazines at the end of the counter. "Unless someone has taken them out, those magazines have a map of Pattaya in the center. They show all of the hotels."

Nuang took the one from the top. The date she noticed was

two months old. It didn't matter, the hotels would be the same. She flipped it open to the middle, the map was still there. "Can I borrow it? I promise to bring it back later."

"Sure, go ahead," the girl answered. "Keep it if you want. It's an old one anyway."

"Khop khun mahk ka," Nuang thanked her.

"Mai pen rai," the girl replied, and then added. "It's not easy to find work in Pattaya, unless you know someone. Most of the better jobs go to friends and relatives. Come back and see me if you don't have any luck. Maybe I can help."

"Thank you, I will." Nuang smiled.

Outside, the sun had baked the city into a sweltering inferno. It wasn't yet nine but it was already suffocating. Chiang Mai and Phitsanulok were never this hot so early in the morning. Nuang studied the map of Pattaya. It was all in English but that was okay. Like she had told the girl, her English was pretty good.

She walked to the end of the street and looked at the signs to get her bearings. She located Soi 6 on the map, and then counted the number of nearby hotels. There were fifteen within a few blocks. With so many hotels, surely one of them would need extra help through the high season. Her hotel, she noted, wasn't listed on the map; she wasn't surprised. She set off up the street toward the heaviest concentration of hotels.

In a moment she crossed the road and walked in the shadow of the buildings. Nuang, like most Thai women, preferred her skin to be as white as possible. White was beautiful and the color of the rich. Brown was the color of farm workers and common laborers. She was sure the hotels would want to hire light-skinned girls

As she walked, she thought she recognized things from the last time she was in Pattaya. But that had been a long time ago, so she wasn't really sure. She kept her pace slow but steady. She didn't want to waste any time, but she didn't want to sweat either.

Fifteen minutes later she arrived at a circular intersection with two top-class hotels within a block of each other. She picked the most expensive looking one and walked through the front gates. The security guard gave her a sidelong stare, but said nothing except a polite hello.

Nuang had never been in a place so luxurious. The marble floors were spotless and the heavy woodwork was carved with such detail it must have been done by the finest craftsmen in Thailand. A fountain with multicolored fish and lotus flowers filled the center of the lobby. Farang's, acting rich and confident, ambled casually to and from the restaurant located at the far side of the room. The hotel employees wore uniforms reminiscent of traditional Thai dress. She was intimidated by the scene. Everything looked so perfect.

She looked down at her clothes. They were someone else's castoffs, clothes she had been given at the temple. They didn't even fit right. She took a deep breath and approached one of the girls working at the reception counter. "Excuse me. May I see the manager?"

The girl behind the counter looked up and smiled. "The manager isn't here at the moment." Her eyes inspected Nuang with a single glance. "May I help you?"

Nuang was so nervous it was all she could do to maintain her composure. She hadn't thought what she would say if the manager was out. "I want to apply for a job. I can cook and I can clean. My English is very good."

"Oh, I can help you with that," the girl smiled. "I don't know if the hotel is hiring or not, but you can fill out an application and leave a copy of your curriculum vitae for the manager."

Nuang stared dumbfounded. "Leave my what?" She wondered if the girl meant a copy of her I.D.

"Your curriculum vitae. You know, the story of your life, your resume. Where you went to college, where you have worked, and things like that. It must be in English because the manager doesn't read Thai."

Nuang could feel her smile dropping despite her efforts to keep it in place. She didn't have a curriculum, much less a vitae. She reached out and took the application the girl pushed in her direction. "Yes, of course," she said as sophisticated as possible. "I just didn't hear what you said. I'll take the application with me and bring it back later with a copy of my curriculum vitae."

Nuang thought she saw a look of smugness in the girl's eyes. Even with her lighter than normal complexion and her better than average English, the girl had somehow identified her as someone too low class to work in this hotel.

"Thank you for your time," she said in the best English she could muster, then turned and strode out of the lobby. She kept her back straight and her head erect. Once through the gates of the hotel, she sat at the edge of the street and cried.

In a few minutes she composed herself and walked to the next hotel. After that she went to the next hotel and the next hotel. Everyplace was the same, except she did get talk to the manager at a few of them.

No place was hiring. Everyone would keep her application on file and call if anything came up. That wasn't likely since she was leaving fictitious names and phone numbers everywhere she went. When anyone asked for her I.D. or a resume, she said she would bring them back later.

By noon she had been to all of the *best* hotels in North Pattaya. Then she started stopping at every hotel she passed, whether they were on the map or not. If anything, the people at those hotels were even worse than the employees at the classier places. One farang manager politely told her he had a job for her, if she was willing to do something for him. The way he ogled her body left little doubt as to his meaning. Politely, Nuang told him to fuck himself in both English and Thai.

By five o'clock she was tired, sweaty, and starving. She hadn't found a job and she had wasted the whole day doing it. Nuang had experienced plenty of rejection in her life, but never so much in such a short time. She was close to her own hotel and decided to go there to get clean, put on dry clothes, and then get something to eat. Her shoulders slumped forward with defeat as she entered the hotel lobby.

The morning girl was still at the front desk. "Sawasdee ka," the girl said, very soft and very polite. "Pattaya is a cruel town."

Nuang looked up at the young woman who had just spoken with wisdom far beyond her age, or perhaps from lessons hard learned. Whichever it was, it was the cold truth.

"It's none of my business," the girl continued, "but your face resembles that of a man I have seen in Pattaya. Do you have relatives here?"

Nuang's heart did a quick summersault. "No, I don't know anyone in Pattaya. My family is from near Laos." It was a lie, but she had told so many lies today that one more wouldn't make any difference.

"Don't mind me," the girl smiled, "I'm just being nosy. I can tell by your mood that you didn't find a job. I'm glad you came back before I left for the day. My sister was here earlier and said the bar where she works needs more girls. They are paying 2,500 baht per month plus tips. I think it must be easy work, if you're interested."

Nuang mentally recounted the money in her purse. "What do I have to do?"

"My sister says all she has to do is smile and be nice." The girl didn't mention the other things her sister did to make money. She knew the bar owners expected the girls to go with the farang tourists, but they didn't make them do it. If a girl didn't go with the farangs, she would be treated less than fair by the owners, but she wouldn't be fired unless someone complained loud enough. "Go to Soi 2 tonight at eight o'clock and ask for Lek; she and her sister own Toy's Bar. That's where they need more girls."

"Thank you," Nuang replied, "but I'm sure I can't do that. I think right now I'll just get clean and go out for something to eat."

"I can recommend a nice outdoor restaurant near the Big C Shopping Center. It's very cheap and it's just across the street from Soi 2. Who knows, maybe you'll change your mind about working at Toy's Bar."

"Or maybe not," Nuang replied as she walked away from the reception desk.

She bypassed the elevator in favor of the stairs. The four flights her floor seemed higher than tallest skyscraper in Bangkok.

The shower hadn't improved any during the day. If anything, it had become worse. Eventually she had washed away the sweat and grime from her job search and was ready for food. Her conversation with the girl replayed itself. If she wasn't forced to go with a man, maybe working in a beer bar wouldn't be so bad. She could still use her days to look for a real job, and the evening work would help stretch her small supply of money.

She pulled a pair of jeans from her clothes box and wiggled her way into them. They were tight—real tight. She looked herself up and down as best as she could without a full length mirror. Probably what the farangs would call sexy, she thought, amused by the idea. She put on new make-up, a colorful blouse, and a pair of well worn high heels. After combing her hair and inspecting herself one last time, she left the room.

The young girl was gone and the boy she had seen that morning was back on duty. He gave her a casual glance but said nothing. Nuang wasn't sure he even recognized her. He probably thought she was just another lady of Pattaya. At the age of 36, it seemed like a compliment.

Outside, the evening sun had slipped over the horizon leaving an orange glow in its wake. Nuang headed in the direction of Soi 2. She saw the outdoor restaurants as she neared the Big C. She hoped the food was as good as the girl said.

She ordered a simple fish and noodle soup for dinner and a coke to drink. She took in the surroundings while she waited for her food to arrive. To her left was the Big C Shopping Center, to her right were more sidewalk restaurants. Across Second Road and a little south of where she sat were the beer bars of Soi 2.

It was still early, but already there were foreigners sitting at the bars. She watched the men as they drank their drinks and put their hands on the bar-girls. Nuang wondered how those girls could do that every night, never knowing who or what they were going home with.

A sharp memory pierced her self-righteous bubble. Not so long ago she, too, had gone home with a farang, so who was she to judge? But that had been different, she struggled to convince herself. That farang had been her sister's lover, so he wasn't a total stranger. And she had done it just once and only because she had promised her sister she would. But it had been exciting, thrilling, romantic, exhilarating. That day she had experienced a climax with a man for the only time in her entire life.

Nuang's food arrived and she turned her attention to her stomach. For the moment she lost interest in the bars, the farangs, and the bar-girls. Either the food was exceptionally good or she was exceptionally hungry. It was delicious. She finished the soup and ordered a second cola. Then she sat there deciding what to do.

Her hopes of finding a job at one of the hotels had dimmed considerably. The girl at her hotel had said the bars were looking for help. She was certainly dressed for the job, and she doubted anyone would care who she was or where she was from or if she had ever gone to school. She could start making money tonight.

She glanced back across Second Road at the open-air bars. They didn't look like much. Tin roofs held up by steel poles provided cover for rectangular shaped bars lined with well worn stools. Inside the bars were coolers, a cashier, and the ever present bar-girls. Nuang noticed a small sign hanging from the eave of one bar. Help wanted, it read in Thai, 80 baht per day. It wasn't much, barely enough for food, but more than she was making now. She was sure she couldn't sleep with a different stranger every night, but she wasn't ready for starvation either.

At that moment she made up her mind. She would work as a bar-girl for one night, and if it was okay she would work there every night. Maybe she would even find a farang who would give her another climax. She blushed at the thought.

Chapter 20

Mike Johnson was one of the first in line to board the plane from Tokyo to Bangkok. He stowed his carry-on and sat down.

The seat beside him stayed empty for a long time. A bit of inane excitement built inside him. To Mike, sitting in business class with an empty seat beside him was almost as good as first class. If no one showed up, he might even sit in the window seat. He passed on the Beefeaters and ordered a glass of tomato juice instead. He had already consumed enough alcohol for one day and figured a little vitamin C wouldn't hurt.

Just before the plane backed from its docking area, an Asian woman stopped beside him and pointed at the window seat. Mike stood to let her in. She was about five feet three inches tall with long black hair. She was well built and attractive. Actually she was more than attractive, she was beautiful. Mike studied her face. He guessed her to be in her late twenties. She looked vaguely familiar, but he was sure he didn't know her. She could have been Vietnamese, Cambodian, Laos, or Thai. Considering they were on their way to Bangkok, he decided on Thai.

"Sawasdee krup," he ventured, "Sabai dee mai? How are you?"

"Sabai dee, khop khun ka. I am fine, thank you."

"My name is Mike."

"I'm pleased to meet you," the lady responded in near perfect English.

"Your English is very good. Do you live in America?"

"I lived in Scotland and England for a while. Now I'm going home to Thailand."

"Going to visit relatives?" he asked.

"No, I am going home to live," she answered then shifted the subject. "What about you?"

"I'm going to Thailand on business for a few months. I'll be working in Pattaya." Immediately, he regretted his choice of words. Many Thais don't like to think or talk about Pattaya because of the things that go on there; things not polite. Some didn't even consider it a part of Thailand. "Have you ever been there?"

"Yes, my husband used to work there."

"Oh, you're married then?" He glanced at her ring finger. It was bare, but for Thais that didn't mean anything.

"I was married," the woman said. "Our marriage is finished now."

"I'm sorry," Mike said with polite sympathy.

"Never mind. It's been a long time. I'm okay."

The stewardess came past collecting glasses and checking seat-belts. A minute later the plane raced down the runway toward the evening horizon. The woman turned to look out the window. Within minutes she was asleep.

Mike slept on and off during the flight. Darkness caught up with them just as his internal clock said it should be getting light. When they passed into Vietnam airspace, he had an overwhelming urge to look down. At that instant he wished he had the window seat. After all of these years, he still carried vivid memories of the time he spent there during the war. He wondered how much Vietnam had changed or if it had changed at all. Someday he would return but he didn't know when. He didn't even know why.

Thirty minutes from Bangkok he went to the lavatory. He brushed his teeth, shaved, and cleaned himself as best as he could in the cramped compartment. When he finally exited the toilet, he got dirty looks from a few of the waiting passengers. He mumbled apologies and rubbed at his lower stomach. They let him pass. The lady was gone when he got back to his seat.

As the plane started its descent, wind turbulence shook it hard. Mike slid his TV monitor into its slot and fastened his seat-belt. He wondered if it was raining in Bangkok.

A minute later, his seatmate stumbled her way down the aisle of the jumping craft. She lost her balance and pitched forward as she arrived at their row.

Mike reached out and caught her. He felt the smooth softness of her body. The scent of fresh perfume filled his nose. He had smelled that same fragrance a hundred times before. Sharp images of Math shot through his head. He fought down the urge to take the woman in his arms. "Are you okay?"

She struggled to regain her footing. "I am sorry. I'm so embarrassed. Please forgive me."

"Mai pen rai," he answered, smiling. "Catching you was my pleasure." He stood to let her inside. "I like your perfume. It reminds me of someone I once knew."

"Thank you. It's my favorite, too."

Outside, the plane broke through a layer of clouds. Bangkok was to their left, to the southwest. City lights twinkled upwards. The plane banked in that direction in preparation for final approach. The flight crew went through their routine of making sure everything and everyone was secure for landing. Again Mike had trouble adjusting to the pressure change. This time the pain was exquisite. The plane had parked at the terminal before his ears finally cleared.

The woman was out of her seat and stepping across Mike as soon as the fasten seat-belt light was turned off. By the time he pulled his bag from the overhead, she was gone.

Everyone shuffled forward, anxious to be off the plane. As he neared the exit, the unmistakable scent of Thailand drifted inside. He breathed deep.

A minute later he was headed toward immigration control. He had made this walk a few times before. He picked up his pace. He wanted to be one of the first in line.

His hurry was wasted. He stepped into the shortest long line and waited. His ex-seatmate stood two rows away. She was eighth in line. Jim Dowling was in the same row as her, but closer to the back.

Mike counted the people ahead of himself. Fifteen. It wouldn't take long unless the immigration officers decided to give someone a hard time. A monk, a young couple with backpacks, and man wearing an Arafat-looking war bonnet were in front of him. The others were less conspicuous. He timed the officials as they processed passports and paperwork. An average of one person per minute.

The line to his left had come to a complete stop while the immigration officer demanded more and more identification from the man standing at his station. After a few tense minutes and a phone call, the man's passport was stamped and he passed through immigration control.

No one in Mike's line was given more than a cursory glance. It moved smoothly. Mike had a ninety day work visa and the official barely looked at him as he stamped, initialed, and stapled. Thirty seconds. It was a record of sorts.

Just before he stepped onto the escalator leading down to baggage claim and customs, he waved at Jim and motioned he would meet him downstairs.

The first of the luggage appeared on the carousal as he entered the area. Without even noticing, he ended up standing next to his seatmate. "Hello again," he said when he realized she was there.

She looked up, "Oh, hello. Sorry, I don't remember your name."

"My name is Mike. You never told me yours."

"I am Thichakorn. My friends call me Itta."

"Do you live in Bangkok?"

"No, my hometown is north of here."

"Chiang Mai?"

"No, but my sister lives there. My home is in Phitsanulok. Oh, there's my suitcase." She pulled it from the carrousel and hurried away.

Mike's heart jerked frantically. Math had been from Phitsanulok. He wondered if this woman knew her. He wanted to follow her and ask, but his legs wouldn't move. He watched as she wrestled her luggage onto a cart and headed toward customs. Suddenly, he found himself walking in her direction. She had exited the baggage area before he came within voice range.

"Do you know anyone with the family name of Bongkot?" he shouted.

She stopped and looked over at him. Her own surname name was Bongkot. Why would he ask such a question? "What?" she shouted back. The customs agent ordered her to keep moving.

"If you know the family, tell them I think of them often."

His words stunned her. How could he know her family. This was all too weird. Itta passed beyond sight.

Mike thought he saw recognition on her face when he said Bongkot. He wondered if she did know the family. Probably not, he decided, and returned to the baggage area. Jim had arrived and was watching the endless circling of suitcases and boxes.

"My offer of sharing the taxi is still open, if you're interested," Mike said as he approached.

"A man on the flight said it could be dangerous going to Pattaya this time of the night. He said there was a hotel next to the airport. I have decided to stay there if my ride doesn't show up. I think right now I need a good night's sleep. I appreciate the offer, though."

"Mai pen rai," Mike responded. "It can be dangerous going to Pattaya at any time. Look me up when you get into town and I'll show you around. I'm staying at the Amari Orchid Hotel. If you don't find me there, try Toy's Fun Bar at the corner of Second Road and Soi 2."

Jim nodded, they shook hands, and Mike walked away.

The air outside the terminal clung like a wet blanket. It was overcast but it wasn't raining. The breeze was slight to none. Exhaust fumes stung his eyes. Sweat formed like magic on his forehead and scalp. He went to the taxi stand and hired a driver to

Pattaya. Within minutes they were moving down the freeway toward Bangkok and beyond. The rear seat of the taxi was small and uncomfortable but at least it was cool. The air conditioning made up for any shortcomings. He watched as the driver steered his taxi in and out of traffic. The young man liked to speed but he didn't take risks. Mike relaxed, he had a good driver.

The sprawling metropolis of Bangkok slid past on both sides of the vehicle. He strained his memory to recognize the shape of the skyline. Beyond an occasional landmark, he drew a blank. Had Bangkok changed so much in the year he had been gone, or was he just getting forgetful? He supposed it was a bit of both.

Within thirty minutes they had passed the heart of the city and were moving south and east toward Chonburi, Sri Racha, and Pattaya. The road was lined by a continuous stream of gas stations, roadside shops, and outdoor restaurants. The old contrasted sharply with the new. Traditional Thai food cooked over glowing charcoal embers while gas pumps filled Mercedes Benz tanks. Ramshackle buildings stood in the shadow of modern high-rises. Pink fluorescent lights merged with mercury vapor yellow.

The traffic thinned as they left the outskirts of the city. The driver pushed his speed up to 120 kilometers per hour and held it steady. Not far from the Chonburi bypass they stopped at a gas station. Mike bought two beers and a soda while the driver relieved his bladder. When the driver returned, Mike handed him the soda and offered a cigarette. He accepted both. They stood outside and smoked before returning to the coolness of the cab. They reached the northern edges of Pattaya at one o'clock in the morning.

Chapter 21

It was just after nine o'clock when Nuang finished her dinner. She waved the waitress to her table, paid her tab, and left the street-side restaurant. Her heart raced at what she had decided to do. She was going to get a job as a bar-girl.

The idea grated hard against her morals but she pushed it aside. She didn't know for sure, but she suspected her sisters Itta and Math had done the same thing. How else would they find rich foreigners to love and take care of them? Maybe she would find one who could help take care of her baby and Somjit.

She braced herself and crossed Second Road to Toy's Fun Bar. She approached hesitantly. For a few moments no one noticed her, or even acknowledged her presence. Finally, just as she decided to leave, a woman came to where she stood.

"My name is Lek," the lady said, appraising her coolly. "Can I help you?"

"I am Kamonal," Nuang lied. "Everyone calls me Ann. I saw your sign for help. Can I have a job working in your bar?"

"Where are you from, Ann?" Lek asked, maintaining her aloofness. The high season was getting under way and Lek needed extra help, but the girl needed to understand what was expected and who was the boss. "Have you ever worked in a bar before?"

"I am from Chiang Mai," Nuang answered. "I have never worked in a bar."

"Do you speak English?"

"Yes, I've studied English a lot. I thought I would visit a friend in America, but I never did. My English is better than most."

"Have you ever had sex with a farang?"

Nuang blushed and lowered her eyes away from Lek.

"You do know what sex is, don't you?" Lek pushed the issue.

"Yes, I know," Nuang stammered. "I had sex with a farang one time. He was my sister's boyfriend."

Lek smiled. The girl wasn't young but maybe she had more to offer than she first thought. "How was it? Did you like having sex with him?"

"He hurt me," she said, remembering her labor pains. "He was the biggest man I ever had," she added to stem more questions on the subject.

Lek laughed aloud. "They're not all so big or maybe you are just very small."

Nuang blushed again. She was sure she wasn't so small now that she had given birth to a seven pound baby. "I like big men, even if they do hurt a little."

"Then maybe I'll hire you," Lek said, sure she had a boyfriend-stealing slut ready to work for her. "Do you know what I expect of you if you work here?"

"To have sex with farangs?" Her words came out as a question instead of a statement like she intended.

Lek smiled briefly and then turned serious. "I will hire you for a couple of nights to make sure I want you working here. I expect my girls to take good care of my customers. Talk to them, entertain them, get them to stay and buy more drinks. If a man wants you, I expect you to go with him, even if you don't like him or think he's ugly or smells bad. I won't make you go with anyone, but if you want to make money, it's what you should do. If I think a man is dangerous, I will tell you. I will pay you eighty baht for every night you work. If a man buys you drinks, I'll pay you twenty baht for each. If a man pays your bar fine, I will pay you fifty baht. Whatever the man pays you to have sex is your money to keep. Understand?"

"Yes, I understand," Nuang answered. She didn't know if it was a fair deal or not. "What is a bar fine?"

Lek couldn't stop herself from laughing. "If a man wants to

take one of my employees away from the bar to go dancing or to dinner or for sex or for anything, they must pay me two hundred baht. Otherwise all of my help would be gone by ten o'clock and I would have no business. Sometimes men only want to take a lady for a short-time. When that happens, you can come back to work and maybe have another man pay your bar fine. Some of my girls make two thousand or three thousand baht in one night for everything."

Nuang's eyes grew wide. Two or three thousand baht! If she could do that, in two nights she would make as much as she would earn in a month at another job. She would do anything to make that much money. She could get rich in just a few months. "You will hire me then?"

"Yes," Lek replied. "But first I must see your I.D. I need to make sure you're who you say. Besides, some hotels won't let you go to a man's room unless you have an I.D. to leave with the security guards."

Nuang fumbled briefly inside her purse. "I must have left it in my room," she lied again. "Can I bring it tomorrow?"

Lek stared. "Okay," she finally conceded. "I need girls or I wouldn't do it. Just make sure you're not lying to me or I'll see that you never work anywhere in Pattaya. Do you understand me? I know everyone in this town."

Nuang nodded her head yes, wondering how she would cover her lie about her name. "I understand. What do I do?"

Lek's expression softened a little. "Usually, I start new girls inside the bar for a few nights until they are comfortable and until they learn some English words. But I think you're not so young and you say you can speak English already. I will start you outside the bar because that's where I need help. Men from all over the world come to Pattaya for holiday. Your job is to keep them happy while they are at my bar. I'm in the business of selling beer, whiskey, and fun. Just so I know, do you like German men, English men, Belgium men, or what?"

"You mean I have a choice?" Nuang asked incredulously. "Are

there Americans here, too? I think I would like an American man."

"You don't have too much choice," Lek answered. "But since you're new, I'll introduce you to someone you will be more comfortable with. Tonight you are lucky, because there is one American here. Not many Americans come to Thailand."

Nuang's face brightened. She glanced around the bar. "Which farang is the American?"

"He's the man sitting over there, at the far end of the bar." Lek raised her hand casually in his direction without pointing directly. "He comes here two or three nights a week and sits in the same place every time. He's a nice man, but reserved."

Nuang looked to where Lek had motioned. The man was middle-aged, about forty-five. He wasn't fat like many of the other farangs sitting at the bar. He was clean shaved and distinguished looking, almost handsome. She turned back to Lek.

"His name is Jonathan. He's been working in Thailand for three or four months. If he has taken a girl from the bar, I'm not aware of it. He says he has a girlfriend in America and they will get married when he goes home. I don't think he will take you from the bar, but he will buy you drinks. Be nice to him and he might leave you a tip."

"Thank you," Nuang said. She fidgeted with the strap of her purse for a moment before adding, "I'm embarrassed to ask this, but what do I say to him?"

"I'll introduce you," Lek smiled. "What you talk about is up to you. Just make sure you keep him entertained."

She led Nuang outside the bar to where the American sat sipping his beer.

"Jonathan," she spoke above the music. "This is my new girl. Her name is Ann. She started work just tonight. She is very shy. I thought you would want to meet her. She speaks English very good."

Nuang/Ann pressed the palms of her hands together in prayer-like fashion, positioned them in front of her face with the tips of her fingers at eye level, then bowed slightly. "Sawasdee ka, good evening, Khun Jonathan," she stumbled slightly at the unfamiliar feel of his name on her tongue. She blushed. "'I'm sorry if I say your name wrong."

"Mai pen rai," Jonathan replied, his Thai much worse than her English. "You can call me Jon. I think that would be easier for you to say."

"Khop khun ka. I think I can say that better." She paused then said, "Jon. Did I say it correct? "

He laughed. "You said it perfect. Would you like to sit down? I'll buy you a drink. What you would like? Beer, whiskey, coke, Lipo, or what?"

Nuang/Ann sat on the bar stool next to Jon. "Please talk slowly. I can speak English a little, but I cannot understand when you talk so fast."

"Sorry," Jon said. "Ja derm arai dee, nah?"

Nuang looked at him, questions lined her face.

"Phom poot Thai. Ja derm arai dee, nah? Khow chai mai?"

It took her a moment to realize the farang was speaking Thai. His words were horribly accented and monotone. Still, she understood him. Her eyes widened in surprise. "Oh, you speak Thai."

"I don't think very well," Jon smiled sheepishly. "What would you like to drink?"

"I want water," Nuang answered in English.

"Bad idea. I think Lek won't pay you if you have only water. I will buy you a lady drink *and* a bottle of water. You can throw the lady drink away if you don't want it."

"Okay," she giggled at the idea of getting paid to drink water, or to do anything else for that matter. "I'll have a lady drink and water."

He ordered her drinks and another beer for himself. "So, this is your first night here, huh? Where did you work before?"

"I worked as a seamstress in Chiang Mai. But that was a long time ago."

"I mean what other bars have you worked in Pattaya?"

Nuang blushed, "I have not worked in a bar before. I came to Pattaya just today."

He let her words sink in as he took a sip of beer and lit a cigarette. "You've never been to Pattaya before?"

"I have been here two times before. One time when my sister was killed in a motorcycle accident and once when her boyfriend invited me to a Buddhist ceremony for her spirit."

Jon reached out and touched her arm gently, and then pulled his hand away. "I'm sorry about your sister's death."

He was silent for a moment, then noticed Nuang staring at his cigarette. "I'm not polite. Would you like a cigarette?"

"Mai aou ka," Nuang answered. "I do not want; I was only looking. I don't smoke."

He shrugged his shoulders. "So you're from Chiang Mai? I've heard it's very beautiful."

"No, I'm not from Chiang Mai," Nuang answered. "I worked in Chiang Mai before, but my home is in Phitsanulok."

"Phitsanulok?" Jon's face pinched into a look of intense thinking. After a moment he said. "I don't know Phitsanulok. Where is it?"

"North of Bangkok, it's very far from here. Almost twelve hours by bus."

"In Thailand, almost everything is twelve hours away by bus," Jon mumbled wryly under his breath.

"I don't understand what you say. Please say again."

"Never mind," Jon responded. "It's not important. Why are you in Pattaya? Where do you live?"

Nuang squirmed nervously on the bar stool. What should she tell him? Certainly not everything. She decided to tell him bits of the truth.

"Please excuse me, if I don't know all of the English words to tell you, but I will try. I have a baby at my home in Phitsanulok." She blushed at the distorted truth she was about to tell. "Now the economy in Thailand is not so good and I cannot find work. I have not much money, but I must take care for my baby. Really, I came to Pattaya to work in a hotel or restaurant, but I'm not so young anymore and every business wants young women with big educations to work for them. I thought I would work here until I find another job. I don't think I will be good bar-girl because I'm not beautiful or sexy. I am too old."

Nuang didn't mention that she had a husband, and she hoped the farang wouldn't ask any questions about her baby. She didn't like to lie, but she could lie with the best when she wanted. She had proved that today at the hotels.

"You don't look so old to me," Jon replied. "You can't be more than thirty."

"Khop khun ka, thank you," Nuang's smile widened at the compliment. "But I'm much older than thirty."

"You shouldn't make jokes with us foreigners," he returned her smile. "By the way, you never told me where you live in Pattaya."

"I have a hotel room for tonight," she said. "It's not very nice and it doesn't have air con or a TV or anything except a bed."

"How much do you pay for one night?"

"Just a little," Nuang answered, "One hundred fifty baht."

Jon stared at her. That was less than five U.S. dollars. It had to be worse than a dump, and it was still probably more than she could afford. He changed the subject, "I'm sorry, but I don't remember your name."

"Nuang. My name is Nuang."

He lifted his brows. "Are you sure? I don't remember what Lek told me, but I'm sure it wasn't Nuang."

Her smile froze. She had worked as a bar-girl for less than an hour and already she had been caught telling lies. She glanced over at Lek and then back at Jon. She leaned forward and whispered. "I lied to Lek. I told her my name was Ann. My real name is Chalamsee and my nickname is Nuang. I don't want my mother to ever find out that I'm working as a bar-girl. You understand, yes?"

Jon took a sip of his beer. When he looked back at Nuang, his expression had turned to total seriousness. "Which lie do you want me to believe?"

J. F. Gump

Nuang stared at his face. Deep lines creased the corners of his eyes and across his forehead. There was no smile. Nuang could barely hear the music or the voices in the background. Her own smile faded to nothingness. "I want only for you to believe the truth," she answered, lowering her eyes from his face. There was a long moment of silence before she added, "I think you don't want to talk to me anymore so I will leave you alone."

She turned her seat away from the bar and stood. "Thank you for the drinks."

Jon reached out and took her by the arm. "Wait. I'm sorry if I insulted you. I didn't mean to do that. Please stay and finish your drink."

She allowed herself to be pulled back. His seriousness was gone and a sincere pleading had taken its place. The slightest trace of a smile pulled at his lips. She felt the heat of his hand on her arm.

"I am embarrassed," was all she could think to say.

"So am I," Jon replied. "I want to know more about you, if you'll let me."

She looked around the bar at the drunk farangs and the bar-girls. The cold realization of where she was assailed her. If she walked away from this man, Lek would expect her to sit with another. Maybe the next one wouldn't be so nice. The thought frightened her. "Are you sure you want me to stay?"

"Yes, sure, one hundred percent."

Nuang returned to her seat and they talked. Picking her words with the greatest of care, she told him small bits and pieces of her life. She told no lies except by failing to tell the whole truth.

When Jon told her about his life and his job, she knew he wasn't being honest, either. Lek had said he had a girlfriend in America, but he never mentioned it and neither did Nuang. After all, there was much she hadn't talked about, too.

Nuang and Jon sat together for a long time. Sometimes they talked, sometimes they listened to music, and sometimes they just watched the activities at the bar. Jon continued to order drinks for

118

both of them and Lek didn't pressure Nuang to move from her seat. Whenever Lek wasn't looking, Jon would toss Nuang's drink into bushes and refill her glass with water. By midnight Nuang had made a hundred baht from the drinks Jon had bought her. The girl at the hotel had been right, it was easy money and she was actually having fun.

At midnight, two of Jon's fellow workers arrived at Toy's bar and everyone was introduced all around. Nuang blushed at the talk about her being Jon's new girlfriend. The men told Jon they were going to another bar just down the street and asked him to join them.

Jon looked over at Nuang, and then turned back to his friends. "Do you mind if I bring her with us?"

No one objected.

Jon called Lek over, "I want to pay her bar fine."

Lek's eyes widened in surprise. "Okay," she barely managed say. She took Jon's money for the drinks and bar fine, and then spoke to Nuang in rapid Thai. "Come inside the bar for a minute."

Nuang's eyes were as wide as Lek's. This was happening too fast. She never thought she would go with a farang on her first night in Pattaya. She was terrified. Her head spun as she stepped inside the bar. Lek came and stood beside her.

"Either you are very good or very lucky," Lek said just loud enough for Nuang to hear. "He has never taken a girl from my bar before. If you can do this every night, you will make a lot of money here."

Nuang knew she should feel good at Lek's words, but she couldn't bring herself to smile. "What do I do?"

Lek laughed, "Have fun."

Jon and his friends didn't go far, only across the street. The bar was indoors. Its main attractions seemed to be loud music, air conditioning, and half naked dancers on a small raised stage. The girls, Nuang noticed, all wore numbers on their skimpy dance uniforms. She wondered why but was too shy to ask.

J. F. Gump

Everyone ordered beer except Nuang; she ordered a lady drink and water. She wondered if she would receive a tip from this bar, too.

The men talked so fast in English that Nuang couldn't keep up. Sometimes she understood entire sentences, but more often she recognized just a word here and there. At times the men would turn to look at her and laugh. It made her uncomfortable. She wondered what bad things they were saying about her.

No one spoke to her and, except for an occasional glance, no one even acknowledged her presence. The men drank beer, talked amongst themselves, and watched the girls dancing on stage. They flirted with any lady who came within shouting distance. By one o'clock they were ready to leave. One of Jon's friends was paying to take a dancer from the bar. The way the two smiled, Nuang was sure this wasn't the first time.

Jon's mind wandered while they waited for the dancer to put on her street clothes. This morning's phone call to his fiancée entered his thoughts. He had been away from home less than four months and Julie had already found another man. She had rambled on about being lonely, that life was too short, and other bullshit. She made a point of telling him it had nothing to do with sex, but he knew that was a lie. It always came down to sex.

He glanced over at Nuang and realized for the first time how much he had enjoyed her company this evening. Her English was good—better than most he had heard in Thailand—and she had been easy to talk to after their rocky start. He hadn't learned much about her, only enough to know she wasn't an average bar-girl.

When he had asked her to teach him a few Thai words, she had seemed more than happy to do it. She had been very patient and didn't laugh at his thick-lipped attempts at pronunciation. For reasons he didn't completely understand, he had an overpowering urge to take her home with him. He didn't need a sex partner, but after Julie's bombshell he desperately needed female attention to boost his ego.

THAILAND - COLD RAIN

He wondered if there was some way to get her to go home with him without seeming like every other stiff prick cruising the bars of Pattaya. He searched through his beer hazed mind for some plausible excuse. There had to be something she could do for him besides laying on her back and spreading her legs, especially when that wasn't an option for him anyway.

He had a drunken inspiration—she could teach him to speak Thai, just like she had done tonight. As stupid as the idea sounded, it was the only one he had.

"We're going back to Toy's for another drink," his words slurred a bit. "You can go with me if you want, but I think that's not such a good idea. If we go back together and you don't go home with me, Lek will expect you to go back to work. Do you understand what I'm saying?"

Nuang nodded.

"I'll give you a thousand baht for coming here with me, and then you can do what you want. If you want to go to your room, you can. If you want to go back to the bar and work, it's up to you. If you would like a decent place to sleep, I have an offer. I live in a condo with two bedrooms; I only use one. If you want, you can get your things from the hotel and stay in my extra bedroom. But there's something I need you to do for me."

Nuang understood his words, but wasn't sure she understood his meaning. She forced a smile to her face despite the fluttering in her stomach. "Do you mean you want me to go home with you?" she asked. "Do you want to sleep with me and have sex?"

Jon laughed. "No, you don't have to sleep with me. I really do have two bedrooms and I do want something from you, but it's not sex." He pulled a thousand baht bill from his wallet and handed it to her. "If you decide to come to my condo, you can wait for me in the lobby. If not, at least get a better room than you have now. And find another place to work. Okay?"

On impulse, he took a second thousand baht bill from his wallet and added it to the first. "Just so you don't feel pressured to make an immediate decision."

Nuang was stunned; two thousand baht in less than a minute. She never dreamed she could make so much money in such a short time. "I don't know where your condo is."

"Oh yeah," Jon mumbled. "I didn't think about that." He searched through his wallet and extracted a worn business card and gave it to Nuang. "This is where I live. Will you come?"

One side was written in English and the other in Thai. Nuang could read both. "I don't know what I will do," she said.

The dancer returned looking even sexier than she had in her skimpy bar uniform. Jon smiled and left with his friends.

Once they were gone, a waitress came and asked Nuang if she needed anything.

"Can you change this into smaller bills," Nuang asked, holding out one of the thousand baht bills.

"Maybe," the girl said and walked away with the money.

A minute later the waitress returned with the change. Nuang left a small tip then exited the bar and reentered the nightlife of Pattaya.

Two thousand baht, she thought. Two thousand baht and she hadn't even taken off her clothes. She wondered what Jon could want from her if not sex. What could she possibly do for him that was worth so much money? Her imagination ran wild.

"Need a ride?" A motorcycle taxi driver shouted at her from across the street.

"How much?" she shouted back.

"Twenty baht," the man responded.

Small money compared to what she had in her purse. They arrived at her hotel in less than five minutes.

Nuang walked quickly through the hotel lobby ignoring the desk clerk's hello and the two Thai ladies with farangs sitting at the small lobby bar. There was an "out of order" sign on the elevator door—she wasn't surprised.

She trudged up the four flights of stairs to her floor. By the time she arrived she was sweating and breathing heavily. Her room was even hotter than the stairwell and hallway.

Nuang tried repeatedly to bring the overhead fan to life, but managed only to get her hands black from the dust that edged the blades. When she went to wash her hands, nothing came from the faucet. The water, like the elevator, had finally died. She wiped her hands on a dry towel but the dust clung to her skin. She tried the faucet again. Still no water came out. This place was awful.

Earlier she had decided to wait until tomorrow before making a decision on Jon's offer to stay in his condo. Now, she was deciding to make her decision tonight.

Small beads of sweat swelled and trickled through her hair. She liked to be warm, but not this warm. The overhead florescent light made a loud hissing, zapping, buzzing noise and then joined the fan in death. The smell of burnt ballast soured the air.

Nuang repacked her cardboard box in the dim light that filtered in through the dirt stained window. She trudged back down four flights of stairs, through the lobby, and out the door. The desk clerk didn't speak as she left. A baht-bus was sitting at the curb.

"How much to this address?" she asked, showing the driver the card Jon had given her earlier.

"Fifty baht," he replied.

Nuang nodded her agreement. She would have paid twice that much to get away from the hotel.

Jon's condo turned out to be less than three blocks away. She felt like the baht-bus driver had tricked her, but she kept her mouth shut. After all, a deal is a deal. She would know better next time. She paid with a five hundred baht bill and waited while he dug through his small hoard of money to give her change. She was sure he would have to waste time at a shop or gas station to renew his supply of change before taking another fare. She didn't offer a tip. The man gave her a sour look and drove away.

Nuang entered the lobby of Jon's condo carrying her box of belongings. A young girl sat at the reception desk. A security guard stood near the counter watching a comedy show on TV. She approached the girl. "Sawasdee ka, good evening," she said politely.

The girl looked up, noting Nuang's dress and the box she carried. "Sawasdee ka. May I help you?"

Before Nuang could speak, the girl added politely but pointedly, "We do not rent overnight rooms to Thais. I'm sorry."

"Mai pen rai, never mind," Nuang replied. "A friend has invited me to stay in his condo. His name is Jon. He's an American. Is he here?"

The girl glanced up at the row of keys hanging on a board behind the desk. "He's not here. Are you sure you have the right place? The American who lives here never brings women to his room."

Nuang showed the business card to the girl. "I am sure. May I sit in the lobby and wait for him to come home? He told me I should wait if he wasn't here."

The girl hesitated for a moment before answering, "It's not allowed."

Neither spoke. The desk clerk's embarrassment was as real as Nuang's indignity. The girl squirmed in her chair for a moment before breaking the silence. "If you sit and be quiet, I think no one will notice. If Khun Jon comes home and tells you to leave, you must go without question or I will call the police. Do you understand?"

"Yes, thank you," she answered. "My name is Nuang."

"And I am Jahl," the desk clerk said in return.

Nuang carried her box of clothes to a wicker chair away from the reception desk and the guard. For a while she watched as people, mostly farangs, entered and exited the lobby. Sometime after two o'clock in the morning, she fell asleep. She dreamed of her husband, her baby, and Somjit.

Chapter 22

Mike Johnson arrived at the Amari Orchid Hotel at one o'clock that same night. It had been a long trip from Pittsburgh to Pattaya. He overpaid the taxi driver and walked into the reception area.

Three men, all farangs, sat at the lobby bar sipping beers. Mike didn't recognize the barmaid. He didn't recognize the girl at the front desk, either. He used to know them all, but that was long ago.

He filled out the forms, showed his passport, collected his key, and went to his room. By one-thirty he had showered and put on clean clothes. He knew he should go to bed, but he knew it would be pointless. He needed to unwind before he could sleep. He left the hotel and walked south toward the nightlife of Pattaya.

The walk from the Amari Orchid to the cluster of beer bars at Soi 2 was longer than he remembered. Either that or he was feeling the effects of his long trip. Or maybe he was just getting too old to handle it. He decided he would have two or three beers and then go back to the hotel.

At the corner of Second Road and Soi 2, he stopped and stared down at the cluster of bars. Even though he hadn't been here in nearly a year, he recognized everything as if it were yesterday.

The open-air bars were stacked side by side and front to back for a solid square block. Pink fluorescent bulbs and strings of Christmas tree lights lit the scene. Smiling bar-girls of every age, shape, and size went about their jobs of luring passing tourists inside.

"Hello sexy man, come sit with me," a girl shouted in his direction. He smiled and shook his head no.

He focused his attention on Toy's Bar, his old stomping

grounds. The worn red vinyl on the bar rail had been replaced with a medium blue, and the two-man band he had come to love was gone. Everything else seemed the same except the faces. He didn't see anyone he knew. Bao, Som Jai, Naow, and the rest of the old crew were gone. He didn't even see Toy, the owner, or her sister, Lek. He wondered if they had sold out to a new owner. He wouldn't be surprised. In Pattaya anything could happen.

He took a step toward Toy's bar then changed his mind. There was nothing for him there. He crossed Second Road and continued south. New beer bars were everywhere. A block south of Alcazars, he reached the Music Lover Bar. It hadn't changed at all. He took a stool beneath an oscillating fan.

Music Lover's wasn't near the popular bars and their business was thin. "Kaw bier Heineken kort neung krup," he ordered his beer in Thai. It had been a while since he had attempted speaking Thai. He hoped his words were understandable.

The barmaid stared at him stupidly.

"Heineken," Mike shortened his order to one word. No doubt his Thai was in need of practice.

The girl hurried away and then returned a moment later with his beer.

"Where is Wan?" he asked in clear English.

Again the barmaid stared stupidly.

"Khun poot angrit, chai mai? Do you speak English?" Mike tried his Thai again.

The girl shook her head no, but her eyes lit up with understanding. She turned and shouted to another barmaid.

"Dee chan poot angrit, I speak English," the new girl smiled. "What name you?"

"Phom cheur Mike, my name is Mike," He said in both Thai and English.

"Oh, you speak Thai?" the girl's smile widened.

"Nit noy, just a little," Mike answered then changed the subject. "Do you know a lady named Wan? She used to work here as the manager. She was my friend. I don't see her."

"Yes," the girl answered, "I know Wan. She no work here now. She marry Thai man and go Lop Buri."

"Too bad, I would like to see her again."

"You like play game?" the girl asked, her face hopeful. "Dice, connect four, jinga?"

Mike shook his head. "Mai, khop khun krup. No, thank you. I want only my beer. Maybe later."

"Okay. Never mind," the girl responded. "Maybe later." She turned and left him alone.

It was hot. The oscillating ceiling fan offered only intermittent relief. He sipped his beer and eased into his world of jet lag.

This bar and the condos behind it held more memories than would ever leave him. He had once lived there with a woman named Math, but that was a long time ago. They had stopped at this bar more times than he could remember. Conflicting emotions assaulted him as scenes of those days paraded through his head.

His first beer went down fast. He ordered another and it quickly joined the first. After that he slowed to a more normal pace. He sat there thinking, watching the ladies behind the bar, and listening to the music. Three songs later he was ready to leave.

As he finished his last beer, a man walked in from the street and sat next to him. Immediately three girls hurried to the bar, their smiles wide. The man ordered a beer for himself and drink for each of the girls. He flirted drunkenly with the giggling girls.

Mike was surprised to hear the very familiar accent of the man's words. When his initial excitement ebbed to a normal level, he turned toward the man, "Are you from Greene County?"

The man looked at Mike for the first time. He didn't speak, but only stared open-mouthed. Mike wasn't sure if the man was shit-drunk, totally dumbfounded, or both.

After a long second the man found his voice, "You mean Greene County as in Pennsylvania?"

Mike smiled. "Yeah, that one. I used to work with a man from Greene County. His accent was just like yours. If you had said no, I'd have guessed northern West Virginia. By the way, my name is

Mike."

"I'm impressed."

"Pleased to meet you, Mr. Impressed," Mike laughed at his own odd humor. "I'm from Pittsburgh. What about you?"

"I'm from Dayton, Ohio, but I grew up in Greene County. Pennsylvania that is. My name is Jonathan—Jonathan Yeager. Everyone calls me Jon."

"You here on business or pleasure?"

"Business. I'm doing some work for a steel mill in Chonburi. What about you? Business or pleasure?"

"Both," Mike smiled. "Mostly I'm here for a project at a refinery in Rayong. You been here long?"

"About four months. Not too long, but it seems like a year. I've almost forgotten what my life in America was like. And you?"

"I've been in Thailand for about three hours. The jet lag thing is really kicking my ass. My head thinks it's about two in the afternoon but my eyes think it's the middle of the night; the rest of me don't know what to think. I came out to have enough beer to put my head to sleep. It's not working yet." Mike paused, lit a cigarette, and then continued, "So, you've been here for four months, huh? You must be an old-hand by now."

"Hardly," Jonathan said. "Don't have time. Work keeps getting in the way. If your company is like mine, you'll understand soon enough."

"I know already. But I'm only here for a few weeks, so I don't care. Besides, I'm too old to be doing much nightlife anyway. In another five or six years you'll understand what I mean."

"I know what you mean already, too," Jon laughed.

Mike only smiled. "So, how do you like Thailand?"

"It's okay. I would like it better if it wasn't so damned hot. I spend half of my life sweating, taking showers, and changing clothes. I spend the rest of my time drinking cold beer and hanging out in air conditioned places. When I'm not working, that is."

Mike wiped his forehead with the back of his hand. "Yeah, I know what you mean. Any problem working with the Thais?"

THAILAND - COLD RAIN

"Not since I quit trying to change them. I wasted my first two months here trying to westernize their work habits. They have their own way of doing things, most of which makes little sense to me. I became so frustrated I nearly grew an ulcer. My best advice is to let them do what they want because that's what they're going to do anyway."

Mike remembered the years he had spent here. The Thai way was annoying. They would make a short term effort to please you, and then go back to their old habits. You either learned to deal with it or you left Thailand. There was no middle ground. "Sounds like good advice."

Jon nodded but offered nothing further on the subject. "Can I buy you a beer?" he asked.

"Maybe another time. I have to get to bed. Like I said, this jet lag is kicking my ass." He turned to one of the bar-girls, "Ghep tung krup."

The girl totaled the bills from the wooden cup sitting beside his empty beer bottle. "Two hundred sixty baht," she said in very clear English.

Mike handed her 300 baht and turned away indicating she should keep the change. The smile on her face told him he had just made a friend.

"This isn't your first time here, is it?" Jon asked.

"No, I've done this once or twice."

The two men stared at each other but said nothing. Strange how they had met halfway around the world at a second-class bar on Second Road in Pattaya, Thailand. Mike stuck his hand out to Jon, "My pleasure to meet you, Greene County."

He shook Mike's hand firmly, "You can call me Jon."

Mike smiled and stood to leave. "You'll always be Greene County to me. I'm staying at the Amari Hotel. Stop by some evening and have a beer or two. Ask for Mike Johnson, someone will find me."

Chapter 23

Mike's steps were less steady than he thought they should be. He had drunk only four beers, certainly not enough to make him intoxicated. Must be the jet lag, he decided, as he walked north on Second Road.

It was after two in the morning, but the music and the tourists were still going strong. As he neared the cluster of bars on Soi 2, a few of the left-over girls stared in his direction. They were waiting for him to get within hearing distance. He took a deep breath and shuffled onward.

"Hello sexy man", "I love you too much", "I want love you long time", and all of the other things the girls had been taught to say drifted to his ears. Mike smiled at the attention but didn't look at them. He knew that would be a mistake.

Not far down the street he saw Toy's Bar. A couple of girls looked vaguely familiar but he doubted they were anyone he knew. The bar-girls in Pattaya came and went on a regular basis. Sometimes they never came back.

In a moment he saw Lek and Toy, the bar owners, going through their routine of welcoming and attending their customers. He hadn't seen them earlier but they were here now, wringing every last baht from the tropical night. If either saw him, they didn't acknowledge it. They were too busy to notice a lone farang still two bars away. He decided to stop and say hello.

He fell in behind three men heading in the same direction. He stayed several steps back, and kept his head lowered to make his face less visible. He wanted to surprise Lek and Toy both, but mostly he wanted to surprise Lek.

THAILAND - COLD RAIN

Mike considered Lek his best friend in Pattaya. At one time he had considered her as something more than a friend, but their relationship had fizzled almost as quickly as it had started. Still, he had strong feelings for her.

The three men entered Toy's Bar ahead of him. Lek, the consummate bar hostess, swooped in on the men and led them to empty seats at the bar. Toy stopped what she was doing and headed in their direction to help. Mike turned around, putting his back them. He listened as the women welcomed their newest customers. He peeked over his shoulder once he was certain they weren't looking in his direction.

Lek was busy talking with the men she had pulled into the bar and Toy was happily introducing them to her ladies. Lek made sure everyone had a drink.

Mike slipped unnoticed toward the end of the bar opposite of where Toy, Lek, and the three men sat. He took a seat near the far back. It was a perfect location. Lek and Toy were hidden from his view by a cheap mirrored column that disguised one of the roof's steel support posts. He studied the faces of the girls. There was no one he knew.

He ordered a beer from one of the ladies and relaxed. He passed the time nursing his beer, listening to the new three-man-band and waiting for Lek to make another of her endless rounds.

Mike had always found Lek to be an interesting woman. When she was younger, she had been married to a police captain, had taught school, and had a comfortable life. All of that changed after her son was born. Her husband had left her for another woman and her teacher's pay was barely enough to make ends meet. Her sister, Toy, had opened a bar in Pattaya and had asked Lek to help run it. Lek's personality and business acumen had made the bar one of the most popular at the north end of Second Road.

While Mike had lived in Thailand, he had become entranced with Lek. After weeks of wooing her, she finally decided she liked him, too. Their relationship hadn't lasted, but their friendship had survived. He was anxious to see his old friend again.

After about fifteen minutes, Mike caught a glimpse of Lek as she slipped away from the men and started another circuit of the bar. He turned slightly to keep his face hidden from her view. In a moment he heard Lek's voice directly behind him.

"Hello darling," she was saying. "What your name?"

He turned and came face to face with her. "My name is Mike."

Her eyes opened wide, her hand leapt to her mouth to stifle a scream. For a moment, he thought she might faint.

"How are you, Lek?" he asked, when she didn't speak. "I've missed your beautiful smile. Did you miss me?"

"I don't believe it," she said loudly, recovering from her surprise. She threw her arms around Mike and hugged him furiously. "Yes, I missed you, too."

When she finally eased her grip, Mike was able to pull away for air. "What a welcome," he said. "I didn't expect you to be so happy, but I'm glad you are. Please, sit down; I'll buy you a drink."

"No wait," Lek responded, "You must say hello to my sister. Toy, come quickly," she shouted above the music. "Come see who has returned to Thailand."

Toy repeated the scene Lek had already made. He was embarrassed, but didn't protest. Actually, he liked the attention and was embarrassed by his embarrassment.

Mike sat with Lek on one side and Toy on the other. They talked about old times and the people they knew in common. He bought Lek and Toy drinks and they bought him drinks. In a while Toy wandered off to take care of other customers leaving Mike and Lek to talk alone.

"How are your wife and family?" Lek asked.

Mike tensed despite his exhaustion and the several beers he had consumed. "My wife is dead," he answered, his smile fading.

"I know that already. She died over a year ago. You told me that when you came for her sympathy ceremony. But that was your mia noy. I mean, how is your American wife?"

He took a deep breath. "She is dead, too."

Lek just stared, as if not sure how to respond. Finally she said,

"I'm sorry. Please forgive me for asking. Are you okay?"

"Almost. I'll survive whether I deserve to or not. But let's not talk about that. How are you? Have you been well?"

"I'm very happy," her smile turned to a beaming radiance. "I'm in love with a man from Canada. His name is Chris and he has a business in Pattaya, a computer business. He is very smart, very handsome, and very rich. He is good to me too much."

For some reason her happiness made him feel even lonelier than he had felt before. If it hadn't been for the beer, his smile would have disappeared altogether. "I'm very happy for you," he lied. "Can I meet him someday? I would like to meet the man who has stolen your heart from me."

Lek hit him playfully on the shoulder. "My heart will always belong to you, Mike. But for now my love belongs to Chris."

"Well, at least I have something." His laugh was artificial. If Lek noticed, she didn't mention it. "I really need to get back to my hotel. I'm about to fall asleep right here with the sexiest girl in the world sitting next to me. I should be trying to make you forget your boyfriend, but all I can think about is a soft bed."

"With me in it?" Lek smiled seductively.

This time his laugh was genuine. "Yeah, that too. But not tonight, I'm too tired. Maybe tomorrow." He stood to leave.

"Okay then, tomorrow. I like handsome men to pay attention to me. I will wait for you. Come early and I will introduce you to Chris. Be careful going home."

"Thanks, Lek, I will." He started the long walk to his hotel.

He fell asleep as soon as his head landed on the pillow.

~~~

Jonathan "Greene County" Yeager had two more beers before deciding he should go to bed. He really didn't need his last beer but he drank it anyway.

He politely ignored the bar-girls and passed the time thinking about the man he just met—Mr. Mike Johnson from Pittsburgh. He was impressed at the way the man had picked up on his accent. Thousands of miles from home and someone had pegged his background to a small spot on the Pennsylvania map.

Funny, he thought. He could have passed the man on the streets at home and they never would have met. But put them half way around the world in a backwater tourist trap and they couldn't pass the chance to talk. Familiar strangers. Jon had met a lot of them here in Pattaya, but Mike Johnson was the first to be from so close to his hometown. Definitely the first one to know he was from Greene County, Pennsylvania. One day he would look Mr. Johnson up for a beer at the Amari.

Jon paid his tab and left the bar. The number of beers he had consumed during the course of the evening was apparent as he wobbled toward home. It was a short walk to the condo lobby, but every step was a staggering challenge. The security guard watched bemused at Jon's efforts to maintain a sense of soberness. The night boy was asleep, his head on the counter behind the front desk. Jon reached over and pushed at the boy's arm.

"Key," he said as clearly as his thick tongue let him.

The boy jerked awake and handed Jon his room key.

"Thanks," Jon mumbled, walking away.

The elevator was open and waiting. As the doors shut, he saw a Thai woman asleep on a chair in the lobby. Her head was turned away so he couldn't see her face. The door closed and the elevator inched its way to his floor.

He heard the phone ringing as he struggled to unlock his room. *Julie*, the word jumped into his beer-pickled brain, she was calling to confess her sins and to beg his forgiveness. In a moment he was inside and picked up the phone. "Hello!"

"So sorry," a male voice said. "Lady wait you in lobby." It was the boy at the front desk.

Jon heard the words but they didn't registered. "Arai, na? What?"

"Thai lady," came the answer. "Want come you room."

Thai lady? Thai lady? Thai lady? he repeated to himself. *What*

THAILAND - COLD RAIN

Thai lady? A vague recollection wormed its way inside. "Okay," he said without thinking. The phone clicked dead.

Jon sat at his kitchen table and waited. In a moment there was a knock. He toe-heeled his way to the door and pulled it open. "Come in," he mumbled without really seeing who was there.

Nuang stared at him. This wasn't the same man she had met just a couple of hours before. This was a very drunk farang. She stood in the hallway not moving.

"I think I have the wrong room," she said, turning to leave.

His eyes focused on her face and his memories blossomed into drunken recognition. "Wait," he said very loud then softened his tone. "I promised you a place to sleep. Take your things in there." He pointed toward the room he never used. "That's where you sleep. I'll sleep in there." He pointed toward his own bedroom. "I'm drunk and I'm going to bed now. Just leave my stuff alone. Okay?"

With that he staggered to his room, flopped unceremoniously onto the bed, and fell asleep. He left his door wide open.

Nuang stared at him for a long time. She wondered who was crazier, herself for being here, or him for letting a total stranger into his room and then passing out. Earlier, when she decided to come here, she was sure he would want to have sex with her despite what he had said at the bar. Now she was sure he wouldn't. Or more correctly, he couldn't. She was surprised. For her entire life she had heard that all farangs were sex maniacs, able to have sex even if they were falling down drunk. Obviously this farang couldn't. He was the same as Thai men when they drank too much.

She struggled with herself deciding what she should do. He had paid her two thousand baht for something. He said it wasn't for sex but he hadn't said what it was for. She was confused.

Finally she went to the room he said was hers and pushed the door shut. Five minutes later, she was curled under a blanket. Just before falling into a deep sleep, she had a fleeting dream of her sister, Itta. She had no way to know that at that very same instant Itta was at their mother's house and having a dream about her.

Chapter 24

When Thichakorn "Itta" Bongkot left Bangkok's Don Muang International Airport, she went directly to the train station and boarded the last train heading north. As happy as she was to be off of the plane, the train didn't seem much better.

Itta's flight had been long and grueling. Instead of going east across Europe from Scotland to Thailand, she had been routed westward through America and Japan. It wasn't by choice but by financial necessity.

One of her regular customers at the restaurant in Scotland ran a courier service that sent time sensitive materials from Europe to America and the Far East. He had arranged a series of flights which had been incredibly cheap, but on a route that took her three days to travel. Thankfully she had been put in a business-class seat on the last leg of her trip.

She had dropped a package at the airport in New York, and then collected another in Chicago which she delivered to a man in Tokyo. It had been a marathon journey that left no time for hotels. She never even left any of the airports. She hadn't bathed since leaving Scotland, but she had washed, changed clothes, and doused herself with deodorant and perfume at every stop. She had slept some in the airports and on the flights, but it wasn't restful sleep, not even in the business-class seat. She was exhausted.

The smells that were Thailand drifted through the train car. They filled her nose and put her at ease. She leaned back into her seat and closed her eyes. Images of her seatmate from Tokyo to Bangkok drifted through her head. What was it he had said? *Do you know the Bongkot family?* or something like that. *Tell them I think of them often?* She wasn't sure of his exact words yet they haunted her. In a while she succumbed to her exhaustion and fell into a fitful sleep. She slept during most of the ride northward.

When she arrived at the Phitsanulok depot, her family was there to greet her. Her mother Nui looked just like she remembered. Her brothers, Anan and Yai, and sister her Neet had changed, but not much. Their reunion was full of smiles and tears. She felt good to be with people who loved her. It took a long time before she stopped crying at her happiness.

Itta and her family squeezed into a single taxi and headed home. It was crowded but no one seemed to mind. Itta, especially, didn't mind. She felt at peace for the first time in years.

As they rode to her mother's house, the family discussed Nuang's mysterious disappearance. It had been six weeks and still no one had heard from her. During that time, their initial worry had shifted to fear, then sadness, and finally to numbness. Everyone still cared, but their emotions had callused. Itta vowed to find Nuang, but in reality she had no idea how. It was one of those things people said to make others feel better.

After washing up she lay next to her sister and fell into a fitful sleep. That night Itta dreamed about her sister Nuang. Her dreams were so vivid they might have been real.

The next morning, Itta was awakened by the annoying crow of a neighbor's rooster. She looked toward the window; dawn had barely touched the morning sky. She glanced at the clock on the dresser; not yet seven. She had slept less than two hours.

Her sister, Neet, snored soft beside her. Itta moved her hand until it touched her sister's back. She could feel the warmth of her body and the gentle motion of her breathing. Having her sister so near made her feel good. She closed her eyes and tried to fall back asleep but couldn't. The land of dreams eluded her.

Finally she slipped from the bed, walked through the living area, and stepped outside. It had been dark when she arrived and had seen only what showed in the taxi's narrow headlights. Now daylight was coming and she could see the landscape forming through the night's shadows. It was a familiar world she had seen a thousand times before on mornings like this. It was her home.

Home! It didn't seem real. She breathed deep the air of Phitsanulok. She would recognize its scent anywhere. Coconut palms lined the dusty road. The smell of newly lit charcoal drifted to her nose on a soft breeze. In the distance she could hear the roar of trucks and motorcycles as they hurried their way through the early morning streets. The neighbor's dog barked one obligatory yap then ignored her completely. The smells, the sounds, the houses, and everything overwhelmed her. She had been away for so long that her own home seemed almost alien.

A faint noise hummed in her ears. It sounded like chanting monks, but she knew that wasn't possible. The nearest temple was kilos away. Not even the loudest of chants would travel that far.

Abruptly the noise stopped. She strained her ears to hear more but it didn't continue. She wondered at the strange phenomenon. Maybe it was an omen of some sort. The thought sent chills down her arms.

She hurried back inside, put on proper dress, and left the house. On the front stoop she slipped on her shoes and then hurried down the street. It was a short walk to the main road. She flagged down a taxi and directed the driver to the morning market. The cabby waited while she bought fruits and sweets, and then continued toward the temple.

Itta hadn't been to a real temple since moving to Scotland. Her memories of the customs were clear, but she had been away for so long. She hoped God and Buddha would understand.

When she entered the temple grounds she expected to hear chanting but all was quiet. Ahead she saw a young woman sitting near one of the many spirit houses erected around the temple. She supposed the woman was praying. When she got closer, she heard soft crying. The woman held a baby but it was deathly quiet.

Itta hesitated for a moment before moving forward. She knew this temple often took in abused women for a night or longer. She wondered if this woman had arrived too late for anyone to notice or help her. She hoped the baby was okay. She walked nearer.

"Sawasdee ka," she said quietly when she was within speaking range. "Are you okay?"

The woman looked up, anguish etched her face. "No. My life is all wrong." Her cries went from low sobs to not so low wailing.

Itta fought back the urge to run and comfort her. Only God knew why this woman was here or what might happen if she got too close. "Is your baby okay?"

The woman looked down at the baby as if seeing it for the first time. Immediately her crying stopped. "I don't know." She held the baby out toward Itta. "Dear Buddha help me, I don't know."

Itta's heart pounded as she took the baby in her arms. It was warm but limp as a cloth doll. She put her ear to its chest then turned her cheek toward its nose. Soft puffs of breath brushed her face. The baby was sound asleep. She breathed a short sigh of relief. "Your baby is okay."

It was then that Itta got her first clear look at the baby. It was Thai and not Thai at the same time. She looked up at the woman. She was attractive and well built. Most likely a Bangkok whore who had been stupid enough to get herself pregnant.

"Sawasdee krup." A male voice came from behind them.

Itta turned to see a middle-aged monk. Still holding the baby, she managed a proper wai. As expected, the monk didn't return her gesture. He ignored her completely.

"Somjit," the monk said to the woman. "Please go to your room. You and the baby need rest."

Obediently she took the baby from Itta's arms and walked toward a small building near the main temple area.

When the woman was out of sight, the monk turned and said, "Somjit has had a hard life. Yesterday was especially hard. She will be better tomorrow."

"She seems very sad."

"People she love have moved on with their lives. She thinks they have deserted her."

"What do you think?" Itta asked, surprised at her boldness with the monk.

"What I think is not important. What she believes is all that matters. After the others left, Somjit came here to pray. She was praying for death. I watched them all night to make sure they were okay."

Itta's mind reeled. The woman had been praying for death. Surely neither God nor Buddha would grant such a plea. She wondered if this was the reason for her omen. Was this why she had heard the chanting when it was too far away to be heard, and even when the monks had been silent?

"I think Buddha sent me here to help her," she said. "Is there anything I can do?"

"Not today; she needs rest. Tomorrow would be better."

Itta nodded. Images of the sobbing woman and her sleeping baby slipped through her thoughts. The baby wasn't Thai. Her curiosity overcame protocol and she said, "Her baby is farang, I saw it."

"It's not her baby," the monk replied. "She is only taking care."

"Oh!" Itta's face flushed at her wrong assumption. She picked up the plastic bags and held them toward the monk. "I have gifts for the temple."

His hands remained at his sides. "You can leave them there." He motioned toward a low table near one of the stone buildings.

She blushed even harder at her bad manners. "Khop khun ka," she said, wai'ing politely. She carried the plastic bags to the table then hurried away from the temple grounds.

She sat outside for a while thinking about what had just happened. Surely fate was rolling the dice for her and the woman, but she didn't know why. She wondered what it would bring. She was tempted to go back inside the temple but didn't. She said silent prayers for strength and then went home.

Her mood was sullen the rest of the day. She told her family she was exhausted from the trip, even though it wasn't entirely true. Images of the crying woman and the farang baby haunted her every thought. She went to bed early, but lay awake wondering if they had returned to the shrine to pray for death again. When she slept, her dreams were filled with nightmares.

Early the next morning, before anyone else was awake, Itta went to the temple. The courtyard spirit house stood alone; she breathed a sigh of relief. At least one of her nightmares wasn't true.

She entered the building where the monk had sent the woman the day before. The hallway was mostly deserted and the doors were mostly shut. She stopped one woman and said, "Do you know a girl here who has a young baby?"

The woman stared briefly before responding. "Several women here have young babies."

Itta smiled. "Of course. I'm looking for a girl named Somjit."

"Is she a friend or relative?"

"No. Just someone I met. I've been told to help her. Do you know her?"

The woman's face softened, "Follow me."

In a minute they entered an open area that served as the kitchen. Several women were busy peeling, slicing, and cooking. Itta spotted Somjit immediately. She was one of the fruit peelers. She walked to stand beside the girl, picked up a knife, and proceeded to help with the work.

"Sawasdee ka. Good morning," Itta said momentarily.

Somjit glanced up. Dark circles ringed her bloodshot eyes. "Good morning." Her words came out dull and mumbling.

Minutes passed before Itta spoke again. "I saw you yesterday when I came to the temple. Is your baby okay?"

Somjit managed a small smile even though she was clearly uncomfortable at Itta's intrusion. "Yes, the baby is fine. Another woman is caring for her while I help with the morning meal. Thank you for asking."

"Never mind. Your baby is very beautiful." She didn't mention the light colored hair or pale skin. "What's her name?"

"Her name is Tippawan."

"What a coincidence, my sister's name was Tippawan."

Somjit's heart jerked at the woman's comment. Nuang, too, had once had a sister named Tippawan; the baby was named in honor of her. She changed the subject. "What's your name?"

"I'm sorry. I didn't think to introduce myself. My name is Thichakorn but my nickname is Itta."

"How long will you stay here, Itta?" Somjit asked, keeping the focus from herself. "You don't mind if I call you Itta, do you?"

Itta laughed, "Actually, I rather if you did. Thichakorn is far too proper. Itta sounds friendlier to my ears. I'm not staying here; I will go back to my home before noon. What about you?"

Somjit wasn't sure how to answer. Since she had arrived, the question had never entered her head. "Not long," she responded, knowing it was the right thing to say. None of the women ever stayed long. She watched Itta's hands paring the rind from a melon. "You're very good with a knife."

Itta looked down then back at Somjit. "Oh, that. I worked in a restaurant for a while. I've had lots of practice."

Somjit nodded and turned back to her work.

In a short while they were finished, and the women carried the food to where the monks would eat. Somjit turned and left the kitchen. Itta hurried to catch up with her.

"Aren't you going to eat?"

Somjit stopped and turned. "We cannot eat until the monks are finished, but my baby can eat now. You wait with the others."

Itta felt a soft bite in Somjit's words, but she understood. "I know. I only wanted to tell you something. Yesterday Buddha brought me to this temple. He wanted me to meet you. I knew it the moment I saw you and your baby at the shrine. I've been sent to help you, but I'm not sure what to do."

Somjit wondered if the woman was some sort of a nut case. The world she knew didn't come with guardian angels or good Samaritans. Her world came with pain, depression, and desertions. If Buddha had sent the woman, it wasn't to help her. Buddha had abandoned her a long time ago. "You can let me feed my baby."

Itta nodded and watched as Somjit disappeared through a doorway. She felt foolish at her handling of the whole situation. She was sure the woman was her mission, but all she had managed to do was to scare her away.

Maybe she had everything wrong. Maybe the girl didn't want or need her help. Maybe Buddha had sent her here for another reason. Maybe something as simple as making up for the years she had been away. At that moment Itta wasn't sure why she was at the temple. Maybe Buddha hadn't sent her at all. Maybe it was just her imagination running wild. She turned and walked back to the kitchen.

The women were talking and laughing amongst themselves. A few munched on fruit, even though it wasn't proper to do that until the monks had finished eating. Itta watched for a few minutes then decided to leave. She had no more business here today.

As she crossed the courtyard, a monk walked toward her on an intersecting course. When they met, she stopped. It was the same monk she had seen yesterday morning. She wai'ed and waited for him to speak.

"Did you find what you seek?" he asked.

Itta wasn't sure how to answer. "I have found that I don't know what I'm seeking."

A faint smile formed at the monk's lips. "I think that makes your search very difficult."

"Maybe impossible," she responded to his smile.

"I watched you talk with Somjit. She is a very nice young woman, but she's confused right now. She is hurting and doesn't trust anyone. You should come back tomorrow and see her again. She needs a friend."

"I have already decided to do that."

"Then I'm happy for Somjit. I must be going now. I have things I must do."

"I must be going, too. My family wants me to help find my sister." On impulse, Itta pulled a picture of Nuang from her purse. "Have you seen her? It's an old photo, but I think she hasn't changed much."

The monk took the picture from her hand. After a moment of study he said, "She left here yesterday."

Itta heart raced at his words. "Are you sure? Do you know where she went?"

"No, I don't know," he answered. "I only know she is gone."

Itta's head spun. Nuang had been here just yesterday. Her excitement overwhelmed her. She had to tell her mother and her sister and her brothers immediately. Without so much as a wai or a goodbye, she turned and ran. Over her shoulder she shouted, "I must tell my family right away."

"Maybe you should talk to Somjit," the monk said as she sped toward the gate. "She is tending your sister's baby." His words never reached her ears.

Chapter 25

The day after his drunken night on the town, Jonathan Yeager slept until almost noon. He was surprised he wasn't hung over. After all of the beer he had consumed the night before, it was what he deserved. His head pounded but he didn't feel nauseous.

He lay in bed for a minute to shake off his wakening daze. A deep breath triggered a spasm of smoker's cough that threatened to leave a lung on the pillow. A wad of phlegm landed on his tongue. He tasted it for blood, found none, then spit it into a tissue.

He got up from his bed and stumbled to the bathroom. There he relieved himself and made noises in an unrestrained manner as people sometimes do when there is no one around to hear. He turned on the shower and then looked at himself in the mirror.

He looked like death warmed over. What little hair he had was pointing in all directions; his eyes were blood-red splotches with a dab of green thrown in the middle. Sleep creases etched across his forehead. The skin around his eyes was dark and puffy.

He splashed water on his face hoping that would help, but it didn't. He stepped into the shower, adjusted the temperature, and waited for himself to come back to life.

Nuang awoke to the sound of someone coughing very loudly and very harshly. It took her a long moment to realize where she was. She had come to the farang's condo last night. After a few minutes she remembered his name was Jon.

She dropped her legs over the side of the bed and sat up. Her bladder was stretched to the point of exploding. Since having her baby, her bladder control had been less than ideal. She needed to use the toilet and very soon.

As she stood, the sound of someone passing gas echoed into her room. For some reason she found the noise funny. Her attempts to suppress a giggle made her need for the toilet more urgent.

She hurried to the door and peeked outside. The man was nowhere to be seen. She stepped into the short hallway in search of the bathroom but stopped at the sound of the shower starting. The man was occupying the room she needed most.

As she eased her way toward the sound, she heard the shower curtain slide shut and the sharp pitch of spraying water became muffled. She eased her face around the door-frame and looked inside. Thank Buddha he was in the shower. The curtain was heavy but she could see his outline moving inside. She was deciding what to do when she felt her bladder control slipping. She hurried through the doorway, pulled down her panties, and sat on the toilet. She hoped the man couldn't see out through the curtains any better than she could see in.

She was only half finished when the shower stopped. She tried to stem her flow, but couldn't. Without the hiss of the shower to cover the sound, the noise of her urination seemed as loud as a waterfall. She glanced up at the shower curtain just in time to see it snap open.

A soaking-wet, naked farang stared out at her. The alarm on his face matched the horror on her own. She turned her head away from his nakedness, but not until she had seen his private parts. The seconds felt like hours as she finished relieving herself. Her face flushed beet red. With as much dignity as she could find, she wiped herself, slipped her panties up, and walked out the bath. She went back to *her* room and shut the door behind her. At that moment, she could have easily died from embarrassment.

~~~

Jon let the water pour down against him. It felt good. After a minute he rubbed the water from his face and turned his back to the spray. At that moment, he caught a movement from the corner of his eye. He looked in that direction, staining to see through the shower curtain. The material was too heavy to see more than indistinct patches of dark and light. A second later he heard the faint sound of water streaming above the noise of the shower. His heart skipped a beat as he realized someone was on the other side of the curtain using his toilet.

He turned off the shower and opened the curtain in one continuous motion. A Thai woman sat on his commode. Her eyes sweep the length of his body before she looked away. Shock kept him from doing anything except stare back. In a moment the woman stood and left the room as if she hadn't seen him.

What the hell was a Thai woman doing in *his* condo using *his* toilet? And who was she, anyway? Her face was familiar but she wasn't anyone he knew. By habit more than purpose, he pulled a towel from the rack to wipe himself dry. His mind searched for any hint of what he might have done last night while he was drunk. Small bits of memory sparked, but they were too vague to recognize.

By the time he finished shaving, he remembered meeting her at Toy's Bar. By the time he finished dressing, he remembered his drunken idea to have her teach him the Thai language. By the time he arrived at her bedroom door, he remembered inviting her to stay at his condo. But as hard as he tried, he couldn't remember her name or her coming home with him.

He knocked softly at her door. "The bathroom is yours if you want to shower. I'll be watching TV. When you're finished, we need to talk."

He returned to the living room and turned on the Asian version of MTV. The volume was loud enough, but he didn't hear the music. He was too busy figuring how to get out of this situation. Then he wondered if he wanted out. He did want to learn Thai, and now that Julie had dumped him, who cared if his teacher lived with him or not.

Julie! The name dredged up the reason he had gotten so drunk the night before. Yesterday he had called her when he came home from work. It had been Saturday evening his time, but seven o'clock in the morning American time. The male voice that answered the phone had caught him completely off guard. He'd almost hung up, but didn't. Instead he asked for Julie. He had hung up when he heard her voice. She'd called back within minutes and she was crying. He had listened to her explanations, believing none. He had tried to laugh and pretend that whatever was happening at her apartment in Dayton wasn't important, but it didn't work.

"Does he make you feel good?" he had finally asked, his voice oozing sarcasm hot as molten steel.

"I'm lonely, Jon," she'd answered after a short silence. "How he makes me feel physically means nothing. I just can't stand sitting home cooped up all the time. I think it would be best for both of us if I stop pretending I can wait for you. You are a kind and wonderful person, but for now I think we should just be friends. You do understand, don't you?"

The odd thing was that he did understand. What did he have to offer her anyway? Certainly he couldn't offer a stiff throbbing penis like her stud muffin was giving her. She had a need he couldn't fulfill. He understood her completely, but it didn't make his pain any less.

"Yes, you're right," he had answered. "We were always better friends than lovers anyway."

He had hung up the phone and left the condo before she had time to call again. By the time he arrived at Toy's Bar, he'd become numb to the fact that Julie had dumped him. She wasn't the first to do that, only the latest.

The sound of a door closing caught his attention. He wondered if it was the front door or the bathroom door. In a moment the sound of the shower answered his question. He figured she would be in there for a few minutes so he left the condo and went downstairs to buy a newspaper and a pot of tea. The shower was still running when he returned.

He tapped lightly on the door. "I have hot tea, if you want some." The shower continued unabated.

Jon sat at his kitchen table and read the Bangkok Post. He found it interesting to read about America and Europe as viewed by the Asian press. He couldn't help but feel it was a more accurate account than what he got from his hometown paper in America.

After a long while the shower stopped. He wondered if there was any hot water left in Pattaya. A minute later the woman stepped out wearing the same clothes she had worn the night before. They stared at each other for a second before he spoke, "I don't remember your name."

"I am Nuang," she answered. "Your name is Jon."

He laughed despite the pounding in his head. "As amazing as it may seem, I can remember my own name. But that's about all I remember. Do you know why I invited you here?"

Nuang fidgeted with the towel she held in her hands. Her face flushed. "You want to have sex with me? You can, if you want. I am clean now."

This time Jon blushed. "Is that what I told you last night?"

She shook her head. "No. Last night you said I could sleep in your condo, so that's what I did. I didn't touch your stuff, either."

As good as her English was her answer confused him. "What stuff are you talking about?"

"I don't know. It's what you said. I don't know the English word *stuff*, but whatever it is I left yours alone." She remembered seeing him naked in the shower. She wondered if that was what the word meant. "Maybe I saw your stuff, but I didn't touch it."

"Stuff is slang for what belongs to me. Things like my clothes, my money, my passport, and my airplane ticket."

"Oh." Her face reddened even more. "Then I didn't see your stuff either. It was something else I saw. I only thought maybe it was your stuff."

Jon wiped his hands across his face. He felt like they were

talking in circles. He understood every word, but had no idea what she was saying. "What stuff did you see?"

"I didn't see any stuff," she lowered her eyes from his. "I only saw you in the shower. Now I know that wasn't your stuff."

Jon cleared his throat and changed the subject, "I'm hungry. I think we should get something to eat."

Nuang was happy they had stopped talking about his stuff. "If you have food, I can cook for you. I'm a very good cook."

"I have food in the refrigerator, but nothing I would trust eating. There's a restaurant nearby. They have American and Thai food. I think it's safer if we eat there. We'll go shopping while we're out. Then you can cook dinner for both of us. It's been a long time since I've had a home cooked meal."

Nuang nodded and smiled. She wondered if this was why he had invited her to stay with him. Maybe he wanted his own Thai cook. He had certainly paid her enough for something. If he wanted a cook, she would make him the best Thai meal he had ever eaten.

They got plenty of stares from the condo employees as they walked through the lobby. No one said anything, but their sly smiles made their thoughts clear. Jon broke into a sticky sweat from the heat of his blush. He had an urge to introduce her to everyone but he didn't. He could do that later.

After a leisurely lunch they went shopping. First he bought her some clothes which he thought were more appropriate for his new employee. It dawned on him that this was the first time in his life he had ever taken a woman shopping for clothes. He was surprised at his realization. He could tell by the look on her face that his small generosity made her happy.

Next they went to the grocery section. Jon turned the cart over to her and told her to buy anything she wanted. Then he went to the book rack and busied himself finding something to read. When she returned with the cart filled with fruit, bread, milk, snacks, and a lot of Thai things he didn't recognize. He frowned at the cart.

Nuang shifted nervously from foot to foot. "Have I bought the wrong things?"

Jon stroked his chin thoughtfully. He wasn't concerned about what she bought but the quantity gave him pause. The idea of lugging kilos of food in the midday heat made him grimace. He looked at her face. Her anxiety was obvious. He was sure she would cry if he said anything. He let a small teasing smile pull at his lips. "You forgot to buy me beer." It was a lie; he had seen several bottles in the cart, but she didn't know that.

Her return smile was priceless. "I bought you beer already." She moved a few items and extracted a bottle of Heineken. "See? I think of everything."

"You sure did," Jon laughed at her excitement. He was sure she hadn't thought about carrying everything back to the condo. He put his book in the cart. "Let's go then."

The total cost at the checkout was inconsequential compared to the number of plastic bags it took to hold everything. Nuang glanced nervously at Jon as the number of bags grew. She wished she had bought only one cantaloupe instead of two. Same thing for the pineapples and banana bunches.

Jon pocketed his change and began gathering plastic bags in his hands. Nuang did the same. She was careful to let Jon get the heavier ones. The cashier had to help pick up the last two bags.

The other customers watched their efforts in amusement. One man applauded as Nuang and Jon left the store.

The plastic straps cut sharp into the bends of their fingers. They stopped three times before they reached the mall exit. They could rest the bags on the ground but they couldn't let go, else they would never get them all picked up again.

At their last stop inside the mall, Jon told Nuang they would take a baht-bus back to the condo. One was always parked outside.

A minute later they arrived at the spot where the baht-bus always sat. It wasn't there. Jon took a deep breath, "We'll catch one at the street."

He knew that wasn't a sure thing at this time of the day, at least not one with enough room for them plus all their bags. He started toward the condo and Nuang followed close behind.

Every baht-bus that passed them was nearly filled with passengers. The drivers didn't slow down or even look in their direction. The sun was merciless. Sweat trickled through his hair and down his back. Salty drops burned his eyes.

"My fingers hurt too much, Khun Jon," Nuang whined.

"So do mine," he said back. Actually, his hands hurt like hell and they weren't even halfway home. "Let's rest for a minute."

Nuang didn't need any encouragement. She stopped and plopped her bags to the sidewalk. The relief was instant. She wiggled her fingers to make sure they still worked. They tingled with a mixture of pain and delight.

Jon put his load on the ground. The pain in his fingers eased but his sweating didn't. He managed to keep hold of the bag handles as he rubbed at his eyes with body of his tee shirt. It helped, but only for a second. He looked back at Nuang. She was sweating, too. He smiled to himself. He knew it was hot when a Thai sweats. After a minute he was ready to continue. "Are you ready?" he asked Nuang.

Clearly she wasn't but she nodded yes anyway. She stood and started forward.

As Jon lifted his bags, one split at the seams and the beers clanked to the sidewalk. Two bottles broke.

"Shit fucking bags!" he said loudly. He looked at Nuang and lowered his voice. "Okay, never mind. I'll buy more later." He turned and walked away.

He had gone several meters before he realized Nuang wasn't behind him. He looked back to see her struggling to slip unbroken bottles into her own bags. He was impressed at her ingenuity and her selfless act. In a moment she stood and continued forward with her extra load. He waited for her to catch up.

"Thank you," he said, meaning it.

"Mai pen rai, ka," she smiled at his words. "Let's hurry. It's too hot in Thailand today."

THAILAND - COLD RAIN

She set off at a fast walk and he followed close behind.

They dropped their bags inside the front door of the condo. Jon rushed to the bathroom and washed the sweat from his face and eyes.

Nuang grabbed a tissue and dabbed daintily at her face. Her make-up was ruined already. She looked at the mounds of food strewn across on the floor. Then she looked at the refrigerator. She wondered if it would all fit.

Jon returned from the bath. "I think we have too much stuff," he said.

"You can never have too much stuff, Jon, even if it's more than you can carry."

Somehow he found her logic indisputable. Together they found a place for everything.

Afterwards, Jon took a shower. When he finished, Nuang did the same. By the time she stepped from the bathroom, Jon was asleep. As quietly as possible, Nuang began preparing dinner. She took her time. She would let Jon sleep for a while before waking him to eat.

Without distractions Nuang was able to think. She pondered her situation. Less than two days in Pattaya and already she was living with a farang. An image of Surat flashed. It was followed by a sharp pang of guilt.

She wasn't really living with the farang, she reasoned with herself. She had only slept one night in his extra room. Besides, she and Surat were finished now so what difference did it make. She hadn't planned to move in with a man when she left the temple, it had just happened. She had done nothing wrong. He had already said he didn't want sex but maybe he was joking. Or maybe not. She didn't know. She had no idea what he wanted from her. If it was a cook, he had one now.

Chapter 26

Mike Johnson awoke that same Sunday a few minutes past noon. He would have slept longer if it hadn't been for the hotel cleaning crew. They weren't intentionally noisy, but they weren't intentionally quiet either. They were just doing their jobs.

He showered to shake off last night's beers and the jet lag. Later he ordered a sandwich from room service. It wasn't very good, but it didn't cost much, either. It sort of balanced out.

It was two o'clock when he finally emerged from his room. Work was still two weeks away and for now he was officially on vacation. He hadn't yet figured a way to charge his personal expenses to his company, but he would think of something.

He stopped at the hotel Lobby Bar and had a beer before catching a baht-bus south on Beach Road. The afternoon air was hot and humid, almost suffocating. The cool season was coming, but not fast enough. Smells of warm seawater and hot blacktop permeated the scanty breeze. He saw the sign for the Tahitian Queen, the TQ.

A long time ago the TQ had been his favorite go-go bar in Pattaya. There they played good old rock-n-roll and they had the best looking dancers in town. More importantly, it was air conditioned. He rang the buzzer for the driver to stop.

The TQ was dim to the point of darkness. It took a minute before he saw anything other than shadows. The bar seats were all taken. He stumble-felt his way to one of the elevated tables surrounding the dance stage. A hostess took his order and returned a moment later with his drink.

The go-go girls were tempting as hell, but he had no desire to take any of them home. In fact, he had felt no sexual urges at all since Susan had died. Not even the early morning erections he used to have.

One girl came by and asked if he wanted company but he declined. He wasn't here to get laid, he was here to cool off and have a drink or two.

Customers came and went, but mostly they came. In a while nearly every seat in the bar was taken. The tables on both sides of him were occupied by young German tourists oozing money and hormones. The bar-girls swarmed around them like fruit flies to bananas.

By the time he finished his third beer he was ready to leave. He waited for an opening through the crowd, and then started his exit. He sucked in his stomach and inched his way from his seat. His ribs slid across the tabletop as he moved. When he was sure he was at the bottom of the elevated area, he stepped toward the aisle. He stepped into empty air.

Mike fell hard but his chest remained perched atop the table. The table was bolted to the floor and didn't move. The impact bit savagely into his rib cage and knocked the breath from him.

Immediately bar-girls were holding him and asking if he was okay. After a few breathless seconds his wind returned and he inhaled deep. The pain in his left side was fierce. He tried to smile at the hostesses but it came out more like a grimace. He hurried to the toilet thinking he would be sick from the intensity of the pain.

He stayed in the restroom until his nausea eased. He examined his chest and ribs. Except for a fast-forming bruise, everything looked normal. It hurt like hell every time he breathed. He practiced standing straight and moving without wincing. After a minute he was sure he could walk without anyone noticing anything was wrong. Wearing his best smile, Mike exited the toilet and left the TQ.

Outside, the heat had increased to a broil. It almost took his mind off his ribs. He headed down a side street toward Second Road to catch a baht-bus back to his hotel. Each step jolted a fresh reminder of his *accident* at the Tahitian Queen. He felt stupid it had happened to him. He could imagine explaining to people that he had hurt himself falling off a bar stool. Actually, most people who knew him wouldn't be surprised. The thought made him laugh; the sharp pain made him stop.

Mike passed a small store with coolers of cold beer and a plastic case filled with cigarettes. Considering his pain, he figured he might need something to help him sleep.

He stepped inside the shop and bought a pack of Marlboro Lights and two beers. Then, on impulse, he got two more beers. Emergency supply, he reasoned. The shop lady put everything into a plastic bag. He paid and continued down the street. The weight caused enough pain to make him wish he hadn't bought the extra beers.

When he reached Second Road, he flagged down the first baht-bus that came by. In Pattaya the baht-buses come in two styles. One has a high cap on the back and can be boarded standing up. The other has a low cap and requires some bending to enter. This baht-bus had a low cap.

As he bent to step into the back, a strange click-pop echoed through his body. The pain didn't seem any worse but the sound panicked him. *Jesus*, he thought, *I must have broken a rib*. It haunted him all the way back to his hotel.

He was more careful exiting the baht-bus but the click-pop happened again anyway. He paid the driver and eased himself through the lobby of the Amari Orchid Hotel.

In the privacy of his room, Mike examined himself closely. He discovered he could cause the click-pop just by breathing deep. Not only could he hear it, but he could also feel it.

He drank two of his beers while deciding what to do. He knew there wasn't much anyone could do for broken ribs except wait for them to heal. He also knew if the break was bad enough he could end up with a punctured lung or worse. By the time he finished the second beer his pain hadn't eased, and a visit to the hospital became a good idea.

THAILAND - COLD RAIN

One hour and multiple x-rays later the doctor confirmed the broken rib. He also confirmed there was nothing he could do except prescribe something for the pain. Mike paid his bill, collected his medicine, and returned to his room. He washed down a pill with beer and waited.

When the pain persisted, he took another pill for good measure. The pain never went away, but in a while he didn't care. The beer and drugs did their jobs remarkably well.

He tried lying down but couldn't get comfortable. He hurt less when he was sitting or standing. On a whim he set up his laptop computer to play a game of solitaire. His conversation with the young man on the airplane drifted through his thoughts.

"It's an incredible love story," the kid had said. "You should write a book."

By the time his computer finished booting up, Mike had decided the young man was right. He opened his word processor and wrote his first sentence. In a state of alcohol and pain killer mindlessness, words flowed like magic from his fingertips. By the time he stopped, he had written his first 7,000 words. That night he slept sitting up because it was too painful to lie down.

The next morning the pain in his side was excruciating. Sitting, standing, breathing, and even going to the bathroom hurt. He took multiple pills and drank the over priced beer from the mini bar in his room. In a while the pain eased and he returned to his writing.

Mike didn't know it at the time, but pain killers, alcohol, and writing was to become his daily routine for the coming days. Also, he didn't know that his future was being cast by events hundreds of kilometers north of Pattaya.

Chapter 27

The day after Laht left the Buddhist temple, his family had a party to celebrate the end of his religious devotion and the beginning of his new career. Laht smiled through it all even though he didn't feel like smiling. He was still hurting from Somjit's blunt rejection.

His father, Isara, didn't mention their meeting of ten days before and neither did Laht. They talked only about his future as a doctor. Within a month Laht would be joining the staff at the Chiang Mai Hospital and opening his own practice not far away. His father was arranging everything. Laht knew he should be excited but he wasn't. It took a concentrated effort just to act enthusiastic at the polite congratulations everyone offered.

As the party wound down, Laht was introduced to a beautiful young lady—an engineer his father had casually pointed out. Laht had no choice except to talk with her, but his mind was elsewhere.

The woman made it clear they could be very good friends. She even asked him to join her for a drink at her place after the party. He made excuses then apologized to excess hoping he hadn't hurt her feelings. At the end of the evening Laht went to bed alone.

He lay awake letting his thoughts wander. They always came back to Somjit. He was embarrassed by how he had let himself believe she had loved him or that he had loved her. He must look like the ultimate fool to his father and everyone at the temple. No one, including his father, had said a word but he could imagine what they were thinking and how they must be laughing at him.

He had fallen in love with a common Thai and she had rejected him. It was the worst thing he could imagine. A man of his stature, his education, and his future, turned away by a Thai nobody. That night he cried for his broken heart and his loss of face. When he finally slept, he dreamed of Somjit.

Laht spent the next two days at his parent's house. He never left the grounds, not even to take his new car—a present from his father—for a drive. He spent most of his time in his room sorting through everything that was his life. He packed the things he wanted to take with him and boxed up the things he couldn't throw away. A trash can collected the rest.

It was early on Saturday morning when Laht left his parents' house to start his new life in Chiang Mai. His new Toyota purred like a kitten and jumped whenever he stepped on the throttle. His father had bought top of the line.

Before leaving Phitsanulok he drove to the temple but didn't go inside. Instead he sat in his car and waited, hoping to catch a glimpse of Somjit. He fingered the envelope laying on the seat. The letter inside said things he couldn't say in person. He wanted Somjit to have it and not have it at the same time. He wasn't sure what to do. Just as he decided to leave, a fellow monk, the one who always seemed wiser than the others, appeared at the entrance of the temple. Laht took the envelope and exited the car.

"Sawasdee krup, good morning," he said smiling, wai'ing politely.

"Sawasdee krup," the monk responded but without a wai. He glanced at Laht's Toyota. "I see you have returned to the world of human desires."

Laht smiled sheepishly. "I promised my father that I would heal all of Thailand. I can't do that so easy in a monk's robe."

The monk nodded his understanding. "I wish you well in your noble quest. You must come back to visit us when you have time. I will say prayers for your success and your safety."

"Thank you," Laht said. "I need all the help I can get." He hesitated for a second before adding, "I was hoping you could do something for me."

The monk raised his eyebrows and waited for Laht to speak.

Laht pushed the envelope in his direction. "I would like for you to give this envelope to Somjit. You know her. She's the woman whose baby died. I want to tell her goodbye."

"Maybe you should tell her yourself. Don't you think that would be better?"

Laht shook his head, "No, I don't want to see her right now. It's very complicated. It would be best if you give her my letter."

The monk stared for a moment before taking the envelope. "Love is always very complicated, isn't it?"

Laht blushed, "More complicated than you can imagine. Thank you for your help." He glanced at his watch, "It's getting late. I have to be in Chiang Mai this afternoon so I must be going. Thank you for giving Somjit my letter. I'm forever in your debt." He wai'ed respectfully and returned to his car.

The monk waved as Laht drove away. Then he continued on his way to the city for his morning routine of exchanging prayers for gifts of food. He would deliver the letter later.

Chapter 28

Three days had passed since everyone had deserted Somjit. She was returning to her room from the midday meal when she was stopped by one of the monks. She knew him but didn't know him at the same time. She had seen him almost every day since she had been here, but he'd never approached or spoken to her.

"Please stop," he ordered more than asked. "I must speak with you."

Somjit hurriedly presented him with a wai and then waited. She wondered why he wanted to talk to her.

"I have something for you," he said. He removed an envelope from his personals bag and handed it to her. "It's from the young man named Laht." He turned and walked away.

Somjit's hands shook as she raced back to the women's quarters. Her imagination ran wild at what he might have written. She didn't stop to get the baby from the afternoon caregiver, but went straight to her room instead. Carefully she tore off one end of the envelope and shook loose its contents. Ten 1,000 baht bills slid out followed by a single piece of paper. She ignored the money and unfolded the handwritten note.

"Somjit," it read. "The money is to help you and Nuang care for the baby after you leave the temple. If you need a place to go, you can come to Chiang Mai. I can be reached at the number below. Laht."

Somjit wasn't sure what she expected, but she had hoped for more than she found. Not for more money, but for more substance. She had prayed to see "I love you" written on the paper but it wasn't there. She reread the short note, "If you need a place to go, you can come to Chiang Mai."

She mulled his words, trying to understand his intent. Was he making another offer or was he just being kind? If he wanted her to come to Chiang Mai, he could have just bought her a bus ticket. That would be a lot cheaper than the ten thousand baht he'd put in the envelope. Maybe the money was only a bribe to make her go away and his letter nothing but banal politeness. Actually she was surprised he had written at all.

She remembered the day Laht had left the temple. He had asked her to go with him and she had told him no. It hadn't been intentional. She hadn't even realized what he had said until after he was gone. Her answer had come from her throat but not her heart. The memory made her angry.

She read the letter again. "If you need a place to go, you can come to Chiang Mai."

No, that wasn't banal anything. He was asking her to come to him and the money was for her to get there. The more she thought about it, the more she knew it was true.

She packed her and the baby's few belongings, and then collected little Tippawan from the sitter. It was almost dark when Somjit and the baby left the temple. She flagged down the first taxi she saw.

She made one stop to buy disposable diapers and a few snacks for herself before directing the driver to the Phitsanulok bus terminal. The next bus to Chiang Mai wasn't scheduled until early morning. She found a comfortable spot and settled in for the night.

It was five o'clock in the morning when the baby vomited for the first time. It was five-thirty when the diarrhea started. By the time she boarded her bus, she had changed the baby's diaper several times. The trip northwards was filled with alternating bouts of vomiting and diarrhea.

The vomiting stopped three hours outside of Phitsanulok, but the diarrhea continued until past noon. That was about the time when the baby became very quiet. Its skin felt clammy. It had been hours since the baby had nursed. Somjit was sure the baby must be dehydrated. She attempted to breastfeed, but the baby didn't respond.

She dampened the corner of a small washcloth with bottled water and squeezed a few drops into baby's mouth. She couldn't tell if the baby swallowed or not, but the water didn't come back out. Every few minutes she repeated the routine. She prayed to Buddha that the water was safe. She prayed even harder for the baby to be okay. She wished she hadn't left the temple.

Somjit's bus arrived at the Chiang Mai station at two o'clock in the afternoon. The temperature outside the terminal was suffocating. She hired a three wheeled tuk-tuk taxi to the nearest pharmacy and had the driver wait while she bought more diapers, an eyedropper, and a bottle of infant electrolytic drink. Then she told the driver to take her to the nearest affordable hotel with air conditioning. She had to get the baby out of the heat. A thundering downpour arrived just as she entered the hotel lobby. It was three o'clock.

During the next four hours Somjit managed to force an entire bottle of liquid into the baby, one eyedropper at a time. The baby seemed less clammy now, and was breathing easier. She was sure Buddha had answered her prayers. In a while, the baby fell asleep.

Somjit rushed through a shower and put on fresh clothes. Afterwards she checked the baby's diaper. The diarrhea had started again. She wasn't sure what to do, but she knew she had to do something. Her first thought was to call Laht. After all, he was a doctor. More than that, he was the baby's doctor.

The phone in the room was out of order. She tried to wake the baby but couldn't. Somjit panicked. She ran from the room leaving the baby lying on the bed. She had to move fast and she couldn't do it with a baby on her shoulder.

In the lobby she approached the receptionist. "The phone in my room is broken and I must make a call. Do you have a phone I can use? It's very urgent."

"I'm sorry," the girl behind the desk responded. "The hotel phones have been out of order since the storm. There's a pay phone down the street to your right. It's only a couple of blocks. Maybe you should try that one."

Somjit ran full speed despite the thick closeness of the night air. She arrived in less than a minute. The phone was dead. She saw another one down a side street and ran there. It was out of order too. So was the next one and the one after that. She wanted to scream. She stopped a passing teenage girl, "Where can I find a working phone in this city?"

"What?" The girl looked at her like she was from another planet.

"A phone. I need a telephone. This is an emergency. Where can I find one that works?"

"I think the storm wiped them out," the girl answered. "This one still works though." She pulled a cell phone from her waistband. "If it's a local call, you can use mine."

Laht answered on the second ring. Somjit nearly fainted at the sound of his voice. "I need help, Laht. I only came to see you, but baby Tippawan is very sick and I need help." Her voice rang with hysteria.

"Calm down. Everything will be okay," he said confidently. "Where are you now? Tell me where you are and I'll come to you."

Somjit looked around. Her panic grew when she didn't see the hotel anywhere. "I don't know." She handed the phone to the girl and asked her to tell Laht where they were. She listened to the one-sided conversation while the girl explained. In a moment the girl returned the phone to Somjit.

"Stay where you are," Laht ordered. "I don't have my car but I'm not far away."

The phone went dead. She handed it back to the girl, thanked her profusely, and then waited for Laht to arrive.

Chapter 29

Weeks had passed since Surat Duansawang had been demoted to the taxi circuit for his *unauthorized use of a company vehicle* infraction. He had worked hard for the last year to become one of the "privileged" drivers, but he had ruined it all with his frantic trip to Phitsanulok. He had expected to be fired but was put on taxi duty instead. If he didn't mess up again, he would get his old job back in a few months.

Without Nuang around, he had fallen into the habit of working double shifts. Since she had emptied their bank account, he needed the extra money. It had been nearly two months since she had vanished, but to Surat it seemed like yesterday. As often as possible, he would drive past their house to see if she had come home.

He felt foolish driving through his neighborhood five or six times a day, but he did it anyway. He wondered how long it would be before he gave up on ever finding Nuang. He was sure it wouldn't be anytime soon.

The day had been miserably hot. At three o'clock a monsoon downpour swept through the city. Heavy sheets of rain split the air and filled the storm sewers to overflow. Traffic slowed to a crawl as cars and motorcycles died with flooded ignitions. The electricity went off for a short time and sections of the city phone system died altogether. Pedestrians sought shelter inside shops and beneath umbrellas.

At four o'clock the sun returned to bake wisps of steam from the rain soaked streets. The tropical heat in Chiang Mai became thick enough to slice.

J. F. Gump

Even after the sun gave way to the night, the hot dampness continued to press against everything within reach. Surat kept his air conditioner running only enough to keep the taxi comfortably cool but without causing his windows to fog. The shiny faces and sweat mottled clothes of the people outside made him happy he was working tonight.

He had just dropped two farang tourists at a downtown hotel and was headed back to the airport when he saw a Thai man and woman waving at his taxi from the other side of the street.

Normally he wasn't interested in local fares, but this man's clothes and posture spoke of money. He waved through the window to let them know he was coming back for them. Surat had a nose for good tippers and this one smelled like a hundred baht minimum. He did a u-turn at the next intersection and hoped another driver wouldn't beat him to the waiting couple. Seconds later he coasted to a stop and they entered the back seat.

The man directed him to the Dee Lek Hotel. Surat nodded and drove in that direction.

The Dee Lek was one of the seediest hotels in Chiang Mai. He knew they weren't going there for dinner so it had to be for an early evening tryst. He smiled at the thought but said nothing. As long as they gave him a generous tip, what they were doing was none of his business. He eavesdropped on their conversation.

"How long has the baby been sick?" the man asked.

"Since early this morning," the woman replied. "I'm very scared. Nuang left her baby with me because she believed in me. If anything happens to the baby, I will kill myself."

Nuang? Surat's heart stutter-stepped. That was his wife's name. He knew there must be thousands of Nuang's in Thailand but he had never met one.

"If anything happens," the man was saying, "it's not because you're a bad mother. Do you have any idea where Nuang might have gone?"

"No, I don't know how to contact her. I told you before that she just disappeared. She left me a note and said she would be back soon. I couldn't wait at the temple any longer. You understand that don't you?" A small sob followed her words.

The man put his arm around her and lowered his voice to a soothing tone, "Yes, I understand why you left the temple, but I don't understand what Nuang did. I was sure she would return to her family once she had time to think. I guess I was wrong. "

Surat stopped in front of the hotel and turned off his meter. He got out and opened the door for his passengers. He smiled his best smile and waited for the man to pay.

"Can you wait here for a minute?" the man asked. "I might want you to drive us someplace else. I'll make it worth your while."

Surat nodded. After the couple entered the hotel, he slid back into the taxi and resumed the meter. As he waited, he replayed the overheard conversation. Nuang! The name had to be a coincidence. There was no way two complete strangers could be talking about his wife and his baby. On the other hand, it was a baby and its mother's name was Nuang. Anything was possible.

He thought hard for some way to get more information from them but nothing came. He would listen with both ears wide open when they came back—if they came back. The idea that they had cheated him out of his fare crossed his mind. He shoved the thought aside. The man had too much class to pull a cheap trick like that.

His wait was short. They were back in less than five minutes. The man was carrying a baby and the woman was crying.

"Take me to the Chiang Mai Hospital," the man ordered as they slid inside the rear seat. "I'll pay an extra 1,000 baht if you hurry. This is an emergency."

Surat needed no encouragement. The very idea that he could be saving a baby's life was all he needed. The notion that he might be saving his own baby's life caused his foot to push harder on the gas pedal. The tires squealed as he pulled into traffic and sped toward the hospital. He kept his ears glued to the back seat.

"Don't worry." the man was saying. "Everything will be okay."

"We have to find Nuang," the woman replied through tears.

"I will if I can," he said. "Do you know her family name?"

"She told me her given name is Chalamsee but I don't know her family name. She said she had a brother in Pattaya and that she was from Chiang Mai."

Surat's ears nearly popped from his head. It was all he could do to keep quiet.

"That isn't much," the man said. "I'll call my father; maybe he can help find her. He's good at that sort of thing."

The woman pulled the baby close to her breast and cried, "Laht, I'm so scared."

The man put his arm around her. "Everything will be okay. Please trust me."

Minutes later they arrived at the hospital. When the man tried to pay, Surat refused his money. "Please, you must take care of the baby. You can pay me later. I'll wait for you here in case you need another ride."

Surat fought back a powerful urge to follow them as they disappeared through the emergency room doors. He parked his taxi away from the entrance then returned to wait.

His heart pounded as he remembered what the woman had said. She wanted to find a woman whose name was Chalamsee and whose nickname was Nuang. Her Nuang had a brother in Pattaya, she was from Chiang Mai, and she had a baby—all the same as his wife. It had to be her. Everything fit. As impossible as it seemed, he had found his baby because he had stopped to give the man and woman a ride in his taxi. But where was Nuang? It was obvious the couple didn't know, but the man had said something about his father finding her.

My father is good at that sort of thing, the man had said. Surat hoped it was true. Maybe this whole nightmare would be over soon.

Surat wondered how long they would be inside the hospital. He didn't want to lose them and would wait all night if necessary, but what would he say when they returned? Would he have the nerve to come right out and accuse them of having his baby? He blushed at the thought of such rudeness at a time like this. The baby was sick; at least the man had said so. He should be praying for the baby's health instead of planning how he would take it away from them. The notion that the baby might die clawed through his head. The thought terrified him. He lit a cigarette and waited.

Twenty minutes later the man returned to where Surat stood. "Thank you for waiting, but I think we could be here for a long time. We have taken enough of your time already. Here's the thousand baht I promised you." He held the money out toward Surat.

"What about the baby? Will it be okay?"

"I don't know. I think everything will be okay. Look, I don't mean to be impolite but I must hurry. I'm the baby's doctor." He pushed the money at Surat again.

Surat took the baht bills and watched as the man walked back inside the hospital. A fluttering pressed at his senses. He wondered what he should do. It only took a minute for him to decide. He would stay until they went home. He hurried to his taxi, moved it to a spot where he could see the hospital entrance, then sat back and relaxed.

He fell asleep before midnight.

Chapter 30

Strictly speaking, Laht wasn't the baby's doctor, but as a soon-to-be staff physician he had been allowed to take part in treating Nuang's baby. Somjit waited in the emergency room lobby.

The baby's dehydration was less than he had expected, and the hospital doctors had treated a thousand other infants with the similar symptoms. Laht had the American book learning, but these doctors had the real-life experience. He didn't interfere.

The doctors worked with practiced confidence and like magic the baby's temperature dropped and the diarrhea ended. By four in the morning, the baby had drunk and retained enough liquids to satisfy even the most cautious of doctors. Laht asked the night nurse to call them a taxi.

As he and Somjit waited at the curb, he remembered the taxi driver who had brought them to the hospital. He wondered at the cabby's concern. Maybe the man had a baby of his own or something. He was sure that must be it. In less than a minute their new taxi arrived and the other driver was forgotten.

"I want you to stay at my place where I can keep an eye on the baby." Laht said to Somjit as they entered the cab. When she didn't respond, he gave the driver directions to his condo. "Tomorrow we can get your things from the hotel."

Somjit only nodded. Inside she was a mass of conflicting emotions. She was depressed about the baby being sick and exhausted from being awake for the last thirty hours. Still she was elated because Laht had asked her to stay with him. Despite exhaustion, her thoughts of being with Laht flooded her with a rush of desire. "Khop khun mahk ka," she said, lowering her eyes in deference. They rode the rest of the way in silence.

Laht wondered if his offer to Somjit was a beginning or an ending. A powerful need burned in him, an urge like he had never felt. He remembered past thoughts of his naked ass humping through a monk's robe. He wondered if she ever had sexual thoughts about him, too. Did she ever touch herself and wish it was him.

By the time they arrived at his address, an unwanted erection pushed against the front of his pants. It waned as he fumbled for his wallet. By the time he exited the taxi, it had softened enough that no one would notice.

Laht carried the baby to his condo and Somjit followed close behind.

Somjit was in awe of where he lived. She had never been inside the barriers that separated the very rich from the poor. The lobby area of his condominium was like a palace. Being in a place so clean and well kept made her feel like royalty.

In a moment they reached his unit and Laht opened the door. The furniture was basic but tastefully so. There were no pictures on the walls or magazines on the coffee table or anything else to make it feel like a home.

Suddenly Somjit realized she was totally alone with him for the first time ever. "Is the baby still asleep?" she asked to cover the urges gathering inside her.

"Yes, I will lay her in my second bedroom. She's too young to move much, but I'll prop pillows around her anyway. She will be safe like that. The master bath is there if you want to shower or anything." He pointed to the door at the end of a short hall.

Somjit did want to be clean. If she had her way, there were reasons she wanted to smell good. The bathroom was spotless. She adjusted the water to just below scalding and took a long shower. When she finished, she wrapped a towel around herself and stepped into his bedroom. Laht was in bed and asleep, or apparently so.

She considered what to do. With only the slightest hesitation she let the towel fall away and she lay down completely naked. She pulled the sheet over herself and waited for him to move toward her.

"I can sleep on the sofa if you want," he said in the darkness.

She moved closer and put her arms around him, "I want you to stay with me."

"Are you sure you?" he whispered.

"Yes," she whispered back. "I'm sure."

His hand stroked her arm hesitantly. "Okay."

She felt his fingers tremble. His caress was awkward and rougher than she expected. She waited for him to touch her in other places, but he didn't. It was as if his hand was frozen to her arm.

After a moment she slid her hand across his chest and down his stomach. A second later she slipped her fingers beneath the elastic of his underwear and pushed her hand inside.

He tensed and pulled away at her intrusion.

"Are you okay, teeluk?" she asked.

"I'm embarrassed," he answered very quiet.

"I have wanted you since the day you saved my life. Tonight I want you more than ever. There is no reason to be embarrassed. This is the way Buddha wants it to be."

"I have never been with a woman before. I know what to do, but I've never done it. I'm afraid I won't do something right."

Somjit rose to her knees. "Don't worry, you will be perfect."

She proceeded to undress him in the faint glow of the light filtering in from outside. Using everything she had learned from Nong, she seduced Laht. She kissed and touched and sucked him until he was ready to explode. At the same time she rubbed herself into a state of total lust. By the time he entered her, she was already in the throes of an intense orgasm. He finished less than a minute later, but she was completely satisfied. His erection faded but didn't die. They fell asleep still mated together.

THAILAND - COLD RAIN

When Laht awoke her at nine the next morning, he was already dressed. "We should get your things from the hotel now."

She remembered last night, but kept herself covered in feigned shyness. "What about little Tippawan? We can't take her out in the heat."

"I had one of my nurses to come and help. She will take care of the baby. We can go when you're ready."

After checking to make sure the nurse was properly tending the baby, Somjit showered and put on the jeans and tee-shirt she had worn the day before. She could smell odors drifting up from the armpits. She could hardly wait to be in clean clothes. She waited for Laht in the living room.

When Laht emerged from the bedroom, he was dressed to the max. His fine silk suit was sharp pressed and his face clean shaved. He looked handsome.

"Miss Somjit," he said politely formal, "we should hurry," His eyes flicked toward the nurse who was tending the baby. "I have much to do today."

"Of course," Somjit responded just as formal. "I'm ready."

Their first stop was his new office. Laht wasn't due to open for business for another three weeks, but his father had already hired a staff to organize everything and Laht felt obligated to make a daily appearance. He spent some time inside with his staff while Somjit sat in the waiting room. From there they drove to a store and bought baby things.

At ten-thirty they arrived at the hotel where Somjit had stayed the night before. For no reason other than impulse, they made love in her hotel room. This time Laht seemed more relaxed, more confident. By eleven-thirty, they had checked out of the hotel and were back at the condo.

Laht shooed the nurse off into the bedroom with the baby. Once she had closed the door, he turned to Somjit.

"I have made a decision. I'm taking some time to help with the baby. I'm not officially on the hospital staff until the end of the month, and my practice isn't scheduled to open for a while. The staff my father hired is bored just sitting around, so I have given them two weeks off with pay. They're happy to have a holiday."

"Are you sure, teeluk? I feel guilty, like I am interfering with your future."

He pulled her close and placed a sniffing Thai kiss on her cheek. "You are my future. Everything else can wait."

"You're too nice to me."

"I could never be too nice to someone I love."

Later, Laht called his father and explained everything about Somjit, Nuang, and the baby. Isara sounded tense during their conversation. Laht figured his father was coming to grips with him taking up with a common Thai. In the end Isara agreed to help find Nuang.

Chapter 31

Surat awoke when the morning sun touched his eyelids. For a moment he didn't know where he was. He rubbed his face to shake off his drowsiness. Suddenly he remembered; he was at the hospital and waiting for the couple with the baby.

He left his taxi and hurried inside. The woman at the information desk looked familiar. After a second he realized she was the same woman who had been on duty the night he had come looking for Nuang.

"Excuse me. I'm looking for someone."

The woman's eyes flashed recognition. "Your wife still hasn't returned, if that's who you're looking for." She punched at her computer keyboard. "And your bill hasn't been paid either. The cashier is just down the hall." She pointed to her left.

He ignored her comments and her tone. "I'm looking for a woman and a baby who came here last night."

"Your wife?"

"No, not my wife, but my baby."

The woman eyed him warily. "Just so I understand: You are looking for a woman who isn't your wife, but who has your baby." Her expression was cold. "Mr. Duansawang, it's none of my business, but I want you to know I don't approve of men having mistresses. And I certainly don't condone men making babies with anyone except their wives." Her unforgiving stare drilled holes through him.

"You don't understand," he sputtered. "The woman isn't my mistress." He thought quickly, "She's my babysitter."

"You mean you got your babysitter pregnant? That is

disgusting."

"No, my baby was ill and my babysitter brought her here."

The woman's face softened, but not much. "I know the woman you mean. She left here over two hours ago. She probably went home. Maybe you should look for her there."

"Do you have her name and address?"

"I'm not allowed to give out that sort of information," she answered tersely. "Besides, I think you would know her address if you're who you say you are." She pushed a button on her desktop and glanced at the front door. "I don't know what your game is, Mr. Duansawang, but I think you should leave."

Surat looked over his shoulder and saw a security officer headed in their direction. He turned back to the woman. "Thank you for your help," his words were polite but his tone sarcastic. "You're right, maybe I should go now."

"Is there a problem?" the security man asked when he reached speaking distance.

Surat turned to face him. "No problem," he said as evenly as he could. "I was just leaving." He walked to the exit.

The security guard followed but didn't interfere.

Outside, Surat cursed himself for falling asleep. If he had been awake, he would have seen them leave and he wouldn't have made a fool of himself with the hospital lady.

He glanced at his watch. If he hurried, he had time to go home and clean up before checking in at work. He wanted to take the day off but couldn't afford to take the risk; his boss still wasn't over the *unauthorized-use-of-a-company-vehicle* thing. He started the taxi and went home.

After a cursory washing and quick change of clothes, Surat reported for work. If anyone noticed his haggard appearance, they didn't mention it. His bossed assigned him to the airport circuit.

At his first opportunity Surat drove to the hotel where he had taken the man and woman the night before. He put on his friendliest smile as he approached the receptionist.

"Sawasdee krup," he said with humble politeness.

"Sawasdee ka," the girl returned. "May I help you?"

"Last night, I gave a woman a ride in my taxi. She had a young baby with her. By accident she left some keys on the seat. I have come to return them to her." It was a lie, but it sounded like it could be true. "Do you know the woman I mean?"

"Yes, I do," the girl smiled. "She checked out about fifteen minutes ago. I'm sorry you missed her. It's most honorable of you to return her things."

Damn the luck, Surat thought to himself. It was all he could do to keep the smile on his face. "Can you tell me her name or where she's gone?"

"Sir, I'm not allowed to give out that sort of information. But if you want to leave the keys, maybe she will come back when she realizes they're missing."

"Never mind," his smile faded. "I'll go to where I took her last night. Maybe she'll be there. If she's not, I'll bring the keys back here." He turned and left the hotel lobby.

Surat spent the rest of the day and most of the evening making airport runs. After dropping off each customer, he would drive through a different section of Chiang Mai hoping for a glimpse of the woman or the man. By the time the evening flights had stopped, Surat had given up ever finding them. For the second time in two months, he had lost his wife and his baby. His mother-in-law was right, he was a loser.

Chapter 32

Pajeeka Wasiwat was a patient investigator. Four days had passed since her meeting with Lieutenant Viboon, and her patience had finally paid off. It was a good thing because the information from her friend in Bangkok hadn't amounted to anything.

Viboon had called earlier and asked her to meet him at six o'clock that evening. His tone had been polite but his words were terse. They agreed to meet at a restaurant near the police station.

Pajeeka showered and put on clothes appropriate for the restaurant and her meeting with the Lieutenant. On the way she stopped at the bank and withdrew money from her business account. She arrived at the restaurant at five forty-five.

She took a table and asked the waitress to watch for the Lieutenant. She knew it wasn't proper to select a table on her own, but it was her nature to bend the rules of etiquette.

Viboon arrived fifteen minutes late, his face tight. He carried a thin folder in his left hand. He murmured a brief hello, took his seat, and ordered Singha beer. He put the folder on the table but didn't offer it to Pajeeka. She waited for him to speak.

In a minute his beer arrived in a pitcher with a large chunk of ice frozen to the bottom. He poured himself a glass and drank half. "Please excuse my bad manners. I've been very busy the last few days, but I think I have fulfilled your request."

He picked up the folder and handed it to her.

Pajeeka held it for a moment before flipping the cover open. The first page listed the members of the Bongkot family starting with Supit and Nui and followed by their six children from youngest to oldest. A footnote at the bottom of the page stated that

Nui and Supit were living separately but weren't legally divorced. The subsequent pages contained short bios of their children.

Pajeeka skimmed the pages on the Bongkot family, except for the woman named Nuang. She read Nuang's page carefully. She wanted to see how close it came to what she knew as fact. Most of it matched with what she had learned on her own. The report ended with Nuang running away with her baby. The Lieutenant must have had contact with the Bongkot family to learn that tidbit of information. The page on Math was conspicuously blank.

"I'm surprised, Lieutenant. From our conversation I thought you'd have more information on the woman named Math."

Viboon squirmed in his seat. "I have a separate report on her. It has information Khun Isara might prefer to remain confidential."

Pajeeka pursed her lips in annoyance. Isara had already told her that anything she learned was to be kept secret. She forced a smile back to her face. "I understand. I appreciate your concern for my boss's privacy and well being—I defer to your judgment. By the way, I don't see anything in here about the Duansawang family. Couldn't find anything?"

Viboon cleared his throat, "Look, I don't understand everything that's going on here, but I do know that if Isara Horungruang is interested in this, there's either money involved or it's extremely personal. I found few facts about the Duansawang family and fewer still about Surat. But I heard plenty of rumors that could be true. I made a list of them so Khun Isara can check them out if he wants. I put the Duansawang report together with the one on the woman named Math."

"I trust you will deliver those reports to my boss at your earliest opportunity."

He smiled. "I have delivered them already. If I can be of further assistance, please contact me." He stood to leave.

"Wait," Pajeeka rose to her feet. "I owe you 30,000 baht."

"I can't take it."

Pajeeka was confused, "Why? It's not illegal and it's what we agreed. What about your father's new motorcycle?"

"This has nothing to do with legal or illegal. My father's old motorcycle will have to last a while longer."

Pajeeka had never met a Thai who wouldn't take easy money. "I'll hold on to it for a while in case you change your mind."

"You can keep it, I won't change my mind. If you get a chance to read my reports, you will understand. Please enjoy your holiday." He walked away without waiting for her response.

Pajeeka glanced at her watch. It was six thirty-five. She was sure Isara had already left the office for the day but she called anyway. The automated phone system answered her call. She keyed Isara's extension and got his voice mail. She exited that and dialed her own mailbox. There was one message. It was from Isara. It was short, sweet, and weird. "Come to my office at seven in the morning. I'm sending you on a pre-holiday holiday."

What in Buddha's name was a pre-holiday holiday? It sounded suspiciously like an out-of-town assignment. No doubt it had to do with Lieutenant Viboon's private report. She wondered if Isara would let her read what Viboon had learned. Most likely he would just tell her what she needed to know and turn her loose. That was his typical mode of operation.

She called the waitress to the table and ordered dinner. She studied Viboon's report as she ate. She memorized each detail he had written. She paid special attention to the two pages on Nuang. She would give the report to Isara in the morning, when he told her about her pre-holiday holiday.

Pajeeka was waiting when Isara arrived at his office at seven o'clock. He led her directly to his office, not wasting a second on pleasantries or small talk. He took his seat behind his desk and motioned her to a chair.

"I'm sending you to Pattaya on a short assignment."

"You want me to find Nuang?" Pajeeka reached her conclusion via a short leap of logic.

"I want you to find a woman named Anya Duansawang." He handed her an overstuffed envelope. "It's all the information I have. Since you're familiar with Pattaya, I think it's enough."

She chastised herself for her wrong conclusion. She took the envelope, "Are you sure the woman is in Pattaya?"

"This is Thailand; nothing is ever certain. A private source said she's there. If she is, I want you to find her and then set me an appointment with her."

"Is this a rush job or just something to do at my leisure during my pre-holiday holiday?"

Isara smiled, "You know me better than that. I don't like to waste time. I've booked you a flight leaving for Bangkok at ten o'clock. A car and driver from Thai Limousine Service will take you to Pattaya. I have also reserved you an executive suite at the Amari Orchid Hotel. Find the woman, set my appointment, and then call me. After that you can relax and have fun at my expense. When I'm sure I don't need your help anymore, I will send you on holiday wherever you want. Anyplace within Thailand that is."

That answered her question. It was a rush job and he wasn't being stingy about it. She glanced at her watch, "If I'm going to catch a ten o'clock flight, I must hurry." She stood to leave.

"In your spare time," he interrupted her departure, "find the woman from the temple. The one named Nuang."

She looked at him coolly, smiled, and presented him with a very proper wai. "I'll call after I've set your appointment."

Anya Duansawang! Isara didn't know the woman but he remembered the name. He had been fifteen years old at the time and she had been the talk of Phitsanulok. She was the first woman in town to get pregnant by an American soldier. It had churned the rumor mill for months. Isara had wondered if her baby was a boy or a girl or if it had ever been born at all. Now he knew it had been a boy and his name was Surat.

Lieutenant Viboon's report was thorough. He had covered the Duansawang and Bongkot families in more detail than seemed possible. Nuang Bongkot had married Surat Duansawang and moved to Chiang Mai. Recently she had given birth and run away.

Isara knew Nuang had ended up at the temple for a while before going to Pattaya, and that she hadn't taken her baby with her when she left. That wasn't in the report, nor was the fact that her baby was now living in his own son's condo in Chiang Mai. There was no way for the lieutenant to know anything about that. Also, there was no way for him to know that Laht had called just two days ago asking for help finding Nuang. The whole situation had taken on a life of its own.

According to Viboon, Anya's last known address was Pattaya. Attached was a three year old tax form. Isara's instincts said that she was still in Pattaya somewhere.

Nuang had gone to Pattaya, too. For a while he had considered that she may have gone to her brother's house, but then discarded that notion. If she had gone there, Viboon would have found out. He supposed she could have gone to Anya's house. Not likely but anything was possible, and it was his only lead to finding Nuang. If she hadn't gone to Anya's, he probably would never find her. He didn't know what that meant for his son Laht, if anything.

He had sent Pajeeka to find Anya because she would be easier to find than a woman determined to stay hidden. He hoped Nuang was with her. There were issues that needed discussed.

Viboon's report had carried unsettling news, too. Tippawan "Math" Bongkot was dead, killed in a motorcycle accident more than a year ago. The news of her death depressed him. Images of his deceased brother Jum flooded his thoughts. Math had been Jum's daughter, conceived out of wedlock with a woman named Nui, the mother of the Bongkot family. It was a secret that few people knew; two had been Math and his brother Jum. They were both dead now and couldn't tell a soul. He was sure that Math's farang lover knew, but Mr. Michael Johnson was at home in America, and would probably never return to Thailand. Even if he did, the chances of him ever meeting Laht were minuscule. Except for himself, Nuang was the only person who knew his family's secret. He had to make sure she never told Laht.

His first client arrived and Isara attended to business.

Chapter 33

Nuang sat on the sofa inside Jon's condo and flipped aimlessly through the channels on the TV. She finally stopped on a Thai news station. The weatherman was predicting a heat wave for Pattaya and Phuket, while a cold front was overtaking Chiang Mai and northern Thailand. She knew that meant rain.

Thoughts of Surat drifted through her head. Rainy days were always bad for the business of driving tourist to the temples, elephant farms, and floral gardens. She figured he was probably at home alone, cursing her and the weather.

It had been two months since she had seen Surat, and more than a week since she had left the temple in Phitsanulok. She pondered everything that had happened during her stay at the temple. Most of her memories were fuzzy, but little Tippawan, Somjit, and the young monk sparked unforgettable imagines. They also triggered sharp feelings of guilt and depression.

Since leaving the temple her life had taken a new course. Any possibility of returning to Surat or her family had disappeared the night she moved into Jon's condo. She recalled the events of the last few days. It was like a fairy tale. If she hadn't lived it herself, she would never have believed it could happen.

From the very night Nuang arrived in Pattaya, she and Jon had lived in the same condo but they'd never slept in the same bed.

Jon was a very kind and generous man. He bought her expensive clothes and enough food for three women, yet he never once asked for anything in return, except his daily Thai lessons. On top of everything, he had paid her a month in advance. It was the most relaxed she had felt in months, and the most frustrated as well.

Jon had never tried to have sex with her. From what she knew of men, that wasn't normal. He seemed to like her, but he had never so much as touched her, not even in private. Really she didn't care, or so she kept telling herself.

On impulse she went to the bathroom, took off her clothes, and inspected herself in the mirror. Except for the loose skin on her abdomen, her body looked as good as ever. Her face had a few wrinkles but she didn't look old. Jon, nonetheless, seemed oblivious to the fact that she was a woman. It bothered her to the point of frustration.

By the time she finished putting her clothes back on, she had decided to ask him what he found so repulsive. She had all afternoon to think about it, and none of her thoughts were good. She decided the direct approach would be best.

~~~

Jon had had a shitty day. Everything that could go wrong did go wrong. It was one of those days that would make Murphy and his laws proud. By the time he left work he was ready for a relaxing night at home. A couple of beers, his daily Thai lessons, and maybe some music. He would use the headphones for the music so Nuang could watch the Thai soap operas she had become addicted to. When he opened the door of his condo, Nuang was waiting but she wasn't smiling.

"Why do you think I'm ugly?" she demanded without so much as a hello.

Jon stepped back. Obviously Murphy wasn't finished for the day. "What are you talking about?"

"You think I'm not young enough or sexy enough. That's it, isn't it? You think I'm an ugly old woman."

His mind whirled, searching for a response that made more sense than her accusation. "That's not true. I don't understand why you even think that. You are very beautiful, and the sexiest woman I've ever met."

"Goh hoak! Bullshit!"

It was the first time he had ever heard Nuang swear, either in Thai or English. Something was going on, but he had no idea what. And after the day he'd had he wasn't in the mood to listen anyway. "Well, bullshit to you, too. If I thought you were an ugly old woman, I would never have talked to you in the first place."

She dropped her eyes from his. "Then I am the one who doesn't understand. If you think I'm sexy and beautiful, then you would want to make love to me. That's how men are. But you don't want to, so I think you're lying." She turned to move away.

Jon reached out and pulled her back. "Look, I'm telling you the truth."

She struggled against his grasp for a moment, then gave in and allowed herself to be held. Her thoughts were blurred. How could a man want her and not want her at the same time? He didn't make sense. Tears gathered and slid down her cheeks. "I don't understand." She rested her head against his chest.

Jon felt her tears where they dampened his shirt. He was amazed at the whole situation. He had invited Nuang to live with him only because he wanted company and someone to teach him Thai. He had never considered that she would feel rejected because he had never tried to have sex with her. Certainly sex had entered his thoughts but for him it wasn't an option.

"As much as I like you," he finally said, "I can't make love with you."

"I don't blame you," she replied, dejected. "No one could. I think I should sleep now. I want to be alone."

He wondered if she had understood what he had said. "Listen to me. It's not you." His face contorted and flushed bright red at the confession he was about to make. "I can't make love with any woman."

"What do you mean? Do you have some illness, or an injury?"

His blush deepened. He let his arms relax and slip away from her. He stared at a spot high on the wall. "Nothing like that. I just can't."

Nuang struggled for something to say but nothing came. Images of the shower and his limp manhood flittered through her head. She put her arms around him and whispered, "I understand."

She held him for a long moment then went to her room. She lay there thinking how sad he must be. She felt sad, too. And so alone. She cried for both of them.

Jon sat awake for a while and thought about what had just happened. As much as he had enjoyed her company these last few days, he knew she would have to go. He didn't want to live with someone who wanted him in a way he could never be. He couldn't deal with a repeat of Julie and the others. He would tell her tomorrow. He fell into a depressed sleep.

~~~

It was after midnight when Nuang went to the toilet. The light beside of Jon's bed was still on. She walked quietly to turn it off. Jon stirred as she reached for the switch. She looked down at him. He was naked from the waist up. The rest of him was covered with a blanket. She clicked the light off and headed toward her own room. Then, on impulse, she went back and slipped into bed beside of him. She wasn't thinking about sex, she only wanted someone to be close to.

As she lay there, she could feel the heat of his body. It reminded her of Surat and that comforted her. In a while she fell asleep.

Later that night, Nuang awoke with a start. Something had disturbed her sleep but she wasn't sure what. A second later she felt a hot pressure twitch against her thigh. She knew immediately what it was. Jon's manhood had come alive. He had said it wasn't possible, but it was happening anyway. She wasn't sure what to do. The twitch became a hard steady throb, a burning desire focused between her thighs.

She reached down and touched her womanhood. The wetness surprised her. She rubbed briefly and her heat exploded into raging need. Quickly, quietly, Nuang got to her knees and straddled him.

"Dear Buddha, forgive my human desires," she whispered as she guided his erect member into her waiting passion. Her womanhood spasmed. The sensation took her breath away. She saw his eyes coming awake, but she didn't stop her self-absorbent undulations.

Jon had been dreaming he had to pee. Before he could find a toilet he found himself naked and surrounded by women touching and loving him. He had to pee so bad he wished they would stop. At the next instant he didn't have to pee; he was erect, and having sex with one of the women. He couldn't see her face.

Suddenly the dream ended and he was awake. Nuang was atop him, moving rhythmically against his hips. Her head was tilted backwards, her hands rested on her naked thighs. He glanced down between their bodies and saw his manhood sliding easily into her body.

Dear sweet Jesus, his heart raced, how had she managed this miracle. For a full minute he watched as Nuang worked to satisfy her yearning. He waited for himself to go soft or climax, but he did neither. Hormones coursed through him, heady and intoxicating, a sensation he hadn't felt in a very long time.

Nuang sensed he was completely awake now. She waited for him to stop her, but he didn't. She pulled her pelvis tight against his and oscillated her hips in short rocking motions. A small sound escaped her throat and she increased the speed of her thrusts. In a second she moaned and pressed harder against him. She nearly fainted at the pulsing contraction of her orgasm. She held him like that for a few brief moments as the rippling inside her faded. She had never felt such intense pleasure. It left her drained.

Jon was still erect, he could feel it. Watching Nuang's climax sent his own desires soaring. He let his hands slide down her back and across her buttocks. He pulled himself halfway out before stopping and easing back inside. He repeated the motion again and again, reveling in the bliss of their union. In a minute Nuang responded to his steady stroking. All sense of time deserted him. His body, his mind, his very soul was consumed with pure lust. There were no thoughts, only burning passion. This woman was surely a goddess or a sorceress to have worked such a miracle. He closed his eyes and let hot waves of pleasure rush through him.

Suddenly he pulled her tight against him and in one quick motion rolled her onto her back. She spread her legs wide and succumbed to him. He pushed himself into her as deep as his manhood let him. He held like that for a long moment before continuing his urgent lunging. Nuang lost herself in the throes of his overwhelming desire. Touching, kissing, and moaning they shared a climax that left them both sweating and breathless.

"I love you, Nuang," Jon whispered. "God how I love you."

Nuang knew it wasn't true, but she needed to hear the words. "I love you, too, teeluk," she lied. "Thank you for making me feel like a woman."

Later they fell asleep in each other's arms.

The next morning, Jon left for work before Nuang awoke. All day, the events of the night before haunted his thoughts. Sometimes he smiled and sometimes he didn't. Last night was the first time in years since he had made love with a woman. He had decided long ago that he was impotent. Even after what had happened, he still believed it. Yesterday's lovemaking had been a fluke, a trick of nature, an evil joke by the gods of love. He knew it might never happen again.

He had relished their intimacy, and he was sure she did too. That was what bothered him. What if she wanted to make love again and he couldn't? On the other hand, what if she didn't want to do it again? He didn't know which humiliation would be worse. By the end of the day he had decided he didn't want to face either alternative.

After work he didn't go straight home. Instead he stopped for a few beers with his co-workers. If he could have found a good excuse, he wouldn't have gone home at all. With each drink he became more convinced he should end their relationship before she learned just how dysfunctional he was. He would tell her she should leave and that they should just be friends. He didn't want to do that but it would be the best thing for both of them. He didn't want to live with the constant fear of failure and humiliation.

By his sixth beer, he had steeled himself enough to end their living arrangement. By his seventh he had decided he would do it in a way that wouldn't hurt her. By his eighth beer he was thinking it might be possible that he could have sex again. By his ninth, he had decided to try one more time before throwing everything away. Maybe Nuang really was magic.

It was almost nine o'clock when he let himself into the condo. The lights were off and the living area lit only by the harsh flickering of the television screen. Nuang sat on the sofa, a blanket wrapped around her. She didn't acknowledge his presence.

"Are you okay?" he asked, his words slurred. He wondered if she was naked beneath the blanket.

"I'm not well, Jonathan." Her tone was soft, subdued.

She hadn't used his full name since the night they had met. He figured she was pissed because he was so late coming home. "I stopped for a few beers with my friends. I'm sorry if I worried you. I didn't think you would mind."

She looked up at him. "It's not you, it's me." Tears filled her eyes and she turned away.

Her mood wrenched at his alcohol-numbed brain. "Hey, what's going on?"

"There are things you don't know about me. Bad things. I have decided to leave before you get hurt. I've packed already. I waited until you came home so you'll know what I've done."

Jon's drunken thoughts spun. He was the one who was supposed to be ending the relationship, not her. "What are you talking about? Did you leave a trail of dead bodies from Bangkok to Pattaya or what?"

"It's worse than that. I have a husband and a baby. I have shamed them both. I have shamed myself even more. "

Jon blinked at her pronouncement, barely believing his ears. "You told me your husband was dead and your baby was living with your mother. Isn't that what you said?"

She covered her face and cried. "I lied to you. I have lied to everyone. I even lied to myself."

He knelt down and reached for her hand but she pulled away. He searched for something logical to say. Something to pull reality back from the edge of this nightmare. "I love you," was what came from his mouth.

"You can't do that and I can't do that." Her blush showed in the dim light. "I'm a married woman. I have a husband and a baby."

"I'm confused. If you have a husband and a baby, why are you here in Pattaya? Please be honest with me."

She took a deep breath to brace herself and then told Jon everything right down to the smallest detail. When she finished, she stood and hurried toward her room.

Jon caught up to her before she reached the door. He took her firmly by the arm and spun her around. "Listen to me. You're not a bad person; you're only human. I can't make you stay, but I don't want you to leave." He let an impish smile form on his lips, "Besides, you still owe me two more weeks of Thai lessons."

She looked up at him. "I will have to leave someday."

"I know," he answered. "But you don't have to go tonight."

Her expression twisted with uncertainty. Her eyes studied him as if hoping to find an answer in his face. "Then I will stay until I have finished your lessons. I want to sleep now."

"So do I," he answered. After she closed her door, he went to his own bed and lay down. He smelled her perfume on his pillow. He held it tight and drifted off to sleep.

Chapter 34

In the days following their emergency trip to the hospital, Laht and Somjit lived as man and woman, husband and wife. The feelings they had suppressed at the temple blossomed into fiery hot passions. Their desire for each other grew to undeniable love.

Little Tippawan had recovered nicely and demanded constant attention. Laht spent as much time with the baby as Somjit did. He discovered how it felt to be a father and he liked it. He was usually the first to pick up little Tippawan when she cried, and he was always the last to leave her crib before going to bed.

Somjit spent her days cleaning the condo of non-existent dirt, helping care for the baby, and paying intense attention to Laht. He treated her like someone special, almost like a queen, and she responded in kind. Every emotion from her past paled in comparison to what she felt. She glowed with a love she had never imagined possible. She prayed to Buddha it would last forever.

Every day Laht would go shopping and bring back something for either Somjit or the baby. Clothes, toys, jewelry, shoes. He enjoyed watching Somjit's face light up at his little gifts.

Almost every day they took the baby for short strolls. Somjit would walk proud beside of Laht as she pushed little Tippawan in the carriage. In her new clothes and with Laht at her side, everyone smiled with a respect she had never experienced. Her confidence and self-esteem grew with each passing day.

On Thursday a cold rain arrived and they were confined to the condo. Laht and the baby fell asleep shortly after lunch. It was three o'clock before the sun reappeared. Little Tippawan awoke but

Laht didn't. On impulse, she decided to take the baby for a stroll. She left a note for Laht and went outside. The air was cool for a Thailand afternoon. It was a good day to walk. Baby Tippawan soon fell back asleep to the gentle rocking of the carriage.

~~~

Surat had spent most of that same morning ferrying passengers all over Chiang Mai. Business had been steady but he hadn't made much in tips. With the cold rain, everyone wanted a real taxi and not the open-sided tuk-tuks and motorcycle taxis. Most of his fares were locals going short distances and giving him even shorter tips.

At two o'clock the clouds thinned and the sun peeked through. By three o'clock the sky was clear and the north air crisp.

Surat had just finished a downtown run and was on his way back to the airport taxi-stand when he saw her. She was pushing a baby carriage in the same direction he was driving. If she hadn't looked toward the street, he would never have seen her face. Even then, he wasn't sure it was her.

He slowed his taxi, pulled to the curb, and waited for the woman to catch up. He studied her face through the rear window as she approached. There was no doubt—it was her.

After she had passed by, Surat exited the cab and hurried toward her. She noticed him when he entered the periphery of her vision. She stopped and turned.

"Good afternoon," he said. "Do you remember me?"

Somjit studied him. "No, I don't know you. If you will excuse me, I must be going. I'm late already."

"You and a man rode in my taxi the night your baby was sick."

Suddenly she did remember. She didn't remember his face, but she remembered the taxi ride to the hospital. "Of course. How impolite of me to forget."

"Never mind," he replied, his eyes focused on the carriage. He couldn't tell if the baby looked more like him or Nuang. "Is your baby better now?"

"Yes, thank you for asking. She's much better."

Surat smiled. "She is very beautiful. What's her name?"

"Her name is Tippawan. She's named after her aunt."

The woman's words, though softly spoken, pounded against him like a jackhammer. Nuang's sister's name had been Tippawan. It was all he could do to maintain his composure. He took a deep breath, "Is her aunt deceased and was she nicknamed Math?"

Somjit's heart fluttered. How could he know that? She knew he must have overheard her and Laht that night in the taxi, but she didn't remember saying anything about Nuang's dead sister. She struggled to remain calm. "Do you know Nuang? Are you a relative or something?"

"She is my wife."

Panic exploded inside her chest. "You're mistaken, Nuang doesn't have a husband. She told me so herself."

Surat kept his voice low, composed. "Nuang has one brother who lives in Pattaya. She has another brother and a sister in Phitsanulok. Her mother lives there, too. She likes to wear her hair in braids."

He paused to gauge her reaction. Her expression spoke louder than words. There was no question; they were talking about the same Nuang.

"When she was pregnant, she sometimes heard voices whispering in her ears. Maybe she still does. She thinks they are evil spirits. Does that sound like the same Nuang you know?"

"Yes! But that's not possible. This baby's father is farang. Nuang told me that. Anyone can see it's true."

"I don't understand what you mean."

Somjit slipped the cap off the sleeping baby. Its hair wasn't blond, but it was far from Thai black. "Her eyes are blue," she said.

Surat paled as he backed away from the carriage. He couldn't believe what he was seeing. The baby was half farang. There was no doubt about that. His head swam. Maybe the woman was right. Maybe the Nuang she knew wasn't his wife. But too much was the same; it had to be her. But this didn't have to be his baby. At that instant he saw everything crystal clear—the baby wasn't his.

Nuang had been to Pattaya just before she learned she was pregnant. She must have had sex with some farang while she was there. All this time she had let him believe the baby was his. An extreme urge to hurt someone raged inside, but he kept it in check.

"You're right," he lied to hide what he now knew to be the truth. "I must be mistaken. It must be a different Nuang."

"Yes," Somjit responded, edging away from the cabby. "I must go. People will worry if I'm gone too long."

Surat returned to his taxi as Somjit hurried towards her condo.

Somjit shook as she fumbled the key into the lock. The cabby had terrified her. She pushed the door open and came face to face with Laht.

"Are you okay?" he asked.

"I don't know. I think I just met Tippawan's father."

Laht tensed. "Are you sure?"

Somjit told him about her encounter. "What if the man comes back? What if he knows where we live. What if he really is Nuang's husband?"

Laht pulled her close to her, "Don't worry, teeluk; he won't come here. Everything will be okay. My father is looking for Nuang. I'm sure he will find her soon."

Somjit's emotions ran rampant. She wanted to find Nuang, but, at the same time, she hoped she never would. She buried her face against Laht's chest and cried.

He held her for a minute then pulled away. "Listen to me Somjit. I love you, but it's time for this to an end. Not us, but our situation with Nuang and her baby. The longer you and I and little Tippawan live as a family, the harder it will be for everyone."

Somjit was quiet for minute then said, "I know you're right, but I'm so afraid that man will come and take her away and I will never see her again."

"I don't know who the man is, but he clearly isn't Tippawan's father. Maybe he isn't even Nuang's husband. For all we know he is some crackbrain who happens to know Nuang. I don't think he will come around again."

"Who knows what a crazy person might do?" Somjit responded.

Her comment gave him pause. She was truly scared. Actually, he was too, but he couldn't let it show. "If that man ever comes close to you or the baby again, it will be the last time. I think we should leave Chiang Mai for a few days. We can go to Phitsanulok. Maybe someone at the temple has seen Nuang, or knows where she went. We can stay at my parents' house. I want them to meet you."

The thought of meeting his parents terrified her almost as much as the cabby. She knew it would have to happen sooner or later if she and Laht stayed together, but she wasn't ready, not yet. "Teeluk," she whispered, "can we stay at a hotel?"

Laht laughed despite the situation. "Yes, we can stay at a hotel."

She glanced down at baby Tippawan and then back up at Laht. "Can we leave now?"

Her worry was contagious. He looked up at the door. "Pack our things while I make a couple of calls. We'll leave as soon as you're ready."

~~~

When Surat left Somjit and the baby that same afternoon, he drove aimlessly through the streets of Chiang Mai. Anger and depression twisted his mind into a worthless pile of elephant dung. Images of Nuang having sex with a hairy, stinking farang sifted through the mayhem inside his head. As clear as day, he could see her eagerly taking an oversized penis into her mouth, and then helping guide it into her womanhood. He could hear her moan in sexual pleasure. He watched as the farang exploded his seed into his wife.

"Noooooo!" he screamed at the top of his lungs and pulled the taxi to a stop. He slumped over the steering wheel and smashed his fist against the dashboard. Tears burned his eyes and streamed down his face. It was the first time Surat had ever cried as a grown man.

In a while his sobs gave way to nausea and he vomited at the side of the road. Afterward he felt empty and numb. He steered back into the flow of traffic and headed home. Now more than ever he wanted to find Nuang. He didn't want to hit her, shout at her, or even hate her; he only wanted her to see how much she had hurt him. Then he would leave her alone.

Surat hadn't touched alcohol in months, but he needed a drink now. He stopped at a small outdoor restaurant and ordered a beer. He felt its impact within minutes. His earlier images of Nuang with her farang lover returned to haunt him. He almost cried but didn't. Several beers later, the scenes from his imaginary world had become facts in his mind. His mood sank from hurt to loathing. At eight-thirty he paid his tab and left the bar.

Chapter 35

Isara glanced at the clock hanging on the far wall. It was after three and as was typical for his Friday afternoons no appointments were scheduled for the rest of the day. He closed the open folder and stacked it on the corner of the desk with the others. Wasana would make sure the folders were delivered to the appropriate people for follow-up.

He gazed around the office. It was stark to the point of ugliness. The room had been stripped bare two weeks earlier in anticipation of a makeover, but like everything in Thailand it was late. His *new* office would be a combination of old favorites, new furniture, and his annual rotation of Thai paintings. He truly missed some of the decorations, such as the large wooden elephants that stood constant guard at either side of his desk. He had bought them the first day he opened for business and believed they brought him good luck. They were Pajeeka's favorites, too.

Pajeeka! He had been trying not to think about her, but it hadn't been working. It was like his mind found reasons to dredge her to the forefront every hour or so. She had been gone for almost a week and hadn't yet checked in. He wondered if sending her to Pattaya had been a bad idea. He knew her background with the drugs, alcohol, and prostitution. Pattaya was the last place she needed to be—the temptations might be more than she could handle. He shook the thought from his head. Pajeeka was a strong-willed woman and she had walked away from that life once already; she wouldn't backslide. He dismissed the whole idea.

He picked up the stack of folders and left his office. He paused at Wasana's desk long enough to instruct her who should get what file, and then continued his way to the elevator. Wasana caught up with him just before he stepped inside the lift.

"You have a phone call. It's Pajeeka."

Isara hurried back to his office. "Hello," he said into the phone. "Where have you been? What took you so long contact me?"

Pajeeka's sighed noisily. "The impossible is ever easy. Sometimes it takes longer than anyone would expect. And I'm fine, thank you for asking."

Isara sighed back. "It's just that I was worried about you. Have you had any luck?"

"I have found the woman named Anya," she answered. "She has agreed to meet you tomorrow afternoon. I'm sorry for such short notice, but she was hard to find, and getting her to meet with you was almost impossible. When I mentioned your name, she looked like she had seen a ghost. What is that all about?"

Isara took a second to compose his response. He understood her prying, but it annoyed him nonetheless. "I already told you it's personal. Did you find the woman named Nuang? Was she with Anya?"

"No, I haven't seen Nuang. If she's in Pattaya, she isn't with Anya. Maybe her bus ticket to Pattaya was nothing but a ruse to fool anyone who might come looking for her. She's smart enough to invent a trick like that. I assume you'll be here tomorrow?"

He glanced at his watch. It was too late to catch a flight, but he could be there by midnight if he went by car and if he didn't run into any traffic delays. "Reserve me a room at the Royal Cliff, and one for my driver at the hotel where you're staying."

"Yes sir," she said answered smartly, a touch of sarcasm in her voice. She hung up the phone without waiting for a response.

He knew from her tone that she resented his double standard with the hotels, but he had an image to maintain. She knew that as well as anyone.

For the second time in less than five minutes he stopped at Wasana's desk. "Call my driver and tell him to go home and pack for a short holiday. Have him meet me at my house in thirty minutes."

"Will you be gone long? Where are you going?" Wasana asked, and then quickly added to cover her nosiness. "In case I need to reach you."

"You can call me on my cell phone. If that doesn't work, you can reach me at the Royal Cliff in Pattaya. I should be back by Monday."

"Do you need me to pull any client files?"

Isara frowned at her left-handed prying. "This is personal business."

"I'll call your driver right away."

Isara rode the elevator to street level and took a taxi home.

Anya! As recent as ten minutes earlier, he had hoped that Nuang might have gone to Anya's house. Clearly it had been a false hope. He suspected that the missing wooden elephants had affected his intuitive skills.

Isara wondered if his self-serving interference amounted to stepping into a nest of scorpions. Was he concerning himself with things that really didn't matter to anyone except himself? Would his prying hurt others more than his family pride would be saved? He would forget the whole thing and leave it alone, except for Laht being involved with that woman Somjit, who was involved with Nuang, who was involved with Surat, the son of Anya.

He had always figured that Laht's affair with Somjit would end when he left the temple, and for a few days it had; but it didn't last. Deep inside Isara had always known it would turn out this way, despite his hopes to the contrary.

Anya! Now that he knew Nuang wasn't with her, he had nothing to gain from meeting with the woman. All he had were things to tell her, things she probably didn't want to hear. She could tell him to go to hell as easily as she might thank him. He would find out tomorrow.

~~~

J. F. Gump

Laht and Somjit were in Phitsanulok two days before Laht finally convinced her that his parents would be happy to meet her and would accept her as part of their family. Meanwhile they didn't do much except keep to themselves inside the hotel. Somjit insisted she wasn't feeling well, but he knew she was afraid she might see ghosts from her past if they went out. On Thursday Laht drove to the temple alone to ask if anyone had seen or heard from Nuang. No one had.

It was late on Friday when they went to his father's office. His father never had appointments on Friday afternoons so there would be no interruptions; it would be a good time to introduce Somjit. They arrived at four-thirty. Somjit was such a bundle of nerves that Laht took little Tippawan from her for fear that she might drop the baby. He handed her back just before they entered the office.

Wasana, Isara's secretary, brightened when she saw Laht. "What a surprise. Isara didn't tell me you were coming."

"I didn't even know it myself," Laht said. "If my father isn't busy, I would like to see him for a few minutes."

"He's not here. He left over an hour ago. You can call him on his cell phone." Wasana's eyes shifted to Somjit and back.

"I'll just go to his house. I can talk to him there." He smiled toward Somjit and the baby. "Mother will want to meet my future wife, too."

Wasana focused on Somjit. " Congratulations young lady. I have known Laht since he was a boy. You're a lucky girl." She turned back to Laht. "Your father isn't at home either. He went to Pattaya on business. He should be back by Monday."

Laht's expression showed both disappointment and relief. "Thank you, Wasana." He nodded toward Somjit, "I guess I will wait until Monday to tell everyone."

"You should tell your mother right away, she will be surprised and happy. Your lady is very beautiful."

"I need to tell father first. That is the polite thing to do."

Wasana smiled. "Then I will see you Monday morning? Your father doesn't have an appointment until nine-thirty."

Laht smiled back. "Yes, Monday. By the way, her name is Somjit." He noticed Wasana staring at little Tippawan. "We're babysitting for a friend," he added to put her nosiness to rest.

After leaving his father's office, Laht and Somjit had an early dinner at the hotel. They were back in their room by six o'clock.

Laht had been thinking since talking with Wasana. He knew his father sometimes went to Pattaya for business, but he couldn't remember a single time when he had ever gone there on a weekend. He wondered if his father had really gone to Pattaya on business, or if he had found a need for younger women in his middle age. The thought of his father having sex with someone besides his mother didn't surprise him, but it did irritate him.

By ten o'clock, he had decided that something wasn't right about his father's trip to Pattaya. Perhaps it was sexually inspired, or perhaps it wasn't. By the time they turned off the TV and the lights, he was convinced that his father had located Nuang but for some reason hadn't told him. "Somjit," he whispered in the dark, "tomorrow we are going to Pattaya.".

Chapter 36

Weeks had passed since Nuang and Jon had bared their most personal secrets. Their confessions had changed their relationship and it was for the better. Unspoken limits had been set and both respected them. Without the expectations of physical intimacy, they had become more comfortable in each other's company. There was lots of warmth and laughter and they easily became friends. Still, their words and smiles and body language churned with an undertow of desire waiting to explode.

Today was Friday which meant she and Jon would go to a nearby German restaurant for dinner and then to a movie at the Big C. After that they would go to Bud's for ice cream. That had become their Friday night routine and Nuang enjoyed it.

She was deciding what she would wear when the phone rang. She jumped at the unexpected sound. It was the first time it had rang while she was in the condo alone. She wasn't sure whether to answer it or not. It wasn't her phone and she had no idea who might be calling. For all she knew it might be Jon's ex-fiancée. The ringing persisted. Finally, she picked up the receiver.

"Hello," she said hesitantly.

"Hello, Nuang. This is Jon. I have a surprise for you, a good surprise. I'll tell you about it at dinner. Put on that new dress I bought you last week. Tonight we're going to a fancy restaurant."

Nuang was excited by Jon's excitement. "Do you mean the German restaurant?"

"No, I mean a really fancy restaurant. This surprise is so good that it calls for a special dinner."

"What surprise could be that good?"

"I will tell you later. I'll be home by six."

Nuang spent the rest of the day primping and preening. The butterflies in her stomach made her feel giddy. *A surprise!* She wondered what it was. *A good surprise!* She loved and hated surprises at the same time. *A surprise so good it calls for a special dinner.* Her heart fluttered in anticipation. By the time Jon arrived, she was dressed and ready to go.

"Wow!" he said, when he entered the condo. "You look absolutely beautiful."

"Khop khun mahk ka," she smiled. "What's your surprise?"

Jon laughed, "Later, after dinner. I'll get cleaned up now."

At seven o'clock they arrived at the new upscale restaurant at the Royal Garden Plaza. By eight o'clock they had finished dinner.

"What's your surprise?" Nuang asked at a quiet moment. "Can you tell me now?"

"Okay, but I need to explain something first. Before I met you, I tried to learn Thai but couldn't. For some reason, the little games we play while you teach have made it easier for me to learn. Some of the men at work are surprised at how much Thai I've learned so fast. When they asked how I did it, I told them I had the best teacher in Thailand.

"Guess what happened; they want you to teach them Thai, too. But that's not the surprise. The surprise is that our company is going to pay for everything, forty thousand baht per month. It will only be for six months but it's a start. If the men learn, other companies will do the same thing. In fact, tomorrow I'm calling a friend, an American who works at the oil refinery near Rayong. He might be interested in private lessons. Maybe he will say no, but it never hurts to ask. What do you think?"

Nuang wasn't sure what to think. She wasn't sure what she had expected, but she hadn't expected to get a job making forty thousand baht per month. Dear Buddha! With that much money she could afford a nice apartment here in Pattaya for her baby and Somjit. They could come as soon as she received her first check. Her excitement soared. "Do you think I can do it? I'm not a teacher. There's much I don't know about English."

He looked toward the waiter, "Kaw thort krup, excuse me," he said. "Ghep tung krup. My check please."

The waiter nodded and hurried away.

He turned back to Nuang, "Yes, but there is much you know about Thai. And if you can teach me, you can teach anyone."

For a moment Nuang thought she would cry. She tried to speak but no words came. "Thank you," she mouthed with her lips.

Jon saw her emotions. "Let's get out of here. I'll buy us a nightcap at one of the bars by the condo."

Neither spoke as they rode north on Second Road. Nuang replayed the evening through her head. She didn't understand why Jon was helping her so much, but she was glad he was doing it. Jon was one of the kindest men she had ever met. Truly he was a gentleman. She felt a strong need to give him something in return, but she had nothing to give except herself, and they had both agreed not to do that again. But now, after what Jon had just done, her resolve faded like a wisp of incense on a monsoon wind.

As they passed the Pattaya Klang intersection, she turned to Jon, "Have you heard about that new medication for men?"

"What are you talking about? You mean the stuff that makes your hair grow?"

"It makes something grow, but not your hair." She felt herself blush. "It's called Viagra or something like that."

"Oh," Jon said. He had heard of it, but he had never tried it. He had always been too embarrassed to talk to his doctor about his problem. "I thought we agreed to just be friends."

"Yes, we did," her blush deepened. "I was only making conversation."

Jon knew she was lying. He wondered if she was going to try to seduce him again. He wished she would. Tonight he felt closer to her than he had felt toward any woman in a very long time. What he had felt for Julie didn't compare. As much as he had been pretending it wasn't happening, he was falling in love with Nuang.

Memories of the night they'd made love drifted through his head and left a comforting glow in its wake. Maybe Nuang would be the magic that would make him whole again.

"When I find the right woman," he said, "I will see a doctor. Maybe I'll do it tomorrow."

Nuang squeezed his hand and smiled, "You're a good man Jonathan Yeager."

They stopped at the Sandy Bar for their nightcap. Jon practiced his newest Thai phrases with the bar-girls and their earlier conversation was forgotten.

Jon had just ordered their second round of drinks when Nuang felt eyes at her back. It was an eerie feeling that made her shiver. She hadn't felt anything like it since her baby was born. She turned to see who or what was staring at her. It took but an instant to recognize her brother's face. Immediately, she looked away, wondering if he had seen her.

"Do you see the Thai man behind me?" she asked Jon, as calmly as she could.

He glanced over his shoulder. "I don't see any Thai men anywhere."

Nuang turned around and looked, the man was gone. She stood from her seat, ran to the sidewalk, and searched up and down the street. No one! She wondered if she had been hallucinating. Maybe her sickness was returning. She put her hand to her head; it felt normal. She sensed Jon standing beside her. She looked up at him.

"Are you okay?" he asked. "You look as if you've seen a ghost. Who do you think you saw?"

"A man from my nightmares," she answered. "I'm ready to go home. Suddenly I don't feel so good."

Jon paid their bill and they left the bar. He asked if she wanted him to hold her for a while and she said yes. They lay together in spooning fashion, but Jon didn't make any advances and she was happy for that. She waited for the voices to return but they didn't. Her dreams were nightmares of imminent doom.

Chapter 37

At eight o'clock that same evening, Peebanlat "Anan" Bongkot finished his last sales call. The hotel manager had made him wait until he was sure the Friday evening dinner guests were being properly attended before taking time to meet with him.

Anan's wait had been a complete waste of time. The manager had declined to renew his advertising. It was the third customer he had lost this month. Anan had barely kept his anger hidden behind a professional posture.

The last few months had been disastrous for his business. After struggling for four years to make his business grow, he was practically back to where he had started. The upswing he had experienced when his sister Math had been selling for him had eroded completely during the last year. He would be lucky if he could cover next month's costs. If he lost another major account, he would lose his business. The time and money he had spent traveling to Phitsanulok to talk to his mother about Nuang's disappearance hadn't helped anything, either.

That thought reminded him of his promise to his family. They had some notion that Nuang might come to Pattaya, but Anan doubted it. If she wanted to hide from everyone she knew, she would go to Bangkok or Phuket or some other city where no one knew her. Nuang wasn't so stupid that she would come to Pattaya, but he had promised to look for her and he would keep his word.

During the day, while taking care of business, Anan had looked at every woman he passed. In the evenings he had cruised the bars along the main streets of Pattaya City searching for Nuang. He'd never seen his sister but he had seen a lot of young

Thai women laughing and kissing farangs in public. It wasn't polite and he hated it.

For the last week he had been stopping at a different cluster of popular bars each night and wandered from one establishment to another, never ordering anything and never staying more than a few seconds at any one place. He knew he would never find Nuang, even if she were in Pattaya. There were too many places for one woman to be, and too many places for one man to search. He felt stupid for even trying. He had already decided this would be the last night he would waste his time looking for his sister. He started his motorcycle and drove from the hotel parking lot.

He rode south on Beach Road wondering where he should stop. At Pattaya Klang he turned left for one block then joined the flow of traffic heading north on Second. He had already stopped at the most popular places from Central Road to South Pattaya, but he hadn't yet stopped at the cluster of beer bars on Soi 2. That was where he would go tonight. It would only take a few minutes to search the area and he would be home by nine o'clock.

Three blocks south of Soi 2 he neared the condominium complex where his sister Math had once lived with her farang lover. A few beer bars lined Second Road directly in front of the condos. They weren't crowded tonight, but then they never were. He had never bothered to stop at these bars because he could see everyone and everything clearly from the street.

As he drove past, he scanned the faces of the bar-girls and their customers. That's when he saw her, sitting beside a farang at one of the bars farthest from the sidewalk. At first he thought his eyes were playing tricks on him, but after a second look he knew it was Nuang. He pulled to the side of the road and pretended to adjust his motorcycle helmet.

He wasn't sure what to do. If Nuang had been alone, it would have been an easy decision, but the farang complicated things. Who was the man and why was she with him? His conclusion left him cold. Nuang had moved to Pattaya and become a bar-girl. The farang was her customer for the night. His sister had stooped to peddling her body for money.

For a moment Anan thought he would be sick. Then he wondered about her baby. Most bar-girls who had children left them at home with relatives while they plied their trade. At least those were the rumors he had heard. He didn't know any bar-girls personally, only their faces from passing them on the street. Nuang hadn't left her baby with relatives and it wasn't with her now. That narrowed things down. Either the baby was alone in some cockroach-infested dump or she had given it away or worse. He flinched at the thought.

Surat had mentioned that Nuang had been acting strange during her last months of pregnancy. Extreme paranoia, hearing voices, and other things that weren't normal for Nuang, or anyone else for that matter. If she was capable of walking away from everything she had ever known, maybe she was capable of destroying every link to her past, including her baby.

Anan drove up the street far enough to be out of sight and then parked his motorcycle. He propped his helmet on the seat, padlocked the rear wheel, and walked back toward where Nuang was sitting. He stopped at the edge of the building next to the bar area and peeked around the corner.

They were still there, less than twenty meters away. They talked and smiled but they didn't touch each other. Neither seemed drunk, although the man was drinking a beer.

Anan's mind raced, rehearsing what to say when he confronted her. He wished she wasn't with the farang. He took a step in Nuang's direction.

At that moment she turned and looked directly at him. The shock in her eyes stopped him in mid stride. He fought down a powerful urge to run. He stood frozen for what seemed like hours. When Nuang looked away, he ran. He bypassed his motorcycle and ducked up a dirt lane at the end of the block. His heart pounded from the exertion. Suddenly he felt foolish for running away. He felt even more foolish for trying to approach Nuang in the first place.

He had reacted on impulse, a stupid thing to do. He should have called his mother and his sisters in Phitsanulok immediately to let them know he had found Nuang. But he hadn't really found her; he had only seen her. He didn't know where she lived or if she was even with the farang. He needed to find out where she went when she left the bar.

A street vendor with a cart of food and hot charcoal passed down Second Road. Anan followed the smells of cooking to the mouth of the dirt alley. He spied around the corner; neither Nuang nor the farang were among the people on the sidewalk. He hurried to the street and fell in behind the food vendor. They arrived at the bars in less than a minute. Nuang and the farang were gone.

Anan stepped from behind the cart for a better view. He glimpsed their backs as they entered the condo parking lot. When they were out of sight, he hurried toward the building. He stopped when he saw the security guard. He smiled at the guard then turned and walked away. From the corner of his eye he saw Nuang and the farang enter the elevator and all of his doubts became facts.

He knew Nuang had seen him just minutes earlier and figured she would disappear again as soon as she finished with the farang. It was up to him to make sure she didn't. First he would call his mother in Phitsanulok. Then he would find a hiding place where he could keep an eye on everyone who entered or left the condo.

He went to the bar where Nuang and her farang had been sitting. He took a seat and ordered a Lipo. He would need all of the power he could get to stay awake for the night. While he waited for the girl to bring his drink, he called his mother.

"I have found Nuang and she's living with a farang." he said very plainly when she answered. "Call my cell phone when you arrive in Pattaya." He hung up without waiting for her response. He knew she would be on the next bus south. The thought made him smile.

Next he called Surat, Nuang's husband, his brother-in-law. He had never liked Surat much, but he wasn't sure why. Maybe it was because his mother had never liked Surat. He had even picked up his mother's despicable habit of taunting the man. He knew it made his sister angry, but he did it anyway.

"I have found your wife," he said, when Surat answered. "She is in Pattaya and she is with a farang. A big, ugly, hairy, farang. I bet his penis would make two of yours. Come to Pattaya and I'll show you. Nuang is at the condos on Second Road, just south of The Alcazar Show. Call me when you arrive."

Anan hung up before Surat had a chance to respond. He could almost see Surat going crazy with jealousy while deciding whether to steal his company's taxi again or not. He couldn't help but laugh.

Finished with his calls, he turned off his cell phone. He couldn't remember when he had last charged the batteries and he needed to conserve power. After finishing his drink, he found a place where he could keep an eye on the entrance of the condo without being seen.

He wondered which floor Nuang and her farang lover were on. Thoughts of his sister having sex with a shit-farang made his skin crawl. It was after midnight when he fell asleep in his hiding place.

Chapter 38

Nui had just drifted off to sleep when she was awakened by Anan's call. It took a moment for her to understand what he'd said. He ended the call before she could respond. She called Anan's cell number but got a busy signal. She waited a minute and then called again. This time she got a message saying that the phone was either turned off or out of range.

Anan's cryptic message puzzled her. He said he had found Nuang, but he didn't mention talking to her or how she was or anything about her baby. He also said something about Nuang being with a farang but he must be mistaken; Nuang would never be with a farang. Something wasn't right, but she wasn't sure what.

She dialed Anan's number every few minutes for the next half hour. Finally she decided she was wasting time. Anan had told her to call him when she arrived in Pattaya. She didn't know anything about Pattaya but her daughter Itta did. She would take Itta with her.

She glanced at her watch; it was nine o'clock. Itta had gone to her sister's house earlier and hadn't returned. Neet didn't have a phone so there was no way to reach either of them. She stepped outside, slipped on her sandals, and hurried to Neet's house.

"Anan has found Nuang in Pattaya," she announced breathless as she burst through the door. "We must go there right away."

She repeated what Anan had said, even the part about Nuang being with a farang.

Itta knew Pattaya best, so she laid out their plans.

~~~

Surat had fallen into an angry depression after confronting the woman with Nuang's baby. For the last three days he had gone to his job but had spent more time drinking than he did working. Today he had his first beer at two o'clock and was staggering drunk by eight. By luck more than skill, he had maneuvered his taxi home. His cell phone rang as he unlocked his door.

"Hello," he slurred.

"I have found your wife." It was Nuang's brother Anan. "She is in Pattaya and she is with a farang."

The words stung at Surat's ears. "Arai na? What?"

"A big, ugly, hairy, farang. I bet his penis would make two of yours." Anan sounded almost happy at his pronouncement. "Come to Pattaya and I'll show you. Nuang is at the condos on Second Road, just south of The Alcazar Show. Call me when you arrive." The phone clicked dead.

Surat's head spun. Everything he had suspected now rang with undeniable truth—Nuang had a farang lover. In a jealous, drunken frenzy he turned his house into a shambles. By the time his rage ebbed, clothes were scattered everywhere and Nuang's sewing machine, her most prized possession, lay busted on the floor.

He stepped back and stared, amazed at the damage he had done. He barely remembered doing any of it. A strip of aluminum foil swung from the ceiling. He snatched it down, wadded it into a tight ball, and threw it across the room. On impulse he gathered up the clothes that belonged to Nuang and loaded them into the taxi. He didn't want anything near him that belonged to her. He didn't want to be reminded every day of her lies and infidelities.

He shut and locked his house, and then drove south toward Phitsanulok, Pattaya, and Nuang. He knew his boss would fire him, but he didn't care.

Surat was halfway to Phitsanulok before his anger induced high slipped away and exhaustive depression filled the void. It was all he could do to keep his eyes open. Twice he had awakened just in time to steer his car back onto the highway. He stopped at a gas station to fill his tank and to get a few minutes rest.

It was after two o'clock in the morning when the night manager ordered him to leave. He hadn't meant to sleep so long and was glad when the man awoke him, even if he wasn't very polite about it.

Bleary eyed, he steered his car onto the road heading south. He arrived in Phitsanulok at five o'clock in the morning.

Surat still hadn't decided exactly what he was going to do with Nuang's clothes and things. Last night, when he left Chiang Mai, he was determined to go to his mother-in-law's house and dump everything on her doorstep. He had even practiced what he would say to the old witch. Now that the time had come, he didn't want to confront her. Nui had a sharp tongue that could lash with the best of them. Despite his mood he wasn't up to doing verbal battle with Nuang's mother.

He decided to go to Neet's house instead. He would dump Nuang's things there and tell Neet everything he knew. He would also make sure she understood exactly how he felt about Nuang and the things she had done.

It was still dark when he parked in front of Neet's house. He was surprised to see her door open and the lights on so early in the morning. The rest of the neighborhood was still asleep. Maybe it was for the better, he thought, at least he wouldn't have to wake her. He gathered an armload of clothes from the back seat and started toward the house. As he neared the doorway, Nui stepped out. Their bodies bumped, but not hard.

"What are you doing here?" she demanded, seeing who it was. There was no smile on her face. She wondered if Anan had called him, too. She was sure he had, else he wouldn't be in Phitsanulok at this time of the day. "You almost knocked me down."

He cringed at his recognition of her voice. She was the last person he wanted to see. "Where's Neet?"

"That's none of your business. What sort of trash are you bringing in here?"

"It's your daughter's trash. I want it out of my house and I want her out of my life." His words came out bitter-cold. He dumped the clothes on the ground.

"Why would you do that to your own wife? Nuang is the best woman you'll ever know."

Surat stared at her. Ever since he and Nuang had met, Nui had been nothing but a pain in his ass. She had never approved of his marriage to her daughter, and there had never been a formal wedding with family and relatives to help celebrate. If Nui had ever said one kind word to him, it was because she wanted something. He didn't really hate her; he was just sick and tired of the whole family. "Don't play stupid with me. Anan called me and I'm sure he called you. But I know something you don't, and it's going to kill you."

Nui tensed. "If you know anything, it will be the first time in your life."

"I have found Nuang's baby and now I know the truth."

"What do you mean? You're not making sense. Is the baby okay?"

"No, the baby's not okay," he spit his words at her. "The baby is farang!"

"Oh dear Buddha," Nui paled and stumbled toward a chair.

Surat didn't move to help her. Instead he picked up his verbal assault. "Nuang has been having sex with farangs and now she has given birth to a farang baby. She probably doesn't even know which farang is the father." His volume increased to a shout, "Your daughter is nothing but a fucking whore."

Nui's face burned red and her anger exploded. "It's your own mother who was the whore."

Surat glared. "You old lizard, I should hurt you for that."

"I'm telling the truth," she screamed.

"You're a liar," he screamed back. "My mother was never a whore. She was married to a Thai soldier. He died in battle; he was a hero. She died giving birth to me. It's true because my grandmother said it was true." He lowered his voice to a snarl.

"Don't ever try to pass the sins of your daughter onto my mother."

"You're a fool," she hissed back. "I'm going to tell you some truths before lives get ruined."

"Lives have been ruined already and you know it," he retorted in disdain. "What do you know about truth? You have spent your whole life twisting simple truths into grotesque lies. You have done everything you could to make me look like an idiot and a fool. You never even accepted me as your daughter's husband. To you I was nothing but something to be mocked and scorned. Nothing I did ever pleased you. You have always hated me and I don't even know why. What did I ever do to you?"

"You were born the son of a farang," Nui spat out the words. "You are the piece of foreign bird shit that married my daughter."

"Fuck you," Surat hissed through clinched teeth. "I am not foreign bird shit. My mother and father were Thai and so am I." Veins pulsed at his temples. "Fuck you and your whole family." He turned to leave.

"Fuck your mother," she screamed back.

Surat stopped. His hands balled into fists.

Nui ignored his threat. She spoke fast and harsh, "I know your mother. We grew up together. It was during the Vietnam war. Your mother slept with half of the American soldiers stationed here before one of them was stupid enough to fall in love with her. He got your mother pregnant and you were born. You are half farang. If Nuang gave birth to a half-farang baby, it came from your seed. My daughter is not a whore."

Surat looked down at his hands. They weren't as dark as some who drove for a living. Neither was his face. He had always taken pride in having the complexion of the upper class. Other than his naturally light skin, he was Thai, 100% Thai. If Nuang had given birth to a half-farang baby, it wasn't his. "You're a liar."

He ran to his car and threw what was left of Nuang's possessions into the street. He gave Nui one last sneer and then drove away. He headed south toward Pattaya. Nui's words haunted him every kilometer.

Neet arrived home less than two minutes after Surat had left. Nui was standing on the front stoop staring at the clothes, handbags, and junk jewelry littering the street. Her face was frozen into a mask of shock and depression.

"Mama, are you okay?" Neet was the first to speak.

"No," Nui answered. "I'm not okay. We must get to Pattaya right away. Did you get our tickets? What time do we leave?"

Neet looked away from her mother's penetrating stare. "We couldn't get a bus with three open seats until tomorrow. Itta used the money to buy herself a plane ticket to Bangkok. She has gone to your house to pack her suitcase. She will be in Pattaya by tonight. I hope you aren't angry."

Nui gave her a disapproving stare but bit her tongue. "Maybe it's just as well. Itta knows Pattaya and I don't. I would only slow her down." Images of Surat's angry face burned in her mind. "Let's go to the temple and pray for her safety, and for Nuang's safety, too." Her instincts told her Nuang would need all the prayers she could get.

Chapter 39

Laht and Somjit checked out of their hotel at six o'clock that same morning. Ten minutes later they were beyond the city limits of Phitsanulok and heading south. The kilometers rolled past in quiet monotony.

They were just north of Bangkok when the rain came. The traffic continued to move but at a much slower pace. Laht drove as fast as he felt comfortable, but stayed in the slow lane and let the more daring drivers pass him by. Glancing in his rear view mirror, it was clear that others agreed with his precaution. Trailing him was a Honda, a Mercedes, and a string of other vehicles.

As they cleared the first tollbooth on the Bangkok freeway, Somjit announced that she had to stop. Laht was irritated that she hadn't thought of that before but said nothing. He cut through a narrow gap in the traffic and exited the highway. At a gas station Somjit took her pause while Laht bought them milk and snacks.

It took forty-five minutes of stop and go traffic before they reentered the freeway. It was bumper-to-bumper madness that inched forward only slightly faster than the vehicles on the snarled streets below. He glanced at his watch: it was almost four. At the rate he was moving he wouldn't be in Pattaya for hours. For that matter, he might not even be out of Bangkok for hours. He sighed deep and glared at the long line of cars ahead.

~~~

Surat was away from his mother-in-law and driving south by six o'clock. Traffic was light and he made good time. About eighty kilometers north of Bangkok, he stopped to stretch and buy fuel.

He hadn't slept much the night before and he was tired, a little hung-over, too. He considered a nap but was afraid he wouldn't wake up any time soon if he slept. The sky had grown overcast, looking more like a long steady rain than a hit-and-run storm.

As he pulled back onto the highway, the first drop of rain splattered on his windshield. He raced along in the fast lane until he felt his tires hydroplane on the wet pavement. He edged his way behind a mini-van that was moving at a more cautious pace. He stayed in the impromptu convoy until he reached the first tollbooth on the Bangkok freeway. There he flared away from the others, looking for the shortest line to pay his toll. It was congested, but he was through in less than two minutes.

As he exited the tollbooth, he glanced to his right looking for an opening in the flow of traffic. In the car next to him he saw the woman from Chiang Mai, the woman with Nuang's baby. The man was there, too, driving the car.

Surat's mind raced. Why were they here in Bangkok? It occurred to him that maybe he was the reason they were here. Maybe they were running away from him. Maybe he had scared them so much that they were afraid to stay in Chiang Mai. Then a second thought came to him. Maybe they were headed to wherever Nuang was hiding; maybe they had found her. He remembered the man saying that his father was good at finding people. He squeezed his taxi into the lane directly behind their fancy Toyota.

He had followed them for less than two kilos when the man suddenly veered to his left and exited the freeway. Surat tried to follow and almost had an accident in the process.

"Shit," he said aloud, and then regained his composure. It really didn't matter if he caught up with them or not. All they had was the baby, and it wasn't his. They might have led him to Nuang, but maybe they wouldn't have, either. Losing them was no great loss, except now he would have to deal with Nuang's brother Anan. It wasn't a thought he relished, but one he could live with as long as he got the chance to tell Nuang to fuck-off in person.

Chapter 40

Nuang awoke on Saturday morning to the sound of the condo door opening and closing. She glanced up at the clock; it was after ten. She turned toward the noise and saw Jon standing in the doorway. He was smiling.

"I have another surprise," he said.

"Your company wants to give me a car?" she joked.

Jon laughed. "Even better, I hope." He pulled a small plastic bag from his pocket. Inside were five blue pills, diamond shaped.

"Are those drugs?"

"It's Viagra."

Nuang blushed as his shameless intentions unleashed a wave of hormones that left her tingling. "How does it work?"

"I don't know."

"I will take a shower."

"And I will take a Viagra." He slipped a pill into his mouth.

"Thank you, teeluk," Nuang giggled as she ran tip-toe to the shower.

She hurried through her bath and went back to the bedroom. "Is the pill working yet?"

"I don't know," Jon answered. "Maybe it won't work. I'll take a shower and give it some time."

"Okay, teeluk. I'll wait for you." She prayed to Buddha that the pill was potent.

Nuang allowed her imagination to run wild while she waited for Jon to return. She hadn't felt so sexually aroused since the night she practically raped him. But now she felt an emotional need as powerful as her physical desire. Both intensified with each passing second. She hoped the Viagra worked as advertised.

Nuang feigned nonchalance when Jon lay down beside her. In a moment she slid her arms around him.

"I would like it if you touched me," she urged, pulling his hand to her womanhood. She moaned softly as his fingers found their mark.

She moved her own hand to his manhood. It was swollen yet soft and flexible. *"Please dear Buddha,"* she said to herself in Thai. *"Please let the Viagra be magic."* Her prayers were answered as his penis grew larger and stiffened in her hand. She squirmed as his fingers rubbed incessantly at her clitoris.

"Please take me," she whispered.

Her heart pounded wildly as he slid between her legs and joined his body with hers.

Afterwards, Jon held her close and whispered loving things in her ear. His words made her happy inside. Later, when he told her he never wanted her to leave, she knew he meant it.

They make love twice again before the afternoon passed into early evening, each time was as passionate as the first. By the time the Viagra lost its effect, both glowed with a closeness far more intimate than friendship.

Nuang felt safe with Jon holding her tight in his arms. Her terror from the night before had faded as she allowed herself to believe that Jon would always be there to protect her. For the first time since running away from Chiang Mai, she felt at peace.

Later, when Jon suggested that they go out for dinner, a small pinprick of apprehension crept back inside, but when she looked into his eyes she knew everything would be okay. She spent the next hour making herself beautiful for Jon. Night had fallen by the time they left the condo.

~~~

Anan had spent most of most of that Saturday morning

sweating, shooing flies from his face, and battling the hordes of tiny ants that had taken a liking to his hands and clothes. He was hot, tired, and irritated. Except for the few times he'd dozed off, he had spent the night keeping an eye on the entrance to the condo.

It was possible Nuang had sneaked away while he slept, but more likely she was still inside getting her pussy reamed by the farang. The mental image triggered an erection. He got to his feet and moved about, forcing down the urge to masturbate. He looked at his watch; it was after noon.

At one o'clock he bought chicken and rice from a passing food cart. Shortly after two o'clock, he succumbed to his exhaustion and fell asleep.

Anan's afternoon nap was interrupted by an extreme fullness in his lower abdomen. A clammy sweat wet his face. He had experienced food poisoning before and knew what was coming. If it was bad enough, the next few hours would be misery. For the moment he needed a toilet and he needed it fast. He cursed the street vendor for selling him tainted food and sped his motorcycle toward the Amari Orchid Hotel.

Inside the hotel he went directly to the restrooms. The mess that poured from his body smelled worse than the entire Pattaya sewer system. Eventually his symptoms subsided and he felt almost normal. Gingerly he cleaned himself and left the toilet. He glanced at his watch—it was seven o'clock.

As Anan strolled through the hotel lobby, he noticed a familiar face at the bar. He was almost to the exit before he realized who the man was. His name was Mike Johnson, the farang lover of his dead sister Math and the person he blamed for her death. He couldn't imagine what the man was doing in Pattaya. Probably here looking to fuck any Thai girl who would go with his ugly farang ass; same as he had done to his sister. Suddenly he saw a chance to even things up; to return the hurt this farang has caused him and his family. He walked to where Mike sat and took a seat.

J. F. Gump

~~~

Mike had been cooped up in his hotel for three weeks. At first he had stayed inside because his ribs hurt so much that he could barely move, then later because he had become so engrossed in writing the life story of Math that he didn't want to leave his room. He was surprised by how much he had written—over 100,000 words if his word processor was correct. He was amazed at what could be accomplished when working fourteen hours a day.

He had finished the story's rough draft hours earlier and now he was bored stiff. His chest still hurt but less than before, and his ribs no longer popped when he took deep breaths. He figured he had healed enough to go out. He showered, shaved, and put on fresh clothes.

At seven o'clock he entered the open-air lounge of the Amari Orchid Hotel. It was the farthest he had ventured since breaking his ribs. He took a seat at the bar, ordered a beer, and then found a position that didn't put pressure on his left side.

Mike gazed casually at the other customers. All were westerners except for one Thai lady and she was sitting with a westerner. The overhead fans moved enough air to be felt, but not enough to chase away the heat. An annoying dampness gathered on his forehead and upper lip. The other faces in the lounge glistened with the same uncomfortable stickiness.

He wiped at his brow with a thin paper napkin. It came away less wet than he expected. He lit a cigarette, leaned back, and pretended that tropical heat didn't bother him. He knew the others were doing the same thing. He smiled to himself at the thought.

Halfway through his first beer he sensed someone sliding onto the stool next to his. Nonchalantly he turned to look at the newcomer expecting to see another round-eye. He was surprised to see a Thai man. He was even more surprised to realize he recognized the face.

"Sawasdee krup, Khun Mike," the Thai man said, his smile disarming. "Do you remember me? I am Anan, brother of Math."

"Of course I remember you." Shock was the mildest emotion racing through him. Anan was the last person he either expected or wanted to see. If it had been any of Math's family besides Anan, he would have been excited beyond joy. As hard as Math had tired to make him friends with her brother, it had never worked. Neither had budged beyond superficial politeness. It was a mutual dislike. Mike managed a smile. "How are you and your family?"

"We are fine," Anan answered. "I never expected to see you again. Can I buy you a drink?"

"No, let me buy. I can charge it to my company."

Mike waved down the barmaid. She took their order, put the beers in front of them, and then moved away.

"Chok dee krup, cheers and good luck," Mike said, and both men drank.

Anan wiped his mouth daintily, "Are you here for business or on holiday?"

"Business, but only for a month or two. Speaking of business, I hope yours is booming."

"My business is very good. I'm moving into a larger office next month." It was a lie. His business was falling apart and he was behind on all of his payments. But he wasn't about to let this farang know that. It might take the edge off of what he was about to say.

"That's great." Mike reached over and patted him on the shoulder.

Anan almost recoiled at the farang's touch but managed to keep his smile in place. "Thank you for asking."

"What about your sister Nuang. I hope she is well."

Anan tensed despite himself. "I haven't seen her for a while, but I think she's okay."

"That's good. Next time you talk to her, tell her I said hello."

"Sure, I will tell her. She will be pleased to know you asked about her. By the way, I have found some things that belonged to my sister Math. If you want, I'll bring them to you. I know you loved my sister. What I found are more your memories than mine."

Mike had images of unsent love letters, pictures, and other bits of sentimentality valuable only to him. "What did you find?"

Anan leaned forward and began his tale of lies. "Last month I was at my mother's house in Phitsanulok. I found a diary hidden in my brother's room. It belonged to Math. I'm embarrassed to say this, but I read what she wrote. I think it was meant to be private."

Mike's eyes opened wide. "Math kept a diary? She never told me. What did she write? Did she say anything about me?"

"Yes, she did." Anan paused and sighed deep, as if not sure of what to say. Finally he said, "It's hard for me to say this, but my sister never loved you." His lips formed a sadistic smile as he added, "She only wanted your money."

Mike blinked involuntarily. Of all the things he expected Anan to say, this wasn't one of them. All the little doubts he ever had about Math whipped through his head. Why had she loved him? Or had she ever loved him? She had been beautiful and half his age. She could have had any man she wanted yet she had picked him. For his money? Not likely! "You're lying."

Anan leaned away. They were unpredictable animals, these farangs. He wasn't sure how the man would react to his next words. "Then why did she write it in her diary? Why would she call you names like monkey, water buffalo, and lizard? Why would Math write insulting things about you while writing loving words about her Thai fiancé? Why would she say she wanted to marry you only so she could get everything you have? I wish I were lying but I'm not. I'm ashamed of my sister."

Mike felt his face burning. Not so much for what Anan had said, but for knowing it could be true. His ego denied it all. "I don't believe you," his voice rose involuntarily.

Anan stood from his seat. "I only wanted you to know the truth. I'm sorry to be the one to tell you, but I am the only one who could. You will thank me later." He took a step away. "I will bring you her diary tomorrow. Enjoy your stay in Thailand."

Anan hurried from the bar. He had hurt the farang more than he had hoped and it was good. He was bursting with pride at his performance. It was the best he had felt all day.

THAILAND - COLD RAIN

Mike didn't move. He wanted to chase Anan down and thrash him, make him say he was lying, but he couldn't force his legs into motion. His left arm worked superfine as he lifted his bottle from the bar and finished it in one long swallow. For a moment he thought he would be sick but it passed quickly. He waved toward the barmaid and she brought him another beer. This one he drank slower as he let his emotions digest what Anan had said.

Mike had heard all of the stories about Thai women taking advantage of westerner's perceptions of love. He knew how they pretended to love lonely farangs while fleecing them of everything they had. But Math hadn't been like that, had she?

The disease! His conversation with the boy on his flight from Detroit rippled through his thoughts. His not-so-little doubts grew to undeniable facts and he knew that Anan was telling the truth. What had once been love turned as cold and brittle as cheap china.

He signed for the drinks and went to his room. Suddenly he hated himself for coming back to Thailand, for thinking it could ever be the same, for imagining he was something special. Math, the woman he had loved with all his heart had made a fool of him. He couldn't believe he had been so gullible. She had only pretended to love him so he would give her whatever she wanted. Tomorrow Anan was bringing her diary as proof.

He wondered what else he would find in her diary. How many other farangs had she lied to just so she could get their money? He was sure he wasn't the only one. At that instant he crossed the thin line that divides love and hate. The transition was painful.

When his hurt eased, it was replaced by conflicting emotions he didn't understand. His thoughts seemed crystal clear but they made no sense. On one hand he wanted to pack his clothes and head to Bangkok. On the other he wanted to hit every bar in Pattaya and act like the ugliest American anyone had ever seen. It took only a second to make up his mind—he would get drunk. If he felt the same way in the morning, he would tell his fat-assed boss Jess Ankrom where to shove his fucking job and then he would go back to Pittsburgh. He washed the oily sheen from his face and left the hotel. It was eight o'clock.

He stopped at the first bar he came to and ordered a beer. It went down fast. He handed the waitress a hundred baht note then went to the bar next door. There he repeated the scene before heading south.

He kept his eyes pointed straight ahead as he passed Toy's Fun Bar. Toy's was the last place he wanted to be; he didn't want to see anyone he knew, not tonight. He caught a baht-bus south to Soi 6.

He had walked up and down Soi 6 a thousand times, but he had stopped here only once before and that had been a long time ago. It had been the day when he had first suspected Math might be a common bar-girl. That night she had convinced him he was wrong, but now, after his conversation with Anan, he knew his instincts had been correct. The whole mess disgusted him. He took a seat outside of a nondescript bar and ordered a Heineken. Out of habit he lit a cigarette. His beer arrived in a styrofoam cooler and his bill in a wooden cup. He downed the beer quickly and ordered another. A smiling girl came to sit next to him but he rudely chased her away. He scowled at the others and none came close.

~~~

After leaving the Amari Orchid lounge, Anan headed back to his hiding spot at the condos. He was less than halfway there when his insides went into spasms. This time it was more than a hot fullness. This time it was a gut wrenching pain accompanied by an urgent need to vomit.

He parked his motorcycle on the sidewalk by Big C Shopping Center and ran to the public toilet. The food poisoning escaped violently from both ends of his anatomy. Each time he tried to leave, the spasms stopped him. Anan was in the toilet for a long time. He didn't know it, but he was about to miss the very events he had set into motion.

Chapter 41

Itta's taxi from Bangkok airport barely missed the traffic jam of the year. It was a monstrous disaster, even for Bangkok which spent most of its existence in traffic gridlock. A heavy downpour had started it, and the steady rain which followed added to the misery. The streets flooded and the traffic snarled. Vehicles moved forward with alternating spurts of gas and brakes.

It was only by luck that her taxi was on the southern edges of Bangkok when the rains came. The radio announced multiple accidents on the stretch of freeway she had just passed. Itta didn't see any accidents, but the traffic slowed to a stop and crawl pace anyway. It finally smoothed out when the storm cleared and the taxi reached the far outer fringes of the city.

It was nearly seven o'clock before she arrived in Pattaya. She had the driver take her to a hotel on Soi 6. She knew it was a dump, but it was cheap.

Once in her room she called Anan's cell phone but got the irritating *"turned off or out of area"* message. She knew Anan was not out of Pattaya and not out of cell phone range. If his phone wasn't working, it was because he had intentionally turned it off or he'd forgotten to charge the battery. There was no way she would find Nuang without Anan's help. Pattaya isn't a large city, but it has more places to hide than a Bangkok whore has lies. She wasn't sure what to do, so she did nothing. She laid on the bed and tried to relax. Every few minutes she called Anan, but he never answered.

By eight o'clock, Itta had decided Anan wasn't going to answer his phone any time soon. She knew she should stay in her room and keep trying to reach Anan, but the thought of being back in

J. F. Gump

Pattaya after all these years held an irresistible attraction. Besides, she hadn't eaten since morning and she was starving.

She remembered the sidewalk vendors who set up evening food carts on Beach Road not far from her hotel. The thought of food made her mouth water. She put on new makeup and left the hotel. Fifteen minutes later she was sipping on a cold Coca-Cola and waiting for her dinner.

Beyond Beach Road, moonlight glimmered across the watery crests of the Gulf of Siam. In the distance she saw the running lights of a fishing boat. She had seen this scene a thousand times before. It was as if nothing had changed. Music—Thai music— drifted to her ears. It was coming from a beer bar just south of where she sat. She had been gone for years, but the way she felt at the moment it could have been yesterday. The roaring motorcycles, honking baht-buses, and hordes of sweating tourists were exactly as she remembered. The pink neons, the happy music, and the scent of sea air matched her fondest memories. The lights, the sounds, and the smells that are the essence of Pattaya had not changed. Its allure rushed through her.

When her food arrived, she gave it her undivided attention. She was tempted to order more but didn't. As she waited for her change, she considered what to do next. She had more than few baht in her pocket, certainly enough for a couple of drinks. It would be interesting to visit some of her old haunts. She didn't care about the farangs; she had had her fill of them a long time ago. But the idea that she might see faces from her past excited her. As anxious as she was to return to the Pattaya nightlife, she decided to do it slowly. She would have a drink at one of the quieter bars before going to Soi 2 and the places she knew best.

As she neared the intersection of Soi 6 and Second Road she noticed a farang sitting alone at a table outside one of the bars. When she got closer, she realized she knew him. He was the man who had sat next to her on her flight from Tokyo. The same man who had said something about her family in Phitsanulok. Her curiosity overcame common sense and she headed in his direction.

Chapter 42

Pajeeka met Isara at his hotel at five o'clock that same afternoon as planned. She had set his meeting for six so they had plenty of time. She was miffed that he had put her up at the Amari Hotel while he stayed at the Royal Cliff, but she kept her thoughts to herself.

Isara was unusually quiet as his driver steered them through the late afternoon traffic. Whatever reason Isara had for setting this meeting, it clearly upset him. Pajeeka couldn't recall ever seeing him so tense before.

When they arrived at Anya's house, Isara instructed Pajeeka and the driver to stay in the vehicle while he went inside alone. The meeting lasted more than two hours. When he finally came out of the house, his face was as expressionless as when he went in. She couldn't tell if his meeting had been good or bad. She wanted to ask but didn't. Whatever this was all about, it was none of her business. If he wanted her to know, he would tell her. If he didn't tell her, she would find out on her own. She was good at that sort of stuff.

On their way back go the hotel, Isara invited her to dinner.

"Thank you, but I cannot," she declined politely. "I want to see a few old friends—if they are still here that is."

"Stay out of trouble," he said, his tone demanding, his expression fatherly.

"Don't worry about me," she smiled. "Pattaya is like my second home."

"I know," Isara sighed. "That's what worries me."

Pajeeka smiled. "I'm sorry I can't have dinner with you, but I'll let you buy me breakfast in the morning." She turned to the driver, "I'll get out here." He braked to a stop, and she slid from the car. She waited until Isara was out of sight before heading toward the bars on Soi 8. She glanced at her watch—it was after eight.

She wandered through the maze of smiling ladies and drinking farangs hoping to see any of her old friends. Tonight was no different than the night before, or the night before that. Everyone she had ever known from her rowdy days at Soi 8 was gone. So were many of the bars which had been torn down to make way for a new hotel. She supposed it was some farang's idea of progress. She caught a baht-bus north toward her hotel.

~~~

Somjit's legal husband and the killer of her baby had been in Pattaya since the night he assaulted her. Nong sometimes wondered if Somjit and the baby had survived his attack. He thought about it more than he wanted, but he didn't let it bother him. It'd been her fault for getting pregnant in the first place.

Nong had been staying with a man he had known since their school days. His friend had lived in Pattaya for nearly two years and knew everything about the city. He worked as a dancer at one of the "boys clubs". Nong had been desperate when he arrived in Pattaya but he hadn't been that desperate. But his friend had contacts that Nong understood very well—yaba and ganja, speed and pot, meth and marijuana. Since arriving in Pattaya, Nong had made a living peddling drugs to the bar-girls and the farangs. It was easy compared to what his friend did for money.

Nong was on cloud nine this evening. He had just sold 15 grams of ganja and ten yaba pills to a farang for five times what he'd paid. He had even smoked a ganja cigarette with the man. His head buzzed high, his pockets were full, and he was thirsty. A cold Singha beer would taste real good.

He signaled the baht-bus driver to stop at the small bar complex on the right. He crossed Second Road and took a seat at a place called Music Lovers. There was one Thai woman and a few farangs sitting at the bar. No one noticed his arrival, not even the barmaids. They were too busy flirting with the foreigners. His drug-high shifted to irritation as the seconds ticked past without service. Finally he shouted at one of the girls. He ordered a beer when she looked in his direction. The farangs turned, stared at him briefly, and then continued their conversations with the girls.

It was been a minor incident, but it had ruined his good mood. He drank the beer fast hoping to recapture his euphoria. It didn't work. The alcohol only intensified his frustration. He searched his pockets and found a yaba pill. He downed it with a swallow of beer and waited for happiness. In a while he decided he needed something stronger to lift his mood and he wouldn't find it here. He decided to leave as soon as his beer was gone.

Chapter 43

The sun had set by the time Surat arrived in Pattaya. His unexpected encounter with the man and woman from Chiang Mai had faded during the two hour drive, but the thoughts still lingered.

Surat had never been to Pattaya before and didn't have a clue where Second Road was, much less a place called the Alcazar Show. He followed a sign pointing toward Beach Road. He knew Pattaya was a seaside resort and figured that was the direction he needed to go.

A minute later he maneuvered his taxi through a busy traffic circle. Ahead he could see water. In all he life he had never seen the ocean. The closest he'd ever been to the Gulf of Siam was downtown Bangkok. He pulled to the edge of the street and stared at the dark expanse of water. Moonlight glimmered across the low waves. In the distance, lights bobbed in the water. A boat, he imagined.

Surat exited the vehicle, crossed the street, and stopped at the edge of the sand. The air lay stagnant. Every picture he had ever seen of the beach clearly showed the trees swaying in the breeze, but typical of his luck he had come to Pattaya on the only day out of hundreds when the wind didn't blow.

He slipped his cell phone from his belt and called Anan. He got a recording saying it was either turned off or out of range. Surat sighed, irritated. Anan had told him to call when he arrived, but the lizard didn't even have the courtesy to leave his phone turned on. It crossed his mind that Anan had played a trick on him. Maybe he hadn't found Nuang at all. The thought chafed at his already worn nerves. He replayed his conversation with Nui in

Phitsanulok. If the old woman knew anything about Anan finding Nuang, she hadn't let it show. Surely Anan would have called Nui if no one else. The more he thought the more he was convinced that Anan had been lying. Before long he felt stupid for coming to Pattaya in the first place. There was no Nuang, no baby, or anything else for him here. Anan had cast the bait, and like a fool he had swallowed it. Anan was probably someplace drinking a beer and laughing his ass off.

What else had Anan said? Come to the condos on Second Road or something like that. It was possible that Anan had trouble with his phone. Surat decided he would go to the condos if he could find them. If Anan wasn't there, he would track him down and teach him a thing or two about lying to people. He took one last glimpse at the ocean and then turned away from the beach. A couple of motorcycle taxi drivers were parked at the curb. He walked to them.

"Excuse me. I'm looking for the condos on Second Road, the ones just south of the Alcazar Show. I've never been to Pattaya before and have no idea where I'm going. Can either of you help?"

"Do you have a cigarette?" one of the boys asked.

"I don't smoke," Surat answered. "But if you'll give me directions, I'll buy you a whole pack." He pulled sixty baht from his pocket.

The directions the boys gave were easy. The condos were on Second Road, on the right just beyond Soi 6, behind some beer bars. If he passed the hospital or the Big C, he had gone too far. If he came to a traffic circle, he should turn around and backtrack. It seemed easy enough. If the boys weren't lying, he would be there in minutes. Surat handed over the money, returned to his taxi, and drove south. He turned left on Pattaya Klang and then left again on Second Road.

As he moved up the street he saw a bar complex on his right but he didn't see any condos behind it. He figured it wasn't the place he was looking for. A second later he passed the hospital and the Big C. He grunted in annoyance. A minute later he was edging his way around the same roundabout he had passed on his way into Pattaya. As he exited the circle heading south, he saw the Toyota he had lost in Bangkok, the one with the woman and the man and Nuang's baby. Surely this was no coincidence. Something was going on and he was going find out what. It was time to bring this whole crazy affair to an end. He steered in behind the Toyota.

~~~

Laht's drive from Pitsanulok to Pattaya had taken forever. First the rain, then Somjit's untimely stop in Bangkok, and then the traffic jam from hell. They were halfway to Chonburi before the road cleared enough to go the speed limit. Somjit fell asleep as they passed through Sriracha. They reached the northern outskirts of Pattaya at eight-thirty in the evening.

Laht saw a sign that said Beach Road and turned in that direction. If there were hotels in this town, they would surely be near the beach. He was in the far left lane when he came to a traffic circle and was forced south on street called Second Road. He sighed in annoyance then shrugged his shoulders in resignation. Probably there would be hotels on Second Road, too.

Laht had never been to Pattaya because he had never a reason to come. He had heard stories about the nightlife of Pattaya, but this was the first time he had ever seen it. He had once gone to Patpong in Bangkok when he was eighteen, but it had been nothing like this. Pattaya was like a hundred Patpongs sitting side-by-side and back-to-back.

He stared at shops, bars, and restaurants that lined both sides of the street. He couldn't keep his eyes from the bar-girls. They were mostly young and pretty. Many, he guessed, were Isaan. Certainly, they were someone's daughter or wife or mother. He wondered how they could sell their bodies for a few baht, sleeping with a different stranger every night, putting their health and their lives at risk. Coming from a wealthy family, Laht couldn't imagine what their home lives must have been like to push them to this.

THAILAND - COLD RAIN

In the near distance he saw a sign advertising an establishment called The Alcazar Show. Its parking lot was busy with people, cars, and buses. He figured it was a place of entertainment for tourists. A horn honking to his right caught his attention. It was a taxi and the driver was making angry motions for him to pull aside.

It took a second for Laht to recognize the man as the taxi driver from Chiang Mai, the crazy man who claimed to be baby Tippawan's father. Laht's mind whirled. Had the man been following them since confronting Somjit? He had no idea what was going on, but it was time for it to stop. He pulled to the side of the road. The taxi stopped behind him.

Immediately Laht was out of his car. Adrenaline coursed uncontrolled. He was going to kick the taxi driver's ass. At that moment he heard a woman shouting that someone was stealing a car. He turned in time to see a young Thai man easing himself into his Toyota. For a moment he was stunned to inaction. He found his legs as his car sped away.

~~~

Nong had just finished his beer when he noticed a Thai man exiting a new-model Toyota stopped at the front of the bars. The man wore clothes that spoke of money, lots of money. His face looked vaguely familiar but Nong couldn't place it. The man headed straight toward the taxi parked behind him. He didn't close his car door and he left the engine running; his face was red with anger.

Nong's figured the two men had had a minor accident and now there would be some screaming and cursing for entertainment. Maybe there would even be a fight. His next thought was pure inspiration. He could jump inside the unattended car and be gone before the man could stop him. Normally he wouldn't be so daring, but the yaba, marijuana, and beer had made him invincible. He wouldn't be caught; he was far too cunning for the police.

J. F. Gump

He stood from his seat and walked toward the Toyota while keeping a close eye on its owner. The man continued his threatening strut toward the taxi. Nong smiled to himself. As he slid into the driver's seat, he heard a loud shout coming from the bar behind him. It was the girl who had given him such shitty service. The whore was telling everyone he was stealing the car. Nong slammed the door shut and sped away.

A shrill scream came from the back of the car. He hadn't thought there might be a passenger. In the mirror and he caught glimpse of a woman in the back seat. Her screaming raked harsh across his ears. He couldn't get rid of her here, but he could shut her up. He floored the accelerator for an instant and then jammed the brakes. The woman launched forward over the front seat. His fist struck a sharp blow to the back of her head and her screams stopped immediately.

The nerve-rasping cry of a baby broke the momentary silence. It was more irritating than the woman's scream. He reached behind the seat, his hand scrambling to find the baby. Through the rear window he saw the well-dressed man charging full speed toward the car. He had to get out of this traffic or the man would catch him. He forgot about the wailing baby and raced down a narrow side road to his left. He had never been down this street before. He hoped it went somewhere.

~~~~

Laht chased after his own car with a stranger in the driver's seat and Somjit and little Tippawan in the back. Despite sprinting at top speed, he couldn't catch up with the vehicle. Somjit's terrified face looked back at him through the rear window. He could hear her loud shrieks of terror. He redoubled his effort to catch the car. At that moment the thief squealed to a stop. Laht hoped that the man had changed his mind. Then Somjit's face disappeared from the rear window and the Toyota continued down the street going faster than before.

Laht knew he would never catch up on foot. He needed a ride. He looked for a motorcycle taxi but none was within shouting distance. His helplessness grew as his Toyota disappeared down a side street. A honking horn grabbed his attention. It was the taxi driver from Chiang Mai. The last thing he wanted was continue his confrontation with a crazy man.

"Leave me alone," he shouted. "I don't have time for you right now."

"Get in," the taxi driver shouted back. "Or you'll never catch them."

After a moment's hesitation, Laht slid into the passenger seat and the taxi driver sped in pursuit of the Toyota.

~~~

Pajeeka was on her way to the bars at Soi 2 when she saw a flurry of activity as she neared the normally quiet cluster of beer-bars just south of the Alcazar Show. People were shouting and pointing. She pushed the buzzer signaling the baht-bus driver to stop. She noticed a taxi and a new model Toyota parked illegally at the curb. At that instant, tires squealed and the Toyota sped away. A man on the sidewalk ran after it. She got a clear look at the man's face. It was her boss's son Laht.

She threaded her way through the traffic and across the street, angled south in the direction that Laht was running. As she made the other side, the taxi raced past her. It stopped long enough for Laht to climb inside.

She didn't know what was going on, but she knew it wasn't good. She flagged down a passing motorcycle taxi. "One thousand baht to catch that taxi," she shouted.

The motorcycle driver didn't need more encouragement. Once Pajeeka was aboard, he tore away at a frightening speed. She shouted at him to slow a little and he did. She wanted to catch the taxi but she didn't want to die in the process.

As the motorcycle roared down the narrow street, Pajeeka

called Isara from her cell phone but got his voice mail. "It's eight forty-five," her voice shrilled. "There's a problem and I think Laht is involved. Come to the bars just south of Alcazars on Second Road. I'll meet you there."

As she clipped the phone back on the waistband of her jeans, she accidentally turned it off.

~~~

Nuang had been on high alert from the moment she and Jon took a seat at the Sandy Bar. She fully expected to see her brother Anan make an appearance like he had the night before. After a few minutes and all stayed normal, she allowed herself to relax. She figured she was worried for nothing. Last night had only been her imagination.

She noticed the Toyota as it stopped in a no-parking zone at the edge of the street. She watched as the driver exited his car and walked toward a taxi parked behind him. She had seen the man's face before but wasn't sure where. Suddenly she realized who he was—he was the young monk from the temple. His head was no longer shaved and he had on civilian clothes, but it was him. She slipped from her seat and hid behind the bar.

"What are you doing?" Jon stared down at her.

"Do you see that man? The Thai man there by the taxi?"

A girl at another bar shouted something in Thai. Jon looked up to see a new-model Toyota speed away with a Thai man chasing it on foot. "Not any more. He just ran away. Who is he anyway? Is he the same man you saw last night? Is he your husband?"

"No, he's a monk," she answered.

From the corner of his eye he saw a Thai woman dash across the street and chase after the man who was chasing the Toyota. "He didn't look like a monk to me. Do you know the woman, too?"

"What woman?"

"The one chasing the *monk*."

The taxi pulled away from the curb, tires screeching. By

instinct Jon knew the taxi was part of whatever was happening. Even more, he knew that Nuang was part of it, too. An uneasy chill slid down his back. "What the hell's going on? Who are those people?"

When she didn't respond, he reached down and took her by the arm. "Get up here and talk to me."

Nuang peeked over the bar as she stood. She didn't see anyone except the usual evening crowd. "I don't know what's going on." She wondered if the woman Jon had seen could be Somjit. Who else would be here in Pattaya with the young monk. If they were both here, she knew her baby would be here, too. "Was the woman carrying a baby?"

"I didn't see a baby. Now tell me what's going on?"

"I told you I don't know."

Without warning Nuang twisted her arm from his grasp and darted away.

It took a moment for Jon to react and chase after her. He caught her at the curb, grabbed her shoulder, and spun her around. "Stop this bullshit and tell me something."

Nuang almost fell when Jon grabbed her. She glanced down the street just in time to see a woman speeding away on the back of a motorcycle taxi. If it was Somjit, she wasn't carrying a baby. Her panic grew like wild bamboo. She swung her arm and dislodged Jon's hand from her shoulder. "Leave me alone."

He grabbed her by the wrists. "No, I won't leave you alone. What's wrong with you? If you tell me who those people are, I'll help you find them."

She balled her fists and thrashed her arms to escape his grasp. When her right hand came free, it was moving furiously toward his face. It landed full force against his nose.

Jon staggered backwards. By reflex he raised his own fist but held it in check. He lowered his hand and cupped it over his nose.

Nuang turned and ran down the sidewalk.

Jon stared dumbfounded as Nuang raced away. His mind tried

to rationalize what had just happened. She hadn't meant to hit him, or at least he didn't think so. Just hours ago she had been his lover, but now she was acting like a total stranger. That man, the *monk*, had triggered something. He wondered what the truth was.

He felt a slick dampness on his fingers and looked down. Blood streaked down his arms and dribbled dark spots onto his shirt and the dusty concrete below. He needed to get home. He pulled a handkerchief from his pocket, clamped it over his nose, and hurried toward his condo. The bar-girls stared wide-eyed as he passed.

Nuang reached the side-street less than a minute after escaping Jon's grasp. Neither the taxi nor the motorcycle was in sight. She wasn't sure what to do. Images of her fist colliding with Jon's nose burned in her mind. She hadn't meant to do that. She needed to tell him she was sorry.

She ran back to the bars but didn't see Jon anywhere. She figured he had gone to his condo. She took a few steps in that direction before stopping. She couldn't go to the condo; Laht and Somjit might come back while she was gone. She ran back to the street and hurried down the sidewalk. Her eyes inspected every vehicle that passed by.

Chapter 44

Nong smiled as he steered the Toyota down the side-street; no one would catch him tonight. He turned left at the next intersection. The street widened and he recognized where he was. He glanced at the dashboard clock. It was almost nine. He would be rid of the car and a lot richer by ten.

The baby's crying continued unabated. The woman dangling across the seat moaned and coughed. She was coming awake. Nong swerved up a narrow lane lined with deserted tin huts and overgrown fields. He switched off the headlights and braked to a halt.

The woman felt light as a feather as he dragged her from the car and tossed her into the weeds of a vacant lot. Next he opened the rear door, grabbed the baby by the arm, and yanked it toward him. There was a small popping sound and the cry became more intense.

A motion caught his attention. He turned to see the woman pushing herself to a standing position. His heart stutter-stepped. It was Somjit. "What are you doing here?" he shouted.

"Put the baby down." Somjit's words came out thick-lipped.

Nong looked down as if seeing the screaming baby for the first time. "Is this mine?"

"No, it's not yours," she put her hands out in a begging fashion. "Please put the baby down."

Nong eyed her, "You're lying." He glanced down at the baby dangling from his fist. In the dim light of the deserted street, he saw the baby was more farang than Thai. He reached an instant conclusion: his own wife had given birth to a baby that was not his. She had whored around with some farang, and he had fed and clothed her while she carried another man's child. Nong needed no drugs or alcohol to fuel his anger. He tossed the baby aside like yesterday's trash. The crying stopped instantly. "This time I will kill you both."

"No, you bastard," Somjit hissed. "This time I will kill you." Before she could move Nong charged at her, his fist lashed out a wild swing.

Somjit ducked and his blow glanced off the side of her head. His momentum carried him past her. Immediately she was on his back clawing, biting, and pounding with every ounce of fury inside her. Nothing would stop her until he was dead.

Nong twisted violently, trying to throw Somjit from his back. There was a sharp pain at his left ear. When he reached up, his hand landed on her head. The bitch was biting his ear off. He grabbed a handful of hair and pulled, but he couldn't remove her from his ear. Desperate, he jumped up and backward. They landed hard on the ground with him on top, his back against her chest. Her grip loosened. At once he was on his feet. Blood trickled down his neck from his mangled ear. He stepped forward to finish what had been started months ago. He kicked out at her with his foot. This time he aimed for her head and not a pregnant stomach.

Despite having the wind knocked from her, Somjit found the strength to spin away. Nong's foot missed her by millimeters. As she rolled, her hand touched something cold and hard. Even without seeing it, she knew what it was. She had held thousands of them in her lifetime, a length of concrete reinforcing steel—rebar.

She looked up in time to see Nong start another kick at her face. By reflex she lashed out with the rebar putting it on a collision course with his leg. The force of the blow nearly knocked the heavy metal from her hand. The sound of hard steel meeting shinbone cracked loud in the night. Nong fell close beside her, his face livid with pain.

Again Somjit rolled away and came to her feet; her breath had returned. She brandished the rusty metal rod like a Siamese sword.

THAILAND - COLD RAIN

The hatred in her eyes left little doubt about her intentions.

Nong tried to stand but his right leg buckled under the weight. "Please," he pleaded, crabbing away from her. "Please don't hit me again. I'm your husband."

Somjit close in, now holding the steel rod like a baseball bat.

"I'm the father of your baby," Nong whimpered.

Somjit unleashed two savage swings. The first shattered the arm Nong held up to protect himself. The second glanced off the side of his head and peeled away a bloody flap of skin and hair. She raised the rebar for the third time, ready to deliver her final revenge. From nowhere a hand snatched the rusty piece of rebar from her grasp. She spun to attack whoever had interrupted her moment of vengeance.

~~~

The Toyota had had a big head start. It was only by luck that Laht had seen it turn left. When they reached the intersection, the car was nowhere to be seen. They sped down the street even though there was nothing to chase.

Laht glanced up each lane and driveway they passed. Suddenly, he saw his car in a dirt alleyway to his right. "Stop!"

He jumped from the cab and raced up the alley. Ahead he saw Somjit standing over a man who was cowering on the ground. She held something in her hand, but in the dim light he couldn't see what it was. Then she swung the object like a cricket player and the impact was loud enough to be heard from meters away. Immediately, she swung again.

Laht was nearly upon them, close enough to see a rusty metal rod clutched in her hands. As she raised it for another strike, he wrenched it from her hands. "No! Stop."

Somjit threw herself at him, her arms flailing, her hands grabbing insanely for the length of rebar.

"I said stop," Laht screamed.

This time Somjit obeyed. She threw her arms around him and

burst into tears.

"Where is the baby?" he asked.

Somjit pointed toward the field to her left but refused to look. Her crying became loud wails of grief.

Laht looked where she pointed but didn't see anything that looked like a baby. If it was crying, he didn't hear it. Behind him, a motorcycle roared up the street and stopped. Its headlights lit the scene. He turned to look. "Look out!" came a shrill voice just before his world went black.

~~~

Pajeeka had guessed right when she told the motorcycle driver to turn left. Three blocks ahead she saw the taxi at the side of the road. She caught a glimpse of Laht as he darted up a narrow lane.

"Hurry," she shouted. The front wheel of the motorcycle lifted from the pavement as it shot forward. He slowed only a little when he entered the alley. Ahead sat the stolen Toyota. He slowed the motorcycle to a stop and aimed his headlight at the scene.

The faces of Laht and Somjit turned toward her. A movement behind the couple caught her eye. It took a moment to recognize what she saw. A limping figure was edging toward Laht and Somjit. It was like something from a horror movie. Blood covered his face, his left hand dangled useless at his side, his right held a thick piece of wood. He raised it to strike.

"Look out!" Pajeeka screamed.

The club cracked against Laht's head. The man lifted the club for a second blow aimed at Somjit. Pajeeka reached Somjit just in time to push her to the ground. The club barely missed them both.

Pajeeka scrambled to her feet. "You just made a big mistake, lizard dick," she hissed. She picked up a heavy metal rod laying at her feet. With one swing she destroyed his remaining good arm. By reflex she swung again. This time the rebar embedded itself deep, just above the man's left cheekbone.

Pajeeka's eyes went wide with horror. The man was dead. She

knew it as sure as she knew her own name. She stepped back, recoiling from what she had done. Without warning, gut wrenching nausea washed through her and she vomited again and again. It could have been seconds, minutes, or hours before a honking horn invaded her world of shock. She looked up expecting to see the motorcycle but it was gone. In its place was the taxi.

~~~

Surat had watched out the rear window of his taxi as Laht disappeared down a narrow lane. Just as he started to back up and follow, a motorcycle came roaring toward him. He braked and waited for it to pass. At the last instant the motorcycle braked and swerved up the same alley where Laht had gone. Surat sped the taxi back to the intersection and followed.

Just ahead sat the Toyota with its lights off and the motorcycle with its lights on. When he approached, the motorcycle raced away. Surat's headlights shined on two women. One he recognized as the woman from Chiang Mai, the other he had never seen before. He didn't see the young doctor anywhere. He didn't know what was happening but instinct told him it wasn't good.

He got out of the taxi and ran to where the women stood. To his right lay the doctor. Not far away he saw a mangled body with a metal rod protruding from its head. He turned toward the women. "Where is the baby?"

Somjit pointed and walked to her left. When she stooped and picked up the limp body, he didn't interfere. She pulled the baby close to her breast and released a wail unlike anything he had ever heard. It put cold bumps on his skin.

He took Somjit by the arm and pulled her toward the taxi. He wanted to take the baby from her but he was afraid of what he might find. Once Somjit and the baby were in the back seat, he went back to get the woman who was vomiting and the young doctor who lay quiet as death.

"Help me get this man to the car," he shouted.

The woman, Pajeeka, took a deep breath. "Give me a minute. I've never killed anyone before."

Surat struggled to gather the dead weight of Laht in his arms. "Please, I need your help now. We may not have minutes."

Pajeeka's mind recovered a small degree of normalcy. "You're right. We may not have minutes." She helped Surat carry Laht to the taxi. They left the dead body of Nong in the grass and rubble.

"Turn right," Pajeeka said when they reached Second Road. "The hospital is there."

Surat kept his attention on the traffic and his hand on the horn.

Somjit stared out through the car window as they passed down the street. That's when she saw Nuang. She was in view for less than an instant. Two blocks later, they arrived at the hospital. Somjit jumped from the taxi and carried little Tippawan inside. Surat and Pajeeka wrestled Laht from the rear seat.

A doctor took the baby from Somjit as she entered the hospital. She tried to follow but a nurse stopped her. A moment later attendants whisked Laht's motionless body inside. A single loud wail sprang from her throat. It was all she could do to stop another. She pulled her arms tight to her chest and swayed back and forth. Small whimpers escaped her lips.

Surat's body shook as he took a seat in the hospital waiting area. He cradled his head in his hands. The last fifteen minutes had drained him. He had come to Pattaya to find Nuang, but instead he had found limp bodies and dead people. It was a nightmare. He wished he had stayed in Chiang Mai. If he had, maybe none of this would have happened.

Pajeeka stood to one side away from both Somjit and Surat and made two calls. The first was to the police. "I have killed a man," she said calmly, then told them where to find the body. "I'm at the Pattaya International Hospital with the people he attacked. I'll wait here." Her second call was to Isara.

Chapter 45

Nuang had been pacing frantically up and down the sidewalk on Second Road since the night had gone crazy and everyone had disappeared. She didn't know where Laht and the taxi, or the girl on the motorcycle had gone except down the now deserted side-street. She didn't know what to do. Maybe they would come back to the bars by the condo. Maybe Jon would too. Jon had said he would help her if she told him what was going on, and she needed his help now. She hurried back toward the bars.

She hadn't gone far when she heard a horn blaring and tires screeching. She turned to see a taxi racing zig-zag through the heavy traffic. Through the front window she saw a woman she didn't recognize; the driver's face was turned away. As the vehicle sped past, she noticed the taxi was from Chiang Mai. Through the rear window she saw Somjit's face. Her heart leaped to her throat. She hadn't seen the driver's face, but she knew it was her husband Surat. She wondered if her baby was in the backseat with Somjit.

What little reason she had left evaporated and she ran after the taxi. Her terror spiked when the taxi turned toward the hospital. People only went to the hospital when they were very sick, very hurt, or dying. She tried to run faster but her legs wouldn't cooperate. By the time she reached the road to the hospital, her muscles ached and her lungs burned. She slowed to a walk when she saw the taxi in the hospital driveway.

A man and a woman were struggling to pull a limp figure from the back seat. Somjit was carrying a baby through the emergency room doors. Nuang knew it was little Tippawan. As she watched, two hospital workers came outside with a gurney. When the cabby turned, she got a good look at his face and all doubts disappeared; it was Surat.

Nuang was torn between running away from Surat and running to the hospital to make sure her baby and Somjit were okay. A loud cry came through the sliding doors as Surat and the others wheeled the man inside. The eerie wail made up her mind; she ran to the emergency room entrance and stepped inside.

Directly ahead stood Somjit, her face twisted in anguish. To her left was the woman from the front seat of the taxi. To her right sat Surat with his head resting in the palms of his hands.

She ran to Somjit, "Where is my baby? Please tell me little Tippawan is okay."

Somjit looked up, her eyes streamed tears. "I'm a bad mother," she moaned.

Nuang's took Somjit by the hand. "What happened?"

Surat's voice interrupted. "You have shamed me. That's what happened. I should kill you."

Nuang cringed. Surat had never talked like that to her before. Despite her need to see little Tippawan and make sure she was okay, she turned and ran from the hospital.

Surat wasn't sure what he felt as he watched Nuang disappear through the exit. He glanced over at Pajeeka and then at Somjit. Both stared wide-eyed but neither spoke. Surat left the hospital as fast as his feet would carry him. Outside he didn't see Nuang anywhere. He sprinted down the driveway in pursuit of nothing. As he reached the street, he was stopped by two policemen.

Nuang was sure Surat would follow her from the hospital and she knew he could outrun her. Halfway down the drive, she veered to her right and hid behind a bush. A second later Surat burst through the doors and headed toward the street.

She heard someone shout "halt" and all noise stopped. A second later she heard men talking but too low for her to hear. She peeked through the bushes and saw two policemen escorting Surat back inside the hospital.

Once Surat and the policemen were out of sight Nuang hurried back toward Second Road. She collided with an older man in her haste. She mumbled an apology and caught a baht-bus south toward Jon's condo.

The security guard and the night boy smiled politely as she passed through the lobby. She tried to smile back but couldn't. She stepped off the elevator on the third floor. Her footsteps echoed off the marble floors and the hard plaster walls. She tapped lightly at Jon's door and waited.

Chapter 46

Isara Horungruang was in his hotel room taking a shower when his cell phone rang. He didn't realize Pajeeka had called until after he had dressed for dinner and checked his voice mail. "It's eight forty-five," her message said, her voice was shrill. "There's a problem and I think Laht is involved. Come to the bars just south of Alcazars on Second Road. I will meet you there."

He phoned back right away but got her voice-mail. He called his driver. "Do you know a place called Alcazars?"

"Yes. It's not far, sir. Maybe ten or fifteen minutes."

Five minutes later they were creeping their way up Second Road. Baht-buses, tour buses, motorcycles, and cars stretched as far north as Isara could see. He settled back into his seat and recalled the events that had led him to this place at this time. His deceased brother Jum came first to mind. If not for Jum, he would be home in Phitsanulok. Next he considered the Bongkot family, especially Math, his brother's illegitimate daughter, and her sister Nuang with the braided hair. Isara knew her, too. Because of Jum he knew the whole family.

By a twist of fate his son and a young woman named Somjit had become entangled with his brother's past. Isara wanted to make sure the past stayed secret. What would Laht think if he ever learned that his Uncle Jum, the monk to whom he had paid six month's of tribute, was the legitimate father of Nuang's illegitimate sister. It would taint memories and he couldn't let that happen. He had to find Nuang and her husband. He had to talk to them before either of them talked to Laht. After what he had learned from Anya, he knew they needed to talk to him, too. Pending doom gnawed at him. He hoped Pajeeka was wrong and that Laht was still in Chiang Mai. His driver edged them north toward Alcazar's and the beer bars.

His cell phone shook him from his thoughts. "Hello."

"Did you get my message?" came Pajeeka's voice. "Where are you?"

"I'm stuck in traffic. Why did you turn off your phone?"

"Forget that now." Her response was tense. "I'm at the Pattaya International Hospital with Laht. I think he'll be okay."

He jerked at her words. Horrifying scenes of smashed bodies raced through his head. "Hospital? What are you talking about?"

"There was a fight. Laht was hurt, hit on the head with a club. He's still unconscious."

"This is crazy! Laht has never been in fight. I'm at the light at Pattaya Klang. Am I far away?"

"No. You're very near. Your driver will know. I have to go now. A policeman wants to talk to me. I think I have a big problem." Her phone clicked silent.

"Policeman?" he shouted into the dead connection. "What policeman?" He turned off his cell phone, took a deep breath, and forced himself calm. To his driver he said, "Get me to the Pattaya International Hospital as fast as you can."

Once past the stop light their speed picked up and held steady at about four kilometers per hour, only slightly faster than he could run. His driver pointed ahead and to their left. "There," he said.

Isara looked. A glowing sign appeared briefly between buildings. The hospital was less than four blocks away. Two blocks later the traffic came to a standstill.

"I'm walking the rest of the way," Isara said and exited the car. "Meet me at the hospital."

Isara entered the emergency room area just as Pajeeka was being escorted to the exit by three policemen. "Excuse me," Isara stopped them. "This woman is my employee. What's the problem?"

"Murder," one officer responded. "I saw the body myself."

"He was going to kill Laht," Pajeeka interjected. "You know me, Khun Isara. I may be crazy, but I would never kill anyone unless I had to."

Isara nodded, his smile thin. He slipped a business card from his pocket. "I am Isara Horungruang. Tell your boss I'll be calling him later. He knows who I am." He nodded toward Pajeeka. "You will take good care of her." It was not a request, it was a command. "I don't want her strip searched, I don't want her questioned without me present, and I don't want her in a common jail cell. I want her in a decent hotel room. I will pay for everything. Bonuses for the room guards. Do you understand?"

The policemen exchanged nervous glances. One officer spoke, "I guarantee she will be treated with the utmost respect."

Isara let his smile brighten a little. He slipped slipped a wad of bills from his hand in his pocket and pealed off four 1,000 baht-bills. He motioned the man aside. "I'm sure you've had a stressful night. I want to buy dinner for your families." He folded three bills tight and slid them into the officer's shirt pocket. "May I speak with my client in private for a minute?"

The officer smiled and nodded his consent.

Isara pulled Pajeeka to one side of the waiting area. He kept his tone low but his tenseness showed plainly. "What happened?"

Pajeeka related the evening as accurately as she remembered. Her stomach turned as she recalled the fatal blow.

"Do you know the man you killed?" Isara asked soft, soothing.

"No, but I'm sure he was Somjit's husband. That's Somjit over there." She glanced in the direction of the woman who was standing with her arms wrapped tight around herself. "I think he deserved to die, but I get sick when I think about it."

Isara looked briefly at the woman then turned back to Pajeeka. "I understand. Are there other witnesses?"

"That man over there." She raised her hand slightly in the direction of Surat. "He is Nuang's husband. Nuang was here earlier but she ran away. The police kept him for questioning but they're not arresting him. His surname is Duansawang. I'm sure of that."

Isara nodded. He handed the last baht-note to Pajeeka. "In case you need anything. Don't worry; we'll be back in Phitsanulok by tomorrow evening."

Pajeeka nodded and then asked, "What about my vacation?"

Despite the situation, Isara couldn't stop his laugh. "I haven't forgotten. I want to see Laht now. I'll see you later tonight. "

He stepped aside and let the officers resume their duties. "Take good care of her," he said as they left the hospital. He went to the registration desk, "I want to see Laht Horrungruang. He's my son."

The nurse made a brief call then said, "Dr. Phansak wants to see you first. His office is there."

Isara walked in the direction she pointed.

Inside the room sat a young doctor. The man stood and wai'ed when Isara entered. "I am Dr. Phansak. I'm pleased to meet you. You don't know me, but your son is my friend. We met in medical school. Laht will be okay. He's had a nasty blow to his head but there is no internal bleeding. He's awake and coherent."

"I would like to see him."

"You can see him later. Right now he's getting a few stitches. We'll be keeping him overnight just to be safe. I think he can leave tomorrow. You can relax; we'll take good care of him. Like I said, he's my friend and I look forward to talking to him myself."

"Could you have the nurse tell me when he's in his room?"

"Yes, and I'll also let him know you're here."

"Thank you," Isara said and headed back toward the waiting room. As he entered, he saw a nurse leading Somjit into the treatment area. Surat was already gone. He went to the registration desk. "Is that young woman okay?"

"I think she'll be fine," the nurse smiled. "The doctor will examine her just to be safe."

"Where's the man who was here? I think his name is Surat."

"If you mean the man who talked to the police, he's outside."

Isara walked to the door and looked out. The scene he saw set him in motion.

Chapter 47

Jon's nose had stopped bleeding by the time he got back to his room. He went directly to the bath and inspected himself in the mirror. Blood was everywhere, on his face, his hands, his arms, and his clothes. No wonder everyone had stared at him. He looked like he'd been beaten half to death.

He stripped off his blood-mottled shirt and pants and washed himself clean. He put his clothes in the basin and filled it with cold water. It probably wouldn't help, but it was all he could think to do. If the laundry couldn't get the spots out, he would throw the clothes away.

He grabbed a beer from the fridge and took a long swallow. It didn't do much to calm his nerves. He hadn't smoked pot in years but wished he had a joint now. His hand shook as he lit a cigarette.

He replayed the events from the bar. It had all happened so fast. One minute he and Nuang had been talking to the bar-girls and the next minute she had gone wild. Who in the hell had those people been? She had said the man was a monk, but that was an obvious lie. If the man wasn't her husband, he was probably her brother or a boyfriend. He figured the woman was probably a sister or some other relative. She had already admitted she'd run away from her husband and abandoned her baby. God only knew what else she had done.

For the first time since he had met Nuang, he wondered what he had gotten himself into. If she was cold-hearted enough to desert everyone she loved, she might be capable of anything. She might even be crazy.

He had calmed a little by the time he finished the beer. After a few minutes of self debate, he decided to go back to the bars. He needed to know what was going on and he wanted to make sure that Nuang was okay. Even if she was crazy, he didn't want anything to happen to her.

He had just slipped into a clean pair of jeans when there was a light tapping at the door. Instinctively, he knew it was Nuang. With heart pounding, he yanked the door open.

Nuang pushed past him in total silence. Her face was set with determination. She pulled the liner from the trashcan, went to the closet, and began shoving her clothes into the bag.

"What are you doing?" he asked, ignoring the obvious answer.

"I'm leaving," she said without looking up.

After sex, power, and money, the fear of loss is one of man's mightiest driving forces and Jon was feeling it now. It came unexpected and with uncontrolled frenzy. Minutes before he would have been relieved to have her gone. Now he would give anything to make her stay. His mind reeled with conflicting emotions. "Why?"

"I don't want you to get hurt." She continued filling the bag.

"Who are those people?"

"I told you already!" The bag was full but there were still clothes in the closet. She swapped a dress for a pair of jeans, tied the bag shut, and then stood and ran from the room.

Jon's heart stopped. His need for her to stay became paramount. He chased after her. She was already on the stairs when he stepped into the hallway. "Wait. You can't leave like this."

Nuang looked back at him. Tears filled her eyes. "You don't understand. I can't stay like this, either." She continued her flight down the stairs.

"I love you," he shouted as she disappeared from sight. There was no response.

He ran back to his condo. Quickly he finished dressing and went outside. A fast scan of the bars proved that Nuang wasn't there. He sprinted to Second Road. He looked up and down the street but didn't see her. He turned toward the bars and one girl pointed north. Jon hurried in that direction.

He had no idea where he was going but he kept moving. He searched every bar all the way to Dolphin Circle. She wasn't at any of them. She had disappeared.

At that moment he realized Nuang was truly gone. His emotions darkened to depression. Nuang wasn't the only woman who had ever run away from him, but she was the first one who didn't say goodbye. Suddenly, he wished he had never come to Thailand. He would be glad when his job here was finished.

Chapter 48

Itta was stopped by one of the bar-girls as she approached the man sitting alone on Soi 6.

"I think he's drunk," the girl said. "He wants to be left alone. You don't work here so you should just keep on walking."

"I know him," Itta responded. She stared at the girl as if daring her to disagree. When the girl didn't respond, she added, "Bring me a Singha, and one of whatever he is drinking." She flipped her long hair over her shoulders and went to stand beside the farang. "Do you remember me?"

"Go away," the man grumbled without looking up.

"I bought you a beer."

The farang looked up. After a short pause he said, "I met you on the flight from Tokyo. I'm sorry; I don't remember your name."

"Never mind. I am Itta. I was just thinking about what you said to me as I was leaving the Bangkok airport. Something about the Bongkot family in Phitsanulok. I thought maybe you know my brother Anan. He lives here in Pattaya."

"Who are you?" he whispered.

"My name is Thichakorn Bongkot, but everyone knows me as Itta. I'm the second oldest sister of Anan."

Itta watched his reaction. His shock was unmistakable. She knew about her brother's sexual preferences and had accepted it long ago. She figured this man and Anan had once been lovers, or maybe they still were.

"Does he have a sister named Math and a mother named Nui?" Mike asked.

A strange, fluttering feeling invaded her. She had often

J. F. Gump

wondered what sort of men her brother found attractive, but she had never expected to meet one of them. This man didn't look gay at all. "Yes, it's the same," she nodded.

"Your sister was a cunt and a whore," Mike hissed. "Get the fuck away from me."

Itta's head spun trying to make sense of what he had said. "If you have some problem with my brother, I don't care, but you can't talk like that about my sister."

"I have a problem with your family. They are all liars and pieces of shit."

A powerful rage tore through her. "Who are you to say anything about my family? A farang coming to my country to have sex with my brother and Buddha only knows how many other boys." She stood from her seat. "I think I know who the piece of shit is."

"I hate your brother. I once loved your sister but now I hate her too. I hate anyone named Bongkot and that includes you. Now get away from me."

Itta's head swirled. "What do you mean you once loved my sister. Do you mean Math? Who are you?"

"My name is Mike Johnson and your sister was a cunt. Now leave me alone."

Itta struggled to make sense of what she was hearing. Sitting here was the man she had heard so much about. The man her sister Math had once loved and planned to marry. Something was going on but she couldn't imagine what. "I don't understand any of this. How can you hate someone you loved, and someone who loved you in return?"

"Your sister never loved me. She only used me to get my money. I'm sure I'm not the only man she's fucked over. Thank God it will never happen again." He stood to leave.

Itta stared, dumbfounded by his response. Something was wrong, terribly wrong. Math had called her many times and there had never been any doubt about her feelings for this man. Math would have done anything and sacrificed everything for him. If her sister had used him, she didn't understand how. Unless Math had lied, this was the man she wanted to spend her life with. Itta reached out and put her hand on his arm. "That's not true. My sister loved you."

Her light touch stopped him from walking away. He kept his voice low, even, and distinct as he spoke, "You're a liar, just like your sister. I saw Anan today and he told me the truth. Math made a fool of me and I will never forgive that. Forget what I said at the airport about the Bongkot family. Those were phony words from a false dream."

Suddenly Itta understood what had happened. "So, you have seen my brother? He told you that Math never loved you, and you believed him? Anan is the biggest liar in Thailand. I swear to Buddha, my sister loved you with all her heart."

Mike turned back to her. He knew it could be true. He had never liked Anan, and he was sure Anan felt the same about him. What if it was all a lie? What if Anan had only been trying to hurt him. He could imagine Anan doing that. His angry scowl gave way to a pleading expression. "Jing-jing?"

"Chai, yes, jing-jing." She waved at a barmaid with her free hand and pulled Mike back to his seat with the other. "Please sit with me for a minute. I will tell you everything I know."

Mike stared at her for a second and then sat back down. He wanted to hear that he hadn't been duped, that he wasn't a fool. "I'm listening," he said.

Itta ordered two more beers from the waitress. Then she told Mike of every conversation she ever had with her sister. She held nothing back, not even Math's doubts about his love for her. Once or twice as she spoke, Mike's eyes filled with tears. His memories must be very strong, she thought. In a while she finished talking, leaned back, and waited for him to speak.

"I want..." he started, but didn't finish his sentence. Tears filled his eyes and he turned his head away from her.

Itta was surprised. She had seen men cry before, but it was usually when they were very drunk. She had never seen a man cry in public. A few of the bar-girls looked in their direction, but they said nothing. She laid her hand gentle on his back. "I'm sorry if I hurt you. I thought it would make you feel better to know how much Math loved you."

He took a deep breath, turned, and spoke in a low, husky whisper, "I want to thank you for being here. When I saw Anan, I believed everything he told me. Now I know it was nothing but lies. You have made me a happy man."

On impulse she pulled him toward her and he didn't resist. She held his face against her shoulder. His tears dampened her blouse. She wished she could stop his pain.

After a minute Mike sat erect and rubbed hard at his face. "I'm sorry; I feel better now. I loved your sister and it's important to know that she loved me, too."

"Mai pen rai, never mind," she spoke softly. "I understand."

He wiped at his eyes with a bar napkin. "Why are you here? I mean, I'm happy you are here, but I thought your home was in Phitsanulok."

Her thoughts rushed back to everything that had happened since she had returned to Thailand. "I came here to find my sister, Nuang. Do you know her?"

"Yes, I know Nuang. I met her when Math and I were in Chiang Mai." He had seen her again at the sympathy ceremony he'd had for Math, but he didn't mention that time. It was a secret better left unspoken. "Is Nuang here in Pattaya?"

"Yes," Itta answered. She knew he was lying about how well he knew Nuang. She knew he had returned to Pattaya after her sister Math had died because Nuang had called her in Scotland and told her about the ceremony. Nuang had seemed quite enamored with this man. He was practically all she had talked about. An ugly thought entered her head as she remembered what her brother had said about Nuang and a half farang baby and a foreign lover. Dear Buddha, could this be that man? "I guess you haven't seen her?"

He hesitated slightly before he answered, "I haven't seen Nuang in over a year. I've only seen your brother. Is she living with him?"

Itta wasn't sure how much she should tell him. If he wasn't involved with Nuang then this was none of his business. It was a family matter. Somehow, her logic didn't seem right.

"I don't know where she lives." She twisted the napkin in her hand. "Nuang has run away. She took her baby and ran away."

"Baby? Nuang has a baby?" Memories of one year past flooded his senses. "How old is her baby?" He prayed she would say *just born.*

Itta started to answer but was interrupted by a loud horn and the screech of tires. She was happy for the distraction. She looked toward the noise and caught a brief glimpse of a taxi speeding erratically up Second Road. "Crazy drivers," she said.

"Yeah," Mike smiled. "I think Pattaya does that to people."

"What did you ask me? I forget."

"I forget, too," Mike was happy for the chance to change the subject. "Hey, look, Soi 6 isn't exactly my favorite place in Pattaya. I'm getting out of here as soon as I finish this beer. Wanna come with me?"

Itta smiled. She wanted to continue their discussion about Math and Nuang. "Sure, why not?" She picked up her beer and finished it in one long swallow. "I'm ready whenever you are."

Mike chugged his beer. "I have to use the toilet first." He laid 500 baht on the table. "Take care of the check-bin. I'll be right back." He winced as he stood.

"Are you okay?"

"I fell and broke my ribs a couple of weeks ago. It still hurts when I move the wrong way." He walked away from the table toward the toilet.

Minutes later they were on their way north up Second Road toward Soi 2 and Dolphin Circle. They had gone less than a block when Itta stopped and pointed.

"Do you see that woman?" Her voice was shrill with sudden excitement.

"Which one? I see lots of women."

"That one there. The one carrying the plastic bag. I think it's my sister. Come on, I have to catch her." Itta set off at a full run.

Mike tried to keep up but his ribs protested at the motion. "Sorry, I can't run anymore," he shouted at her.

Itta stopped. "I can't wait. How can I find you later, in case we get separated?"

"I'm staying at the Amari Hotel. Do you know where it is?"

Itta nodded. "I will find you." She ran as fast as her feet would carry her. Ahead she saw the woman veer left on the Soi leading toward the Pattaya International Hospital.

Mike watched as Itta vanished around the corner. He hurried as fast as his aching ribs allowed. Soon he was walking down the narrow street leading to the hospital. He had gone only a few steps when an eerie sense of danger rushed through him. He had an overwhelming urge to run away as fast and as far as he could. It was checked by a more powerful need to know what was going on. He walked stiff-legged down the sidewalk. When the emergency entrance came into view, he saw Itta. She was talking hard and fast to someone whose face was hidden by shadows. He continued his walk until he was at the edge of the drive.

At that second a Thai man exited the hospital. Mike had seen the man before but didn't know where. Three steps closer and recognition burst clear. It was Math's brother-in-law, Nuang's husband. He even remembered the man's name, it was Surat. Mike wanted to turn and leave, but his legs propelled him forward by their own accord.

Chapter 49

After being questioned by the police, Surat watched the activities taking place around him. The police officers began their questioning of the girl named Pajeeka. The woman named Somjit stood in the middle of the emergency-room waiting area, her arms wrapped around herself. An occasional whimper came from her mouth. He wondered if she was okay.

A few minutes later a middle-aged Thai man entered the hospital. His demeanor and his attire spoke money and power. He went directly to the police and the woman they were arresting. Surat couldn't hear all of their words, but the policemen seemed intimidated. There was no doubt he was an influential man. After a few minutes, the police took the woman named Pajeeka away and the rich man disappeared down a hallway. A short while later a nurse took Somjit away, too.

Surat sat for a time wondering what he should do. No one had told him he could leave, but no one had told him to stay, either. Finally he decided to go outside for some fresh air. Maybe Nuang would come back and he wanted to talk to her. He had a lot more to say. As he stepped through the door, he saw a farang walking toward the hospital entrance. He didn't notice the two women standing in the shadows to his left. When the farang moved under the streetlight, Surat realized he knew the man. It was the American his sister-in-law Math had brought with her to Chiang Mai. Why was he here?

Suddenly his random thoughts gelled and everything became undeniably clear. Nuang had been living with this farang, her deceased sister's lover. For once Anan had told the truth; he was seeing it with his own eyes. Now he could put a face to the images he had only guessed at yesterday—images of a foreigner impregnating his wife. The man walking toward him was the father of his wife's baby. He knew it as sure as his name was Surat.

He felt surprisingly calm. Maybe it was because he had already suspected the truth, or maybe it was because he had had enough time to become hardened against Nuang. Maybe he was simply in shock from everything that had happened. He stood, unmoving, torn between killing the farang or just saying fuck-it and going back to Chiang Mai. His decision took less than a second. He couldn't live with the disgrace of what Nuang had done. He took a deep breath and hurried to his taxi.

As Surat pulled his father's military pistol from under the front seat, he remembered the man's name. It was Mike. Mike Johnson. The images of the man having sex with Nuang assaulted his senses. He turned, stepped forward, and aimed the pistol at the farang. In Thai he said, "Mike Johnson, you are going to die."

Mike looked up and saw the pistol pointed directly at him. "What are you doing?"

Surat didn't understand Mike's words but he saw the look of terror on the man's face. It made him smile.

"Surat!" a shout pierced the scene. "Put the gun down." It was Nuang. "Please, put it down now."

"Stay away from me whore," he cut her short. "Or I will kill you too." He kept his eyes on Mike.

"I'm not a whore." Her face flushed enough to be seen in the pale streetlight.

"And I'm not blind. I've seen your baby and now I've seen your farang lover."

Nuang opened her mouth but nothing came out. She took a deep breath and managed to whimper, "Please, Surat. I love you."

"Fuck you, Nuang. Do you think I'm stupid. I know what you love and it's not me." Images of her having sex with this farang tore through him again. "You have made me the biggest fool in the world and I hate you for it."

264

THAILAND - COLD RAIN

"Please, Surat, I never did that; I would never do that to you."

"The baby's not mine, Nuang. Do you understand what I am telling you? It's not mine. It belongs to your farang." He tightened his grip on the pistol and took another step toward Mike. "You fuck my wife," he spit out the few English words he knew. Hatred boiled through him. In Thai he added, "I will kill you now."

Mike understood the English perfectly. He didn't understand the Thai words, but he didn't have to. The gun said it all. He was about to die for past sins. He held his hands in front of him, as if they could stop a bullet. It was a superman gesture in mortal clothing. His head spun so hard he thought he might faint. Alternating urges of fight or flight assaulted him. His male ego demanded that he attack; his sense of survival ordered him to escape. He staggered backwards and dropped to a crouch instinctively making his target smaller. His mind churned a thousand thoughts. He noticed that his ribs didn't hurt. He searched for reason amidst the madness. "I never fucked your wife," he shouted his defense. He wondered how much English Surat understood. He adjusted his words to pure basic. "No fuck you wife."

Surat narrowed his aim to the Mike's head. He was surprised at the man's fear of death. He was even more surprised that his finger wouldn't respond to his command to pull the trigger. He stepped closer. The sounds of the city faded until he heard only his heart pounding in his ears. He wondered if the farang's bowels would empty before or after he died.

At that instant, Isara stepped through the hospital doors and sprinted down the drive. "Surat! If you pull that trigger, it will be the biggest mistake of your life."

Surat flicked his eyes toward the intruder. It was the older man he had seen inside. "This is none of your business."

"It's enough of my business to know you are about to shoot an innocent man."

"He fucked my wife. This piece of foreign bird shit got her pregnant. My wife gave birth to his baby."

"You're wrong. Your wife gave birth to your own baby. If you want to hate her for that, I can't stop you. But I can't let you kill a man for something he didn't do, even if he is a farang."

"You're lying, rich man," Surat spit his words. "You don't know anything about this. You don't know anything at all. This is none of your affair."

"I know more than you know yourself."

"You're a liar."

"Am I? Are you so sure that you're willing to spend the rest of your life in jail? Are your beliefs that strong?"

Surat didn't move. He stared at the farang cringing in front of him. What if the sharp dressed man was right? What if the farang hadn't done anything. He remembered his confrontation with Nui and steel butterflies flailed inside his chest. For a moment he thought he would be sick. He didn't want to kill anyone, he only wanted everyone to know how much Nuang had hurt him. Slowly, without taking his eyes from the farang, he stooped and laid the gun on the ground.

Isara stepped forward and picked it up. "Surat, look at me."

Surat did look. How could this man possibly know his name? Maybe he did know something. Surat couldn't stop the surrealism overtaking his mind. "Who are you?"

"My name is Isara. Come with me. There's someone I want you to meet." He turned and walked away.

Surat's thoughts collapsed into a wad of sticky rice. Mindlessly, obediently, he followed the sharp-dressed man. Not far up the street sat a Mercedes. When they arrived, Isara motioned him inside and then slid in beside him.

"Take us to Khun Anya's house," Isara ordered the driver. They rode in silence.

Chapter 50

After the older Thai man and Surat were gone, Mike forced himself to stand. He hadn't been so sure of death since that night of hell in Vietnam. The pain returned to his chest and his legs felt like he had just run a four minute mile. He barely noticed when Itta and Nuang came to his side.

"Are you okay?" one of the women said.

He stared dumbly. He recognized their faces but their names wouldn't come. At that moment he wasn't even sure of his own name. He was surprised at the strength of his fear. "Yes," he finally managed, "I'm okay." He leaned forward, put his hands to his knees, and breathed as deep as his ribs let him. "He was going to kill me. It doesn't make sense."

"He is angry," said Itta.

"Why? I've never done anything to him."

"You got my sister pregnant," she answered.

You got my sister pregnant, her words pounded in his head. How could she know? Math said she had never told anyone. "I thought only Math and I knew. I thought it was our secret. She miscarried. I guess you know that, too."

His confession caught her off guard. Itta didn't know about Math's pregnancy and miscarriage. After a slight pause she said, "I have two sisters."

A year-old scene invaded his head—an image of him and Nuang naked together in bed. He knew the sister Itta meant was probably Nuang. Why else would Nuang's husband want to kill him? A lump settled in his chest. "What do you mean?"

Itta was opening her mouth to speak when Nuang took her by

J. F. Gump

the arm and pulled her aside.

"He's not the man who got me pregnant," she whispered in Thai.

Itta stared, "What do you mean?"

Nuang lowered her eyes. "He's not the one. I would rather not talk about it."

A million thoughts flashed through Itta's mind but only one came to the surface. If this wasn't the man, then Nuang had had sex with another farang. She had already admitted her baby was half farang. "Then who?"

"I don't know," Nuang lied. Mike Johnson was the man who had fathered her baby, but she didn't love him and there was nothing to gain by telling anyone that she had used him for her own selfish pleasure. There was no point in making things worse. "I may never know," she continued her lie. "Tell him I told everyone about Math's pregnancy. Tell him thank you again for the beautiful ceremony he had for Math and that I still remember every minute of that day."

Itta stared at her sister hoping to make eye contact, but Nuang kept her head down. After a second she turned back to Mike, "Nuang told our family about Math losing her baby. She wants to say thank you for the ceremony you had for our sister. She also said that she remembers every minute of that day. I guess you do, too."

"I hardly remember it at all," he stammered. "It was a long time ago."

"Yes, it has been just over a year."

Silent embarrassment permeated the night. They both knew the truth.

"I have to go now," Mike finally said. "I'm not feeling well." He put his hand to his ribs for emphasis.

"I still want to talk with you," Itta said. "There are things you need to know, and much I want to know—about Math, that is. Can we talk?"

Images of Surat and the pistol filled his head. "I'm not sure it's safe for me to talk to anyone in your family."

"Please, I promise you'll be safe. I must stay with Nuang and her baby for a while, but I want to talk to you later. Where can we meet?"

Mike knew he should tell her no, but in spite of common sense he didn't. "It's the same as before. I'm going back to my hotel and have a few beers to settle my nerves. You know how to find me."

Itta and Nuang went back inside the emergency room waiting area. Somjit was nowhere in sight. Nuang walked to the registration desk. "Is my baby okay?"

The nurse looked up. "I thought that other woman was the mother."

"She is my baby's nurse mother," Nuang answered. "Her name is Somjit, we are best friends. Is she okay? And my baby; is my baby okay, too?"

The nurse nodded, "They are treating your friend for shock. The doctors said your baby will be fine. Some cuts and scrapes and a dislocated shoulder, but nothing too serious. I think she'll be discharged tonight. She's in examination room B."

Nuang took Itta by the hand. "Let's go."

"Wait," the nurse stopped them. "It's after hours. We have rules."

"But I want to see my baby." Nuang said.

"I understand and you can see your daughter. But the rules say only one person at a time after visiting hours. Your friend must wait here."

"She's my sister," Nuang protested.

Itta took Nuang by the arm and said, "You go ahead. There's something I must do. I'll come back later. You'll still be here, won't you?"

Nuang understood her sister's concern, but it was for nothing. She was tired of running away. She would stay here until little Tippawan was released. Then she would go home. Not to Chiang Mai, but to her mother's house in Phitsanulok. She never expected to see Surat again; that part of her life was finished. She took Itta's hand in hers and squeezed tight. "Don't worry; I'll be here."

Itta nodded and smiled, "Go to your baby. I'll see you later."

Nuang walked to examination room B. Little Tippawan was asleep. Her heart ached at the bandages on her daughter's little body. So much she wanted to pick her up and hold her close. "I love you," she whispered in the dim solitude. A tear welled and slid down her cheek.

A nurse stepped into the room, "Please, the doctor is coming. I think he'll reset her shoulder. It will be easier if you wait in the lobby." Her voice was kind yet firm.

Nuang didn't argue. She went back to the waiting area and tried to get comfortable. She wondered what would the future bring? Would Surat would come back looking for her? She hoped not. If he had been angry enough to kill the American, Buddha only knew what he might do to her. After everything that had happened, she would deserve whatever he did.

The faint cry of a baby in pain reached her ears through the double doors of examination rooms. She cringed at the sound. She cupped her face in her hands and cried.

Chapter 51

As Isara and Surat drove farther from the tourist areas of the city, the lights and sounds that are the essence of Pattaya faded into stillness. The Mercedes turned left, then right, and then left again until Surat was hopelessly lost. Here the streets were unpaved. Here sidewalks were nonexistent. This was the less glamorous side of Pattaya, an area not frequented by the cocky farangs with their bulging wallets and overactive libidos. Here was where the poorest Thais lived and loved and died, far from the beer bars and the discos and the fancy hotels.

The driver stopped in front of a short row of tin-clad shacks that made Surat's house in Chiang Mai seem like a mansion. Isara exited the car and waited.

Surat felt uncomfortable. He was in a strange city, with a strange man, in a seedy part of town. This man obviously had money. The only Thais he knew with money were an unscrupulous and untrustworthy lot. Why had the man brought him here? Something bad was going to happen, he could feel it. He wished he had his gun back. "What are you going to do to me?"

Isara reached inside, took Surat by the hand, and urged him from the car. "Come, I want you to meet someone."

Against his every instinct, Surat allowed himself to be led outside. The sour taste of copper flooded his mouth. His fingers tingled and twitched. His motions were jerky. He was as scared as the farang had been.

Isara squeezed his hand. "You will be safe."

They walked like that, hand in hand. Isara stepped in a puddle splashing muddy water on his shiny shoes and dark trousers. In a minute he stopped in front of a house. "We're here," he whispered. They stepped through the doorway.

Surat expected the inside of the shack to be as stark and barren as the outside. He was surprised to find it immaculately clean and cozy. The small room was lit by two dim incandescent lamps. The inner walls were covered with tightly woven bamboo painted with dozens of true-to-life murals of rural Thai villages and bustling Thai cities. He scanned the paintings. Three characters repeated their appearance in each scene. One was a blond farang man, another was a young Thai boy, and the last was a beautiful Thai woman. Surat stared transfixed. He had seen artwork like that before but he couldn't remember where.

"See anyone you recognize, Surat?"

He turned toward the voice. It was a woman. She was thin but not gaunt. Her face was mature, but in a beautiful way reserved for the lucky few. She sat with her back straight. Strands of gray laced her medium length hair. She looked familiar. "How do you know my name?"

"Do you see the young boy in the pictures?" she asked, ignoring his question.

Surat looked at the wall and then back at the woman. "Yes," he said. "I think I know him from somewhere."

"What about the farang? Do you recognize him, too?"

Surat looked. A hard chill crept up his back. "No. I've never seen him before. Should I know him?"

"He is your father."

Surat's senses reeled. His world turned inside-out. He reached over and put his hand on Isara's shoulder to steady his quavering knees. Sweat formed on his upper lip. Nui's words pounded at his thoughts. "And the woman?" He already knew the answer.

"My name is Anya. I am your mother."

Surat's light brown skin turned chalky white.

When Surat awoke, he was in the woman's arms, held tight to

her chest. She rocked gently. Images of the blonde farang crept through him. It couldn't be his father, that wasn't possible. His father had been a soldier in the Thai army and had died in a border skirmish with Kampuchea. His father had been a hero. He had his father's military pistol and the Thai army metals as proof.

"The farang is not my father," he broke the silence. "And you are not my mother." He wiggled from her grasp and stood. "I don't know who you are. My mother and father are both dead." He turned to Isara, "I want to leave now. I've seen all I care to see."

The woman's face twisted. Tears formed and slid across her cheeks. She stood and reached toward him but stopped short of touching. "Please Surat, don't go. If you hate me, I don't blame you. But please stay for a few minutes longer. Please give me a chance."

"Give you a chance for what? To explain you are a whore and that my father was a farang soldier?" He lined his words with every drop of venom he found within himself. "Nui has explained that already." He watched as the old woman's knees buckled and she sank to the floor. Her sobs pierced every square centimeter of the small room.

Instantly he regretted what he had said. All his life he had dreamed of his mother being alive and loving him, and of them being together. Now that it had happened he had attacked her with his lifetime of resentment. He didn't understand why. His thoughts scattered to the point of nonsense and his emotions ran rampant. He wished he could take back his words. He crouched down beside her and took her in his arms. "I'm sorry mother; I'm sorry if I hurt you. I do love you."

She put her own arms around Surat and held on for dear life. "And I love you, too."

Isara waited until their crying stopped before he spoke. "Tell her about her grandchild, your baby daughter."

They both looked up at Isara; she in confused wonder and he in terrified realization. Surat was the first to speak, "Is that possible? I mean I don't look farang, I only look different." He fell silent as his thoughts cohered into chaotic understanding. He didn't understand the medical facts, but his basic instincts said that if he was half farang then his baby could be half farang, too. After a second he said, "The baby's mine, isn't it?"

Isara nodded.

Surat turned to his mother. "I have a baby daughter who needs her grandmother. Will you come to live with us?" His voice choked with emotion on each word.

Anya tears resumed. This time from joy. "I'd be honored, if it's okay with your wife."

His wife! Dear Buddha, his wife! Panic ripped through him. Nuang was the one who had given birth to a half farang baby. Surely, she must wonder how or why. Maybe she'd had sex with a farang, but maybe she hadn't. He was half farang and maybe the baby was his. Or maybe it wasn't. Maybe he would never know the truth. At that instant, he decided he didn't care about the truth. He wanted his wife back and he wanted his baby. In his heart he knew he was the father. He looked up at Isara, "I need to find Nuang right away. Can we go back to the hospital now?"

Isara nodded.

As they rode, Anya told Surat the story of her life. She held nothing back, not even the things most humiliating. Her story was similar to what Nui had told him, but the details were different. She had fallen in love with an American soldier stationed in Phitsanulok during the Vietnam War. He was an adviser to the Thai army. He had died without ever knowing he would be a father.

In those days Phitsanulok was a cruel town. It hadn't taken long for word to spread that she had given birth to a foreigner's baby. She'd been ostracized by everyone, even her best friends. Worse, the citizens of Phitsanulok had shunned her parents as well. Six months after Surat was born, Anya had fled Phitsanulok leaving Surat behind with her parents. It was her only sane option. Bangkok wasn't a place for a young woman with a baby.

THAILAND - COLD RAIN

Without an education her career choices were limited. Eventually, she took a job as a dancer in nightclub that catered to farangs. That was where she discovered just how much her body was worth.

Like a good daughter she had sent money home. Like a bad mother she rarely came home to see her baby. In time she became too ashamed to ever go home.

As she got older, the farangs found her less desirable. They wanted young girls and by then she was a woman past her prime. From there she had worked as a hostess, a hotel service maid, a laundress, a laborer, and a beggar. Anything to keep her alive. She resigned herself to dying a lonely old woman in some back alley hovel that passed as a house. She had painted scenes on the walls of her home to be with the ones she loved but could never have. It was the closest she would ever come to having a family.

As Surat listened to her talk, he heard the painful repentance in her voice. Whatever resentment he had ever felt toward her dissolved into nothingness. Her life hadn't been easy. She had made the only choices given to her. She had done what was best for him.

He wondered how much different her life might have been if she had never given birth to him. Would she have gone to Bangkok or Pattaya? Or would she have married a good Thai man and raised a family in Phitsanulok? But for him, would she be happy? In her own way she had given up her life for him.

When she stopped talking, he took her hand in his. He tried to speak but his throat clamped shut. He buried his face on her shoulder and cried. In a moment he managed to whimper, "Mama, please hold me." He sounded more like a young boy than a grown man. "Please hold me again." And she did.

By the time they had reached the bustle of Pattaya, Surat had decided he wanted Nuang back, no matter the truth about their child. The baby belonged to his wife and that was all he cared about. If anyone said anything about his child looking more farang than Thai, he could tell them with authority that he had farang genes inside himself. No one could deny his light skin and his green flecked eyes. Suddenly he wasn't ashamed that his father was American.

Then it dawned on him that he probably no longer had a job, but he still had to take care of Nuang and his baby. And now his mother too. He'd have to find new work and soon. He had often thought about starting his own transportation service. He knew the business but lack of money had always been a problem.

He glanced at the rich man sitting in the front seat of the Mercedes and wondered how the man knew his mother, and why he was involved with his life. It was all too coincidental to be anything normal. He wondered just how important he might be to the man. With nothing to lose, he mentioned his plans to someday own a transportation company, if only he had the seed money. He expected instant rejection but it didn't come. The man asked a few basic questions and Surat had ready answers. He was surprised when the man agreed to finance the venture for fifty percent ownership. But the man wanted other things too. Odd things like insisting that he and Nuang stay together and raise their child. Isara also insisted that neither he nor Nuang could ever talk about their pasts when his son Laht was around. Surat wasn't sure what that had to do with anything, but he would make sure the promise was kept. He began making his plans for his family's future.

A few minutes later the car pulled into hospital drive. Isara was the first out of the car. "I must check on my son," he said and hurried away.

Surat slid from the car but motioned for Anya to stay inside. "Please, wait here. I must speak to my wife in private."

She nodded her understanding.

Surat stepped into the emergency room waiting area half expecting that Nuang would be gone. He was relieved when she was there. Her face was buried in her hands. If she had seen him enter, she didn't acknowledge. He fidgeted for a minute deciding what he would say. No coherent thoughts would come. Finally, he decided he would say whatever came out of his mouth. He walked to where she sat, knelt down beside her, and gently put his hand on her arm. "Phom lak khun, teeluk. I love you, sweetheart."

Nuang looked up, her eyes swollen and red. "Why are you taunting me? I know I have shamed you. Why don't you just leave me alone?" Her voice cracked as she broke into heavy sobs.

"Nuang, listen to me. We have spent most of our lives together. I have loved you more during the last year than I loved you when we first met. You may be ready to give that up, but I'm not. When our baby is out of the hospital, I want us to go home and be a family. I want you Nuang. Will you go with me?"

"I don't understand. How can you love me after all I've done?"

"You've done nothing."

"But," she started to protest.

He pressed his fingertips against her lips to stop her words. "You've done nothing except give birth to my daughter."

She pulled him close and her tears fell like a monsoon rain. "I love you Surat. I'll always love you."

"I know," he said. "Come, there's someone I want you to meet." He took her by the hand and led her outside to a Mercedes parked at the entrance. A woman sat inside. Nuang looked up at Surat, questions lined her face. "This is my mother. She is coming to live with you and me and our baby."

Surat caught Nuang when she fainted and laid her gently on the rear seat. "Take care of my wife," he said to Anya. "I'm going to see my daughter."

Anya smiled and nodded.

Surat went to the registration desk, "I want to see my baby."

The nurse recognized him as the man who had come with the others and had been questioned by the police. "And who are you?"

"My name is Surat Duansawang," he said, a touch of pride lit his words. "I am the father of my daughter."

The nursed studied him for a long second then picked up the phone. A long series of *ka*'s followed. She put down the phone and said, "Your baby's being released. A woman is bringing her now."

Chapter 52

Somjit was in an examination room for what seemed like hours while the doctors and nurses poked, prodded, and took blood and urine samples. Finally they left her alone. In a while, she got up from her bed and stepped into the corridor. It was empty.

Laht and baby Tippawan were here somewhere. As quietly as possible, she stuck her head into every room. In one she saw the doctors stitching a cut on Laht's head. He was awake and instructing the doctors on how to do their job. She started to go to him but didn't. The doctors intimidated her. In the next room she found little Tippawan. She had already stepped inside before she realized a nurse was there.

"May I help you?" the nurse asked.

"Is she okay?" Somjit asked in return.

"She is asleep," the nurse answered. "She'll be fine."

Somjit nodded and left the room. She went back to Laht's room and waited outside. When the doctors came out, she stopped them. "Can I see him please? He is my husband." It was a lie but she didn't care. It was almost true.

"We've given him pain medication. He's a little groggy, but you can see him. Let him sleep if he wants."

"Thank you," she said then went inside.

Laht smiled when she stepped into his room. "You look beautiful," his words slurred thick-lipped. "I love you."

She hurried to his side and wrapped him in her arms. "And I love you." She held him until they both fell asleep.

Much later, she was awakened by the sharp cry of an infant in pain. She abandoned Laht and rushed to Tippawan's room. The nurse shushed her outside. "The doctor has reset her dislocated shoulder. There's nothing else wrong except some minor scrapes. She can leave when he is finished. I was told you are her nurse mother. Will you take responsibility for her when she is discharged?"

"Yes," she answered. "I will take care of her."

"Wait here," the nurse said and hurried away.

As Somjit waited for the nurse to bring little Tippawan, she wondered what she would do when she left the hospital. Laht was still here and she had no idea where Nuang had gone. Maybe she would get a hotel room for the night and ask Laht tomorrow what they should do.

The nurse returned and handed little Tippawan to her. Never again would she let anything happen to the baby.

When she stepped into the waiting room she saw the taxi driver, the man who had said he was Nuang's husband. In her heart she knew it was true.

Surat had just turned to face the door to the examination rooms when Somjit appeared with his daughter held tight against her chest. His already-stressed emotions stretched to breaking. How could he face this woman? She had been caring for his daughter, but he had no idea why or for how long. He wondered how attached she had become to the baby. His instincts told him the attachment was strong. He searched for the proper words to say, but nothing seemed right. He knew there would be hurt no matter what he said. He forced a humble smile to his face.

"Sawasdee krup," he presented her a respectful wai. "My name is Surat. We have met before."

Somjit's heart twisted painfully. She knew this moment would come someday, but she had prayed it never would. This man was going to take little Tippawan away and she couldn't stop him. He was Nuang's husband, even if he wasn't the baby's father. She wondered what he knew about his own wife. She steeled herself for the inevitable. "Where is Nuang? Is she okay?"

Surat saw desperation etch the woman's face. He had seen that same look in his own face the night Nuang had run away. It was the reflection of impending loss. "She's outside. I'm taking her home."

"What about the baby?"

"I'm taking the baby home, too."

Somjit grasped at invisible straws, "The baby is half farang."

"So am I," Surat responded, unabashed.

She studied his skin and his eyes and the shape of his face. Now that he had said it, she could see it. Maybe he really was the father of the baby. She tried to speak but couldn't.

"You're welcome in our home if you have no place to go," he said softly. "I don't know everything that's happened, but I think Nuang would want you with us."

Her first reaction was to say yes, images of Laht made her say no. "I think your wife needs time alone with her baby." Tears welled then flowed as she handed little Tippawan to Surat. "Please go quickly."

Surat's emotions twisted tight and hard like wire rope. "Please come with us."

"Please, just go." She turned away from Surat and slumped into a nearby chair. She waved him away without looking. Her shoulders drooped in resignation.

Surat watched her for a minute then walked away. Somehow he would keep in touch with this woman. He knew in his heart that one day she would be known as Aunt Somjit.

He went to the nurse's station. "How much do I owe?"

"You can pay the cashier down the hall."

"I need to know how much. I may have to go to an ATM."

"I'll check," she said then punched at her keyboard. "You owe… hmmm… The computer says you owe nothing."

"I don't understand."

"Your bill has been paid already."

Surat knew it must have been the rich man, Isara. The man had been more than generous with him already. He wondered why?

THAILAND - COLD RAIN

But the why of things wasn't important now. They had already made a business agreement and Surat would keep his promises. "Thank you," he said. "I must go to my wife now." He left the hospital with baby Tippawan in his arms.

Outside, Nuang was still in the backseat of the taxi and apparently asleep. His mother sat in the front passenger seat. "Anya, I mean mother, please hold my baby."

She looked at Surat and said, "I think that tonight, the baby belongs with its mother. She'll wake easily enough for her child."

Surat wasn't sure what to say, so he said nothing. He went to the back seat and nudged Nuang with his hand. "Teeluk, here is our daughter. Will you hold her for a while?"

Nuang awoke. She was in the back of a car, but didn't remember how she got there. Surat filled the open doorway, his outstretched hands held a blanket-wrapped bundle. She took it from him and snuggled it close to her. The baby's scent rushed her senses. It was her baby, it was little Tippawan. In a moment the taxi was in motion. Nuang prayed they were going home. When the lights of Pattaya faded to less than a glow, she spoke to Surat, "Will everything be okay, teeluk?"

There was a moment of silence while he organized his thoughts. "Everything will be perfect. I'm opening a business with the rich man in the Mercedes. It was my idea and he liked it. We're opening a limousine service in Phitsanulok. He has a ready made clientele. I will make so much money that we can buy our own house, a nice Thai house with a kitchen and our own private bathroom and everything. I'm happy we can do this together."

"I was afraid you would hate me. That's why I ran away."

Surat knew what was coursing through her mind. "There is nothing to hate."

She wondered what he thought and what he knew. "Thank you for finding me and for forgiving me."

"There is nothing to forgive."

Nuang blushed. She knew the truth and suspected Surat did too. She changed the subject. "What about Somjit? She will hate me for taking the baby away."

"Somjit will be very busy with her future husband. His father is the man in the Mercedes. I'm sure we'll see them often. "

Nuang leaned forward and wrapped her arms around Surat's neck. She placed a sniffing Thai style kiss on his cheek. "I love you. You are the best husband in the world."

"You should go back to sleep so I can drive."

Nuang lay beside her baby and held on for dear life.

Chapter 53

Laht was asleep when Isara entered his room. A young nurse with a clipboard was writing numbers from the machines. She smiled and motioned for Isara to be quiet. "He's doing very well," she whispered. "The doctor said he can leave in the morning."

Isara stared at his son for a minute before nodding his understanding. He stepped out of the room.

Dr. Phansak, Laht's friend from school, was waiting when Isara stepped into the hallway. "Do you have a minute?" he asked. "There's something you need to know."

"Of course," Isara answered. "What is it?"

Dr. Phansak spoke low and direct. His revelations gave Isara pause. When they finished talking, Isara went to the cashier and made the necessary arrangements for hospital fees both current and future.

A minute later Isara was in the waiting area. To his left sat the young woman his son loved. She was staring straight ahead and didn't see him when he arrived. He took the opportunity to study her. On the outside she was as beautiful as Laht had said. But Isara knew that on the inside she carried secrets that he and Laht could only guess at. He was tempted to give her money and tell her to go away, but the image of his dead brother's face squelched the thought. He would let Laht decide his own future. When she finally noticed him, he walked in her direction.

Somjit pulled her arms tight against her sides and hunched her shoulders downward, as if trying to force herself smaller, or even invisible. She had already lost little Tippawan and now she would lose Laht. She knew it as sure as morning would come. She turned away from his approach.

Isara stopped less than a meter from where she sat. "Look at me," he ordered.

Somjit glanced up. His presence was overpowering. She slid from her seat to her knees and wai'ed in the beggar-like manner suitable to her lot.

Isara ignored her low gesture. "I said look at me. Get up and look at me now."

Hesitantly, meekly, she looked up. "I'm sorry if I've caused your family any problems. It will never happen again."

Isara sighed deep at her groveling. "If you have any intentions of being my son's wife, you need to start acting like you have some self respect. If you love him, you'll get off your knees and look at me."

Somjit stood and pulled back her shoulders, "I do have self respect. Your son gave it to me. I'll always love him for that."

Isara regarded her haughtily. "Only that?"

She paused at his question. For her it was much more. "I love your son for many reasons. I love him because he is good and kind and caring, and I love him because he saved my life. Most of all, I love him because he loves me."

Isara smiled to himself behind his fake mask. "Then you should take care of him. If you'll excuse me, I have things to do before I can sleep. Tell Laht to call me tomorrow." He turned to walk away.

"What about the woman who saved his life? Is she okay?"

"She will be fine. She has the best lawyer in Thailand."

Somjit couldn't help but smile. "I'm sure she does."

At the door he paused and looked back. "You don't know it yet, but you're pregnant. It's my son's child." With that he disappeared into the night.

Involuntarily she put her hand to her stomach. What if it were true? There was no way he could know something she didn't know herself. Yet somehow she knew he was right. She eased past the doctors and entered the room where Laht lay sleeping. She took his hand in hers and squeezed tight. "I will make you a proud husband," she said. "I promise that to you." She pulled herself tall and smiled. "Then I will make you the proud father of our child."

Isara exited the hospital and entered the awaiting Mercedes. "Take me to the Pattaya police station," he said. "I need to get my best investigator out of trouble. I've promised her a vacation and I'm going to make sure she gets it. I think I'll give her a bonus, too."

The driver nodded, smiled, and drove south.

Chapter 54

When Itta left the hospital, she went directly to the Amari Orchid Hotel. True to his word, Mike was there. She wasn't sure what she would say to him. Their earlier conversation flashed through her: Anan and his lies, and Math and her love. Unlike Anan, she had told Mike the truth. She had had no reason to lie. She wondered if he also had no reasons to lie, especially about her sister Nuang. She doubted it. It didn't matter anyway; Nuang had denied everything.

"I'm glad you waited for me," she said, sliding onto the barstool beside his. Her tone was nonchalant. "We were talking about my sister, Math. Is that correct?"

Mike turned and stared at her. Twenty minutes earlier he had almost died and now this woman pretended like it never happened. For a moment he wondered if it had all been a dream. "Yes," he answered. He had no reason to say no.

For the next hour they exchanged personal stories about Math, and about themselves, too. Itta was intrigued by his understanding of her sister. Mike reveled in her stories about Math.

Many beers later their conversation drifted entirely from Math and focused on themselves and their own pasts. Much was revealed, but even more stayed hidden. Mike was entranced with her stories, her smile, and her charm. As they talked, he felt a desire he hadn't felt since Susan and Math had died.

Itta was surprised at how easy she opened up to him. She wasn't sure why. She had had her fill of farangs, but somehow this man was different. He was polite, he was funny, and he wasn't so bad looking. She felt unexpected warmth toward him.

They were both lost souls. One had lost loves while the other had lost dreams. At times it was hard to distinguish one loss from another. In a while they reached a quiet spot in their conversation. Itta broke the silence. "What will you do when your job here is finished?"

"I don't know. I suppose I'll go home. I have no reason to stay."

"Does that mean you have a reason to go home?"

Mike considered her question for a minute. "No," he finally admitted. "I have no reason to go home either. What about you?"

She hadn't seriously considered what she would do with her life. She had been playing with the notion of coming to Pattaya, even before Anan had called. Her search for Nuang had given her a perfect excuse to come here without upsetting her mother. She knew she could find work in Pattaya, but probably not the kind she could brag about to her family.

"I've been thinking about opening my own business," she finally said. "I don't know what, though. Maybe a laundry service or a small restaurant. Whatever I do will have to be cheap; I don't have much money."

Mike nodded his head, "I understand. Everything becomes harder without money. Some things become impossible." He thought about the Pattaya nightlife. "Maybe you should open a bar. I've thought about that myself. A good bar makes a killing during the high season."

"If I had a half million baht, I would do that."

"That seems a little expensive for a beer bar."

"I wouldn't open a beer bar. If I ever go into the business, it will be a go-go bar. If I succeed, it will be money well spent. If I fail, at least I'll go out in style."

Mike smiled at her. "Somehow, I think you would be a roaring success." He considered his next words very carefully before speaking. "I have some money I would be willing to invest in the right opportunity. Let me know if you need a partner."

Itta's eyes widened. "Are you serious?"

"I never joke about money."

"Me, too," Itta smiled.

"Let's move to a table where we can talk in private." He motioned to the barmaid and then escorted Itta to a seat away from the main bar. An old Righteous Brother's song drifted from the bar stereo.

"I'm sorry to ask you this," Itta said once they were seated, "but something has been bothering me all night. What will you do about Anan?"

Mike hadn't expected her question. He felt his good mood fading. She was going to ruin the rest of the evening. "There is nothing to do. You already told me Anan was a liar."

"What if I am wrong? What if my sister really did write those bad things? What if Anan brings Math's diary tomorrow? Would you hate the whole Bongkot family because of it?"

He wanted to say yes, but he knew that would be a lie. "Maybe, but only for a while. I'm not capable of hating anyone for very long." He paused for a moment and then added, "I'm not going to worry about Anan until the day he brings me a diary. And if he does, I'll probably just throw it away. I'm finished talking about that. Let's talk about our new business. I know the perfect location. I'll show you tomorrow. I think we should call it the Suaee Dee Lady. What do you think?"

Itta was caught completely off guard. "I thought you were joking with me earlier." Her expression was priceless.

"Hey," he said, laughing aloud. "I told you before that I never joke about money. If you're serious about opening a bar, then so am I. If I'm going to have a Thai partner, I want it to be you. What do you say?"

"Yes," she almost screamed from excitement. She felt giddy. "I want to be your partner."

"High season is starting soon, we don't have much time. We'll need dancers, and waitresses, and bartenders, and everything. I don't know about all of the legal things. This could take us a long time."

"I can have us open in three weeks. It may cost a little more but I can do it. I still know a few people in this town. I'm sure they will help us."

Mike motioned a waitress to their table and whispered in her ear. She returned a minute later carrying a silver ice bucket, two long-stemmed glasses, and a bottle wrapped in a towel. With great flourish she popped the cork and poured each of them a glass of champagne. She put the bottle on ice and left them alone.

"To the Suaee Dee Lady," Mike held his glass in salute.

Itta lifted her glass and tapped his gently. "To our success."

By the time the bottle was empty they had made their plans—and they were drunk. Mike impolitely asked Itta to spend the night with him and she refused, just as impolitely. He paid the tab and stumbled along beside her to the hotel exit.

A drop of rain put a dark spot on the sidewalk outside. A second fell close beside the first. Then another and another in rapid succession. The wind shifted and a bolt of lightning split the night sky. A heavy rumble followed. Within seconds it was pouring.

"I have two beds in my room," Mike said, very quietly. "I can only sleep in one at a time."

Itta stared at him for a very long moment. He was the man her sister had loved. Math had told her everything about him, even intimate things. Suddenly she realized why Math had loved this man. It wasn't for his money or because he was a farang, it was because he had a good heart. She knew she should go back to the hospital, but at the same time she wanted to stay here. Besides, she couldn't go in the middle of a storm. It would be best if she waited until the rain stopped.

"I can only sleep in one bed at a time, too." She took his hand and pulled him from the rain's over-mist. "But I won't fall in love with you."

Together, hand in hand, they walked to his room. They left their pasts in the lobby of the Amari Orchid Hotel.

Other Books Available
By J. F. Gump

From Bangkok Book House
www.bangkokbooks.com

Even Thai Girls Cry
ISBN: 974-93100-4-7

The Farang Affair
ISBN: 974-85123-6-3

One High Season
ISBN: 974-85129-3-2

From Sabai Books U.S.
www.JFGumpNovels.com

Siam Nights
ISBN 10: 9714855-2-5

Tears For The Thai Girl
ISBN 10: 09714855-3-4

Blame It On Bangkok
ISBN 10: 1440473803

For Details Go To:

www.JFGumpNovels.com